THE CARNEVALE CONSPIRACY

DANFORTH SAGA #7

JOSEPH BADAL

SUSPENSE PUBLISHING

THE CARNEVALE CONSPIRACY
by
Joseph Badal

PAPERBACK EDITION
* * * * *
PUBLISHED BY:
Suspense Publishing

Joseph Badal
COPYRIGHT
2021 Joseph Badal

PUBLISHING HISTORY:
Suspense Publishing, Paperback and Digital Copy, July 2021

Cover Design: Shannon Raab
Cover Photographer: Shutterstock.com/ Jarmo Piironen

ISBN: 978-0-578-88146-1

JOSEPH BADAL'S BOOKS & SHORT STORIES

THE DANFORTH SAGA

EVIL DEEDS (#1)
TERROR CELL (#2)
THE NOSTRADAMUS SECRET (#3)
THE LONE WOLF AGENDA (#4)
DEATH SHIP (#5)
SINS OF THE FATHERS (#6)
THE CARNEVALE CONSPIRACY (#7)

THE CURTIS CHRONICLES

#1: THE MOTIVE
#2: OBSESSED
#3: JUSTICE

LASSITER/MARTINEZ CASE FILES

#1: BORDERLINE
#2: DARK ANGEL
#3: NATURAL CAUSES

STAND-ALONE THRILLERS

THE PYTHAGOREAN SOLUTION
SHELL GAME
ULTIMATE BETRAYAL
PAYBACK

SHORT STORIES

FIRE & ICE (UNCOMMON ASSASSINS ANTHOLOGY)
ULTIMATE BETRAYAL (SOMEONE WICKED
ANTHOLOGY)
THE ROCK (INSIDIOUS ASSASSINS ANTHOLOGY)
GONE FOREVER (NOTHING GOOD HAPPENS AFTER
MIDNIGHT: A *SUSPENSE MAGAZINE* ANTHOLOGY)

DEDICATION

*For my wife, Sara. Your support, encouragement, and love
continue to inspire me.*

ACKNOWLEDGEMENTS

To my readers, thank you for your loyal support. You virtually keep alive my passion for writing. Your kind feedback and suggestions are invaluable, and your reviews make a difference.

I have been fortunate to have had reviews and blurbs for my novels written by many successful and prolific authors, including Mark Adduci, Tom Avitabile, Parris Afton Bonds, Steve Brewer, Catherine Coulter, Philip Donlay, Steve Havill, Anne Hillerman, Tony Hillerman, Paul Kemprecos, Robert Kresge, Jon Land, Mark Leggatt, Michael McGarrity, David Morrell, Michael Palmer, Andrew Peterson, Mark Rubinstein, Meryl Sawyer, and Sheldon Siegel. I know how busy these men and women are and it always humbles me when they graciously take time to read and praise my work.

Writing military/espionage thrillers is a challenging task for several reasons, not the least of which is keeping up to date on technological advances regarding weaponry, aircraft, intelligence gathering techniques, etc. I want to thank Lt. General Charles R. Heflebower (USAF-Retired) for his assistance.

Thanks to several of my friends for allowing me to borrow their names for some of the characters in this book. Just like the real people, their characters here are all good guys.

I especially want to thank John & Shannon Raab at Suspense Publishing for their continued support and confidence, and Amy Lignor for her first-class editing. You guys are the best.

PRAISE FOR JOSEPH BADAL

"Riveting. A secret organization is killing high ranking military and political officials. The lives of at least a thousand people are in jeopardy as the clandestine entity plans to unleash a thousand sleeper cells. After an attempt on his life in Venice, Robert Danforth returns to action in a lightning paced thriller from the masterful Joseph Badal. A superb entry in a stellar series. Highly recommended."
—Sheldon Siegel, *New York Times* Bestselling Author of the *Mike Daley/Rosie Fernandez* Series

"Relentless from start to finish, *The Carnevale Conspiracy* is a tension-filled thriller that will delight fans of Brad Thor, Robert Ludlum, and Daniel Silva. As with the other novels in his *Danforth Saga* series, Joseph Badal masterfully weaves historical context into a modern adventure set in Venice, Italy, replete with villains you will love to hate and heroes you will cheer for."
—Steven Pressfield, Bestselling Author of *A Man At Arms*

"Who can resist an original take on international terrorism, smart bad guys, memorably crafted settings and a high-stakes game of revenge? Joseph Badal's latest soars to a climax at Venice's *Carnevale* that takes "thriller" to breathless new heights."
—Anne Hillerman, *New York Times* Bestselling Author of the *Chee/Leaphorn/Manuelito Mysteries*, Including *Stargazer*

"*The Carnevale Conspiracy* harks back to the golden age of thrillers, a beautifully executed tale that reads like a hybrid mix of Alistair McClean, Robert Ludlum and John le Carre. The sprawl of Joseph Badal's seminal effort is exceeded only by the ambition of this tale where the fate and future of the world are quite literally at stake. *The Carnevale Conspiracy* is a thriller lover's dream, hitting the bulls-eye dead center from first page to last."
—Jon Land, *USA Today* Bestselling Author

"Joseph Badal has produced a terrific new thriller with his latest novel, *The Carnevale Conspiracy*. The seventh entry in the *Danforth Saga* has got it all. An engaging cast of good guys and memorable villains. A tour of the Venice canals and ancient alleyways. And an audacious page-turner of a plot: A thousand sleeper agents trained at the assassins' lair of the Old Man of the Mountain in Iran. All with the same goal, the mass murder of an equal number of military leaders, politicians and business executives—with the Danforths as special targets—in an attempt to disrupt and dishearten the West. As the Italians would say, "moltobene!""
—Paul Kemprecos, #1 *New York Times* Bestselling Author of *Killing Icarus*

"It's a dangerous world in which the characters in *The Carnevale Conspiracy* find themselves. No one does international conspiracy adventures better than Joseph Badal. He's been there."
—Steven Havill, Award-Winning Author of *The Posadas County Mysteries*

THE CARNEVALE CONSPIRACY

JOSEPH BADAL

"They call him Shayk-al-Hashishim. He is their Elder, and upon his command all of thye men of the mountain come out or go in…they are believers of the word of their Elder and everyone everywhere fears them, because they even kill kings."

—Benjamin of Tudela, circa 1165 A.D.

FRIDAY
FEBRUARY 15

CHAPTER 1

The Old Man of the Mountain, Hassan Nizari, preceded his aide and right-hand man, Javad Muntaziri, up the concrete stairs and through the steel door to the roof of the massive stone fortress. He walked toward the south side of the one-thousand-meter-long parapet that ran around the structure's circuitous edge.

"Wait here," Nizari ordered Muntaziri when he was twenty meters from the parapet.

The bull-hide soles of his *giveh* scraped the stone surface as Nizari slowly shuffled to the middle of the two-foot-high parapet wall. Frigid wind penetrated his traditional blouse and pants—the *jameh* and *shalvar*, causing him to wrap the sides of his robe across his chest. He peered from his aerie on the massive rock mesa down at the Cloud Forest. His heart swelled as shafts of sunlight pierced dozens of gaps between the clouds and lanced down into the mist that blanketed the treetops hundreds of feet below. Raptors circled between the clouds and mist, riding the updrafts that came off the forest floor. An antlered stag bounded across a clearing, stopped, raised its head as though to test the breeze, and disappeared into the tree line. Nothing about the view had changed in the last four decades, except for its clarity. The cataracts in his eyes now dimmed the sky's brilliance, the sunlight, and the forest, but didn't impact the memory of the first time he'd stood in this same spot and looked out over his secret domain.

Back in 1981, he hadn't dared argue against the decision to place his headquarters in this secluded area, at the northern edge of Iran's Semnan Province, barely a kilometer from neighboring Golestan Province. Of course, it made sense from a security standpoint. But, after so many years, he still chaffed at the isolation. He would have preferred to be closer to his hometown of Shahroud, where Highways 44 and 83 intersected, where there was a railroad, where he'd attended the University of Technology-Engineering, and where his siblings and cousins lived. But the Ayatollah Ruhollah Khomeini had insisted on this remote spot.

And who was I to object to what the Great Ayatollah wanted? he thought.

Though he'd spent fifteen years in exile with Khomeini in France and was one of the Ayatollah's most faithful acolytes, he knew disobedience, or even questioning the man, could be fateful. After all, the Ayatollah was a *marja*, a source of emulation. His ideas, pronouncements, and even his thoughts were considered sacred.

He reflected on how, after Khomeini came out of exile in France and returned to Iran in 1979, Nizari had entered another form of exile. A man sent by Khomeini delivered a note to him one week after they'd returned to Iran. That note read: *"The Prophet wrote, 'Whoso pursues the road of knowledge, God will direct him to the road of Paradise. Verily, the superiority of a learned man over a mere worshipper is like that of the full moon over all the stars!'"* Nizari understood the words but had been confused about their context. His confusion only grew with the note's final sentences: *"You will study all there is to know about the most revered Hassan-I Sabbah. And, from this day forward, you will no longer use your birth name. You will henceforth be known as Hassan Nizari—Hassan from Hassan-I Sabbah; Nizari from the Nizari Ismailis."* He'd been shunted off to a mosque in Azerbaijan, in a remote village near the Soviet border, in a region that even the most unsophisticated Iranian considered backward.

For a time, he'd contemplated fleeing Iran to find better opportunities elsewhere, when one day, in 1981, everything changed. On that day, he came to understand the Ayatollah's genius and vision. And he finally comprehended that his exile in

Azerbaijan had been to ensure that no one suspected he was to be the man in charge of executing the Ayatollah's most ambitious plan. The Supreme Leader wanted him to be the "forgotten man" so that he could become "Khomeini's Secret Sword." On that day, he'd received another handwritten note from his mentor: *"You will build a new Order of Assassins, patterned after that group that Hassan-I Sabbah formed in the twelfth century. You will recruit one thousand young men and women from all the Prophet's lands to fill the world like dormant seeds that will bloom when the time is right. You will train them as Hassan-I Sabbah trained his followers. They will be intelligent warriors who will be able to meld into their new homelands' societies and cultures. But, most importantly of all, you will ensure they never lose sight of their goal: to eradicate our enemies."*

The note had included other information, including logistics. It ended with the words: *"You are my most trusted and valuable friend. You will have all the Islamic Republic of Iran's resources at your disposal."*

Nizari had harvested young people from across the Muslim world. He and his agents scoured refugee camps in Lebanon and Jordan and orphanages in countries from the Caucasus to Malaysia and the Philippines. But Iran's war with Iraq between 1980 and 1988 generated most of his recruits. During that conflict, boys as young as thirteen were recruited by the Iranian Army. Many of those who survived their service had been radicalized and traumatized to the point where killing became second nature. The war also left tens of thousands of children orphaned. The Iranian government culled the best and the brightest of them and passed them along to Nizari, their surrogate father. His enclave in the Cloud Forest became the home and training ground for myriad disaffected youth. Those who couldn't cope with the Spartan-like regimen were shunted off to child labor camps in Iran. Those who finished the training program became Nizari's—and Khomeini's—warriors.

Now seventy-eight years old and, despite failing health, Nizari reveled in what he'd accomplished. Years of preparation were about to lead to the execution of what Khomeini had envisioned. The Ayatollah died in 1989, but nothing had changed for Nizari.

Khomeini's successors had continued to fund his operations. And this year he would truly become his mentor's *Secret Sword*. The soft pad and cadence of footsteps behind him brought him from his reverie. He smiled but didn't turn around.

"Yasmin, my flower petal, are you trying to sneak up on me?" he said.

"You always hear me, *Baba*. You are impossible."

Nizari turned and took a short intake of breath. His twenty-six-year-old daughter always had that effect on him. Other than her unusually tall stature and her outspoken nature, she was the image of his third wife, the mother who had died giving birth to her. The same hazel-green, almond-shaped eyes; the long lashes; the perfectly formed, black eyebrows; the small, straight nose; the lush mouth; the long black hair that flowed to the middle of her back. Yasmin reminded him of the words from the great Hafiz's poem, *Saints Bowing in the Mountains*. He recited them to her:

"Do you know how beautiful you are?
I think not, my dear.
For as you talk of God, I see great parades with wildly colorful bands
Streaming from your mind and heart,
Carrying wonderful and secret messages
To every corner of this world."

"Oh, Baba, you embarrass me."

Nizari glanced past Yasmin, at Javad, who stood twenty meters away. He saw the man's hungry look. He'd seen it before whenever Yasmin was present. "You can leave us," he told the man. As Javad walked away, Nizari smiled at Yasmin. "Did you need something, daughter?"

"No, Baba. I just wanted to see how you were doing."

He stretched out an arm, inviting her to come forward. She moved into him, side-by-side. He pressed his face against her head, taking in the honey-tinged scent of her hair.

"You seem worried," she said.

He kissed the top of her head and turned her to face him. "Why do you say that, my flower petal?"

She confidently met his gaze. "I think your responsibilities weigh on you." She paused a beat and tilted her head to one side, as though wondering how he might respond.

He tried, without success, to not show the surprise he felt about his daughter's insight. He quickly clamped his mouth closed and shut his eyes for a moment. When he looked back at her, he said, "How did you become so wise?"

Yasmin's gaze didn't waver. "From the time I was a little child, I have listened to all you have said about your grand...endeavor."

He couldn't help himself and smiled. "My grand endeavor?"

"Yes, Baba. I want to join you in punishing our enemies."

"Is that what you think this is about?"

Yasmin's eyes hardened and her lips compressed into a cruel slash. "No, that is merely a means to an end."

"And that end would be?" he asked.

She looked at him as though he were a disappointing subordinate. The girl's expression startled Nizari. For a moment, he didn't recognize his own daughter, as though he was seeing a stranger. A heartless, soulless stranger.

"To destroy the West and take over the world, of course."

His breath suddenly caught in his lungs and his heart seemed to stop. He waited for his breathing to be restored. "Why do you think that's the end game?"

"Because that's what my goal would be."

"You mean ultimate Islamic domination?"

"No, Father. Islam is just the vehicle to achieve domination. It's global, political, and economic power that the mullahs want. They desire the subjugation of all peoples." She breathed loudly through her nostrils and said, "The new Persian Empire."

He was inclined to brush her off as a melodramatic female. But the look on her face stopped him. "How do you propose to help me, my child?"

"I will warn you about the men you should be wary of and identify the ones you should trust."

Nizari smiled. "You think you have the instincts to know men so well?"

"Yes."

"Give me an example of how you might advise me."

Her eyes seemed to light with fire as she stared, unblinkingly, at him. He felt a slight tremor course through him, as though he were being observed by a predator. The tremor stopped when her expression softened, and she said, "The Supreme Leader, Ayatollah Sayyid Noori Hamadani, is a weak link. He doesn't have Ayatollah Khomeini's vision nor President Shabani's backbone. Hamadani isn't a true believer. Sooner or later, he will withdraw support from you. I wouldn't be surprised if he doesn't one day tell the Americans about our location."

"To what purpose?"

"To eliminate the threat that our people pose."

Nizari nodded. "Perhaps, my child, but without Hamadani's support, we would be nothing."

"*With* his support we will surely be finished. If you are beholding to him, or anyone, you are a potential victim. You must eliminate him and his ilk."

"His ilk?"

"All the top mullahs."

He scoffed and showed her a supercilious smile. "And who will support us if they are…eliminated?"

Yasmin's expression changed again. She now appeared scornful. "The mullahs want the same thing Khomeini wanted—domination of the Middle East and all of its oil and gas. They want a land bridge from Iran all the way to the Mediterranean Sea. That's why they support Assad in Syria. Their adventures in Yemen can give them control of the Red Sea. They are using you as a pawn to get what they want. Once they have that, they will have a stranglehold on Europe and Asia. The United States will lose its European and Asian allies unless they can supply them with oil and gas. Those allies will sell their souls for a barrel of oil."

"The Americans are close to becoming petroleum exporters," Nizari said.

She just stared at him.

He narrowed his eyes. "You learned a great deal at those schools in Switzerland."

Her expression now blank, she said, "But I never forgot where I came from or what I believed in."

Beginning to think that Yasmin was out of her depth, Nizari showed a wan smile. "You said the mullahs are using me as a pawn. Explain yourself."

"They will eliminate you and your followers once you succeed in disrupting the West. The Asasiyun will be too dangerous to have around. A horde of killers running loose can be a threat to the mullahs. They will see you and your followers as wild tigers in their midst." After a moment's hesitation, she added, "Remember what King Phillip of France did to the Knights Templar."

"So, being under the mullahs' thumbs could be our ultimate undoing?" He said these words in a condescending tone, now convinced that Yasmin had lost touch with reality.

"That would be true if you didn't send assassins to kill Hamadani and the other mullahs. Cut off the snake's head and the body will wither. Once your mission is complete, you will be the greatest Persian hero of all time. Every man, woman, and child will sing praises to your name and bow at your feet. You will be the man who brings the entire Muslim world together as one unified empire."

"I thought you said that Islam is only the vehicle to achieve political and economic power."

"It is. But it will be the way to conquer the people's hearts and minds. You can achieve ultimate power if you own the people's souls *and* control the political and economic apparatus."

Yasmin's words washed over him like a chill wind. What Yasmin didn't know was that over the past four decades he had placed his agents in Iranian governmental departments where many of them had risen to important positions. He had anticipated that one day he and his acolytes might be perceived as too dangerous to have around. His men and women in the Iranian government were his eyes and ears today but could be the executioners of his enemies at some point. But he had never seen the placement of his agents in the government as a way for him to gain personal power. They were there as an insurance policy in case the mullahs turned against him. He drew in a breath, about to tell his daughter that he would think about what she had said, when she held up a finger.

"First, you should demand a large sum of money from the mullahs. Worse case, if things go bad, you will need funds to survive somewhere outside Iran."

"Leave Iran?"

She said, "Ayatollah Khomeini's vision has almost been achieved. The mullahs won't need you and the Asasiyun much longer. They will cut off our funding and send the Revolutionary Guards and Quds Forces against us."

"So, why would they give us this money you propose?"

"To keep their children and grandchildren safe."

"What?"

"They won't come after us if we have their children."

"Are you suggesting we kidnap children? Are you insane? We kidnap the mullahs' children and we will have targets on our backs. They *will* send the Revolutionary Guards and Quds Forces against us."

"No, Baba," Yasmin said. "Not if they want to get their children back. Besides, they won't know who took their children. I am—"

Nizari raised a hand, cutting her off. "You will never mention such a thing ever again. It is blasphemy…and insanity."

He watched Yasmin storm off and wondered what had happened to the sweet young girl he had raised.

CHAPTER 2

The water taxi plowed through the turbulent Venetian Lagoon as rain peppered the window glass, sounding like a million BBs. Wind whipped up the white-capped waves in the lagoon, rocking the little boat from side to side. Liz Danforth braced her hands against the starboard seats on either side of her and scowled across at her husband.

"Dammit, Bob, whose idea was this, anyway?" she said.

Bob moved awkwardly to the other side of the boat, sat next to her, and wrapped an arm around her.

"You've always talked about wanting to go to Venice during *Carnevale*. Well, here we are. You should be happy that I'm such a thoughtful, loving husband."

Liz frowned. "Did you notice we're the only people on this boat besides the pilot? What's that tell you?" Before he could respond, she answered her own question: "It tells me that people don't travel to Venice when the temperature is in the forties and it rains every other day."

"I wish you had said something before we left Bethesda. I mean—"

Liz cut him off. "Say Carnevale again."

"Why?"

"It excites me when you speak Italian."

"One word?"

"One word, a whole sentence…what difference does it make?"

"My God, you're seventy years old. That's quite a libido."

"You complaining?"

"Carnevale. Carnevale. Carnevale. Carne—"

"Okay, okay. That's enough. I might not be able to control myself long enough to get to our hotel room." She giggled and tried to kiss his cheek, but the boat banged against a wave and went airborne, causing her kiss to convert to a head butt.

"Ow," Bob said, as he rubbed the side of his head.

"Serves you right," she said, as she shifted in her seat, took his head in her hands, and kissed his mouth. She leaned back. "I'm just being grouchy because we've spent the last twelve hours on planes, in airports, in a taxi, and now on a boat shaped like a giant torpedo."

"And you miss your grandson."

She smiled. "That, too. I guess I shouldn't complain, considering Robbie's going through hell at West Point."

"Plebe year at the Point is by no means a walk in the park," Bob said. "But compared to what he went through in Syria last year, it's a breeze."

She shook her head as though in wonder and shuddered as she thought about how their grandson had been recruited out of college by the CIA to go undercover with ISIS in Syria. She looked back at Bob. "That letter he sent last week was nothing but bullet points: '0550 wake up, shave and dress, make bed, clean room; 0630 breakfast; 0700 to 0715 morning formation; 0730 to 1150 four academic periods.' Then lunch, three more academic periods. Sports activities, formation, dinner, restricted to barracks or library to study until 2330, then lights out. My God, how the hell can he survive on six hours sleep?"

"Nice to be young," Bob said, not adding that Robbie probably spent an hour or two more studying in the bathroom after lights out. "Entering the academy in the second half of the plebe year, he more than likely has a lot of catching up to do."

Liz continued to half-heartedly grouse about Robbie's schedule and how the 'damned Army' was going to ruin her grandson's health, but Bob only half-listened. His attention was on a speedboat off their port side. The boat was perhaps sixty yards away in an eight o'clock position to their boat, and rapidly gaining on them. The rain abated and a sliver of sunlight speared the trailing craft, highlighting two men in the partially covered wheelhouse amidships. In years past, when he'd come to the city on Company business, he'd learned that Venetians were some of the most adventuresome boaters on the planet. But it wasn't so much the other boat's speed that had caught his attention. It was the large man—at least six feet, four inches tall, with the shoulders and torso of a weightlifter—who stepped out of the covered pilothouse, seemingly unconcerned about the rain, appearing to laser-focus on their craft. The right side of the man's face appeared to be half-covered with an angry purple stain that could have resulted from injury or was a port-wine birth mark. In any case, the man's size and facial marking made him stand out.

"Bob, are you listening to me?"

"What?" Bob said.

"Where were you? I said your name three times."

"Oh, sorry, honey. Just thinking about Robbie."

"Uh-huh."

Bob glanced back at the other boat as their taxi pilot steered into a tight channel that terminated at a covered slip leading to the side of their hotel. The speedboat had veered away from the channel and disappeared. Bob shrugged, silently chastising himself for an overactive imagination. *Relax, idiot*, he thought, *you're on vacation.* He turned his attention to two young, uniformed men who stood on one side of the slip. They welcomed them to the hotel. One young man whisked away their bags, while the other shepherded them up a steep staircase to the check-in area, which was a desk fronted by two plush chairs. A young woman who was a dead ringer for the actress, Monica Bellucci, checked them in.

Bob thanked her for her assistance: "*Grazie per il vostro aiuto.*"

The woman brightened and answered, "*Spero che tu abbia una meravigliosa visita a Venezia.*"

"*Sono certo che lo faremo.*"

As they followed the bellman to their room, Bob asked Liz, "Do you want to know what that little conversation was all about?"

She squeezed his arm with her hand and whispered, "I couldn't care less. Just get rid of the bellman and put the DO NOT DISTURB sign on the door."

The rain had stopped and sun penetrated their room, bathing it in a golden glow. Bob carefully slipped out of bed at 3:15 p.m., trying not to wake Liz. But she stirred and asked, "What are you doing?" They'd earlier decided to take the fifteen-minute hotel water shuttle ride at 6:00 p.m. to Venice City proper, where it docked at San Marco Plaza, to explore the area, and then have dinner.

"You feel like taking a walk?" Bob asked.

She yawned. "I'm exhausted. I think I'll stay in bed. *You* should come back to bed."

"Good idea, but I think I'll first stretch my legs a bit."

"Sounds like a reconnaissance mission."

He laughed. "I guess I could recon the spa and see if there are any young women wearing Spandex."

She scoffed. "Remember, you had a heart attack recently. Don't overwork the old ticker."

He chuckled. "I won't be long."

Bob dressed, took the elevator down to the lobby, and walked to the bar. He sat at a two-top table in a corner, ordered a Coca-Cola from a waiter, and then, when the man brought his drink and the bill, took out his cell phone and called his old friend, Tanya Serkovic, Director of Central Intelligence at Langley.

"DCI's office, Penelope Simmons speaking."

"Penelope, its Bob Danforth. Is the director available?"

"I'll check. You want to leave your number in case she'll have to call you back?"

"It's nice of you to ask for my number, Penelope, but I know you already captured it off Caller I.D."

Penelope chuckled. "I'll see if she can pick up, Mr. Danforth."

Bob only had to wait a few seconds.

"Hey, Bob. How are you?"

"Good, Tanya. Thanks for taking my call."

"You know better than that."

"How are things there?" he asked.

"Other than terrorism, political battles, Russian interference, Chinese hackers, events on the Korean Peninsula, Turkey's incursion into Kurd country, the Iranian Mullahs, and the like, all's good. Didn't I hear you and Liz were on a trip?"

"We're in Italy."

"So why the call?"

"Do you have anything going on over here? Venice, specifically?"

"You know I can't answer that question, especially with you calling on an unsecure line." She paused a beat, then asked, "Why?"

"I noticed someone who seemed…out of place."

"Paranoia or instinct?"

"*Hmmm.* Maybe a little of both."

"You want a suggestion?"

"Even if I said no, I have a feeling you'll give it to me anyway."

"You're on vacation. Enjoy yourself."

"I had the same thought."

"But you called me anyway."

"Yeah. Thanks for the advice. I'll do my best."

After he hung up, Bob rehashed his conversation with Tanya. Reading between the lines, he knew she had essentially told him the Company had nothing special going on in Venice. This didn't really put his mind at ease. If the tall man he'd seen earlier was "off," so to speak, he could be an unaffiliated agent or someone representing a terrorist group. Or, maybe the guy was just a very large Italian who liked to look at other boats. *Maybe Tanya's correct*, he thought. *I've got to try to relax, to remember that I'm nothing but a civilian now. I don't want to ruin this trip for Liz by conjuring up imaginary boogiemen.* He drank half his soda, sucked an ice cube into his mouth, set the glass on the table, and picked up the bill.

"Holy…" he mumbled around the ice cube. "Ten Euros." *Almost twelve dollars*, he thought. *What the hell is dinner going to cost?*

CHAPTER 3

The night air was crisp and cool as Bob and Liz exited the water taxi that had carried them from their hotel to the boat slip, half-a-minutes' walk from *Piazza San Marco*. They had overdressed in case the temperature dropped: he in a pea coat, purple sweater over a white dress shirt, khakis, and deck shoes; she in a black leather coat over a cashmere sweater, black slacks, black short boots, and a black and burgundy print Hermes scarf wrapped around her neck. Bob carried an umbrella.

There were scatterings of people along the waterfront, but nothing like what Bob remembered when he'd traveled to Venice for the CIA in June twenty years earlier. As they turned into the mouth of the piazza, Liz pulled back on his arm and stopped.

"Oh, my goodness," she whispered. "It's beautiful."

"I thought you'd be impressed. There's something special about it, especially at night, with the lights."

A few young men scattered around the plaza used rubber band-propelled launchers that shot little missiles into the air that lit up and twirled like mini helicopters as they fell back to earth.

"The local Rom vendors," Bob said. He felt Liz's arm tighten on his. "They're harmless, honey." But he knew that just the thought of their son Michael's kidnapping by a Gypsy band over four decades ago while Bob was stationed with the U.S. Army in Greece was enough to set her on edge. He kissed the side of her head. "Let's move on. I want you to see this area tonight." He waved his free hand around as though to take in all that Venice had to offer. "It's more than you can imagine."

Bob pointed out some of the main attractions in and around the plaza, including St. Mark's Basilica, the Doge's Palace, Museo Correr, the National Archaeological Museum, the Bibliotech Nationale Marciana, and the 323-foot-high Campanile Bell Tower.

"I have tickets to tour all of them in the next few days," he said.

Liz gave him a grateful look, then squeezed his arm and kissed his cheek. "You're full of surprises," she told him.

They strolled a bit more around the plaza and window-shopped for a while.

"You getting hungry?" Liz said after half an hour.

"You bet," Bob said.

"What time is it?"

"Does that matter?" he said. "If you're hungry, we'll eat."

"How about a casual dinner? Nothing fancy. Is that okay?"

"Perfect," Bob said. "I suspect jet lag will be our new friend in a couple hours. A long, heavy meal would knock me to my knees."

As they strolled arm-in-arm, toward the plaza's northeast corner, Bob suddenly stopped and stared at a column on their left. He thought he saw the large man he'd spotted on the boat earlier that day. But the man disappeared in an instant.

"What is it?" Liz asked. "You tensed up for a second."

"Uh, nothing. I guess I'm just overwhelmed." He looked around. "I think I could come here a hundred times and never tire of the sights, sounds, and smells of Venice. The city had a bad reputation in the past because of the harbor water's raunchy condition. They've cleaned things up."

"Speaking of smells, is that garlic? My stomach's growling."

"Then I guess I'd better fix that," he said. "You still want something casual?"

"Please. I'll fall asleep at the table if we have a long, drawn out meal."

He slipped his arm out of hers and took her hand. "I know just the place. It's called Tuttinpiedi. It serves take-out."

"Take-out? Like McDonalds?"

Bob chuckled. "Take-out here isn't the same as take-out back home. You'll see."

As they exited the plaza, Liz asked, "You think the restaurant will still be in business?"

Bob grinned. "I checked the Internet." He pointed up the narrow lane ahead. "There it is."

After a quick look at the menu, Liz said, "*This* is what I call 'take-out.'"

The aromas of cooking garlic, tomatoes, meats, and pastas had teased them from outside the little restaurant located on the Corte delle Ancore, a short walk from the plaza. Inside Tuttinpiedi, Bob looked at Liz. The sounds of conversations and the sizzling of meals being prepared; the smells of spices; the sights of already-prepared meals in a small display case; dozens of bottles of Italian wine and beer; and cooks spooning food from pans into white take-out containers all appeared to be having an effect on her. *She looks just plain happy*, he thought.

"*Buonasera*," a man behind the counter said in greeting.

"*Buonasera*," Bob responded. Then he ordered a glass of white wine for Liz, and *Chianti* for himself.

"What do you feel like eating?" he asked Liz.

"Surprise me," she said.

Bob left Liz at the front of the restaurant, near the window that looked out on the corte, and asked the counterman for his recommendation. They conversed in Italian for a few seconds. Bob thanked the man, paid him, took two glasses of wine from the man, and rejoined Liz. He handed her a glass, raised his, and said, "Salute."

Liz clinked her glass against his, sipped the wine, and placed the glass on a small ledge inside the front window. "Nice," she said. "What are we eating?" she asked.

"It's a surprise."

"Come on, I'm too tired for surprises."

"*Ragù di lepre e piselli.*"

She cocked her head, batted her eyelashes, and whispered, "There you go again, getting me all hot and bothered."

"Jeez. Are you getting frisky again?"

"Depends on what you ordered for me."

"Wait until you taste it."

"Are you going to tell me what it is before I take a bite?"

"I thought you wanted to be surprised." He lifted his glass again. She picked up hers and took another sip.

"This is divine," she said.

Bob looked out the window and pointed out the Teatro San Gallo. "We should go to a performance," he said. "They're about the history of Venice."

"Are they in English or Italian?"

"Italian." He chuckled. "Maybe we'd better not go. If you get excited about me speaking a few words in Italian, I can't imagine what would happen to you at an Italian theater performance."

Liz giggled. "It's *you* that gets me excited."

Bob shook his head. "I don't know what I did to deserve you."

"Just lucky, I guess."

The counterman called out, "*Signore, i tuoi pasti sono pronti.*"

Bob placed his glass on the ledge and walked to the counter, where he picked up two take-out containers. As he turned back toward Liz, an outdoor fixture cast a brilliant cone of light on a very tall man in a doorway across the corte. Bob's breath caught in his chest. Then the man moved away and disappeared into the shadows along the little square's far side. Bob stopped and stared, trying in vain to spot the man.

"Sonofa—" Bob muttered. *Who is that guy?*

Liz had also been looking out on the corte and didn't see Bob's reaction. By the time she turned back, he had composed himself and wore a smile. He handed her one of the containers and a fork, and said, "Tell me what you think."

She raised the container to her nose and inhaled the steamy vapors wafting off the food.

"My God, it's heavenly."

She forked up a small portion, tried a wary bite, and rolled her eyes. "Okay, now you have to tell me what I'm eating. It's wonderful."

"*Ragù di lepre e piselli.*"

"Which is?"

"Rabbit ragù with peas."

Her eyes went wide. "I'm eating Thumper?"

"Nah. But maybe a distant cousin of Thumper's."

She shot him a faux-horrified look, laughed, scooped up a forkful, and said, "I'll never again be able to think about *Bambi* in the same way."

"We should try venison tomorrow."

"You're sick, Bob Danforth."

Bob glanced over Liz's shoulder, through the window and at the corte. He felt a twinge of nervousness in his belly and a tingling sensation at the back of his neck. One or two sightings of a particular stranger might be coincidental; three, was a whole other thing.

SATURDAY
FEBRUARY 16

CHAPTER 4

The *Agenzia Informazioni e Sicurezza Esterna* (External Intelligence and Security Agency), commonly known as AISE, is the foreign intelligence service of Italy, akin to the CIA. It's limited to operations outside the boundaries of Italy and protects the country's regional interests mainly using HUMINT (Human intelligence). The Deputy Directors of AISE report to the Director and are, as is the Director, hired and fired by the President of the Council of Ministers. Deputy Directors, by definition, are almost invariably politically astute, well-connected to the "hot rocks" of Italian society, and often wealthy. Occasionally, a Deputy Director is also an intelligence operative with extensive field experience. Giovanni Ventimiglia was both wealthy and an experienced field operative.

Bob and Giovanni had stayed in touch, even after Bob retired and Giovanni had returned to the private sector to work in his family's leather goods manufacturing company. After Bob and Liz made plans to visit Venice, Giovanni was the first person Bob had called. Giovanni and his wife, Anna, had invited Bob and Liz to join them as their guests on February 23 at the grandest Carnevale ball: *Il Ballo del Doge* at *Palazzo Pisani Moretta*. Liz was thrilled at the prospect of attending the ball. Bob was mortified because Giovanni had told him that costumes were compulsory. "The more extravagant, the better," he'd said.

"We should shop for masks and costumes today," Liz told Bob

as they finished breakfast at their hotel.

Bob groaned.

"Poor baby," Liz said. "You've never been big on dressing up."

Bob grumbled something unintelligible.

"What was that?"

"I always hated Halloween. From what I've read about these carnival balls, they're like Halloween on steroids."

"What are you going to do, tell Giovanni and Anna that you don't want to go?"

"The thought crossed my mind. I could fake being ill."

"One reason I always wanted to come to Venice during Carnevale was to go to a ball. Now we're here." She shot him a sour expression. "If you don't want to go, fine. But I'm going. I'm sure Anna can find a young Italian who would be happy to escort me."

Bob raised his eyebrows and rubbed his forehead. "You'd go without me?"

"In a flash, grumpy. Besides, I would probably have more fun if you stayed here in the hotel. You'll spend the entire ball complaining."

Bob was thinking about the psychic price he would likely pay for not going to the ball with Liz when she suddenly stood and announced, "I'm going to the room to get my umbrella and a jacket."

He said, "The ball's not until next Saturday. I'll think about it."

She showed him the sour expression again. "Don't do me any favors."

Bob quickly stood, shoved his chair against the table, and followed her from the dining room to the elevator lobby. He was hoping to mitigate the tension between them when his cell phone rang. Giovanni's name showed on the screen.

"Hello, Giovanni," Bob said.

"Roberto, welcome to Venice. We're looking forward to seeing you. What's your schedule look like?"

Bob put his phone on speaker mode and answered, "We're pretty open, other than a few tours we've signed up for."

"How about dinner tomorrow at our home?"

"Oh, no, Giovanni. Please let us take you to dinner."

"Nonsense, my friend. You're in *my* city."

Bob caught himself before accepting the invitation. He and Liz had long ago agreed that neither of them would commit to social events without conferring with the other. She was already peeved at him. He wasn't about to make things worse. But before he could ask her, Liz was already enthusiastically nodding her head.

"Sounds great, Giovanni," Bob said.

"Wonderful. Anna is looking forward to meeting Liz. How about 8:00?"

"Perfect," Bob said. "Please tell Anna I'm looking forward to seeing her again."

"I'll text directions. You'll need to take a water taxi."

Bob was about to sign off, when Liz said, "Giovanni, would you recommend a shop where I can rent a costume for the ball?"

"Oh, that won't be necessary," Giovanni said. "Anna has already arranged for costumes for both of you. She's on the ball coordinating committee. They have hundreds of outfits that she chose from."

Bob said a grudging, "Thank you." *This is not looking good*, he thought.

CHAPTER 5

Hassan Nizari stared at the computer screen on his office desk. His heart swelled with pride as he followed the success of his agents. Phase One had already begun. Six messages had gone out; five targets had been dispatched.

"My children," he whispered, "you make me proud."

"What was that, Father?"

Nizari turned and smiled at his daughter. "Yasmin, I thought you were resting."

She scoffed. "I am more interested in knowing how things have progressed with the mission. What news?"

Nizari turned back to the computer and tapped the screen. "Five targets eliminated. There will soon be many more."

"I have no doubt, Father. Our agents are the best trained in the world."

Nizari was uncomfortable with his daughter's hyperbole, but he didn't correct her. He knew his assassins were some of the best operatives on the planet, but he also knew there were high-quality killers in many other countries, including military special operatives in the United States, Russia, France, England, and Israel. Where his people were without equal was in infiltration. After all, that's what they'd been trained to do—infiltrate, assimilate, and wait. Then kill.

"When will you release the others?" Yasmin asked.

"Soon, my child. Soon."

"Why not release all one thousand at once? For maximum shock."

He turned back to her and waggled a hand. "I told you *soon*, my dear. I want to see how our enemies react." He chuckled for a moment. "And I want them to think that we are...a smaller organization than we really are. These first attacks are effective, but more diversionary in nature." He chuckled again. "It's misdirection. Do you understand?"

Yasmin narrowed her eyes and nodded.

"I want our enemies to be frightened, but I also want them lulled into believing that nothing more consequential is afoot than scattered assassinations. By watching the Western media and paying attention to what their politicians say, we will know much of what they are thinking and what they might know about us." He scoffed. "Once we've released the first couple dozen agents, the West will be in shock. Then we'll pause. They'll think the assassinations have ended. While they're mourning the first few deaths, and are thinking that the attacks have ended, I'll rain havoc down on them."

Nizari saw his daughter's face flush. He could tell she was frustrated. "What bothers you, Yasmin?"

"I think you're missing an opportunity. Our enemies will be better prepared to defend against our other assassins if we give them time. I think—"

Nizari thrust a hand at his daughter and glared at her. "Perhaps I have indulged you too much, my sweet. I think now would be a good time for you to get some rest."

Her mouth opened, as though she was about to respond, but she quickly snapped it shut, wheeled around, and hurried from the room.

As Nizari turned back to his computer, he thought, *Khomeini was correct. Education corrupts women.*

The skies were gray, the temperature in the mid-forties, as Bob and Liz boarded the water taxi outside their hotel and took seats close to the stern in the boat's covered area. The good news was, it wasn't raining. A spectacular beam of sunlight penetrated the cloud cover and speared the Basilica della Salute's dome at the mouth of the Grand Canal. *Maybe the weather will improve as the day goes on*, Bob thought.

He wanted to apologize to Liz for his earlier comments concerning the costume ball, but a family of six had also boarded the taxi. Based on their Cuban Spanglish, Bob guessed they might be from Miami. The children appeared to range in age from five to fifteen. The father and the oldest child, a daughter, separated from the rest of the clan, as though they wanted nothing to do with them. They took seats on the opposite end of the long bench seat from Bob and Liz. The mother and the three youngest children planted themselves directly across the aisle from Bob and Liz. The woman appeared frazzled—her eyes wide and frequently blinking, her gaze darting and her head jerking from side-to-side, like a spectator at a ping pong match. It took less than thirty seconds for Bob to discover why. The three children across from him were like gerbils in a cage. They careened around the cabin as though they were strung out on a concoction of amphetamines, caffeine, and sugar. When Bob caught the father's eye, the man smiled anemically and shook his head.

Five minutes into the ride to the dock at Piazza San Marco, Bob took Liz's hand and said, "Let's go to the other side." He led the way down the narrow aisle between the bench seats, climbed the stairs to the platform by the wheelhouse, and stepped down into the seating area on the bow side. He waited for Liz to sit, sat down across from her, and said, "Sorry about before."

"That's okay. I know how you feel about—"

He placed his elbows on his thighs and leaned toward her. "How I feel is irrelevant. I know how much you have looked forward to coming here and to Carnevale. I'll do whatever it takes to make this trip a good one." He paused a beat. "But there's no way I'm wearing tights."

She laughed. "But, sweetheart, you have such great legs. You'd look wonderful in tights."

The shuttle boat docked; Bob and Liz walked out onto the pier. The cloud cover had broken up a bit, and sunlight highlighted the Venice skyline in a dozen places. They strolled through the piazza, exited at the rear, and meandered along a narrow lane sporting high-end fashion stores. At the end of the lane, they turned left—back toward the Grand Canal—and found a gondola parked outside the Baglioni Hotel Luna.

"How about a gondola ride?" Bob asked.

Liz's face lit up. "Oh, that would be perfect."

Bob bought tickets at a kiosk, led Liz to a gondola, stepped into the boat, took her hand, and helped her down to a seat. He settled in next to her and said, "You look overwhelmed."

She leaned into him and whispered, "If the gondolier starts singing, I might pass out."

Bob laughed, looked over his shoulder, and told the gondolier, "*Giorgio, la musica per favore.*"

The gondolier turned on a music CD and, in a rich tenor, sang *Santa Lucia.*

"Aw, jeez, Bob. You're killing me."

"Nothing but the best for my girl."

"Say that in Italian and I'll follow you anywhere."

He chuckled, put an arm around her, and opened his mouth to speak, but she placed a hand over his mouth and whispered, "Don't you dare."

After the gondolier finished singing, he pointed out sites along the canal route.

"That's the Teatro La Fenice," the man said as he turned the boat from Rio Delle Ostreghe into Rio Delle Veste. "Many famous singers have performed there."

"Isn't it a beautiful building?" Liz said.

"Uh-huh," Bob said.

She nudged him with an elbow. "Are you paying attention?"

"Of course," he said. "It *is* a beautiful building."

But his concentration was no longer on La Fenice. As the gondola had approached the Calle Delle Veste Bridge, he'd noticed a man standing on the bridge. The man didn't appear to be focused on them. But there was no question it was the same guy he'd seen several times since they'd arrived in Venice: tall—well over six feet, maybe early thirties; he had what looked like a vivid port-wine birthmark on his left cheek; a black ball cap with a Toshiba logo; aviator sunglasses; purple shirt; jeans; and a backpack.

After they passed under the bridge, Bob looked back. The man had disappeared.

"What are you looking at?" Liz asked.

Bob turned back around. "Getting another look at the opera house."

She shot him a skeptical look.

"What?"

"Nothing."

After their gondola ride, Bob and Liz walked to the *Arsenale*, the *Biennale Architettura* venue. The exhibit was vast, a quarter mile-long central corridor with exhibit after exhibit in spaces on either side. Halfway down the corridor, Liz took pity on Bob and suggested they take a break and get something to eat.

"You sure?" Bob asked. "I thought you wanted to see the whole thing."

She grabbed his hand, squeezed it, and waved her free hand around as though to take in the huge building and its massive collection of architectural models. "I can see that you're about to overdose on culture."

"I could eat," he said.

She giggled and said, "Let's do it."

As they turned and headed toward an exit—a good fifty yards ahead, Bob noticed someone scurry into one of the exhibits about thirty yards down on the right side.

"I'll be damned," he muttered.

"What is it?" Liz said.

"Wait here," he said, and fast-walked forward. Just a few steps from the exhibit, the man with the port-wine birthmark leaped into the corridor and sprinted toward the main entrance.

"Bob!" Liz called out.

He ignored her and ran after the man, losing ground with each step. He was still one hundred yards from the main entrance when the much younger man disappeared.

Bob's breathing was labored as he bent over, hands on his knees.

He was still gasping when Liz came up beside him, placed a hand on his back, and said, "Are you all right?"

He raised a hand and gasped, "Give me…a minute…to catch…my breath."

"What was that all about?"

"Probably…nothing. I—"

"Are you sure you're all right?"

He straightened, took a deep breath, released it slowly, and gave her a self-deprecatory grin. "I'm just a little out of shape…I guess."

"Why did you run after that man?"

"What man?"

Liz poked a finger in his chest. "What the hell's going on? What are you playing at?"

Bob raised his hands in surrender, took Liz's arm, and steered her to a bench on the side of the central corridor.

"I've seen the same guy several times," Bob said. "I believe he's been following us." He pointed down the corridor and added, "I just saw him again."

"So, you went after some guy who you thought might be what? An assassin? A terrorist? What?"

Bob touched her arm. "Calm down, honey. I just got tired of being followed."

"By a man who might be a tourist."

He shrugged. "That's possible. It just seems too much of a coincidence that the man keeps popping up."

"You don't believe in coincidences."

"Right."

Liz huffed, stood, slung her bag over her shoulder, and turned toward him. Her jaw went rigid as her eyes bored into his. "Are you intentionally trying to sabotage our trip?" she said, her voice high-pitched and strident. "I mean, what do you think is going on? That some international organization has sent someone to Venice to spy on you? You're a seventy-three-year-old man who's been retired for years. You had a heart attack last year. Now you're running after ghosts in the middle of Venice." She took a breath. "You just can't disengage from the goddamn C-I-A, can you?"

Tears flooded her eyes and her rigid posture suddenly seemed to dissolve. She shook her head, wheeled around, and marched toward the Arsenale entrance.

"Liz," Bob called after her.

She waved an arm in his direction and continued to walk away.

"Wait," he said.

She spun around and pumped her hands at him. "I'm going back to the hotel. I don't want to be with you right now."

Bob watched Liz stride away, her sandals slapping the concrete corridor. When she reached the entrance, turned right, and disappeared, he stood and whispered, "I was just trying to protect us." But then he thought, *From what? Liz is probably right; I'm imagining things.*

He thought about rushing to catch up with Liz but decided it would be best to leave her on her own for a while. After departing the Arsenale, he meandered around Venice, crossing bridges over canals, and passing stores, restaurants, residences, and historic buildings. He stopped at a store and bought a hand-carved cane with a large pinecone-shaped knob handle for Liz's collection: a peace offering. He bought a bottle of water at a kiosk twenty yards from the cane store and continued his disjointed wanderings through the alleys and lanes of Venice, paying no attention to where he was as his mind worked on the man he'd repeatedly seen. After an hour, he found himself on one side of a small square, outside the Hotel La Residenza. The lane he'd come in on seemed to continue for a block or so, but he couldn't tell if it dead-ended or turned. According to his internal compass, it didn't look like it went in the direction of Piazza San Marco, where he needed to catch the water taxi back to their hotel. There was what appeared to be a museum on the left side of the square, but dense, purplish-black clouds had come up suddenly and turned the square midnight-dark, even though it was only afternoon. It was impossible to read the sign on the building from where he stood. There appeared to be an exit from the square on the far-right side, but he couldn't be certain. A few paces away was the opening to an alley. He walked to the top of it but, because of the cloud cover, couldn't make out anything beyond ten yards. Again, it didn't seem to go off in the direction he needed. He did a slow three hundred and sixty degree turn but couldn't spot any exits to the square that would take him in the direction of San Marco. The square was dominated by two to four-story, cheek-to-jowl buildings that Bob guessed were probably apartments. The only exceptions to the residential buildings were the hotel, the museum, and two retail stores—a small café and a nondescript shop of some sort. He seemed to be alone.

Hiding inside, he thought. *At least they have the sense to get out of the weather that's surely coming.* When he completed a full turn, he realized he would have to backtrack until he found a street that would access San Marco Piazza.

Bob placed the plastic water bottle and the cane under one arm, took a map of Venice from a jacket pocket, and moved under a light on the hotel's corner. He tried to find his location on the map, without success. He looked up to see if he could spot a landmark, but it was too dark, and he was too close to the surrounding buildings to see anything beyond their roofs. He squinted up at the hotel to see if the street name was on the building's façade. But before he could read the name in the muted light, he thought he saw shadowy movement in his peripheral vision in the alley to his left. He jerked his gaze and glanced down the alley as he instinctively stepped to his right, behind the cover of the building. But even before he reached the building's edge, he felt foolish, thinking that he'd allowed the paranoia he'd developed from decades with the Company to affect him.

Jeez, what an idiot I am, he thought.

He looked around, wondering if anyone had seen him react as he had. But the tiny square still appeared to be deserted. For a moment, Liz's comment about him imagining things came to mind and he smiled at his own reaction. He was about to turn back to find a street sign when the movement he'd already discounted as nothing grew in shape and substance. A man dressed all in black broke from the alley and strode with purpose toward him. A pistol was held in his right hand.

Bob's heart seemed to stop as the man moved toward him, his pistol-hand extended. He released the map, which the strong breeze carried at the man, smacking his face, distracting him. The gunman swatted at the map, then snatched it away. Bob let the water bottle drop and swung the cane, striking the man's left shoulder. The gunman grunted, then shouted what sounded like a curse. Bob took a step forward, brought the cane back again, and hit the man's right arm. At the same time, he heard the *phfft, phfft* noise of a fired, silenced weapon. A metallic *twang* rang out as a bullet apparently hit something across the square.

When Bob moved forward again, he tripped on a cobblestone, fell, dropped the cane, and rolled against the hotel wall. He tried to gather his legs under him as he reached for the cane. Pressing one hand against the hotel's stone wall, Bob gripped a narrow ledge as he snatched up the cane with his left hand and struggled to his feet. He heard the gunman mutter angrily. Bob again swung at the man, who took the blow with a loud grunt and jerked the cane from Bob's grasp. The man punched him in the sternum, knocking him to the ground again; a loud *oomph* exploded from Bob's lungs. His back seemed to seize as he looked up at the gunman, anticipating the impact of a bullet.

In the low light cast through a window from inside the hotel, he watched the man step toward him. The meager illumination gave Bob a muted view of the man's features: medium height, slim built, a milky-white complexion, and brush-cut, blond hair—a California surfer boy without the tan. The guy flashed a gleaming, toothy smile as he looked directly into Bob's eyes, pointed his pistol, and said in perfect Venice-accented Italian, "I have a message for you from the Old Man of the Mountain."

The gunman stepped forward and came around to Bob's left side. He kicked Bob in the ribs, sending a shockwave of pain through his chest. He placed the barrel of his weapon six inches from Bob's nose, his feral grin a mixture of evil and glee.

Bob gasped for breath.

The man said in a raspy voice, "*Orden pobedit.*" He grinned again and moved the pistol to within an inch of Bob's face.

All Bob could concentrate on was the hole in the end of the noise suppressor as he waited for a bullet to end his life. But a sound like someone clearing his throat came from behind him, causing the gunman to look to his right. Bob saw the man's gun hand jerk upward. He rolled away, but kept his gaze locked on the man's face, on his surprised expression: mouth agape; eyes wide. Then, in an instant, the man's features changed. He appeared to be in excruciating pain. A loud groan escaped his throat, then gurgling sounds as he crashed backward onto the stone pathway. The gunman writhed as blood poured from his mouth, and from around a knife embedded in his throat.

His lungs now working, but his ribs, chest, and back hot with pain, Bob got to his knees, then fought to stand. His body trembled with adrenaline overload as he tried to make sense of what had just happened.

"Are you all right?" a man asked.

Bob spun around and stared open-mouthed at a tall man with a port-wine birthmark on his left cheek.

"You," Bob exclaimed as his heart clenched.

"I suggest you step aside," the tall man said as he pulled the knife from the gunman's throat. He waited for Bob to back up a few steps, moved behind the writhing gunman, and sliced the blade across the man's throat—severing his jugular vein and carotid artery on the right side of his neck. Arterial blood sprayed the cobblestones. The man wiped the knife on the gunman's jacket and then retracted the blade. After returning the knife to his pocket, he took Bob's arm. "I think it would be a very good idea if we left here."

"Who the hell are you?" Bob asked in a half-strangled voice.

"Later," the man said, as he grabbed Bob's arm and moved toward the lane by which Bob had entered the square.

Freeing himself from the man's grip, Bob picked up the cane, the map, and the water bottle, looked at the wall where he'd taken refuge, and wondered about the prints he might have left there.

"We have to go," the tall man said, urgency in his tone.

Bob nodded. As he turned toward his rescuer, he glanced up and finally saw the street name overhead: *Calle Della Morte*. "Street of the Dead," he muttered. "Perfect."

CHAPTER 6

Yasmin Nizari shrugged out of her silk gown, allowing it to fall like a sloughed skin to the stone floor. She watched Javad Muntaziri's reaction—his widened eyes, the flush of his skin, the swipe of his tongue across his lips—and smiled. She also noticed the tenting of the bed sheet over his groin and said, "I believe you're happy to see me."

"Please stop torturing me, Yasmin. Come here."

She slowly moved around the bottom of the bed, to the side farthest from Javad. "You are a very impatient man."

"Oh, God," he moaned. "Your father could call for me at any moment."

She placed a foot on the side of the mattress, which made his skin color even redder. He reached out to her, but she laughed, dropped her foot to the floor, and backed up a step. "Don't be silly," she said. "It's late and my father's asleep. Besides, what are you afraid of? You're the guard force commander. They listen to you, not my father."

Javad huffed and rolled away. He sat up on the far side of the bed and muttered petulantly, "If you're going to play games, I'll go to my own quarters."

Yasmin quickly circled the bed and placed her body in front of him, her breasts level with his eyes. "Don't be that way, Javad."

He placed his mouth on one of her nipples.

"Did you do as I asked?" she said.

"Of course," he mumbled. He pulled back and said, "Our agents are already on the move."

"And what is my father planning as his...*coup de grace*?"

"You should ask *him* that. I'm not supposed to give that information to anyone. I'm—"

An angry expression appeared on her face and Yasmin backed away from the bed. "Obviously, you don't care enough about me," she said.

"Okay, okay, I'll tell you. But you have to keep it to yourself."

"Of course," she said, moving in front of him once again.

His hands moved over her body as he related Nizari's grand plan.

She smiled down at him and, in a sultry voice, said, "Move your hands and I'll show you how I feel about you."

She pressed her breasts against his face and ran her hands through his thick, black hair. She allowed Javad to pull her on top of him as he lay back. While he moaned and smothered her face and neck with kisses, she thought, *He may be only a useful idiot, but he is a gorgeous, useful idiot.*

He grabbed her head with both hands and held her tightly, as he looked intently into her eyes. "Yasmin, tell me how you feel about me."

He dropped his hands to his sides and moaned again as Yasmin moved down his body, kissing and biting his chest, slowly moving lower and lower as she provided the answer.

After leaving the assassin's corpse behind, Bob drank the rest of the water in the bottle and tossed it and the map into a trash receptacle. The cane he'd bought for Liz came in handy as he struggled to keep up with the tall stranger while they walked toward the Grand Canal. They boarded a water taxi at a terminal on the canal and then took the *Cannaregio* Canal to the *Guglie* Terminal. He felt stiff and sore from his encounter with the assassin, and he felt shaky after coming down from the adrenaline high he'd experienced. At the Guglie Terminal, they debarked and walked for ten more minutes. The stranger hadn't said a word during the entire trip, putting Bob off each time he asked a question. By the time they arrived at an apartment building that had seen better days, near *Savorgnan* Park, on the canal's north side, a couple blocks northwest of the Jewish Ghetto, Bob was exhausted; his energy reserves were depleted. They climbed to a fourth-floor apartment where the man handed Bob a glass of cognac, and said, "Drink it."

Bob downed the drink, set the glass aside on a table, and said, "What the hell's going on?"

"Mr. Danforth," the man said, "it's a long story."

Bob noticed the man's distinctly Israeli accent. Seated on a straight-backed chair across a small wood table from the man, Bob spread his hands as though to say, "Go ahead."

"My name is Eitan Horowitz. I was assigned to follow you."

"Assigned by whom?"

"By a friendly agency. I suspect you've already guessed, but I'm not at liberty to divulge my employer."

Mossad, Bob thought.

"Do you want another drink?"

"No. I suspect I should remain clear-headed to understand the story you're about to tell."

Horowitz grinned. "We picked up electronic chatter that you'd been targeted by a group we hadn't heard about before."

"Chatter out of where? From whom?"

"We believe it was an encrypted text message that had a temporary glitch in the encryption, which is how we accessed it. All we could determine was that it came from Rome, mentioned *Asasiyun*, and then listed eighty names of people targeted for assassination. As far as who originated the text, we're unclear."

"Asasiyun?"

"You've surely followed news about a number of assassinations in several countries."

Bob nodded.

"The Asasiyun is responsible for those assassinations."

"Asasiyun, as in assassin?"

"That's a common error that was made as far back as the twelfth century. Asasiyun is what Hassan-I Sabbah called his followers over eight hundred years ago. It literally means 'people who are true to the foundation of the faith.' Sabbah has been immortalized in history as the Old Man of the Mountain."

Bob was more confused now than he had already been. "What the hell does someone from the twelfth century have to do with an attempt on my life?"

Horowitz motioned with his hand to ask Bob to be patient. "Hassan-I Sabbah was a Nizari Ismaili, a branch of Shia Islam. They occupied several mountain fortresses in Persia and Syria. He structured his order into several levels, with the 'Adherents' being the lowest level. It was these Adherents who were trained to become the most vicious and feared assassins the world has ever known. He called these Adherents 'Fida'in,' which literally means self-sacrificing agents."

"Like the 'fedayeen' in Palestine who are willing to sacrifice themselves in their war against Israel and the West."

"Exactly."

"I remember reading about the Old Man of the Mountain. I thought his followers got stoned on hashish before they went off to commit murder and mayhem."

"Again, a common error. Travelers to that part of the Middle East didn't understand the word Asasiyun and thought it was derived from the word hashish. Some of Hassan-I Sabbah's enemies perpetuated that myth, and men like Marco Polo spread the error to the West."

"So, this Asasiyun has been resurrected?"

"As best as we can determine. Your former employer has come to the same conclusion. Like their predecessors, the Asasiyun agents spy on their enemies and intend to assassinate military, government, and other leaders of countries they consider to be enemies of Islam."

Bob puffed out his cheeks as he exhaled. "Doesn't sound any different than what Al Qaeda, or ISIS, or the Iranian government have been about for decades."

"On the surface, that's correct. But there seem to be fundamental differences between the brainwashed idiots that modern terror groups deploy in suicide attacks which target mass casualties, and the Asasiyun...both the original group that operated between the late eleventh and thirteenth centuries and the modern group. The

Asasiyun were experts in disguise, able to sneak into enemy areas where they performed assassinations. The assassin was usually very young and fit, with a strong psychological makeup. They tended to be intelligent and well-read." He shook his head for a long beat. "This is what has us most concerned. The original Asasiyun were extremely knowledgeable about their enemies, their enemies' cultures and customs, and their languages. They were able to easily meld into other societies, where they targeted top-level leaders."

"The perfect spy," Bob said.

"Yes," Horowitz said, "and the perfect assassin. Five assassinations of high-level political and military personnel occurred yesterday in an equal number of countries. The assassins held passports in those countries and were all under the age of forty. They had been educated in those countries and had successful careers. They spoke the local language fluently and no one had a reason to suspect they weren't natives or that they were a danger to anyone."

"I heard about assassinations in Poland and France. In what other countries did assassinations happen?"

"Lithuania, Turkey, and Greece. A sixth assassination was supposed to happen right here in Italy. You were the target."

"That makes no sense."

Horowitz shrugged.

"Were there any other commonalties about the assassins?"

"Just one. It's been discovered that the assassins' documented histories had been falsified. They'd adopted the names of children who had died in their infancy and, somehow, had fabricated family histories and school records. They seem to have been dropped into place out of nowhere."

"I think I'll take that drink after all," Bob said.

Horowitz poured Bob another cognac and asked, "Do you have any more questions?"

"Are you kidding? I haven't even begun with the questions. First, who's behind this group?"

"We've captured snippets of chatter for several years about a shadowy group preparing for something big. Something that would make 9-11 seem like child's play. There was a decidedly Islamic tone to the chatter."

"That could mean any number of countries are behind this," Bob said.

"That's correct and, based on what we know at this point, which isn't a lot, this Asasiyun business isn't an amateur operation. Think about this for a minute. We know there have been six assassinations or attempted assassinations in the past twenty-four hours. In the five attacks that succeeded, the assassins appear to have been sleeper agents who had been embedded in countries for years without raising any suspicions among the local authorities. This leads me to believe that the group behind these attacks is very sophisticated. They turned loose six killers in a coordinated campaign that successfully took out five Western leaders. I suspect that the man who tried to kill you will fit that same description: longtime resident of Italy, good job and education, and his early years a false legend."

"If something big is planned," Bob said, "then the Asasiyun organization must be extremely well-funded. That suggests a country like Russia, Saudi Arabia, or Iran might be behind them."

Horowitz nodded. "What has my people concerned is that they don't believe this is limited to six assassins in six countries."

"How big do they think this is?"

"As I said, eighty names were mentioned in the chatter our people intercepted. If those eighty names are just a piece of the puzzle, there could be hundreds of people targeted for assassination."

"Holy—"

"Almost every one of the eighty people is a current or former Western military, political, intelligence, or business leader. And every one of them directly or indirectly supported military operations in Iraq, Syria, and Afghanistan."

"So, you believe these are Islamic terrorists?"

"Probably. But there is always the possibility the term asasiyun is intended to deflect attention from the group's actual supporters, who might be neither Muslim nor Middle Eastern. But I doubt that. The fact that all six targets to date were involved in one way or another with military operations in the Middle East tells me there is an Islamic component to the Asasiyun."

Bob wondered about what he'd just heard. *The murder of eighty Western leaders would be a big deal. Maybe not 9-11-huge, but it*

would have a dramatic impact on the morale of the Western world.
He felt an electric chill run up his spine.

"In the West, after 9-11, we don't think of a few dozen people
dying in one incident as huge. I know that sounds perverted, but—"

"I know what you mean," Horowitz said. "But remember, just
because we've picked up chatter that mentioned eighty or so names,
doesn't mean that there aren't dozens, or hundreds more."

"But they'd need an army of sleeper agents in dozens of countries
to murder hundreds of leaders. How could that even be possible?
Wouldn't it make more sense to target large groups, *a la* 9-11?"

"Terrorist organizations have learned that grand events, like
what happened on September 11, are difficult to pull off now
that their adversaries have become more aware of the threat and
have implemented security measures and more active intelligence
networks. The West's intelligence gathering capabilities have
dramatically improved in the last twenty years. As I said earlier,
they're following the original Asasiyun's policy of hitting leaders,
not the masses."

Bob thought about what Horowitz had said. It made sense, but
he couldn't quite buy it. He changed the subject and asked, "Why
would I be targeted? It's been a long time since I did anything to
put myself on the radar screen of a terror group."

"We believe that's irrelevant," Horowitz said. "You've been
involved over your career in events that, had you failed, could have
dramatically altered the geopolitical scene in the Middle East, as
well as in the West. We suspect that, although you're retired, your
death would be a major triumph for the Asasiyun. Think about
stories in the media that would have been released had you been
murdered by these maniacs: Former CIA Special Ops Chief; player
in taking down terrorist group in Athens; deeply involved with
anti-terrorism; instrumental in destroying terror cells in Greece
and the United States; and on and on."

Bob snorted derisively. "That's absurd. I—"

"Maybe," Horowitz said, "but we think that's one reason they
came after you."

"How'd you know I was targeted?"

"As I said, we picked up intel."

Bob showed Horowitz a dubious look and said, "What else?"

"Your NSA also intercepted the text and informed your former employer, which asked us to keep an eye on you."

Bob thought about his call to Tanya Serkovic. *Sonofagun*, he thought. *She lied to me.*

"Did you understand what the assassin said to you?"

"He told me in Italian that he had a message for me from the Old Man of the Mountain. Then he said something in Russian, which I didn't understand."

"That much I heard," Horowitz said. "*Orden pobidit*. It means: *The Order will be victorious*. In Arabic, it's *Sawf yantasir alnazam*. Our intel picked up that phrase on several occasions. It seems to be a mantra."

"You said my past life with the CIA was *one* reason I was targeted. What's the other reason?"

"We found it odd at first that you were targeted, considering that there are many others who would have been better targets. I mean, there are those still active in intelligence and military circles who would make more sense to go after. But, after a little homework, something else popped up. You remember that operation in Greece you supervised in 2004, during the Olympic Games? When you took down that terrorist cell, *Greek Spring*."

"Sure."

"You remember the name Musa Sulaiman?"

A shudder went through Bob's body. He didn't like revisiting "wet work" assignments. "Of course," he said. "The guy escaped to Brazil after wreaking havoc in Athens."

"Not for long. You tracked him down there and made him… *disappear*."

Bob stared at Horowitz.

"We believe that Sulaiman was one of the first Asasiyun recruits."

"So what?"

"Musa Sulaiman was a cover name. His real name was Musa bin Abdel bin Hakim. He was the son of Abdel bin Abdullah bin Mohammed bin Hakim, who's a bin Hakim family member. The father emigrated from Saudi Arabia to Switzerland when the son was fourteen. The family became a huge international player in the precious gem business. They locked up the sale of gemstones to the Islamic world and made a fortune. They've been a major benefactor of terrorist causes for decades. Abdel bin Hakim has made dozens of trips to places where bad actors reside. He helps Iran export oil through Russia despite the United States embargo. He runs weapons manufactured in Russia to hellholes all over the world." Horowitz intertwined two fingers of one hand and held the hand up. "Bin Hakim is tight with rogue regimes."

"Are you saying that bin Hakim is the leader of the Asasiyun and that he targeted me because I went after his son?"

"We don't believe bin Hakim runs the group. He's a radical Muslim who believes that Islam will conquer the world. He may be a recruiter for the Asasiyun. But bin Hakim has neither the courage nor the charisma to head up an effort like this. Unfortunately, we haven't been able to determine who's actually running things." Horowitz paused a couple seconds, then added, "As far as you being targeted as a revenge thing, who knows?"

"What do you think these guys want to accomplish?"

"We can only assume they want Islam to dominate the world. My people also think bin Hakim and the Order are after the same things that Hassan-I Sabbah was after: political and personal gain, as well as getting revenge on their enemies. The attack on you fit into that last category. We believe Islam is nothing but the mechanism with which to achieve their ambitions."

Horowitz's cell phone rang. He stood, held up a finger to indicate he'd be a minute, and walked over to a window. After a brief conversation in Hebrew, he returned to his chair.

"We just learned who your attacker was. His name was Sultan Azurbaev, a Chechen. He was raised in Russia until he was fifteen, came to Siena in 2000, where he lived with an uncle and went through high school. But after he disappeared for several years, he reappeared in Siena in 2015, where he's been teaching economics and statistics at the University of Siena."

"So, he fit right into Italian society," Bob said.

"That's right. Even married a local girl and converted to Catholicism. Probably all for cover."

"You said he disappeared for a while. You have any idea where he went?"

"No idea at all."

They looked at one another for a good half-minute, neither saying a word. Finally, Bob asked, "What's next?"

"As far as we know, Azurbaev was on his own in Venice. You should be safe. But, if I were you, I'd go home and hide away until this thing is over."

"When might that be?"

Horowitz shrugged.

Bob stood and paced while Horowitz watched him. After he'd crossed the small room a few times, he stopped and said, "How many people do you believe are on the Asasiyun's hit list?"

"We're not certain. All we've picked up are the eighty names. But if we were to extrapolate from those names, adding men and women in similar positions in other Western countries, we could come to a shocking conclusion. The eighty were all in decision-making positions regarding Western military and or intelligence operations in Middle Eastern countries. We identified every person we could of similar status in over two dozen countries and added in business leaders in the defense industry, politicians, and the like. So far, we've constructed a potential hit list of over eight hundred."

"My God." Then, as an afterthought, Bob asked, "Of the names on the list, I wonder if there are any I know."

Horowitz cleared his throat. "I wouldn't be surprised if you personally know or recognize most of their names." He heaved a sigh and added, "Including your son's and grandson's names."

CHAPTER 7

The Director of the Central Intelligence Agency (DCI) is appointed by the President with Senate confirmation and reports directly to the Director of National Intelligence (DNI). In practice, the CIA director interfaces with the DNI, Congress, and the White House, while the CIA Deputy Director is the internal executive, and the Chief Operating Officer leads the day-to-day work as the CIA's third highest executive.

But, unlike most previous DCIs, Tanya Serkovic came up through the ranks. She was the antithesis of a political appointee. So, in addition to interfacing with the DNI, Congress, and the White House, she shared day-to-day supervision of CIA work with her deputy director (DD/CIA), Clifford Hansen. The combination of these duties created an almost super-human workload.

Tanya felt a bubble of bile burn inside her chest. She reached for the bottle of antacid in her purse, took a long swig, and burped. "This is what happens when my day begins at 7:00 a.m. at the White House," she said in a sleep-deprived, hoarse whisper.

"You say something, ma'am?" her driver asked.

"Just talking to myself, Herb."

Tanya crossed her arms and drummed her fingers on her biceps. "Herb, drop the hammer on this beast," she ordered. "I need to get to my office as quickly as possible." She heard and felt the SUV's super-charged engine kick into another gear as she used her encrypted

56

cell phone to call Clifford Hansen.

"How did it go?" Cliff said without preamble.

"POTUS is…let's say *exercised.*"

"That bad? I assume the DNI took some pressure off you."

Tanya laughed. "Yeah, right. Listen, Cliff, I need you to get the team together. Frank, Raymond, Genevieve, Seth, and, candidly, anyone else you think should be in on this. I'll be back in about thirty minutes."

"As a start, let's go with the names you mentioned," Hansen said.

"Okay. That's probably best."

"There've been more assassinations," Hansen said. "We just received word that the Kuwaiti Defense Secretary and two of their generals were killed in a suicide bombing in Kuwait City. The bomber was a civil servant who'd worked at the Kuwaiti Electrical Company for a dozen years. What's odd is that he seemed to have appeared out of nowhere just before he went to work for the company. The guy was a cipher."

"I heard. That was what sent POTUS off the deep end. If I remember correctly, the Defense Secretary's name was on that list of eighty that we and the Israelis put together."

"That's correct," Hansen said. "However, the two generals who were killed weren't on the list. They may have been collateral damage."

"Or they were targets whose names weren't part of the eighty. If that's true, then that could be further proof that the target list is much bigger than eighty. How's the potential target list coming?"

"Oh, jeez, Tanya, it's daunting. We've put every present and former head of state, defense minister, general, national-level politician, defense contractor CEO, and on and on, from every country that's ever fought against, imposed sanctions against, or even bad-mouthed Islamic fanatics. We're up to over a thousand names and counting. This is a potential nightmare."

"What do our people say about the Asasiyun group's motivations?" Tanya said.

"Based on the targets to date, it's got to be revenge. The targets all had a connection to the wars in Iraq, Syria, and/or Afghanistan."

"What about other common denominators?"

Hansen blew out a loud breath that whistled in Tanya's ear. "The analysts are working on it, but nothing's popped up other than a revenge motivation." After a beat, Hansen asked, "What did the Treasury Secretary have to say in your meeting with the President?"

"She predicts that, if these assassinations continue, stock markets will see a twenty to twenty-five percent correction. And Treasury thinks it will be worse if there are victims here in the States."

Cliff said, "Twenty-five percent. That's not a correction; that's a crash."

"How many victims do we have so far?"

"Not including Bob Danforth, who you know survived an attack, there were five fatalities yesterday and another nine today. Other than Bob and the Kuwaiti Defense Secretary, none of the targets were on the list of eighty. I—" Cliff paused, then said, "Hold a sec, please." He came back on the line after fifteen seconds. "The CEO of a British defense contracting company was just stabbed to death in his home. The killer also murdered the man's wife and two young daughters."

"Was the killer apprehended?"

"No. He was shot and killed by a security guard." Cliff whistled again and added, "Same situation as in Kuwait. The killer was John Doe citizen, late twenties, worked in a bank, and had a fabricated history for the years before he took that job."

Tanya released a long, slow breath. "Cliff, tell Raymond to call General Danforth at Special Operations Command and order him to mobilize every Lone Wolf team."

Michael Danforth had received his second star when he took command of the invasion force that defeated ISIS in Syria. Now, as U.S. Joint Special Operations Command Chief, headquartered at Fort Bragg, North Carolina, he reported to a four-star general who commanded the United States Special Operations Command (USSOCOM) headquartered at MacDill Air Force Base in Tampa, Florida. Since 1998, the JSOC commanders had been lieutenant generals, which boded well for Michael receiving his third star soon. JSOC's mission is to study special operations requirements and techniques to ensure interoperability and equipment standardization; to plan and conduct special operations exercises and training; to develop joint special operations tactics; and to execute special operations missions worldwide.

When Michael took over JSOC, he requested that the Army's Lone Wolf teams be permanently assigned to his command. Created at the CIA's request, the Lone Wolf teams were composed of U.S. Army Special Forces personnel and had, in the past, been deployed only at the CIA's request. Having been a former commander of the Lone Wolf program, Michael understood the teams' capabilities and how they should best be deployed.

It was 8:37 a.m. when Michael ended his weekly staff meeting. On his way from the conference room to his office, he stopped at the desk of his Command Sergeant Major, William Jackson, and inquired about the man's wife who was undergoing chemo treatments for lung cancer. While he talked with Jackson, Michael's senior aide, Major Ronald Darby, continued to Michael's office. It was their custom to meet after every staff meeting so that Michael could offload takeaway assignments to Darby. As Darby entered the office, the "hot line" telephone on Michael's desk rang.

Darby answered: "General Danforth's phone. Major Darby speaking, sir."

"Ron, it's Ray Gallegos. How are things there?"

"You want me to go into detail or just tell you that everything is peaceful and quiet?"

"Lie to me."

Darby laughed. "Okay. Everything is peaceful and quiet."

Raymond chuckled. "Is the general available?"

"Hold on, sir."

Darby put the call on hold, stepped to the office door, waved to get Michael's attention, and held his fist next to his ear. Michael waved back, said something to Sergeant Major Jackson, and moved quickly toward his office. Darby closed the office door after Michael entered. He took a chair in front of the desk, while Michael took his seat behind it.

"It's Raymond Gallegos," Darby said.

Michael nodded and picked up the receiver.

"Good morning, Ray," Michael said. "I expected to hear from you."

"You've been following the intel reports?"

"Of course. What's up?"

Raymond briefed Michael on events of the last few hours. "You'll get intel messages with more details soon. The DCI requests that you put the entire Lone Wolf contingent on full alert."

"All twenty-six teams?"

"You got it."

"Ron Darby is here with me," Michael said. "Okay if I put you on speaker?"

"Absolutely."

Michael put the call on speaker mode. "Okay, Ray. What's going on?"

"This Asasiyun campaign just got worse. We think the potential target list could be around one thousand people. We tried to locate Abdel bin Hakim who we believe could be supporting the Asasiyun. No luck, unfortunately. He's disappeared."

"Have you enlisted the help of the Saudis?"

"Not yet. Bin Hakim is a royal family member. The Saudis will probably circle the wagons and protect him, like they did with the Crown Prince after the assassination of the reporter Jamal Khashoggi in Turkey in 2018."

"A little pressure from the White House might do the trick."

"We'll see," Ray said. "The DCI's on her way back from a White House intel meeting. I'll find out more when she gets here. In the meantime, we'd appreciate you putting together a deployment plan based on what we already have."

"Ray, it's Ron," Darby interjected. "We've got a dozen contingency plans already drawn up, including a couple that address responses to mass assassination campaigns."

"That'll help," Raymond said.

No one spoke for a few seconds, until Michael asked, "Anything else, Ray?"

Ray didn't immediately respond. After a pause, he said, "Yeah. One more thing. Your father was targeted in Venice."

Michael's lungs seemed to freeze. He tried to catch his breath and forced himself to remain calm. "Is Dad all right?" he said.

"What about my mother?" His heart pounded as he waited for Ray's response.

"They're fine. We'd heard noise that he might be targeted and enlisted Mossad's help. We knew they had an agent in Venice because of the annual carnevale event. Several Israeli diplomats were planning to attend. The agent took down the assassin who we learned was originally from Chechnya."

His breathing now almost back to normal, Michael asked, "What happened?"

"Your father spotted the Mossad agent but thought he might be a bad actor. He even called Tanya about the guy. She denied any knowledge about him because she didn't want to worry them. Of course, your father now knows about the Asasiyun plot and is probably pissed off at us for not opening up with him earlier. The Mossad man took out the Chechen just as he was about to shoot your father."

Michael met Darby's gaze and saw concern in his aide's eyes. Anger simmered inside him. His face felt hot. He was about to thank Raymond for the heads-up, when Raymond said, "Listen, Mike, if they targeted your father, where do you think that puts you? You know both your names, as well as Robbie's, are on that list of eighty names we intercepted."

Michael thought about that for a moment. "As commander of JSOC, I would have to be a high-level target." He paused a beat, then said, "I thought that list was bullshit. I guess I was wrong."

Ray cleared his throat. "Your role in the attack on ISIS in Syria raises you to an even higher level than most."

Michael said, "I still don't get how Robbie's name wound up on that list of eighty. How could anyone know his real identity? He operated under an alias in Syria."

"That's what has us worried. Someone must be feeding Top Secret/Sensitive Compartmented Information to the Asasiyun. Robbie and that young woman, Samantha Meek, who were undercover in Syria, were on a classified mission and their identities were buried deep in the CIA archives."

"Yet their names were released," Michael said. His anger now threatened to boil over. "What have you done to protect Robbie and Samantha?"

"Be assured, Mike. I won't let anything happen to them."

"I asked you a question. What have you done to make certain they're safe?"

"I personally spoke with the superintendent at West Point, apprised him of the situation and asked him to take extraordinary action to keep Robbie and Samantha safe."

Michael asked, "Does Robbie know what's going on?"

"The superintendent will brief him."

Major Darby broke in, "I just had a thought. Am I correct in assuming the list of names created from chatter is classified as TS/SCI?"

"Of course."

Darby said, "Then whoever passed classified information to the assassins might have access to that list of names, too. If that's accurate, the killers probably know we're aware of the names on that list. If I were the bad guys, I'd back off targeting those people and go after people whose names we aren't aware of."

"That would possibly give Robbie, Samantha and you, Mike, a reprieve," Raymond said.

"Huh," Michael said. "That could be right unless the assassins are on suicide missions. All the protection in the world won't help a target from a deep cover killer on a suicide mission."

"How many people have access to what we know about the Asasiyun?" Darby asked.

"Oh, shit, Ron," Raymond said, "I can't begin to tell you. The President's Intelligence Advisory Board, the Senate Select Committee on Intelligence, the House Intelligence Committee, people at the FBI, here at the CIA, at NSA, our allies overseas, and so on. The problem is that there are dozens and dozens of staffers on each of these committees and at these agencies who have been granted TS/SCI clearances, many of whom have unlimited access."

Michael said, "Any one of whom could be working for the Asasiyun."

CHAPTER 8

Fifty-nine-year-old Frank Reynolds, a thirty-five-year CIA veteran with an IQ in the stratosphere, had spent much of his career with the Company analyzing intelligence product from the Balkans, Turkey, and Greece, and developing and managing special operations in that region. He'd studied Serbo-Croatian, Turkish, and Greek at the Defense Language Institute, West Coast, in Monterey, California, and received his doctorate of Slavic Languages and Literature from Georgetown University. He knew more about the political systems and parties in the entire region than anyone in the free world. Over the past decade, he'd also built expertise on Iran's governmental organization and its worldwide intelligence operations. He concentrated on the Middle East after the CIA's Special Activities Division and its Special Operations Group became involved in the Operation Icon investigation, and after the rise of the Islamic State. He was later promoted to head up the Special Activities Division. Tanya Serkovic had then promoted him to the position of Director of Intelligence when she became DCI. He'd long ago given up on balancing a CIA career with a personal life. He'd never married, had no siblings or living parents, and was single-minded about his dedication to his country. He'd gained a pound a year since joining the Company and his wiry gray hair looked as though it had never known a comb.

Raymond Gallegos was fifty years old and had the dark, good

looks of a Latin movie star and the intelligence of a nuclear physicist. Although the only exercise he got was walking the halls and stairs at Langley, he was trim and fit. Over the last year or so, his once jet-black hair had finally lost the age battle. His thick, now salt-and-pepper hair not only took nothing away from his looks but made him appear more distinguished. He was a highly-decorated Army veteran with three years in Special Forces. He'd earned his bachelor's and master's degrees in Geography after a tour in the first Gulf War, and spent seven years with the National Security Agency as a cartography expert, before moving to the CIA. He was familiar with every part of Southern Europe and the Middle East the way most people know their own neighborhoods. Tanya Serkovic had recently promoted him from Director of the Special Operations Group to Director of National Clandestine Service.

While Frank Reynolds had always been a bit of a loose cannon, with a communications style that could best be described as acerbic, Gallegos was always "Army-straight" and extremely popular with his associates.

As they walked to the DCI's conference room, Raymond asked Frank, "Cliff tell you anything about Tanya's meeting at the White House?"

"Not much, other than to say that Tanya seemed…out of sorts."

"That's what happens when the most powerful man on the planet gets frustrated."

"Who's frustrated?" Genevieve Salter asked as she walked up to them outside Tanya's office.

The two men stopped and turned to face the CIA's Director of Support Division. Salter was a forty-two-year-old, twelve-year CIA employee who had world-class organizational and logistical skills. The people at the Company who worked with her joked—semi-seriously—that Salter had the looks of Natalie Wood and the personality of Dick Butkus.

"You ought to go into the field, Genevieve," Frank said. "You've got good eavesdropping skills."

She scrunched up her face. "Yuck. I wouldn't make a good field agent. I can't stand sleeping in strange beds and not showering daily."

"Didn't seem to bother James Bond," Frank said.

"That's because he never slept alone," she said.

"She's got you there, Frank," Raymond said.

"After you, madam," Frank said as he stepped aside to let Salter pass.

When they had all entered the reception area, the DCI's assistant said, "Go right in. She's waiting for you. The Deputy Director's already with her."

"Anyone want coffee?" Tanya asked.

They all declined in chorus.

"Okay, let's get down to business." She opened a folder and the others followed suit. "The top document in front of you was put together by Cliff. These are the high-level tasks we are confronted with. I want each of you to weigh in on them and suggest any others that should be on the list. Then I want to discuss responsibility for each one."

She read down the list: "Identify possible targets; Locate Abdel bin Hakim; Identify and locate the Asasiyun's leadership cadre; Identify assassins; Identify possible leaker. Any thoughts?"

No one spoke for a good ten seconds, then, Raymond said, "We should probably add something about coordinating with the intelligence agencies where the surviving members of the original eighty names are located. We should be getting regularly scheduled reports on events in those countries."

"Like who's been murdered since our last conversation with them?" Frank said.

Tanya frowned at Frank but got no reaction from him.

Cliff said, "That's a good thought, Ray, but we're already in constant communication with those countries."

Tanya said, "Anything else to add?"

Genevieve said, "We need to figure out how these assassins infiltrated the countries where they've committed their crimes. They seem to have dropped out of nowhere and assumed local identities. They've been hiding in plain sight, playing the roles of average, everyday citizens for years."

"And they popped up yesterday for the first time and began

murdering people," Frank said. "What has me most concerned is that this organization must have amazing logistical skills and world-class funding."

Cliff said, "I suggest we make goal number one the leaker's identification."

CHAPTER 9

"My God, where have you been?" Liz demanded, as Bob entered their hotel room. Before he could answer, she stepped forward, wrapped her arms around him, and said, "I'm so sorry. I was...." Her voice broke. She swallowed. "Ever since you had that heart attack in Durango, I've been...."

Bob hugged her back and kissed her forehead. "I know, honey."

She pulled back and met his gaze. "You've got to learn to relax." She smiled and added, "You know, there really aren't terrorists hiding behind every bush or around every corner."

"Yes, honey, I know that."

"Then why did you go off after that man?"

He squeezed her hand. "Let's go down to the lounge and have a glass of wine. I have something to tell you."

"About what?"

"Humor me," he said. "This story might be a two-glass tale."

IT consultant Ursan Awan unplugged the stick drive from his computer, pocketed it, and stood behind his desk in his office in the Hart Senate Office Building. He shrugged on his suit jacket, removed his overcoat from a clothes tree, and walked out to the reception area. He was about to tell the receptionist he was leaving for the day, but she preempted him.

"The senator just buzzed me. She wants to see you."

"About what?"

The young woman shot him a sour look. "How should I know?"

Awan nodded and walked past her desk to Senator Deborah Schatz's office. He knocked once and opened the door.

"You wanted to see me, Senator?"

"Oh, hey Ursan. Yes, I want to make certain you've finished installing that network security software."

"Yes, Senator. It's loading right now. That's why I'm taking off early today. While the new firewall is loading, there's nothing I can do."

"Does that mean all the computers in the office are down?"

He smiled. "All the computers of the Senate Select Committee on Intelligence members are down. I sent out an email yesterday warning everyone about the fix I was going to install."

"How long will we be down?"

"It'll be loaded by midnight. I'll come back then to make sure everything's okay."

"Thanks, Ursan. I appreciate your hard work. I don't know what we'd do without you."

He smiled at the compliment, said, "It's my pleasure," and asked, "Was there anything else, Senator?"

She waved a hand. "No, that's all. I guess I'll see you tomorrow."

"Yes, ma'am. Have a good evening."

Awan held his breath when a blast of icy air greeted him as he exited the building onto C Street NE. He raised the collar of his overcoat and slipped on his black watch cap. He took some comfort from the fact that no matter how bad the weather was in D.C., it couldn't come close to the snow, ice, and frigid temperatures of his hometown in Pakistan. He patted a gloved hand against his right pants pocket through his overcoat and suit jacket and felt the tiny bulge of the stick drive. *Like taking candy from a baby,* he thought.

He walked east on C to 4th Street and went toward the southwest corner of Stanton Park. By the time he spotted the white taxi parked near the corner, he was stiff from the cold. But he forced himself to maintain a casual walking pace. When he reached the corner, he opened the cab's left rear door and slid onto the back seat.

"Damn, it's cold out there," Awan said. "Crank up your heater, will you?"

"You're such a wuss," the cabbie said.

"Screw you, Parviz."

"Everything okay?" the cabbie said.

Awan sniffed. "They're idiots. It's a wonder this country hasn't collapsed from its own incompetence."

"Or naïveté," the cabbie said and laughed. "It does make one wonder why the head of the Senate Select Committee on Intelligence would hire a non-citizen from an Islamic country to manage computer security."

Awan didn't immediately respond. When he did, he muttered an Urdu curse, which made the driver laugh again. "You know, Parviz, I've thought a lot about it, and I've concluded that she hired me in the interest of political correctness. She can tell her rich friends how open-minded she is, hiring a Muslim alien."

The driver's tone suddenly changed. "Actually, who gives a damn why she hired you. Do you have the stick drive?"

Awan pulled off his right glove, leaned to the side and dug into his pants pocket. He took out the stick drive and slipped it through the pass-through in the plexiglass separation between him and the driver. Shirazi took it and dropped it into his shirt pocket.

"You want to return to the building?" Shirazi said.

"No, take me to my apartment."

After he dropped off Awan, Parviz Shirazi drove to Reston, Virginia, parked in a pizza restaurant's parking lot, and walked two blocks to the house he and his three brothers rented. He knocked on the front door—two quick raps, followed by a two second pause and three quick raps. He used his key to open the door.

"What kept you?" Yusuf, the eldest Shirazi brother, said.

"Awan was late."

"Did you get it?"

Parviz took the stick drive from his shirt pocket and tossed it high into the air to his brother, who fumbled it and dropped it to the floor.

"What the hell's wrong with you?" Yusuf shouted as he bent

over and retrieved the drive.

"You need to relax, Yusuf. You take everything so seriously."

Yusuf glared at his brother and, through clenched teeth, said, "I think taking out the entire leadership of the Western world *is* serious."

CHAPTER 10

"Don't you have anything to say?"

Liz moved her gaze from her lap and looked across at Bob. Tears flooded her eyes and slid down her cheeks.

Bob stood and moved to sit beside her on the couch.

"I feel like an idiot. I was so upset with you because I thought you were imagining things. But your instincts were correct." Her voice stuttered as she said, "Robbie, Michael, and you. All in danger."

He placed an arm around her shoulders. "It's okay. Everything turned out fine."

"But it might not have." She exhaled a long, shuddering breath. "I think we should return home."

Bob pulled her to him. "Like hell," he said. "No way some pissant psycho is going to make us run and hide. Besides, our new Mossad friend eliminated the man."

"There could be others."

Bob scoffed. He decided to not mention the possibility that he had been targeted because he had killed Abdel bin Hakim's son, Musa, in Brazil. "If this story about the Asasiyun is true, there's no way they'd waste another agent on an old has-been like me. They surely have higher priority targets than a retired bureaucrat."

"I still think we should—"

Bob squeezed Liz's shoulder. "Let's go out to dinner. We'll talk about it in the morning. If you still want to fly home early, I'll make arrangements." He kissed the side of her head and said, "Okay?"

Liz nodded and whispered, "Okay."

While Liz showered, Bob slowly walked around the resort's ample grounds. His body felt as though he'd been in a car wreck. "Tough to get old," he muttered. He dialed Tanya Serkovic's personal cell number and tried to calm his breathing while he waited for her to pick up.

"I can't talk right now, Bob," she answered. "I'm in a meeting—"

"Why the hell did you lie to me about the tail you put on me? And why didn't you tell me that my name, along with Michael's and Robbie's, were on some hit list?"

After a long pause, Bob heard Tanya say, "I'm going to step out for a minute."

A few seconds went by before she came back on the call. "Bob, I didn't think it made any sense to worry you and Liz unnecessarily."

"You don't think my picking up on a tail was worrisome? Or that you brought in Mossad to babysit me?"

"How'd you know about the Israelis?"

"The man I thought might be tailing me turned out to be my savior. He killed a man sent to assassinate me. He told me a long story about some group that has resurrected the ancient Asasiyun, the Order of Assassins. If you'd been candid with me when I called earlier, I wouldn't have been wandering the streets of Venice making myself an easy target." After a beat, he added in an angrier tone, "I wouldn't have exposed Liz."

Tanya exhaled loudly. "I'm sorry, Bob. You're right. Once we discovered your name on the potential hit list, I should have briefed you."

"Yeah, you should have. Now, tell me if I should still be concerned. Should Liz and I catch the first flight back to the States?"

"I don't think there's any place safer than any other. I mean, you're probably just as well off in Venice as you would be in Bethesda."

"Are you kidding me? This group of killers has that kind of reach?"

"Bob, as of fifteen minutes ago, over a dozen high-profile

political, military, and business leaders and several of their family members in ten countries had been assassinated. That includes the CEO of an American defense contractor who was playing tennis at a friend's home in California. He's the latest fatality."

Bob groaned. "My Mossad friend told me that over eight hundred people could be on the group's target list."

"That's based on mathematical modeling but is pure conjecture at this point. Our analysts have come up with an even larger number, but…hell, who knows? It could be twice that number. In any case, I think you're safe. It's highly doubtful this group has enough assassins to go after you a second time."

"But, if the number of people on the target list is eight hundred or more, that means the group has plenty of hit men. If each assassin is considered by the group to be expendable, that would mean at least eight hundred killers. Where in God's name and over what period did this maniacal cult recruit and train so many? This assassination campaign had to be in the works for a long time. How could the Company not have gotten intel about the activities of such a group over the years?"

Tanya cleared her throat, hesitated a moment, and said, "I wish I could answer that. We didn't get an inkling of this group until this month when the NSA and Mossad each picked up electronic chatter about certain people being targeted. The Asasiyun was mentioned, as was the Old Man of the Mountain."

"Tanya, I don't mean to be critical, but how is that possible? How could this group have kept its activities so secret?"

"That's what I'm trying to figure out."

After hanging up with Bob, Tanya returned to her meeting with Cliff Hansen, Frank Reynolds, Raymond Gallegos, Seth Bridewell, and Genevieve Salter. She took her seat at the head of the conference room table. "Sorry about the interruption," she said. "That was Bob Danforth. A man tried to kill him in Venice."

"Is he okay?" Ray asked.

"Yeah, he's fine, Ray. Your suggestion that we ask Mossad for their assistance turned out to be brilliant. An agent of theirs in Venice had been following Bob and took out the assassin."

"Good guys, one; bad guys, sixteen," Frank said.

Genevieve said, "Twenty-one, if you count collateral damage: the family members killed and the two Kuwaiti generals."

Before anyone could respond, Raymond's cell phone buzzed. After he read the text message, he announced, "We may have just caught a break. The Poles captured a guy posing as a waiter at a military conference dinner in Warsaw. He'd just shot the Chief of Staff of the Polish Armed Forces and was turning his weapon on the Polish President when a security man tackled him."

"How's the Chief of Staff?" Cliff asked.

"Dead."

"Who's interrogating the assassin?" Genevieve asked.

"The Polish Intelligence Service, *Agency Viviadu*," Ray answered. "They'll let us know if they get anything."

Cliff looked at Raymond. "I think you should call the Poles and ask if they'd be okay with us sending one of our people to Poland to...help with the interrogation."

"You have someone in mind?" Raymond said.

"Yeah, Vince Loughnane," Cliff said. "He's been with us for thirty-three years."

"He speaks Polish?" Raymond said.

"No. Just Gallic, Arabic, and Urdu."

"That's quite a repertoire," Raymond said.

Cliff laughed. "He emigrated from Ireland as a young man, graduated from USC with undergraduate and graduate degrees in psychology, and joined the Company. We sent him to language school to learn Arabic and Urdu, after which he served for eight years as an interrogation expert in Iraq, Saudi Arabia, and Afghanistan. Although he has no Polish language, he's our best interrogator. We can send a Polish linguist along with him."

Raymond nodded a couple times. "I like it, Cliff."

"Okay," Tanya said. "Let's try to figure out what the end game is with the Asasiyun. We have to develop some focus around these people and their goals."

"You don't think revenge against their enemies is enough motivation?" Cliff said.

"It could be," Tanya said. "But what worries me is that their goal could be something grander. Something diabolical."

"Like what?" Cliff said.

Tanya shrugged. "Maybe picking up where ISIS left off. Creating a caliphate that unites all Muslims."

"Or creating economic chaos in the West," Genevieve suggested. "Or both."

Frank said, "Hell, if they murder dozens of Western leaders, chaos will be a foregone conclusion."

"If they murder hundreds of people, chaos won't even begin to describe the fallout," Raymond said.

"I think our focus needs to be on where the funding for the group is coming from," Tanya said. "Someone's paying to train their killers, to cover their travel and living expenses, to create complex backgrounds, to infiltrate them into western countries with false I.D., etcetera. It can't be a fly-by-night operation. This takes sophistication, planning, and resources."

Raymond said, "Let's make a list of all those countries and organizations who hate the West enough to assassinate lots of people and which have the sophistication to do so."

"And have the wherewithal to fund such an effort," Genevieve added.

"Are you proposing to exclude the proxy organizations, like Al Qaeda, that could be executing this campaign?" Cliff said.

"Initially, yes," Raymond said. "Let's follow the money. If we can identify the funding source, we might be able to follow the money trail to the Asasiyun."

Raymond stood and moved to a whiteboard. He picked up a marker and wrote "Russia" in the top left corner. He turned to the group and said, "Who else belongs on our list?"

Names of countries and organizations were thrown out and added after some discussion about each. After thirty minutes, the list included Russia, Saudi Arabia, Iran, China, Syria, Pakistan, and North Korea. Raymond added Al Qaeda, Hezbollah, the Taliban, and Hamas on the board's bottom right corner in smaller letters. Other countries and organizations initially included on the list were deleted because they either didn't have enough financial resources or had more limited missions in the opinions of the group members.

A few anti-Western multi-billionaires were added to the list just before the group broke up.

SUNDAY
FEBRUARY 17

CHAPTER 11

It was a few minutes after midnight when Ursan Awan returned to his office in the Hart Senate Office Building. He sighed with satisfaction. The new software on the Senate Select Committee on Intelligence's system had loaded without a glitch. He was most pleased when he verified that the worm he'd installed in the system was alive and well. He already knew the CIA had learned the names of some people being targeted. From those initial eighty names that some idiot had included in an unencrypted email, the CIA had extrapolated a huge list of other potential targets. He accessed the database the CIA shared with the Senate Select Committee's members and staffers and brought himself up to date on everything the Company had downloaded since he'd last accessed the database.

"I'll be damned," he muttered. "Maybe the Americans aren't as incompetent as I thought." He read through intel the NSA and CIA had gathered, including new information from chatter. His stomach did a slight flip-flop when he saw that one of the people who had been targeted for assassination, a former CIA executive named Robert Danforth, had been attacked, but managed to survive with the assistance of a Mossad operative. The attacker had been killed.

"Goddamn Israelis," he muttered.

As he read through more Company-generated documents, he discovered that the CIA had communicated with the intelligence services of over thirty countries. Their communiqués advised them to take extraordinary precautions to protect their political, military, and business leaders.

Awan chuckled as he wondered how many of those leaders were *protected* by *trusted* guards who were Asasiyun sleeper agents. He downloaded this new information to a stick drive and pocketed it.

Bob and Liz sat across from one another in their hotel dining room, cups of steaming coffee so far left untouched. Bob waited for her to say something. He knew that pushing her to decide about staying in or leaving Italy would just get her back up. Liz lifted her cup, blew across the top of the hot liquid, and took a sip.

"Hot, but good," she said as she replaced the cup on the saucer.

"You want to go through the breakfast buffet?" Bob asked.

She slowly shook her head. "Let's talk about our trip first."

Bob raised his eyebrows and waited.

Her expression dour, she looked down at her folded hands for a moment, then looked up and said, "This trip was my idea. I'm the one who wanted to visit Italy...especially Venice. But what happened yesterday changes everything." Her eyes became suddenly moist. "You could have been killed. I think we should return home."

Bob didn't immediately respond, making certain she had finished. After a long pause, he leaned forward and whispered, "I honestly believe the danger to me has passed. There's no way the group behind the attack would waste another assassin on me. I couldn't possibly be a high-priority target. Tanya feels the same. If they were going to come after me again—which is unlikely, my location would be irrelevant. They'd search me out in Bethesda, here, or wherever I am."

"So, you're saying that you're as safe here as anyplace?"

"Ri—"

"Or in just as much danger here as you would be anyplace else."

Bob nodded. "Yeah, you could look at it that way." He reached across the table and placed a hand on her folded ones. "But, like I said, I think the danger is past."

"How'd the assassin know we were in Italy?" she asked.

"Sonofa—"

"What?"

"I hadn't thought about that."

Liz cut a narrow-eyed look at Bob. "We don't have social media sites, I made our reservations directly with the hotels and airlines and, other than Michael, we told no one about this trip."

"That's not quite correct. As a former senior level CIA employee, I'm supposed to inform them every time I leave the country."

"You didn't tell the agency when you went overseas last year looking for Robbie."

"No, I didn't. But that was different. I didn't want them to know what I was up to."

"So, you informed the agency about our trip to Italy?"

"I did."

"Which means someone at the CIA might have informed the assassin of our whereabouts."

Bob pressed his lips together in a grimace. "I guess that's possible. But it's more likely that someone hacked the CIA database."

"God in heaven," Liz said.

"Look, honey, if we let these guys chase us away from here, I think we'll regret it for the rest of our lives. We might never get back again and we sure as hell might never have the chance to attend Carnevale. If I truly believed I was in danger or, more importantly, that I was putting you in danger by staying here, we'd be on the next flight to the States."

Liz's expression remained serious. Finally, she said, "Are you sure?"

"Absolutely."

Her eyes were suddenly wet. Tears slipped from her eyes and ran down her cheeks. She took the napkin from her lap and gently dabbed at them. Her expression finally changed. She smiled, her eyes sparkling, and said, "Let's eat."

"Cadets Robert Danforth and Samantha Meek reporting as ordered, sir," Robbie said.

Commandant of Cadets, Brigadier General Douglas Stevens, returned Robbie and Samantha's salutes. "Sit down, Cadets."

Robbie and Samantha took seats in front of the commandant and waited. *This can't be good*, Robbie thought. *Lowly cadets rarely have an audience with the top guy at West Point.*

"We're altering your routines, Cadets," Stevens said. "Information has come our way that necessitates a change."

Robbie sat rigidly as he met Stevens' steely gaze. Out of the corner of his eye, he saw that Samantha sat just as erectly as he did.

"You'll be restricted to post. You won't be allowed to attend off-site social or athletic events." He paused for a couple of seconds and met their gazes. "We want you both to be especially observant."

The commandant looked at Robbie as though he expected him to respond, but Robbie continued to meet the man's stare in silence.

"Aren't you interested in knowing what this is about?" Stevens said as he switched his gaze to Samantha.

"Yes, sir," Samantha said. "But I presume you'll tell us if we have a need to know."

Stevens smiled. "Our's not to reason why, huh?"

Samantha shrugged.

Now looking back at Robbie, Stevens said, "What I'm about to tell you is classified Top Secret. You must not share anything I tell you with anyone. Is that understood?"

Robbie and Samantha each responded: "Yes, sir."

"Good." Stevens sat forward, placed his elbows on his desk blotter, and intertwined his fingers as though praying. "The NSA and CIA have intel on a terror group called the Asasiyun, which is apparently targeting dozens of people, including you two." Stevens directed his gaze to Robbie when adding, "As well as your grandfather and father. The intelligence community believes this group has developed a hit list that could include hundreds of targets in dozens of countries. The common denominator may be anyone who played an important part in damaging Islamic interests or is in a position to do so currently." He paused again and, in a subdued voice, added, "Especially the interests of radical terrorist groups, like Hezbollah, Al Qaeda, ISIS, and the like. For the life of me, I don't know why you two are on the list, but my orders are to keep you safe."

Robbie's eyes went wide as he scoffed. He quickly said, "My apologies, sir."

Stevens waved away Robbie's words. "I can understand your

reaction. It seems far-fetched, doesn't it? That was my reaction, too, until I heard that yesterday an assassin tried to kill your grandfather in Venice."

A chill ran down Robbie's spine. He felt as though he'd been zapped with an electric current. "Is my grandfather all right?" he asked.

Stevens unclenched his hands and pumped them at Robbie. "He's fine. The assassin was killed, thanks to the intervention of someone who stepped up and saved your grandfather. No one knows for sure that you two are targets of this group, but we're not taking any chances."

"You said my father is a possible target? How in the world is that possible? He's on one of the most secure military bases in the United States."

"Remember what Dr. Nidal Hasan did at Fort Hood? He killed thirteen people and wounded thirty. There could be a 'sleeper' stationed at Fort Bragg. Besides, your father doesn't spend every minute of every day on the base."

Robbie nodded. "What about my mother and grandmother?" he said.

Stevens seemed to think for a moment. "As far as I know, the only family members of targeted individuals who have been killed or injured seem to have been…collateral damage, so to speak."

"This Asasiyun group," Samantha said, "are they the ones who murdered people in a bunch of countries? It's been on the news the past few days."

Stevens nodded.

From the commandant's office, Robbie and Samantha made their way downstairs to the dining hall. They walked at quick time, not speaking for a minute.

Finally, Samantha said, "It seems there are risks associated with hanging around you."

Robbie shot her a grim look, but then smiled when he saw her expression. "I recall that you were the one who stabbed that ISIS soldier we threw into a slit trench in Syria. You started that one."

Samantha changed the subject. "I was looking forward to going to the Army-Navy basketball game. Now we're locked up here until who knows when."

"I kind of like it here," Robbie said. "I've gotten used to the verbal and physical abuse from the upper classmen. Now we'll be constant targets. I love to be the center of attention."

Samantha laughed. "You're sick. But, seriously, what do you think about all of this? Are we really in any danger?"

Robbie shrugged. "There are about forty-three hundred students and six hundred staff members at West Point. On top of that, there must be hundreds and hundreds of cooks, vehicle drivers, maintenance people, and so forth. Add to that dozens of delivery personnel and visitors who enter the post daily. All it would take is one crazed man or woman out of all those people to attack someone here."

"Yeah, but do you think you and I are actually targets?"

Robbie stopped and looked at Samantha. "I just don't see it, Sam. We're neither high-value targets nor low-hanging fruit. Why go after us, sequestered on a military installation, when you could take out a defense contractor CEO at a restaurant in Beverly Hills? It doesn't make sense to try to get to us here."

Samantha nodded. "Unless the assassin is already here: a student, a faculty member, an employee."

Robbie reflected on her comment. As they walked into Washington Mess Hall, amid the din of conversations and movement of more than four thousand cadets, he wondered: *How in God's name would anyone be able to identify a sleeper assassin in this mass of humanity?* He was about to voice the thought to Samantha when she stopped and pulled Robbie by the arm into a corner.

"What is it?" Robbie said in a low voice.

"I just had a thought." She swallowed hard, looked around, and said, "I can understand why you might be a target. I mean, going after you could be a way to get back at your father and grandfather. But why me?"

"You and I went undercover with ISIS in Syria last year. That would be reason enough to...."

"Yeah, you see? Even General Stevens doesn't know what we did in Syria. So, how would this Asasiyun group know about us being there? Our mission and our identities were supposed to be classified at the highest level. We operated in Syria under pseudonyms."

"One or more government databases has to have been hacked," Robbie said. As an afterthought, he added, "Our records were supposed to be sequestered at the CIA."

"Which means the CIA's database has been compromised," Samantha said.

CHAPTER 12

Frank Reynolds, Raymond Gallegos, and Seth Bridewell sat at a huge conference table, joined by a dozen CIA employees from Raymond's National Clandestine Service brain trust and Seth's Directorate of Digital Innovation.

Frank said, "Seth, what the hell are we missing? Put aside for a moment the possibility these assassins might be targeting hundreds of people. Even if all they were going after were the eighty mentioned in the intel we intercepted—and we know that's not correct, because they've already attacked people who weren't on the list—that would necessitate at least eighty killers. Because of the geographic locations of the eighty, it would be unlikely that any one assassin would have been assigned more than one, maybe two targets."

Seth Bridewell had a doctorate in computer sciences from MIT and had worked at the NSA for a dozen years before transferring to the CIA when the Company committed almost one billion dollars to its technology operations budget. Seth came over to head up the Directorate of Digital Innovation, which had been covertly operating since March of 2015, but formally began operations on October 1, 2015. That budget number had risen each year since then. He'd recruited hundreds of computer whiz kids and assigned the eight best and brightest of the bunch to a new department supervised by Zachary Grabowsky. When Bridewell discovered that Grabowsky had the interpersonal skills of a rock, he'd elevated Angelina Borden on the team to translate Grabowsky's orders into language the other employees could understand and to deliver directives in a manner that didn't alienate them.

Seth said, "Another reason an assassin wouldn't have more than one or two targets is that there would be a strong possibility that he or she would be killed in an attack."

Frank said, "We've now had seventeen attacks that have killed twenty-two victims. Only four assassins survived their attacks. Two are in critical condition with multiple gunshot wounds and can't be interrogated. The third killed herself after being captured by chomping down on a cyanide capsule inserted under a molar. The fourth is in the hands of the Poles. Vince Loughnane and one of our Polish speakers are on their way to Warsaw to join the interrogation of that man."

Seth asked, "Did the other assassins have hidden cyanide capsules?"

Frank shrugged. "Only a few did."

Angelina Borden raised a hand but didn't wait to be recognized. "Keep in mind that only a few targets were on the list of eighty, which tells us that the target list could be well in excess of eighty." She exhaled a loud sigh. "These guys know what they're doing. They infiltrated the targets' inner circles or were able to be in the audiences to whom several victims were speaking. Their credentials were impeccable, and they'd been citizens of the countries in which they lived for at least a dozen years in each case."

"That's right," Ray said. "You're kind of making my point. Even if we were dealing with only eighty assassins, the Asasiyun would have to be extremely sophisticated. They would have a well-organized recruiting and training operation. They would have to be well-funded. And, they would have been planning this campaign for a long time."

Ray turned to another team member, "Suni, what's new on the statistical analysis side of things?"

Suni Jacob, a Cal Tech graduate with a Masters in Statistics and a Doctorate in Differential Calculus, visibly reddened. Clearing her throat, she responded in her high-pitched voice, "We believe the problem could be much bigger than originally thought. The one thousand or so possible targets could be low by eighty-two-point-seven percent. In other words, we now believe the potential target list could range from about one thousand at a minimum to more than five thousand."

Ray leaned forward, his mouth agape. "That's not even feasible. If our assumption is correct, that each assassin has been assigned to one target, you're saying there could be five thousand assassins."

"That's correct," she said.

"Sonofa—" Ray stood and looked directly at each of the others. "Then our problem may be even bigger than we thought; but that could make finding the kingpin and the funding source behind this group even easier. You can't hide that kind of recruiting, training, and funding operation."

Zach Grabowsky announced, "They've done a pretty good job of it so far."

Javad Muntaziri had been with Hassan Nizari since he was a boy. He was the son of a widow who worked in the kitchen of the Asasiyun's secret headquarters in the Cloud Forest. Muntaziri had been a daily playmate of Nizari's daughter, Yasmin, until she was sent away to private school in Zurich at the age of ten. Initially, Nizari had considered training the boy to be one of his assassins; in the end, he drafted him to be his assistant. Eventually, Javad became Nizari's right-hand man, often transmitting communiqués on Nizari's behalf to his cadre of killers—inside and outside Iran—to the liaison of people inside the Iranian government, and even to vendors and members of the household staff. He'd eventually put Muntaziri in charge of his personal guard force. So, it was now a simple matter for Javad, pushed by Yasmin, to issue orders to assassins who had been recruited from inside Iran and set up as sleeper agents in several parts of the country. When she'd told him what she wanted him to do, he'd initially balked. But, after some memorable cajoling, he agreed.

Thirteen-year-old Soroya was Mullah Bahadur Zarabi's only child. A good Muslim girl, she was her father's delight. He had already begun betrothal negotiations with Rostam Shahzad, the father of a twenty-three-year-old officer in Iran's Quds Force. The elder Shahzad was a wealthy entrepreneur who controlled most of foodstuff importation into Iran. Mullah Zarabi saw the prospective marriage as a merger of the rich and powerful more than even a path to grandchildren. The thought that Soroya might not be pleased with the alliance never came into question.

Zarabi left his office early to make certain all preparations had been made for the dinner he and his wife were hosting that evening for the Shahzads. He was surprised that Soroya didn't meet him at the door, as she invariably did when he entered his home. He simply assumed she must be helping her mother with dinner preparations. One of his servants met him and said, "*Arbob*"—using the term of respect—"may I bring you tea?"

"Yes. I will be in the living room."

Zarabi moved through the house to his favorite room at the back, where he could view the spectacle of Mount Tochal, the thirteen-thousand-foot-high peak that was part of the Alborz Mountains on the north side of Tehran. The view, especially at this time of year when snow covered the expanse, was breathtaking. He sat down facing the large window that gave him the best view, sighed, and waited for the servant to return with his tea. He'd only been seated a minute or so when his wife entered the room.

"How was your day, my husband?" she asked.

"Quite good, Avin. The price of oil went up two dollars a barrel today." He smiled. "The country needs hard currency to support our…global ambitions."

"That's good," she said, obviously disinterested.

"Is Soroya helping you get ready?"

Avin made a clucking sound. "She isn't yet home from school. I called her driver, but he didn't answer. I—"

Zarabi felt a sudden bubble of bile rise from his stomach. "That's impossible." While he stared at Avin, he snatched his cell phone from a pocket in his robe and dialed the driver's number. No answer.

"Did you call Soroya's phone?"

Avin made the clucking sound again and wagged her head. "Ach, that girl never answers her phone. All she does is text, text,

text."

Zarabi was about to text his daughter, when his phone chimed telling him he had received one. He didn't recognize the number.

He opened the message and his heart seemed to stop as he read it aloud: *We have your daughter. She will not be mistreated if you do exactly as we say. If you do not follow our instructions, she will meet the same fate as her driver did.*

He responded to the text with the message: *Who are you?*

A patriot was the response.

Is it money you want? I can—

The text chain suddenly disappeared.

CHAPTER 13

Bob and Liz took a water taxi from their hotel to the Grand Canal, which serpentined its way to the northern Cannaregio area, then navigated the narrow lanes to the Ventimiglia's residence, a renovated medieval-era building located on the Rio di San Girolamo. Giovanni, a short, lean, elegantly dressed man, with thick, all-white hair, pale-blue eyes, and a patrician nose, met them outside at his private dock.

"Welcome, Roberto," Giovanni said.

Bob introduced Liz to Giovanni, who half-bowed and kissed her hand.

Liz said, "Thank you for inviting us. It's good to finally meet you."

"It is our pleasure," he said, as he straightened and met her gaze. He smiled mischievously. "For years I have wanted to meet the woman who could put up with my friend, Roberto."

Liz laughed. "That's exactly what Bob said about your wife."

Giovanni clapped his hands once. "Wonderful. You and Anna already have much in common."

Liz's breath caught in her chest as they entered the foyer. A long, wide, mutely lit hallway ran from the front toward French doors that appeared to open out onto a garden. On both sides of the hallway a wide, marble staircase, with carpeted risers and a brilliant-gold railing rose to a second level defined by the same gold-colored rail. She glanced quickly at the brightly lit rooms on either side of the foyer—their interiors were like no others she'd ever seen outside a museum. Oil paintings and tapestries on the walls, antique furniture, chandeliers, and hand-woven carpets made Liz think of a palace rather than a residence.

A woman entered the foyer from the hallway and skirted a round table with an enormous flower arrangement at its center, highlighted by a quadruple-tiered crystal chandelier. She was a stunning beauty who was at least a couple inches taller than her husband, had a runway model's figure, and classic Northern Italian features: blue eyes, blonde hair, pale skin. She looked to be no more than fifty years old—fifteen years younger than Giovanni.

As Giovanni introduced his wife to Liz, Anna Ventimiglia came forward and said, "Welcome to our home." She kissed Liz on both cheeks. Liz kissed the woman back and thanked her.

"Please come in," Anna said. "I'm sure you could use a drink after that godawful-long taxi ride."

"That sounds good," Liz said, and followed Anna into the richly furnished sitting room off the foyer's right side. Three walls that rose to a fourteen-foot-high ceiling were decorated with dozens of oil paintings. A massive tapestry covered the fourth wall. Damask-covered antique furniture was arranged around a round coffee table inlaid with mother of pearl. Fires in two large fireplaces that bracketed the room made it warm and welcoming.

Giovanni filled four glasses with prosecco and toasted Bob and Liz. They sat and caught up on events of the past few years, after which Anna offered to give Liz a tour of the residence.

"Would you like that?" Anna asked.

"Absolutely," Liz said.

After Anna and Liz left, Giovanni set his glass on the coffee table and moved next to Bob on the couch. In a voice slightly above a whisper, he asked, "What's going on?"

Bob sipped from his glass and met Giovanni's gaze. "What are you talking about?"

The Italian smirked. "I may be retired but I'm neither senile nor out of touch. I've followed the news of the assassinations over the past week. One of my friends in AISE called today and asked if I had heard from you recently." The muscles in Giovanni's cheeks twitched as he stared at Bob. "Don't you think that's kind of a strange question? Out of the blue, this guy calls and asks about you. He told me a body was found in Venice, on Calle Della Morte. The dead man was an Italian citizen who taught at the University of Siena. He came to Italy as a teenager after his parents were killed by Russians during their invasion of Chechnya. He was adopted by an Italian Chechen Muslim family who had immigrated to Italy thirty years ago."

Bob shrugged.

Giovanni now glared at Bob, waiting for him to respond. When Bob remained silent, he said, "Don't you find it unusual that my friend would ask about you and, in the same conversation, mention a dead Chechen Muslim?"

Bob watched his old friend's face redden. Although he hadn't been told by Tanya Serkovic or Eitan Horowitz to keep silent about his near-death experience in Venice, his inclination was always to keep his own counsel. But Giovanni was an old friend and former colleague, and he was interested in knowing what else the Italians knew about the man who had attacked him and about the Asasiyun's operation.

"First tell me what you know about the assassinations that have been in the news."

"Just what I've read—"

Bob scoffed. "If you were about to tell me that all you know is what you've read in the newspapers, I have nothing to tell you."

Giovanni's cheek muscles danced again but, after a few seconds, he smiled. "Okay, my friend, I have been briefed on everything AISE knows. As of an hour ago, twenty-two people had been murdered in a dozen countries. The dead include a few family members and colleagues of men and women we believe were the primary targets. The assumption is that a radical Middle Eastern group is behind the murders because the victims were all involved in some way with the wars in Syria, Iraq, and Afghanistan, or have been participants in anti-terrorism efforts." He blew out a burst of air. "I have to tell you that my government is…highly agitated. The reason that my friend at AISE mentioned your name is because his associates at the CIA informed him that your name came up in connection with planned assassinations. Obviously, AISE is aware of our professional and personal relationships and it, of course, knows you and your wife are traveling in Italy."

"And the dead man?" Bob said. "Why would they assume I had something to do with a dead Chechen?"

"Pure conjecture based on your past. Dead bodies often trailed in your wake."

It was Bob's turn to sigh. "Okay, Giovanni, here's what I know."

Bob related his data about the Asasiyun but mentioned nothing about the dead Chechen. Telling what he knew about the Chechen and how he was killed could jeopardize Eitan Horowitz, not to mention create an international incident if the Italians learned that a Mossad agent was roaming the streets of Venice.

"So, who killed the Chechen?" Giovanni said.

Bob had anticipated the question. He spread his arms and shook his head. "Maybe it was a robbery."

Giovanni scoffed. "The police found a silenced Beretta at the scene. The dead man had a knife wound and his throat had been cut."

Bob grimaced. "That won't be good for tourism."

"You know nothing about the murder?"

Bob narrowed his eyes at Giovanni and shrugged again.

Giovanni nodded and gave Bob a knowing look. He smiled. "I assume you know more than you're telling me but are keeping things close to the vest for good reason."

Bob quickly set the conversation on a new course. "Why are you so interested in all of this?"

Giovanni bit his lower lip and, after a long pause, replied, "As I said, I may be retired but I stay in touch with my old agency. My contacts tell me they believe the assassinations will continue."

Bob blurted a laugh. "We're never really retired, are we?"

"That's a fact," Giovanni said.

It was nearly midnight when they arrived back at their hotel. After Liz went into the bedroom, Bob turned his cell phone on. He found several messages from Michael. He did a mental calculation about the time in Fayetteville—about 4:00 p.m.—and guessed Michael would still be at Fort Bragg. He called his son's cell number.

"Jeez, Dad, it's about time you returned my calls," Michael answered. "Are you and Mom okay?"

"We're fine, son. Everything all right there?"

"We're good. I just checked in with the commandant at West Point. Robbie's good, too. But what the hell happened over there?"

"Probably shouldn't go into detail on this phone. But I suspect you've already been briefed on what went down. I've got nothing to add."

"You're okay?"

Bob chuckled. "I love how roles reverse the older I get. Now you worry about me. I may be old but I'm not decrepit."

"Didn't say you were, Dad."

"Yeah, you did. It came across in your tone of voice." Before Michael could respond, Bob said, "I appreciate your concern, but we're both fine."

After a beat, Michael said, "By the way, I'm attending a conference in Rome this coming week. Initially, I was on the fence about it, but since you and Mom are over there, I'm thinking about going after all."

"It would be great to see you, but it's a long way from Rome to Venice."

"Yeah, but the wrap-up of the conference is a social event. The attendees are invited to Venice for Carnevale." Michael laughed. "I think I'll pass on the masquerade ball. I'd rather spend time with you and Mom."

It was Bob's turn to laugh. "Don't get your hopes up. Mom has corralled me into wearing a costume and attending a ball."

"You're kidding, right? You hate that kind of stuff."

"I do, my boy. But I hate making your mother angry even more."

"You're really wearing a costume?"

"Oh yeah."

Michael chuckled. "I promise I won't tell a soul," he said.

"By the way, what's the conference you're attending?"

"It's a big NATO affair. Planning session and a weapons show.

All the defense ministers, defense contractors, and a gaggle of senior military officers."

Before Bob could react, Liz entered the sitting area and said, "I'm finished in the bathroom." When she saw the phone in his hand, she shot him a questioning look.

"It's Michael," Bob said, as he handed her the phone.

As Liz talked with their son, Bob wondered about the wisdom of putting a bunch of NATO defense ministers, businesspeople, and military officers in one locale. *What a feast that could be for assassins*, he thought.

MONDAY
FEBRUARY 18

CHAPTER 14

Hassan Nizari pulled his robe tightly around him to ward off the wind gusts and chill of the foggy winter morning. He leaned into the wind that threatened to topple him. But, despite the weather, he was committed to taking his daily walk along the parapet and to look down from the stone fortress's ramparts onto what he had for years considered his private preserve. On nearly every day since he'd come to the forest, he woke before dawn and walked to the same site on his fortress's wall. He relished the first signs of the morning, especially when the sun crept up the back side of the mountain peaks on his left, rolled over the foothills, and bathed the valley below in its light. Despite the overcast and fog on this day, his heart beat a little faster as he approached the ramparts. As was his habit, he searched for the great stag that lived in the valley and wondered if the one that now lived there was a descendant of the first he'd seen decades ago. But the valley floor was choked with fog. Even the treetops weren't visible.

He felt stiff from the cold weather and silently prayed that the sun would pierce the dark cloud cover. "I am too old for this," he whispered as a shiver went up his spine.

A sound behind him caused him to startle. He turned slowly and saw Yasmin approaching.

"Hello, my flower petal," he said. He tried to smile but his face was too stiff from the cold. "I am pleased to see you up so early."

She nodded. "I thought I would join you for a change."

"Thank you, my dear. Your company is always welcome." He put an arm around her shoulder and pulled her tightly to him.

They stood together for a minute as an errant ray of sunlight appeared only momentarily on the eastern peaks. Nizari said, "I heard a lot of commotion last night. It sounded like vehicles."

"Uh huh," she said. "Maybe it was just…deliveries."

"After midnight?"

She tipped her head in a noncommittal manner.

Nizari turned and stared at her profile. "What's going on?" he said. "You're hiding something."

"No, I'm not, Father."

He turned to face her head on. "You've always been a bad liar. I demand to know what you're hiding."

Yasmin dropped her gaze for a moment. When she looked back up, Nizari was shocked at the cruel curve of her lips and the hardness in her eyes. "We brought one child or grandchild of each member of the Council of Guardians here last night."

Nizari moved back a half-step, as though he'd been struck. He had forgotten about the cold, the fog, the wind, the stag, and the tremendous joy he usually derived from his mornings here. He knew his mouth gaped, but he couldn't seem to muster the strength to close it.

"What have you done?" he finally shouted. "What in the name of Allah have you done?"

"It's the only way to protect us when our mission has been accomplished. I told you before that the mullahs will see us and all our people as threats. They will eliminate everyone and everything associated with the Asasiyun."

"That is paranoid nonsense," he shouted. "You've ruined us."

"No, Father, I've preserved our future."

Nizari grasped the front of Yasmin's coat and, flooded with anger about what she'd done and with fear of what the Iranian leadership would do to retaliate for the kidnappings, yelled at his daughter as though she were Satan incarnate. "You fool," he screamed. "You demented fool." His words echoed off the mountains.

Yasmin showed her father a toothy, predatorial grin. She

slammed her forearms down on the old man's wrists, causing him to shout in pain as his hands dropped from her coat. She placed a hand on his bony chest, pushed him away, and screamed, "*You're the fool, old man.* Do you really believe the megalomaniacal fanatics in Tehran will be grateful to you for what you have done? What do you think they will do when the West threatens to retaliate against Iran? We'll all be sacrificial goats. They'll claim they knew nothing about the Asasiyun and that you were running a rogue operation."

"You're wrong. Besides, who would believe that?"

He stumbled backward when she pushed him again; his eyes wide, a gasp escaped his mouth.

"I can fix this," he said in a weak, plaintive voice. "The Council of Guardians. I'll call—"

Yasmin quickly moved into him, slamming her hands against his chest, shoving him. His arms windmilling, his robes billowing, he fell over the parapet's edge.

Yasmin watched her father's mouth open even wider than before and heard him wail, "No-o-o," as he disappeared into the fog-cloaked forest.

Footsteps startled her and she spun around. Javad Muntaziri stood twenty feet away.

"I thought you were going to reason with him," he said.

She threw an arm into the air, as though what she had done was unimportant. "The old fool wouldn't listen."

Javad slowly shook his head. "How will you explain your father's death to our people all over the world and to the leadership in Tehran? When they learn he is gone, the assassins might abandon their assignments and the mullahs could pull the plug on the entire project."

Yasmin's complexion turned pale and her eyes went wide. But she quickly recovered. She moved to Javad and wrapped her arms around his chest. "I won't need to do that," she said. "Our assassins and the mullahs rarely communicate with my father and, when they do, it's almost always via encrypted texts or emails. They want to hide the connection between Tehran and us. We'll continue as though my father is still alive. You know all his passwords and how to contact the assassins and the mullahs. You'll act as a go-between."

"What about the ten children we abducted?" he asked.

"We'll keep them hidden until the mission is accomplished. In the meantime, I want you to demand five million American dollars for each child."

"But then the mullahs will know who took their children. They'll storm this place and kill us all."

Yasmin stepped back and chuckled. "We'll pretend to be an Iraqi, or Saudi, or Kurdish group when we demand ransom. Our communications with them will be encrypted. They'll never know who we really are. We'll put funds into a numbered bank account and sanitize the money through the Dark Web."

"You'll release the children?"

She ignored the question completely, stating, "They're insurance against the mullahs turning against us. If they do, we'll threaten to murder their children."

"But *then* they'll know who we are."

"Do you think they'll attack us as long as we have their children?"

Javad stepped into Yasmin, put his hands on the sides of her head, and kissed her mouth. When he pulled away, he said, "That could work." He raised a finger as if a thought had come to him. "And you'll definitely release the children after the mission is over?"

She pinched his arm and laughed. "We'll see." Placing a hand on his arm, she added, "We'll soon be very rich."

Javad looked uncertain. "We'll have to make sure the guard force is with us. If they turn against us, we're finished."

She threw up a hand as though to dismiss Javad's concerns. She thought about the guard captain and the time she'd spent co-opting him, promising him…favors. "Don't waste your time worrying about the guards. They will follow your orders."

"You're awfully confident."

She smiled. "Don't worry, Javad; I'll take care of everything."

CHAPTER 15

Portly, sixty-year-old General Sir Patrick Reginald Cartwright straightened his tie and did another once-over of his uniform and medals. Satisfied that all was in order, he turned away from the mirror in his office's private bathroom, walked out, and smiled at his wife Gwendolyn.

"You ready, old girl?"

Gwendolyn Cartwright cut a scolding look at her husband. "Don't you give me that *old girl* nonsense. I'm twelve years younger than you and look at least twenty years your junior."

Cartwright could tell from his wife's high-pitched, nasal tone that she was still peeved at him for accepting another assignment with the government. She'd pushed him to retire but, as usual, the powers-that-be prevailed on him to accept "just *one* more assignment."

"Come on, Gwenny, let's not go through this again."

"Oh, you want me to be the dutiful Army wife? After all these years, you want me to suck it up and act like a man? Isn't that what you tell your men?"

Cartwright didn't respond. He knew there was no point. She needed to vent.

"I didn't say a word when you were deployed to Bosnia in 1998 and Kosovo in 1999 with the Royal Green Jackets. After that, those bastards in Andover sent you to Afghanistan and then to Iraq.

Still, I kept my mouth shut. I thought it was quite nice when they promoted you to be Chief of the General Staff. But you told me that would be it. You promised me after that assignment you would retire so we could spend time with our children and grandchildren."

Gwendolyn was now in full form. She stood erect, dwarfing her husband by a couple of inches. Her arms moved around her head and shoulders as though storm-tossed, and her eyes blazed with fiery intensity.

"But when the Prime Minister called and said he wanted you to accept the position of Chief of the Defense Staff, you didn't hesitate for a moment."

"Gwenny, I'm a professional soldier. When my country calls, what am I supposed to do?"

"Tell your country to go to hell," she blurted.

She turned her back to him and moved to the window that looked out on the parade grounds where the change of command ceremony was to take place. She scanned the grounds all the way to the spiked iron fence that surrounded the base. Beyond the metal lay wide open fields used for war games and other training exercises, and past the fields were miles and miles of rolling farmland. She thought about her family's estate near Melrose, Scotland, just north of the English border, and wondered if she would ever be able to retire there with her pain-in-the-ass husband.

Cartwright moved up beside his wife, put an arm around her waist, and said, "Gorgeous day out there, don't you think?"

"Yes, Reggie. Thank you for listening to my rant."

"Quite all right, old girl."

She turned into him to scowl over his use once again of the "old girl" sobriquet, kissed his cheek, and moved to step around him, when glass shattered into the side of her face and the top of her husband's head exploded into a mighty, thick spray of blood and gore.

"Not bad," Jeffery Swanson muttered as he broke down the AWM .338 rifle. Designated as the L115A3 sniper rifle by the British Armed Services, the weapon had a stated range of 1,859 yards when loaded with .338 Lapua Magnum ammunition. Swanson knew that his position on top of this water tower on private land to the west of the military base was at the rifle's range limit, but the farther out he was when he took the shot, the less likely he would be discovered. The Old Man of the Mountain had made it clear that he needed to complete his mission, even if it meant sacrificing his own life in the process. But Swanson saw no need to commit suicide when he could take out his target with relative ease and minimal risk to himself. He inserted the rifle into its canvas carrier, slung it over his shoulder, and climbed down the ladder on the outside of the tower. He stowed the weapon in his car trunk and drove around the base's west side to the southern access gate and smiled at the frenetic activity all around. He showed his ID to a guard and said, "What the hell's going on, Sergeant?"

"You'd better report to the commandant, Captain," the man said.

"I just got back from the White House," Tanya Serkovic told the others. "Again." The only surface reaction to her statement was Cliff Hansen's eyebrows rising and falling. Frank Reynolds, Raymond Gallegos, Seth Bridewell, and Genevieve Salter continued to sit stoically in their chairs in the DCI's office. Tanya suspected every one of their blood pressures had spiked at least thirty points. Mentioning POTUS tended to have that effect. Tanya continued: "President Webb is…less than pleased with our progress in identifying the people behind these assassinations." When Cliff opened his mouth as if to object, Tanya held up a hand, "I know, I know. We're doing everything we can, but that's never enough." She looked directly at Seth. "How are the kids doing?" she asked, referring to the young 160-IQers who worked for him in the Digital Innovation Directorate. "Have they turned up anything?"

Raymond shook his head. "Grabowsky and Borden and their staff have analyzed everything we've received to date. First, the captured assassins, including the guy the Poles hold in Warsaw, have been uncooperative. The Ukrainians captured a woman who killed their Secretary of Defense. When they put real pressure on her, she bit down on a cyanide capsule planted in one of her molars and"—Seth snapped his fingers—"she was gone like that."

"Ah jeez," Tanya said. "I thought we'd warned our allies about that."

"I guess the Ukrainians didn't get the message," Frank said.

"Are there commonalties among the killers?" Genevieve asked.

"We're looking into that angle," Seth said. "So far, the only thing we've been able to determine is that they were all citizens of or long-time residents in the country in which they executed their attacks. They had jobs that required higher education and when the locals dug into their pasts, they each seemed to have appeared out of nowhere. We've already learned that some of the killers had appropriated birth names of children who died in their infancy."

"How did they become so radicalized that they would willy-nilly start murdering people?" Tanya asked. "And all within a few days?"

Frank said, "Another question is how in the hell did they acquire the training necessary to pull off these murders? Some assassinations required special training, like in firearms and explosives."

Raymond nodded. "As far as their radicalization is concerned, we don't have a clue. But we've learned that there appear to be gaps in their personal histories."

"Gaps?" Cliff said.

"Yeah. For instance, the individual the Poles have—Roland Kowalski—was hired by a university as a geology instructor. His curriculum vitae showed he'd been educated at a Polish university. His name was Polish; he spoke the language fluently; and he had a background that showed he was born in Zakopane and raised by parents who owned a butcher shop there. When the Polish Internal Security Agency contacted the parents, Antoni and Maria Kowalski, they learned that the couple did have a son named Roland, but the boy had died as an infant. The assassin was using the dead boy's birth certificate. So far, the feedback we've received from other countries where assassinations have occurred follow the same track. In other words, the killers have somehow been able to infiltrate their"—Seth made air quotes with his fingers—"*home* countries with false identities stolen from dead people. The Poles could find no evidence Kowalski had ever gone to school in Poland. His university degree was counterfeit."

"That raises two questions," Genevieve said. "First, didn't the school where he was teaching do a background check before they hired him? And second, how did the guy become fluent in Polish?"

Raymond said, "Both good questions. The answer to the first is that his employer apparently did check Kowalski's credentials. They had a copy of a transcript from his university, along with letters of recommendations from professors there. Turned out, they were all forged. Someone had hacked into the university's computer system and added Kowalski into the database. When Kowalski's employer sent an email request for his transcript and references, they received what they asked for. Whoever actually sent the information is a mystery."

"What about Genevieve's second question?" Cliff asked.

Raymond shrugged. "We have no clue how Kowalski learned Polish or how he became radicalized and trained as an assassin."

"That's mind-boggling," Seth Bridewell said. "If our analysts' estimates are correct—that there could be anywhere from one thousand to five thousand Asasiyun targets—that would indicate there could be as many as five thousand assassins poised and ready to strike. If all those assassins were taught to speak a foreign language, the Asasiyun would have created a language school that would rival the Defense Language Institute in Monterey."

Raymond nodded. "That's about right. What if your people were to try to dig up unusual activity involving the recruitment of language instructors going back fifteen to twenty years?"

"Any particular languages?" Bridewell asked.

"I thought about tracking odd recruiting behavior here in the States, but there must be thousands of Americans who take jobs teaching American English overseas. Everyone from students to PhDs to retirees. It would be almost impossible to identify unusual activity. I think it makes more sense to concentrate on recruitment of teachers of languages like Polish, Greek, Finnish, etcetera. Languages which aren't as common as English."

"Okay Ray," Seth said. "We'll get right on it."

"So, where's that leave us?" Tanya said.

"Actually, it leaves us in a better place than where we were yesterday," Raymond said. He looked over at Seth. "It tells us we might be able to backtrack the computer hacks to their source and, assuming that Kowalski's insertion into Poland is indicative of how the other assassins were put in place in their respective countries, we could conclude that whoever is behind this campaign conducted an extensive language training program. They must have recruited foreign language speakers years ago as teachers. Kowalski spoke fluent Polish without any discernible accent, which would indicate he learned the language at a relatively young age. He's now in his late twenties, which tells me he was probably trained to speak Polish beginning at least fifteen years ago. If the other assassins' backgrounds are similar, there was one hell of a linguist recruiting program going on."

Frank said, "But some assassins were much older than Kowalski. If they were recruited as children, then this program has been going on for, maybe, a couple decades."

"Also," Tanya said, "Kowalski could have been a native Pole. Although it seems unlikely."

"You could both be correct," Raymond said, "but we've got to start somewhere."

CHAPTER 16

Greta Brzynski's first languages were Polish and Serbo-Croatian. Her parents had immigrated to the United States when Greta was seven. She was now twenty-six, a graduate of Georgetown University with a major in Slavic languages, and a recent CIA hire. She was sent to join Vince Loughnane in Warsaw.

Loughnane had flown to Warsaw from Riyadh. He met Brzynski at a company safe house one block east of Ujazdów Avenue, a major thoroughfare running parallel to the Vistula River in Warsaw's downtown district. The safe house was a short walk to the United States embassy—a glass-fronted, unimaginatively designed building that resembled a sheer wall of solar panels implanted on a concrete frame.

"How's your stomach?" Loughnane asked the young linguist.

She frowned. "What do you mean?"

Loughnane hunched his shoulders and shook his head. "You'll see. You ready to go to work?"

"Of course. I didn't fly all the way here for a vacation."

Loughnane stared at her, his expression blank. "You got that right, missy."

Two large Poles dressed in black suits picked up Loughnane and Brzynski with a black Chevy Suburban on the street across from Ujazdów Park and drove them to the General Command

Headquarters on Warsaw's Żwirki i Wigury Avenue. Inside, they were escorted to an underground bunker, briefed by Janusz Mazurek, an agent with the Polish Intelligence Service, and led into a frigid four hundred square foot concrete room. The powerful stench of urine, feces, and sour sweat greeted them. A naked man was secured with manacles to a metal chair bolted to the floor. His head lolled forward; bloody saliva hung in rosy strands from his mouth.

Loughnane studied the bound man for a good thirty seconds, turned to Mazurek, and said, "You get anything?"

"Nothing yet."

"What about family?"

Mazurek cut a look over a shoulder. "His wife's in a room down the hall. A woman from social services is with their three-year-old son in another room."

"Have you questioned her?" Loughnane asked.

"We're letting her stress out. We were just about to start with her when you arrived."

"Does she speak English?"

Mazurek shrugged. "A little."

"Would you mind if my colleague and I talked to her first?"

"Only if we're in the room with you."

Loughnane glanced at Brzynski and noticed she was fixated on the prisoner. Her face had gone gray and she continuously swallowed as though she might gag at any moment. He took her arm and pulled her toward the door. "Let's go."

As they followed Mazurek down a hall, with another Pole trailing them, Brzynski croaked, "What did they…do to…that man?"

Loughnane took her arm again and leaned down to whisper in her ear. "I asked you about your stomach. If you can't handle this, you should wait in the car."

"I didn't sign up to be involved with torture. I—"

Loughnane called to Mazurek and said, "Janusz, give us a minute." After the two Poles walked away, Loughnane turned back to Brzynski and pinned her with a gaze that made her gasp. "Pay attention. You've got two choices. You go out to the car and I'll put you on a plane back to the States as soon as I'm done here. Or you focus on the fact that the prisoner is part of a campaign of murder and mayhem that has already taken almost two dozen lives. If we don't stop them, hundreds, maybe thousands more will die. I need you to talk to the woman down the hall and translate for me. After that, you'll need to translate for me when we go back in with the man. Make up your mind."

"But—"

"But *what*? We're violating his rights? What rights? His right to murder people? His right to destroy families? His right to undermine democratic countries? Suck it up, missy."

When she didn't immediately respond, Loughnane shouted after the two Poles, "Would you have my colleague escorted out to the car?"

Brzynski cleared her throat and, in a phlegmy voice, said, "I'm okay. I'll stay."

Loughnane skewered her with another cold look, twisted his mouth in a disgusted, sour way, turned back toward the Poles, and advanced down the hall.

Roland Kowalski's wife was a diminutive, blue-eyed, blonde named Kamila. She had a low-level position in the Department of Transportation. When Brzynski and the three men entered the room, the woman's already large eyes seemed to bug out. She blurted in Polish, "What am I doing here? I don't understand."

Loughnane said in a rough growl-of-a-voice, "Your husband killed a high-ranking Polish general. You're here because we think you know what your husband had planned and helped him." He pointed at Brzynski and told her to translate. While she did so, Kamila stared wide-eyed at Loughnane.

"That's insane," she finally said. "This is a frameup. Roland is a teacher. He would never—"

The Polish intel officer stepped around Brzynski, bent over—his face even with the woman's—and shouted at her for a good thirty seconds. She seemed in a state of catatonia by the time he'd finished. Her mouth dropped as though her jaws had come unhinged; her eyes were wide with fright. Perspiration broke out on her forehead and above her upper lip. She raised her hands, palms out, as though to prevent the Polish officer from getting any closer. He straightened and backed up a step.

"Th…this can't be true," she squealed. "Roland could never—"

Brzynski had moved to the back of the room with Loughnane, who whispered, "What did he say to her?"

"That surveillance cameras had filmed the assassination and that she was going to be sent to prison and her son would be placed in a government orphanage if she didn't cooperate. He also told her that her parents and siblings would be taken into custody and interrogated."

Loughnane frowned. "That gal doesn't know a damn thing about her husband's extra-curricular activities. I could tell from her reaction to what you and Mazurek told her."

"So, what do we do?"

"Give me a minute to talk with them."

Loughnane waved at Mazurek and walked out into the corridor. When the Pole joined him, he said, "Janusz, we're wasting our time with her. She's clueless."

Mazurek nodded. "I had the same impression. We need to find something that pushes Kowalski's button."

"Based on the intel we've gathered, these people are fanatics. Muslim extremists."

"There's no indication he's a practicing Muslim," Mazurek said.

Loughnane scoffed. "The asshole's doing exactly what's expected of him. It's called *taqiyya*. It's okay to lie, cheat, break Quranic law, whatever, if you're doing Allah's work." Loughnane cleared his throat and ran a hand over his short, gray hair. "You said something about finding a button to push. You open to a suggestion?"

Mazurek made a hand gesture to encourage Loughnane to continue.

It took an hour for Mazurek to transport Kamila Jankowski to a Warsaw "gentlemen's club." He had her filmed with the Albanian proprietor, naked strippers on a runway as a backdrop. During that hour, he enlisted the aid of his brother-in-law, a Catholic priest, and had him brought to the army base. Mazurek had video taken of Roland Kowalski's son being led from the building by his cassocked brother-in-law. With the two videos in hand, Mazurek returned to Kowalski's cell, had a bucket of cold water poured over him, made him watch video of his wife and son, and told him that if he didn't tell him everything, his wife would be turned over to an Albanian trafficker/strip joint owner, and his son would be raised by the Catholic Church. It took Kowalski less than a half-minute to begin spewing everything he knew, including where he'd been trained, where he was from originally, and how he'd been infiltrated into Poland. By the time he'd finished talking, Vince Loughnane's body vibrated with nervous energy.

"Let's get out of here, missy," Loughnane told Brzynski.

Brzynski rounded on Loughnane, poked a finger in his chest, and barked, "With all due respect, sir, if you call me missy one more time, I'll kick you in the balls."

Loughnane laughed, "Now, *that's* more like it, mis…Greta."

CHAPTER 17

The Iranian Supreme Leader, Ayatollah Sayyid Noori Hamadani, sat stone-faced at the head of an oval table in the room reserved for the Council of Guardians. He had appointed six council members and, effectively, had control over the appointment of the other six. He had never seen these men as distressed as they now were. He turned toward the council's senior member and said, "Tell me about the kidnappings."

Abdolkarim Esfandiari's eyes glistened with tears as he looked back at Hamadani. His voice was shaky and hoarse. "They took my grandson, Ismael." He moved an arm around the room, taking in the others, and said, "Every one of us has lost a child or grandchild."

The Supreme Leader slowly looked at each man in turn and finally said, "Have the kidnappers communicated with any of you?"

A council member at the opposite end of the table replied. "We each received a text that said essentially the same thing. That they had our children and would not mistreat them as long as we did exactly as they say."

The Supreme Leader waited until he was certain the man had finished. He asked, "What did they demand?"

"Five million American dollars," another man said.

Yet another man, Sayyid Ghorbani, who oversaw Iran's cyber operations, chimed in, "I had our people try to track the source of the texts, without success. I must tell you, Arbob, this is very unusual. These people must have sophisticated capabilities."

"Are you telling me that you can't track their communications?" Hamadani said, an audible tone of disappointment tainted his voice.

Ghorbani's Adam's apple bobbed as he swallowed. He cleared his throat and said, "Not yet. But we're working on it."

Hamadani said, "Let's hope it's sooner rather than later."

Other than the one man whimpering and the heavy breathing of others, the room went silent. After a minute, Esfandiari began to speak, but Hamadani cut him off with a raised hand. An extended pause occurred before he spoke again.

"Your children and grandchildren are only good to these people as long as they are alive. Iran is not some corrupt Western society where sick men kidnap children to abuse them. We will not pay the ransoms." He glared at Ghorbani. "We will wait to see how these people react. The next time they contact one of you, I presume Ayatollah Ghorbani's people will be able to determine who they are and where they are located."

Hamadani looked around the room, surprised at the stunned silence. No one made eye contact with him. "What is it?" he demanded.

Dariush Gilani, the mullah who oversaw the Iranian Treasury Agency, said, "We already paid the ransom from Treasury funds." His voice broke as he whined, "We couldn't let them murder our children." He spread his arms. "What else could we do?"

Hamadani felt his body temperature rise. "You did what?" he screamed. "You paid these criminals sixty million dollars?"

The council members' bodies looked like question marks as they slumped in their chairs and stared down at their laps.

Hamadani stood and waved his arm as though it was a weapon. He pointed his hand in an erratic pattern at the men, and said, "I give you all one week to return that money to the Treasury, or else." Then he left the room.

"The ransom money has been transferred to the bank in the Caribbean," Javad told Yasmin. He chuckled. "Everything was handled through the Dark Web. The mullahs won't be able to follow the money trail."

Yasmin, seated behind her father's desk, took in a slow, deep breath. She and Javad were the only two people who knew where the money had gone. *That's one person too many*, she thought. *The man is nothing but brawn and testosterone.*

"When do you plan to release the rest of the assassins?" he said. "Are you going to follow your father's plan?"

"With a few minor tweaks."

Javad said, "The agents we turned loose were assigned to single targets. Your father wanted to see how the authorities in different countries would react. And he wanted to leave the impression that the attacks would target individuals versus large groups."

Dear Allah, will this idiot tell me something I don't already know? she thought. She stared at the uneasy look in his eyes and asked, "Is something bothering you?"

"Is there really any place on earth where we will be able to hide from the mullahs or from our enemies in the West?"

Good question, she thought.

"Of course."

He didn't look assured.

She stood, came around the desk and kissed his cheek. "Don't worry, my love, we will have a wonderful and long life together."

He put his arms around her and whispered in her ear, "Let's go to your quarters."

She pushed him away. "Not now, my love. I have things to do first. I will take care of your...needs later."

He frowned like a spoiled child as she stepped back.

Although she had told Javad that soon there would be more assassinations, Yasmin held back the start date of the campaign's "finale." From reading her father's documents, she'd learned that the Ayatollah's original plan was to release seventy-five assassins each week for thirteen consecutive weeks. One thousand killers in all. By the time Easter week arrived, the Western world would be in a state of shock. But she felt that this plan was more symbolic than tactical. She believed it would be preferable to turn all the assassins loose at one time, rather than giving the West the opportunity to build its defenses and possibly discover who was behind the attacks. And, if her instincts were correct, when the campaign was complete, the Ayatollahs would do everything in their power to eradicate everything and everyone associated with the Asasiyun. So, she had decided to let the Ayatollahs think the campaign would end at Easter, which would give her the opportunity to escape Iran before the leadership in Tehran could come after her and her people.

She opened a contact file with the names of several assassins and their targets and sent off an encrypted message. She sat back and watched icons on the computer screen ping as the army of murderers acknowledged receipt of their orders.

Polish Intelligence agents dropped off Vince Loughnane and Greta Brzynski at the park where they'd picked them up. From there, the two CIA employees made their way to the safe house. Loughnane rushed inside the spy-proof sensitized compartmentalized information facility (SCIF) and used the encrypted telephone to call Raymond Gallegos at Langley.

"It's Vince," Loughnane said when Raymond came on the line.

"You get anything?"

"Oh yeah. Whether I believe it all is another question entirely. I mean, what the Polish assassin told us sounds like a Robert Ludlum novel."

"Hold on a second," Raymond said. "I want to patch in the director."

"Maybe you should hear what I have before you bring in the DCI. It could be a fairytale."

Raymond cleared his throat. "How long have you been doing this, Vince?"

"Almost since before you were born."

"How good are your instincts?"

"Okay, Ray, I get it. Bring in the DCI."

After Raymond patched in Tanya Serkovic, Loughnane related what he'd learned from Asasiyun killer, Roland Kowalski.

TUESDAY
FEBRUARY 19

CHAPTER 18

On a Saturday morning when he was ten years old, Russian troops had stormed Mahmoud Lemontoff's village in Chechnya, catching most villagers in the mosque. They had shot poison gas grenades into the building and locked the doors behind them. The oldest child of Aslan and Maaret Lemontoff, Mahmoud had survived the attack on his village because his parents had left him at home to babysit his two-year-old sister, Eliina. When he'd heard shooting, he'd bundled her up and run into the woods behind their home. As the Russian troops swept through the village, Eliina had begun to cry. Mahmoud had pressed a hand over his sister's mouth.

Hours after the Russians left the village, Chechen partisans found him huddled in the woods, still holding his sister's corpse. They'd taken him to an orphanage where his shame became the catalyst for growing his anger. Two years later, the cleric who ran the orphanage had transported Mahmoud on a body-wrenching, hellish, three-week journey by truck, then fishing boat, and then by another truck to a mountainous region. It was there that he discovered his purpose and came to understand how he could expiate his shame and manage his anger, while serving the Old Man of the Mountain. He was taught American English, was schooled in basic medical terminology and procedures, and was familiarized with weapons. After three years, he was transported to Thessaloniki, Greece and put into the hands of an Asasiyun agent who had been in that country for ten years. The agent took Mahmoud to a Greek Orthodox church that managed an orphanage in Thessaloniki. From there, the boy was shipped to the United States where he was adopted by Anton and Martha Pointer, a childless couple in Syracuse, New York.

They lavished love, praise, and guidance on Mahmoud, who they renamed James. His knowledge of English amazed the Pointers and they boasted about their son's intelligence. They wanted "Jimmy" to go to law school and practice law, like his adoptive father. But, while still in high school, the boy had made it clear his interests were in an area other than the law.

"I want to study medicine and become a nurse," he'd told his parents.

"But Jimmy, if you want to study medicine, why not become a surgeon?" Martha would ask.

He'd responded according to the script he'd been indoctrinated with during his years in the Old Man of the Mountain's training school: "I don't want to spend years in school to become a doctor. I want to help people as soon as possible."

His parents weren't overjoyed with his decision, but they weren't completely unhappy with it either. They had to admire his desire to help people. They couldn't quite reconcile his goal of becoming a nurse with his passion for firearms and hand-to-hand combat training, but they indulged him. After all, he was their miracle child. So, they paid for Jimmy to go to karate and mixed martial arts classes, to attend firearms training classes and, ultimately, to get his nursing degree. They were thrilled when he applied and was accepted for a staff nursing position at the United States Military Academy, relatively close to Syracuse. What they didn't know was that Jimmy had been told when he was only twelve that his mission was to become a nurse and get a job at a United States military facility, where he would one day strike a blow for the Asasiyun.

Jimmy Pointer's heart seemed to soar when the message from the Old Man of the Mountain pinged on his burner phone. He immediately entered a code number that destroyed the phone's electronics. He took the phone apart and dropped the pieces into a hazardous waste repository on the wall in the West Point infirmary. Pointer shuddered as he remembered clutching Eliina's lifeless body. His shame and anger resurfaced as the memory scrolled through his brain like a slow-motion video.

He looked at the digital wall clock: 0705. The cadets would now be moving from the dining hall to morning formation. Pointer stared out the exam room window and watched the hustle and bustle of cadre, cadets, and workers as they moved about the campus. He then turned back to the schedule that the medical officer had placed in his inbox. An upper respiratory infection had invaded one of the barracks, laying up a dozen cadets who were now quarantined in a separate building wing. Pointer felt giddy about his luck. The quarantine area and one of his targets' rooms were in the same building.

In response to the communication from the Old Man of the Mountain, he planned how he would execute his mission. As he'd been trained to do, he observed his targets' habits; became acquainted with their class schedules; knew the sports in which they participated. The quarantine would make his task relatively easy as far as the male target was concerned. The female, however, could be more problematic.

It's going to be a long day, he thought.

At 8:00 a.m., Raymond Gallegos and nine of his people joined Tanya, Cliff, Frank, and two representatives from the FBI's Counterintelligence Division, a National Security Branch division charged with protecting the United States against foreign intelligence operations and espionage. They met in a small, second floor amphitheater at Langley.

Tanya opened the meeting with a warning that everything they were about to discuss was classified top secret. Then she looked at Raymond and said, "You're on."

"To ensure we're all on the same page," Raymond said, "I'm going to summarize what we know." He took in a big breath, let it out slowly, picked up a remote device, and pressed the "PLAY" button. A headshot of a man in a tie and jacket showed on a screen. Raymond pointed at the image. "That's Roland Kowalski, the man who shot and killed Polish General Emil Wozniak." He played the surveillance video of Kowalski carrying out the murder. "He was captured by security officers and interrogated by the Polish Intelligence Service."

Raymond paused a few seconds before he continued: "Kowalski was born near Batumi, Georgia, on the eastern coast of the Black Sea. His given name was Merab Ivanishvili. His parents were killed in a car accident when he was eight years old. He was sent to an orphanage funded by the Islamic Republic of Iran and run by Shia clerics. When he was eleven, he was sent to a facility in a mountainous part of what he thinks was northern Iran. He described the facility as a fortress. When he was there, hundreds of children ranging in age from about ten to eighteen were also at this facility. Boys outnumbered girls approximately ten to one, and his impression was that the children were all from Muslim countries. All the children were schooled in Shia Islam and Sharia law. And they were segregated by language."

Raymond pressed the remote and brought up a map of Iran. He pointed a red laser light built into the remote at a location on the map. "This is Semnan Province." He moved the laser marker. "This is the Cloud Forest, where we believe the fortress might be located." He brought up a satellite photograph that clearly showed a structure resembling a medieval fortress. "Kowalski could have been trained there. We've wondered about this facility for years, ever since NRO satellites took pictures of it. We've always assumed it's a military training facility or a school of sorts."

Cliff interrupted Raymond. "Don't limit your thinking to this is *the* training site. It's only one of several locations being investigated."

"Thanks for that clarification, Cliff," Raymond said. Then he continued: "Kowalski claimed that every child at the facility was taught a foreign language and was trained in a specific country's customs, history, governmental structure, food, religion, arts, sports, etcetera. They were given new names and were punished severely if they used their birth names. Some were schooled to be teachers; others were trained as engineers, bankers, doctors, nurses, and so forth.

"They were also given backgrounds that included birth dates, family names and histories, schools they supposedly attended, and on and on. They were each tested daily about their falsified history and, again, were punished severely if they made even the slightest error. They were trained in the art of *taqiyya* to hide their Islamic faith from their neighbors and co-workers when they infiltrated their new countries."

Raymond placed the remote on the lectern. "One other thing Kowalski disclosed was that they received intensive training in physical conditioning and assassination techniques. These involved small arms usage—including sniper training, quick kill skills with knives, bomb fabrication, and use of poisons.

"Before I turn it over to Director Bridewell, I have two items to add. First, Kowalski told our man that there were at least fifty people at the training facility who worked in a computer lab. These people built and perfected the students' legends, and hacked into government, high school, university, and employer databases to back up the students' backgrounds when they applied for admission to schools or for jobs or to get married. The second thing is that he thought the top guy at the facility, a man who everyone referred to as the Old Man of the Mountain, was Iranian-based on his accent. Of course, Farsi is spoken in regions outside Iran—Afghanistan, Pakistan, and Southern Russia, for instance, so the guy might not have been Iranian."

Raymond yielded the dais to Seth Bridewell, who walked the group through the details of Kowalski's history, how he believed it was documented, and how he was activated by an unknown handler.

After Seth was finished, Tanya asked her familiar question, "So where does this leave us?"

Seth said, "Zach Grabowsky, Angelina Borden, and their teammates are working on two projects. The first, with NSA assistance, is to try to intercept communications to and from the fortress in the Cloud Forest. The second project involves trying to hack into the facility's IT system to identify the students trained there and where they were sent."

"What about trying to find out who's funding this diabolical scheme?" FBI Agent Shawn Drake asked.

Raymond nodded. "Frank Reynolds is handling that." He looked at Frank.

Frank mounted the dais and picked up the remote from the lectern. He brought up a PowerPoint presentation that showed an organization chart.

"As you can see, the Iranian government is organized in what seems to be a confused network of offices and departments. What is clear is the fact that *nothing* happens unless the Supreme Leader, Ayatollah Sayyid Noori Hamadani, gives his permission. The Iranian government is an intensively top-down organization. So, we conclude the training, if it's going on at this facility in Semnan Province, or anywhere else in Iran, must be under the direction of Hamadani." He scoffed. "Who else but the *Supreme Leader* could authorize the expenditure of the vast amount of money needed to finance an operation like the one Raymond just described? The cost and organization is mind-boggling. We're trying to find a money trail to Iran's leadership."

Tanya interjected, "Cliff's correct. We shouldn't just focus on Iran. This could be a Russian operation. It sounds almost like a Soviet op. With Putin in power over there, and him being former KGB, the Russians could be behind it."

"What about the Muslim connection?" Frank said.

"That could be misdirection," Tanya said. "The Russians have as much animosity toward the West as do the Iranians."

"We thought about that," Frank said, "but we don't believe Putin would want his or Russia's fingerprints on this scheme. Imagine the reaction in the West if the Russians were tied to the Asasiyun."

"I understand that, but let's not allow our thinking to get single-tracked."

"I agree," Frank said, as he looked at FBI Agent Drake. "You were correct describing this scheme as diabolical. Just think about the convoluted mind that devised the whole thing in the first place, and the patience required of all concerned to put it in place, requiring years of planning, training, and execution. We assume the physical and combat trainers came from the military. If all the trainees came to them the way Kowalski did, it appears that orphanages were used to identify candidates. And they had to recruit linguists who taught the kids foreign languages. Student brainwashing must have involved psychologists and psychiatrists. They found people with the requisite skills to fabricate and document legends and to hack into databases all over the world to support those stories. We're talking about thousands of people, yet not one word leaked about this scheme until we picked up a bit of chatter a couple weeks ago."

Drake said, "Even if we identify the training site and the brains behind the operation, we wouldn't know the names and locations of other sleeper assassins already in place unless we capture someone high up in their organization or hack into their system. We could very well have hundreds or thousands of more deaths across the globe. If Roland Kowalski's experience was typical, we could have sleeper agents buried deep in every Western country, including right here at home."

CHAPTER 19

A couple Advil gave Bob some relief from the soreness left over from the encounter with his would-be assassin. He and Liz toured the Galleria dell'Accademia and the Guggenheim, before taking a lunch break. They wandered into a place named Bar Ai Artisti on the Campo Santa Margherita Piazza. It didn't have much curb appeal, so Liz wasn't enthusiastic about entering.

"I don't know," Liz said. "It looks a bit…worn."

Bob pointed at the sign over the entrance. "Look, they've been in business since 1897. That's a long time to work on getting things right."

"What the hell," Liz said. "I'm too tired to walk around trying to find someplace else to eat."

The aroma that met them when they entered the place was intoxicating. "I don't think I can ever get enough garlic," Liz said.

"I've been meaning to talk to you about that," Bob said. "You're beginning to smell like garlic. Even your clothes—"

"Are you serious?" she said.

Bob chuckled. "I'm kidding, sweetheart." He smiled. "You're so easy."

"You think you're so funny."

He kissed her cheek. As he pulled away, he said, "Boy, you need to do something about your garlic breath."

She gave him a sultry smile. "How would you feel about a life of celibacy?"

Bob held up his hands in surrender. "You win again."

They each ordered a salami and cheese panini and bottles of water. Over lunch they discussed their experiences at the two museums and scrolled through photographs Liz had taken on her phone.

"I'm in museum overload," Bob said.

"This city is amazing," Liz said. "You turn a corner and you find a church, a museum, a palazzo. I'm afraid our energy level isn't a match for the sites."

"You want to return to the hotel?"

She wagged a finger at him. "Not a chance. We've got tickets to the Palazzo Ducale. I don't want to miss that." She stood, took his hand, and pulled him to his feet. "Let's go, Big Boy. The day is still young."

Bob groaned. "You're the most unsympathetic person I know."

"Wa-wa-wa," she said in a plaintive tone, and marched outside. But as soon as Bob joined her, Liz turned and said, "Oh, my God. What was I thinking? You must be in pain after what happened with that man. Let's go back to the hotel. I'm so sorry."

Bob smiled. "I think I can handle one more site before I completely fall apart."

On their walk to the Palazzo Ducale, Bob's mind wandered back to what Michael had told him about attending the NATO conference in Rome and finishing up at Carnevale in Venice. The more he thought about it, the more concerned he became. The terrorists had been attacking single targets, but that didn't mean the group wouldn't capitalize on the opportunity to hit a large group of Western leaders in one massive strike.

When they arrived at the palazzo, Liz excused herself and went to the restroom. Bob took the opportunity to call Raymond Gallegos, who sounded groggy when he answered.

"Did I wake you?" Bob said.

Raymond coughed. "Yeah, you did. But I needed to get up anyway. I've got a meeting in an hour."

"You guys burning the candle at both ends?"

"What candle? The damned thing burned down to nothing days ago. What's up?"

"Listen, Ray, I'm sure you're aware of the NATO Defense Conference starting tomorrow in Rome."

"Of course. Some of our people are…observing the meeting."

"What about Venice?"

"What *about* Venice?"

"Apparently, the Italians have invited the NATO representatives to Venice for Carnevale."

"We were aware of that. How'd you hear about it?"

"Michael's attending the conference. He mentioned meeting up with Liz and me here."

"What are you thinking?" Raymond asked.

"Maybe my imagination's in overdrive, but I'm thinking Venice would be a target-rich environment with multiple general officers and defense ministers here. Not to mention defense contractors, spouses, and support personnel. I've been to conferences in Rome. The Italians are masters at security. There will probably be three cops or soldiers for every conference attendee. But Venice is a totally different venue. It's a rabbit warren of alleys and canals that will complicate security."

Raymond finished Bob's thought: "And the Asasiyun would have a field day in Venice."

"That's what I'm thinking."

"Are you suggesting the group might change its M.O. and go after a group target?"

"It's a possibility. Or, putting all those officials in a small city like Venice will just make it easier for one assassin to rub out a top general or a minister. If you don't mind a suggestion, I'd ask the Italian government where the visitors will be staying, if there are dinners scheduled that large numbers of dignitaries will attend, and if all of them will attend the same Carnevale event? One well-placed bomb could take out a lot of people."

Raymond grumbled something.

"What?" Bob asked.

"I said you're a royal pain in the ass."

Bob laughed. "I won't deny that, my friend. Sorry to add to your burden." Then Bob had a thought. "Are you telling me that none of this occurred to you?"

"The only thing that didn't occur to me was this call and you being involved."

"So, did you suggest to the NATO nations that they discourage their people from going to Venice?"

Raymond didn't respond immediately. After a few seconds, he said, "I gotta go, Bob. It was nice speaking with you." He yawned loudly and added, "Enjoy yourselves over there."

Bob slipped the phone into a jacket pocket just as Liz exited the restroom. He noticed that her eyebrows were arched. She appeared exasperated. Thinking she'd caught him on the phone, he tensed as he anticipated her giving him the third degree. Liz surprised him when she pointed over his shoulder. "Isn't that the man you saw in the Arsenale?"

Bob spun around and spotted Eitan Horowitz leaning against a stone wall on the other side of the *Ducale*'s courtyard. He turned back to Liz, said, "I'll be right back," and walked away. He scanned the courtyard's width and length as he moved toward the Mossad agent, but he saw no one who appeared suspicious or threatening.

Horowitz pushed off the wall as Bob approached. "You're going to love touring the Palazzo Ducale. The Doge's Palace, as it's called in English. There's a lot to see in there. I assume you know that for the price of your tickets you'll also have access to the Museo Correr, the Museo Archeologico Nazionale, and the Biblioteca Nazionale Marciana."

"What are you, in the tour business now?" Bob said.

Horowitz stepped closer and, in a lowered voice, said, "I wanted to talk with you. Sorry to disturb your vacation."

"I assume you wouldn't be here if it weren't important. No apology necessary." Bob smiled and added, "Besides, I owe you big time."

"I understand you and your wife are attending *Il Ballo del Doge* at Palazzo Pisani Moretta."

"Huh," Bob said. "And how would you have come by that information?"

It was Horowitz's turn to smile. "I have a copy of the guest list.

You and Mrs. Danforth are listed as guests of Giovanni and Anna Ventimiglia, the former Deputy Director of AISE." He pronounced AISE like 'ICE.'

"And why would our being on that list cause you to follow us to the *Ducale* on this beautiful afternoon?"

Horowitz closed his eyes for a second. When he opened them again, he said, "You remember my suggestion that you ought to return to the United States until this Asasiyun business is over?"

"Yes, but I came to the conclusion that if the group wants to get me, they can do it just as easily in Bethesda as they can in Venice."

"That's debatable," Horowitz said. "In any case, I recommend you not attend the grand ball."

Bob's internal warning system went on high alert. "Why?"

"We're... hearing things."

"Hearing things or guessing?"

"Okay, it's more conjecture than solid intel. But that doesn't mean we're wrong. The ball would make an inviting target."

"Pretty hypothetical."

"Everything's hypothetical until it isn't, Mr. Danforth."

"It sounds as though you are as paranoid as I am," Bob said.

Horowitz placed a hand on Bob's arm. "Stay alert." He sighed. "When I suggested to my people that they ask the Italians to cancel the invitation for the delegates to come to Venice, they just laughed at me."

"I've been there," Bob said.

"For God's sake, don't go to that ball."

"What was that about?" Liz asked as Bob rejoined her.

Bob wasn't quite sure what was going on and didn't want to go into the matter with Liz...at least not yet.

"That's the man who saved me from the assassin. He just wanted to check up on me." He chuckled. "I guess he's worried about the old fart American."

"That was sweet of him," Liz said.

"Yes, it was." Bob took Liz's hand. "Let's go inside and do the tour."

While Liz slowly admired the art inside The Doge's Palace, Bob trailed slightly behind her and ruminated on his conversations with Raymond Gallegos and Eitan Horowitz. He forced himself to not get lost in his thoughts to the point where he didn't respond to Liz's statements, like, "This is absolutely stunning," or "This is more than I hoped for." When he grunted a reply for the tenth time, she turned to face him. "What's on your mind?"

"Nothing. I'm just overwhelmed with all of this." He waved his arms around to indicate the Sala del Senato's ceiling and walls.

She gave him a skeptical look. "Did you hear what I said about the ceiling?"

Bob looked up and tried to recall what he'd read about this chamber from a guidebook. He dredged up all he could and said, "You mean about Veronese and Titian?"

Liz seemed pleased and turned back to the closest chamber wall. Bob leaned over her shoulder and said, "I'm going to sit down for a minute."

She looked back at him. "Are you okay?"

He smiled. "I'm fine. My feet hurt, that's all."

He took a seat on the wood *banco* along one side wall, watched Liz as she meandered around the great hall, and reflected again on his conversations. After decades with the CIA, he knew how the organization and its senior people worked. He thought about what Raymond had told him…or hadn't told him. His former subordinate had been cagey in his responses. And Eitan Horowitz showing up outside just didn't seem right. He wondered if Raymond had definitive information about the Asasiyun planning to attack the NATO delegates here in Venice, or if he was just being paranoid, too.

An errant thought came to him that made him shudder. *If the Company warned the NATO conference delegates about a possible attack, they would surely call off the trip to Venice. If the trip was still planned, then maybe the Company had not warned the delegates. They could be using the delegates, including Michael, as bait to entice the assassins into Venice. Maybe the Company is setting a trap.*

"That's absurd," he muttered.

"What?" Liz asked as she sat next to him.

"Oh, sorry, I didn't realize—"

"What's going on, Bob?"

"I'm not sure. But I sure as hell am going to find out."

CHAPTER 20

Carlo Severino had been as nervous as a sixteen-year-old on his first date since he'd learned that his boss, Paolo Andreotti, the Defense Minister of Italy, was considering cancelling the Venice portion of the NATO conference because of warnings from AISE. He'd counseled his boss that cancelling the side trip to Venice would make Italy look weak and imply that the country couldn't protect visitors. Nothing had convinced the Deputy Defense Minister to change his mind until Severino mentioned that the press would have a field day about the cancellation and that press coverage would tell travelers planning to visit Italy that it wasn't safe to travel to the country.

His nerves had only become more electrified as the hours, and then a day, went by without a return call from the Old Man of the Mountain. He knew calling the Asasiyun leader was a terrible violation of protocol, but he didn't feel he had a choice. The opportunity was too good to ignore.

"What's wrong with you, Carlo?" Andreotti demanded as he shot Severino a conspiratorial look. "You're acting like a husband who has been caught cheating on his wife."

Severino waved off his boss's comment. "No, no, I'm just concerned about the conference. I don't want anything to go wrong."

Andreotti patted the young man's shoulder. "Don't worry about a thing. You've done a marvelous job." Andreotti's eyes widened.

"It's these assassins that have you worried, isn't it?"

Severino swallowed. "Yes, of course. It would make us look incompetent if one of our visitors was targeted."

"I thought you were against our cancelling."

"I am. I just want everything to go well."

Andreotti patted the young man's shoulder again. "Look around you," he said. "Our security is top-notch. There are more policemen and soldiers here than there are delegates. Everything will be fine."

Severino nodded. "I'm sure you're correct. I—" Severino's cell phone rang. "Would you excuse me, sir?"

"Of course, Carlo." Andreotti smiled lasciviously and said, "Perhaps it's your mistress."

Severino felt his face go hot and smiled back. He moved toward a door that led from the Palazzo del Ministero della Difensa (Ministry of Defense), where the NATO conference was being held, to the street outside—20 September Avenue.

"Severino," he said into the phone.

A man responded with a password and said, "You called."

"Who is this?" Severino said, his body suddenly awash in perspiration. He knew the Old Man of the Mountain's voice, and this was someone else on the phone. He had been one of the few Asasiyun recruits included in the Old Man's inner circle. Since entering the Asasiyun training school, he had been singled out— one of the best and brightest. He also had the advantage of being an Iranian, rather than a recruit from a country which the Old Man considered "second class." The Old Man had handpicked him to infiltrate the NATO establishment via Italy.

"The Old Man ordered me to return your call," the man said.

"Praise be to—"

"Yes, of course," the man said. "What's so important that you felt the need to call?"

"We have an opportunity to…strike a massive blow in…."

"Yes, we know. Why are you calling? You have broken protocol."

"I wanted to…confirm that we are going to…capitalize on this opportunity."

"Why would you need that information?" Before Severino could respond, the man said, "Ah, I see. You want to protect yourself."

"Well, there's that of course. I am a…valuable asset."

"Of course you are. Be assured that we will be in touch."

"Thank you. By the way, I will momentarily text to our leader's cell an updated list of those attending the ball."

Yasmin and Javad met on the parapet. She stared down at the spot where her father had landed after she'd pushed him off the wall and where Javad had buried him. She turned to face Javad and, in an exasperated tone, said, "What's so important?"

"One of our agents, Severino in Rome, called. He wants to confirm our plans." Javad laughed. "He doesn't want to be in Venice during an attack."

Yasmin said, "How would he explain his absence from Venice? His job requires that he be with the Defense Minister and the NATO representatives. If he suddenly left Venice, it could raise questions. People might become suspicious."

"Severino has been an important resource and was a favorite of your father's," Javad said.

"My father is dead, and no one is so important that I will jeopardize our mission."

Javad paced nervously. "What should I tell him?"

"Tell him the attack will happen at midnight on Saturday. That way, he'll think he has time to run away and won't flee until it's too late." She chuckled.

"But what if—"

Yasmin barely kept her voice under control as she jabbed a finger into Javad's chest. "Grow a backbone, Javad."

She turned back inside when her father's cell phone chimed. She took it from her coat pocket and saw a text from Severino. After she got through all the flowery words of greeting praising her father, she saw an updated list of the conference attendees who were traveling to Venice for Carnevale. Halfway down the list, she stopped and turned the screen of her phone toward Javad.

"Look who's on the invitation list. Robert Danforth, the man our agent was supposed to kill in Venice, and his son, General Michael Danforth, the American officer who commanded the assault force that wiped out most of ISIS in Syria last year."

"I'll be damned."

She nodded her head and wondered again why her father had specifically mentioned the Danforths and why it was so important that they be killed. She looked suddenly gleeful. "We'll eliminate a couple hundred of our targets in one stroke."

Javad swallowed hard and cleared his throat. "Yes. But with spouses and hotel employees and aides, it could be five or six hundred."

CHAPTER 21

Abdel bin Abdullah bin Mohammed bin Hakim had never been able to get comfortable in the presence of Iran's Supreme Leader, Ayatollah Hamadani. They were both of similar stature, similar temperament, and about the same age—in their early seventies. But Hamadani's expression never seemed to change, and his mahogany-brown eyes seemed perpetually full of malice. Bin Hakim had spent decades applying the graceful skills of a salesman, while Hamadani had been a fanatical cleric who never had to cajole others to do his bidding. Bin Hakim was an autocrat by nature, but a schmoozer in practice. Hamadani was an autocrat by nature *and* in practice.

"How was your trip, my friend?" Hamadani asked in a neutral monotone, sounding as though he couldn't have cared less about bin Hakim's response.

"Tiring, as usual. The measures I must take to get to Tehran so the damned Americans and Israelis can't track me are tiresome. Zurich to Istanbul. Cyprus, Beirut, and finally Tehran. Changing ID three different times."

Hamadani rocked his head back and forth as though in sympathy. "I appreciate all that you go through in order to assist us in achieving our…long-term goals."

"It is all about victory over the infidels."

"Of course, my friend."

Bin Hakim mused for a moment while an aide poured hot tea

in two small, gold filigreed glasses. When the aide left, the Saudi asked, "When can I expect to hear news about the death of the man who murdered my son, Musa?" Hamadani knew the attempt on Robert Danforth's life had failed, but he decided there was no reason to tell bin Hakim. "There is an event in Venice this weekend that will draw hundreds of high-profile targets. Danforth is one of them, as is his son." He brushed one hand against the other and said, "As the Italians say, '*la musica è finita.*' After this weekend, the West will be irreparably damaged."

"You said 'this weekend'?"

Hamadani again questioned the manic need for revenge that ate at bin Hakim. He had heard rumors that Robert Danforth had tracked down and killed bin Hakim's son, Musa, in Brazil. It's not that he didn't understand the old man's need for revenge on an emotional basis, but his goal was so much larger than exacting retribution on one man.

"That's right, my friend," Hamadani said. "On another subject, I'm sure you're aware that the boycott the West placed on our oil shipments is having serious impact on our economy. Funding the Asasiyun has become increasingly difficult. You can imagine the costs associated with supporting an army of assassins in the field and thousands of support personnel. I would hate for our grand vision to go unfulfilled due to a shortage of funds."

"That would be devastating," bin Hakim said. "How much more do you need?"

Hamadani moved his head to one side and spread his arms. "Our economy is in recession and our people have become restless. If the people revolt, our government could be in jeopardy of being overthrown. We need to inject money into the economy and bring in food and medical supplies in massive quantities." The Supreme Leader grimaced. "And, of course, we will ultimately have to eliminate any surviving assassins and the people at the training center. It won't be cheap, sending Revolutionary Guardsagents to countries around the world to take out surviving Asasiyun agents."

"Why eliminate them? They could be useful down the road."

"Yes, they could. But they could also be a source of information if captured by our enemies." *And they could be a threat to my regime,* Hamadani thought. *Their loyalties are to the Old Man of the Mountain, not to me. The surviving assassins could constitute an elite military force that might become a threat.*

"You didn't answer my question. How much do you need?"

"Five billion dollars."

Bin Hakim closed his eyes and looked up at the ceiling for a few seconds. When he looked back at Hamadani, he said, "Do you understand the risk that comes with selling and transporting that much crude oil? My customers will be afraid they could be compromised. The processing of that much cash will raise red flags in the international banking system."

Hamadani nodded his understanding. "I anticipated that. Of course, we will compensate you and your customers for the additional risk. We are prepared to discount the price by five percent."

Bin Hakim compressed his lips and looked away for a beat, as though he was considering the proposal. When he looked back at the Iranian leader, he squinted and wagged his head, looking embarrassed. "There's too much risk for that price. I'm sorry, but I will never be able to accomplish what you want."

Hamadani forced himself to not show anger. His eyes bored into bin Hakim's. "What sort of discount do you think will…ease your clients' concerns?"

"Fifteen percent," bin Hakim said, after a moment's hesitation.

Hamadani finally responded. "I will try to get the council to agree to twelve percent."

"There is one other requirement I have," bin Hakim said. "You will have your five billion on one condition. I want your commitment that Robert Danforth and his entire family will be dead before the weekend is over."

"I told you the father and son will be in Venice this weekend."

"And the grandson?"

"I understand that he will be…dealt with very soon."

Robbie Danforth envied his roommate. Berto Marinelli could sleep under any circumstance. Robbie felt exhausted, but that seemed to be a perpetual condition for every cadet at West Point. Early wakeups, long physically- and mentally-tiring days, and short nights. Robbie was confident he was on top of all of his academic subjects, but he'd always been driven to be the best, and at West Point being the best was a lot different than it had been back in high school in Fayetteville.

So, after lights out, Robbie closed the door to the bathroom, draped a towel over the bathroom window to prevent light leakage, turned on the overhead light, dropped the toilet lid, and sat down with his differential calculus textbook. By the time his watch neared midnight, he felt that he'd nailed the content of the assigned chapters. Closing the book, he stood and stretched to get rid of the kinks in the middle of his back. He was about to remove the towel from the window when someone loudly double-knocked on the suite door. He heard his roommate growl something, then open the door.

A loud voice said, "Where's Cadet Danforth?"

His roommate said, "Maybe he's using the bathroom, sir."

Robbie moved quickly to the window to take down the towel when the bathroom door was thrown open. With his textbook in one hand, reaching with his other hand for the towel, Robbie felt his stomach clench when he looked at the joyful expression on upper classman Victor Cassidy's face.

"Gotcha," Cassidy said.

Cassidy was a "Firstie," or senior, who was alternately known among the plebes as "Cadet Brutal" (a cadet who has over-absorbed the USMA's culture to the detriment of all around him), "Cadidiot" (short for "cadet idiot"), and "Duke" (West Point slang for a jockstrap). For one reason or another, Cassidy had singled Robbie out for an extra dose of abuse.

Robbie stood at attention and didn't respond.

Cassidy stepped forward, the tips of his shoes just a few inches from Robbie's bare feet. "You obviously don't understand the concept of lights-out, Cadet. Get dressed," he ordered. "You're my 'area bird' for the next four hours.

Robbie stifled a groan. An area bird was a cadet who served punishment by walking on the "quad." This was exhausting, tedius work in good weather. With the storm blowing outside, it would be bitterly painful.

Robbie scrambled from the bathroom and quickly began dressing. As he pulled on a pair of trousers, he caught Berto Marinelli's concerned expression. Then Marinelli said, "Sir, permission to speak."

Cassidy wheeled on Marinelli, glowered, and said, "What could you possibly have to say to me, you low-life plebe?"

"Do I have permission to speak, sir?"

Cassidy muttered something, then shouted, "What is it?"

"Sir, Cadet Danforth has had a bad cough for a couple days and has not been feeling well. He could get pneumonia or worse out on the Quad on a night like this. Just saying, sir."

Cassidy said to Marinelli, "What are you, Danforth's mother?"

"No, sir. Just providing my superior officer with information that might avoid...problems down the road."

As Robbie continued to dress, he watched Cassidy's eyes ping-pong and his mouth twitch as though he was over-caffeinated. He was lacing his boots, when Cassidy made a growling sound and said, "Danforth, thanks to your mother here, you're going to wet-mop the hallway on this floor. You've got one hour to do it, or I'll add a punishment tour out on the Quad."

Cassidy watched Robbie hustle down the hall to a janitor's closet, fill a wheeled bucket with water, and drag the bucket and a mop into the hall. He shouted, "One hour, Danforth. I'll be back in one hour." Cassidy marched down the hall humming: *Heigh-ho, it's off to work I go.*

Robbie thought of Dopey in *Snow White and the Seven Dwarfs* and inadvertently blurted a laugh.

Cassidy must have heard him, because he stopped in his tracks, turned around, and said, "What was that?"

Robbie cleared his throat, coughed loudly, and said, "Just a cough, sir. Hope I'm not catching this respiratory thing that's going around."

As Cassidy turned and walked away, Robbie sent a silent prayer of thanks for Berto Marinelli having the guts to speak up.

WEDNESDAY
FEBRUARY 20

CHAPTER 22

It was a few minutes after midnight when Jimmy Pointer looked through an infirmary window and said to his supervisor, "Looks like it's getting nasty out there."

Major Harold Baker, the duty doctor that night, moved to the window and exhaled a loud breath. "God, the wind's blowing like crazy and there's already a half-foot of snow. We never had weather like this in Arizona."

Pointer laughed. "This ain't nothing, Major. I've seen a lot worse. Maybe I'd better check on the cadets in the quarantine area."

Baker groaned. "I'll go with you."

Oh shit, Pointer thought. "If you want to, sir," he said. "But I don't see any point in both of us freezing our butts off. Why don't I do this one? You can do the next check."

Baker looked positively relieved. "Sounds like a plan. Be careful out there."

"Careful's my middle name," Pointer said, which earned him a chuckle from Baker.

He put on a parka, hefted a medical bag from a cabinet, and waved at Baker as he exited the infirmary. The wind-driven snow pelted his face as he briskly walked toward Grant Barracks. Despite the elements, Pointer felt warm, oblivious to the cold, wind, and snow.

The text from the Old Man of the Mountain had infused him

with a sense of well-being. He was about to execute the mission for which he'd trained. As Pointer moved toward the barracks building, he once again mentally went through the steps he would take. He estimated he would need to falsify the times on the patients' charts to account for thirty minutes spent on taking out Danforth and Meek.

He thought, *I'll be home free, off the base, and ready for my next assignment before anyone even realizes Danforth and Meek have given up the ghost.*

Pointer placed his medical case on the floor inside the Grant Barracks entry door, just outside the area covered by the security camera. He opened the case, removed the tray of medications and other paraphernalia, and extracted a surgical mask and a pair of rubber gloves; a thick wad of gauze was glued to the right-hand glove. He'd practiced the actions he had to take and had become proficient in manipulating the cap on the vial that contained the deadly liquid concoction.

"Gray Death" is what the woman had called the liquid when she'd delivered it to his off-campus apartment. He'd heard about the substance but hadn't realized how powerful it was. "Be extremely careful with this," the woman had told him. "Even a few drops on a finger can kill you." She'd lectured him about the ingredients: "It's a mix of a synthetic opioid compound called U-47700, heroin, fentanyl, and carfentanil. You're probably aware of the potency of heroin and fentanyl, but I bet you've never heard of carfentanil." In a merry tone, as though discussing a dinner recipe, she'd said, "Carfentanil is used as an elephant tranquilizer and can be one hundred thousand times more potent than morphine."

Pointer donned the gloves and lifted his scarf to cover his mouth and nose. With his left hand, he removed the vial from a small frame in the case's bottom. He slowly unscrewed the vial's cap with his right hand, placed the cap on the floor next to the case, covered the vial's top with the palm of his gloved right hand, and tipped it until the liquid covered a quarter-sized spot on the gauze pad. He replaced the cap, inserted the vial in the rack at the case's bottom, and put the tray in the case. After resealing the latches on the case and sliding it into a dark corner, he pulled open the fire door to the emergency staircase, climbed to the third floor, and stepped into the hallway. He was stunned to see a young man with a mop in hand staring back at him.

Robbie had mopped about a third of the hallway in fifteen minutes. He figured he had plenty of time to spare to finish the job within the hour that Cassidy had allotted him. He'd just dunked the mop head into the bucket when he heard the door to the fire exit stairs open. He straightened to see if Victor "Duke" Cassidy had returned to harass him. At first, he was relieved to see that it wasn't his tormentor, but then he leaned on the mop handle and wondered why the guy wore a scarf over the lower part of his face. *Sure, it's cold and snowing outside, but….*

"What's up, man?" Robbie asked.

"Hey," the guy said. "Looks like you got a shit detail."

Robbie didn't respond but continued to stare at the guy as he came toward him.

When the man was about twenty yards away, he said, "I'm looking for Cadet Schmitt's room. He called the infirmary about not feeling well."

Robbie had talked with Schmitt a few minutes before lights out. There had been nothing wrong with him. Robbie's internal threat detection system now vibrated like an out-of-control tuning fork. "His room's three down on the right," he said. "Be careful; the floor's wet."

As the guy came within a few paces of Robbie, he stuck out his right hand, as though to shake hands, and said, "Thanks for your help."

Robbie noticed the guy wore surgical gloves, which would have been worthless against the cold weather. Prior to his service as an undercover agent for the CIA-designed infiltration of ISIS in Syria, Robbie might have taken the man's hand. But the time in Syria had given him what would amount to a decade's worth of experience and paranoia. The guy's lie about Schmitt being ill sealed the deal. Without thinking about the consequences, he adjusted the mop handle in his hands, choked up on it, and poked the handle end at the guy's chest.

"Who are you? What the hell are you doing here?" Robbie barked.

The man knocked the mop handle aside with his left arm, stepped forward, and jabbed his right hand at Robbie. Shifting to his left and ducking under the man's right arm, Robbie choked up on the mop handle and swung it at the guy. The metal frame that held the mop to its handle connected with the right side of the man's head, making a wet, metallic "smack" that reverberated through the hallway. The man staggered back against the wall, gathered his legs under him, and righted himself. He came off the wall, his right hand extended toward Robbie's face, palm open. Robbie used the mop as a pike and rammed it with all his strength into the man's sternum. The blow bent him in half and a huge huff of air exploded from his lungs. He fell back against the wall again and bounced off it. Robbie kicked him between the legs, which dropped the man onto his back. The guy grunted and his face went from strawberry-red to plum-purple.

The guy surprised Robbie when, despite his obvious pain, he roared as he struggled to get to his feet. He'd gotten to his knees, one hand under him, and reached out with his right hand as though pleading for mercy, when Robbie noticed the white gauze pad affixed to the man's glove. Now operating on adrenaline and instinct, he stepped into a vicious kick that caught the man under the chin. The cracking of bone and splintering of teeth resonated through the hall as cadets opened doors and stepped out of their rooms.

Then Victor Cassidy burst into the hall from the fire exit staircase. He pushed his way toward Robbie, knocking aside sleepy-eyed cadets like bowling pins. When he looked down at the unconscious man, Cassidy yelled, "What the hell have you done, Danforth?" He tried to push Robbie away from the prostrate man as he shouted to no one in particular, "Call 9-1-1. Someone get me a towel. My God, this guy could be dead."

But Robbie wouldn't budge from his position between the intruder and the cadets in the hall. "Don't anyone go near this guy," he announced.

Cassidy shouted, "Get out of my way." He gripped Robbie's

right shoulder and tried to pull him away. Robbie reflexively threw out his right arm to knock away Cassidy's hand just as the senior cadet dropped it down. Robbie's arm swung backward, his hand striking the upper classman's mouth, knocking him to the floor. Blood leaked from splits in Cassidy's lips. He cursed and spit out bloody saliva.

Someone in the hallway muttered, "Oh shit."

Cassidy touched a hand against his mouth and looked at the blood on his fingers as though he couldn't understand how it had gotten there. He took in a breath and lisped through his broken lips, "Someone call the MPs."

CHAPTER 23

The West Point Commandant of Cadets, Brigadier General Douglas Stevens, sat at his desk and re-read the report that Cadet Cassidy had filed. When he finished, he dropped it on the left side of his desk blotter and again read the incident report filed by the military policeman who had taken Danforth into custody and, for a few hours, had locked him in an interrogation room in the MP offices. Several cadets who had observed Danforth strike Cassidy had also filed statements. A couple of those cadets had stated unequivocally that Cassidy had grabbed Danforth first.

The part of the incident report that most upset Stevens was Danforth's preventing anyone from assisting the injured man. By the time emergency medical service personnel and Major Harold Baker had arrived, Pointer had expired.

Stevens opened a file labeled "James Pointer," and carefully read the contents. Pointer had worked at the academy as a civilian nurse for the past two years. His performance had been exemplary. A red flag went up in Stevens' mind when he read that Pointer had been born in Chechnya and adopted by an American couple. But there was really nothing in the file that could even begin to explain why Danforth would attack the man.

"Ah, well," Stevens whispered. "Another good cadet goes down the drain." He thought about the call he would make to Danforth's father to advise him that his son was being kicked out of West Point.

He piled the files and statements together on the credenza behind his desk and was about to buzz his assistant when something that had been niggling at the back of his brain resurfaced. He pulled out the MP's statement and scanned it until he came to the part where the MP had written: *Cadet Danforth was calm and non-confrontational when I arrived on scene. When I asked him what had happened, he shrugged and told me there was something off about Pointer. Danforth told me several times that Nurse Pointer's hands should be bagged and that no one should touch the gauze pad on his gloved right hand.* The MP went on to say that even though he thought Danforth made no sense, he did as Danforth had suggested.

Stevens picked up his desk phone and buzzed his assistant. "Get the West Point city medical examiner on the phone for me." He replaced the receiver and waited.

Fifteen minutes later, Stevens' assistant buzzed to tell him Dr. Claire Allen was on the line.

"Hey, Claire, how are you?"

"A little excited."

"Why's that?"

"The body the paramedics brought to us from your place."

"That's why I called you. I—"

Dr. Allen cut him off. "I want you to seal off your infirmary," she told Stevens. "Anything that was in Mr. Pointer's possession or under his control needs to be left untouched and guarded. I've already had the local police post a guard on his apartment here in town."

"What's going on, Claire?"

"You ever hear of something called Gray Death?"

"No."

"We ran the gauze pad glued to the rubber glove on Pointer's right hand. Preliminary results showed the presence of several drugs, including heroin, carfentanil, and something known as U-47700. There might be other drugs on the pad. We're waiting for further test results. In any case, the ingredients we already discovered can kill a person tactilely."

"You want to explain that?"

"If anyone had touched the gauze pad, which was saturated with the stuff I just mentioned, that person, more than likely, would have overdosed instantaneously."

"Overdosed? As in *died*?"

"As in instant death. Whoever put Mr. Pointer out of commission probably saved the lives of some of your people. If the paramedics hadn't bagged the deceased's hands, they would more than likely have died as well. I don't even want to think about what would have happened when the body was brought here if the hands hadn't been bagged and if the EMS guys hadn't warned us."

"Jesus, Mary, and Joseph." Then, after a few seconds, Stevens said, "We found Pointer's medical case under a stairwell. It's under lock and key back in our infirmary."

"Doug, I want you to put a guard on it; don't let anyone open it. You got that?"

Cadet Victor Cassidy reported as ordered to Brigadier General Stevens, who made him stand at attention rather than put him at ease. He stared at Cassidy, noticing the young man's split lips and facial bruises. He didn't say anything more until he saw color leech from the young man's face.

"I read multiple statements, including yours, concerning the incident last night. Is there anything you would like to change in that statement?"

"No, sir," Cassidy responded. "I stand by everything I wrote."

Stevens looked more closely at Cassidy's face and thought, *Damn, Danforth really did a job on him.* "Although you didn't specifically say so, I get the impression you would like to see Cadet Danforth drummed out of West Point."

"That's not my decision to make, sir."

Stevens sat back in his chair and scowled. "I know that. I would like your honest opinion in this matter, Cassidy."

Cassidy cleared his throat. His face regained some of its color. He ran his tongue over his lips and grimaced. "Permission to speak freely, sir."

"That's what I just told you to do, Cadet."

Cassidy took a big breath and let it out slowly. "I think Cadet Danforth is unstable. When I tried to administer first aid to the man he'd attacked, he assaulted me." Cassidy pointed at his mouth. "I think Danforth is a disgrace to the academy and would be a disaster as a U.S. Army officer."

"Are you aware that several cadets who witnessed the incident claim you put a hand on him first and that he accidentally hit you when he tried to knock your hand away?"

Cassidy didn't immediately respond. Finally, he said, "I don't believe that's an accurate representation of actual events." Another pause, then, "His preventing me from administering aid to Nurse Pointer probably contributed to his death."

This cadet sounds like a law student. "Would you change your statement if you were to learn that Danforth more than likely saved your life by preventing you from coming into contact with Pointer?"

"Of course, sir. But that's impossible. Pointer posed no danger to me or anyone else. He was unconscious when I arrived on the scene."

Stevens told Cassidy about the drug concoction on the gauze pad affixed to Pointer's glove. Then he said, "There's a distinct possibility that James Pointer was an Asasiyun agent. I assume you've heard about the group in the news."

Cassidy's complexion turned deathly pale. He babbled something unintelligible.

"Cadet Cassidy, I have a strong opinion that you have singled out Cadet Danforth for abuse. I don't know why. I find your behavior unbecoming of a future military officer. Knowing what I know now about what Cadet Danforth did, I believe your written statement is not an honest representation of what happened. I think it's a biased account intended to bear as negatively as possible on Cadet Danforth." Stevens glared at Cassidy. "You came damn close to ruining the reputation of a fine cadet and, we hope, a future Army officer."

Cassidy now looked as though he might be sick. His posture had slumped, and his mouth gaped.

"What do you think we should do about this situation?" Stevens said.

Cassidy tried to respond but the sound he made was reminiscent of a toad with laryngitis.

"Perhaps I can help you," Stevens said. "What if I make a few recommendations and you tell me if you agree with them?"

Cassidy nodded and croaked out, "Ye-yes, sir."

"First, I think it would be a good idea for you to amend your written statement to reflect *actual* events, including a comment regarding your opinion that Cadet Danforth very possibly saved the lives of multiple persons, including yourself."

Cassidy nodded again.

"Second, I think that an apology from you to Cadet Danforth would be warranted and appreciated."

Cassidy's color had begun to return, causing Stevens to think, *This pissant thinks he's going to get off easy.*

"Next, I want you to change your behavior regarding cadets in my command." Stevens' voice had turned gravelly, tinged with anger. "If your treatment of Cadet Danforth is any indication of how you will treat soldiers in your command, *if* you receive your commission, you probably won't last very long in the Army. In fact, a continuation of abusive behavior here at West Point will cause me to do everything in my power to prevent you from receiving a commission."

Stevens waited for Cassidy to respond, but the only reaction he saw was a moistening of the young man's eyes and a grayish cast to his skin. "Cadet Cassidy, are you capable of understanding what I've told you and changing your behavior?"

"Yes, sir. I will do my best."

"You're excused, Cadet."

Cassidy saluted and did an about-face. But Stevens barked out, "Cassidy," which stopped him in his tracks. He turned back. "Yes, sir."

"One question. Are you resentful about what Danforth did or are you grateful?"

Cassidy said in a strained voice, "Damned grateful, sir."

After Cassidy left the office, Stevens thought, *Maybe the Duke will make it after all.*

CHAPTER 24

Zach Grabowsky and Angelina Borden stormed into Seth Bridewell's office. Angelina took a chair, while Zach paced. Bridewell was used to Grabowsky's eccentricities, so he sat back in his chair and asked, "Do you have good news or bad?"

Zach continued to pace as Angelina said, "We think we found the leak. It was the attempted hit last night on Robbie Danforth that was the key."

"You *think* or you *know*?" Bridewell said.

Zach stopped pacing and said, "What's the one piece of data that had us all stumped?"

"Let's not play twenty questions, Zach."

"Okay. Okay. I'm talking about the Company planting Robbie Danforth and Samantha Meek with ISIS in Syria."

Seth nodded.

Zach continued: "That information was supposed to have extremely limited access. A couple people at the Pentagon, POTUS, Senate Select Committee on Intelligence members, and very few people here at the Company, including the three of us."

"And Bob and Michael Danforth," Bridewell said.

Angelina said, "We eliminated them, of course. But we couldn't understand how Robbie Danforth and Samantha Meek made the assassination short list. His grandfather and father being on that list makes sense. They each have a long history of combating our enemies in the Middle East. Both have public personas. But, as far as Robbie and Samantha are concerned, they're just a couple teenagers attending West Point."

Zach said, "So, how did their names get on the kill list? We figured someone who had access to the SAP file on the ISIS operation in Syria last year leaked it."

Seth gave the two a skeptical look. "Robbie could have become a target because of his father and grandfather. Maybe it had nothing to do with his going undercover with ISIS."

"Okay, but that doesn't explain Samantha being on the list," Zach said.

"True," Seth said.

Angelina said, "We started with the premise that they made the list because of their undercover assignments in Syria. If that was accurate, then one or more people who had access to their classified files had to be a leaker."

Zach paced again. He said, "We sent out an encrypted email to everyone who had access to the file, informing them that the Vice President planned to attend the festivities in Venice this coming weekend, along with his itinerary."

Seth said, "Yeah, I saw that. I didn't realize the VEEP was going to Venice for—"

"He's not," Zach said, sounding impatient. He raised a finger in the air like a teacher making a point. "We embedded code in the message that gave us the ability to detect if any recipients forwarded it or made a copy."

"Well?" Seth said.

Angelina blurted a laugh. "One person copied the message to a disk or flash drive." She paused, then said, "Senator Deborah Schatz, the Senate Select Committee on Intelligence chairman."

Seth cursed under his breath, then said, "You want me to believe that Schatz, a four-term U.S. senator, is a spy for some fanatical group that's murdering people? Give me a break."

Zach's face turned beet-red. He stopped moving and glared at his boss. "Are you going to ignore what we found? This is the best lead we've had. You damn well better do something about it."

Seth exhaled an exasperated sigh as he stood and pointed a

finger at Zach. He opened his mouth as though to respond to the young man's insubordination, but Angelina dragged Zach quickly out the office door.

"Sonofabitch," Seth muttered. He allowed himself a minute to calm down and to consider what he'd just learned, then called Raymond Gallegos, briefed him, and said, "We'd better take this to the DCI."

After Seth and Raymond briefed Tanya on what Zach and Angelina had discovered, Tanya called FBI Director Stan Rictor and asked him to come out to Langley. When Rictor objected, she said, "I'd say this was a matter of national security, but it's bigger than that."

"Give me an hour," Rictor answered.

"One other thing, Stan. I plan to call the Attorney General and the head of Homeland Security about the reason for our meeting. But I thought you and I should meet first to put our heads together."

After a beat, Rictor said, "I'll be there in thirty minutes."

"Holy shit," Rictor said shortly after arriving in Tanya's office. "We need to be careful here. Her making a copy could be totally innocent."

"Not totally."

"What do you mean?"

"The message was stamped with the warning, 'copies of this message cannot be made without the prior consent of the sender.' At a minimum, she violated those instructions."

"Yeah, but that's an entirely different matter from espionage and consorting with the enemy."

"Unless the copy she made winds up in the hands of the bad guys."

Rictor said, "That's true."

"I'd like to make a suggestion," Tanya said, "if you don't mind."

"Go ahead."

"I think, instead of sending a gang of FBI agents to Schatz's office and creating a scandal that'll be front page news in five minutes, why don't you and I pay the good senator a visit at her home tonight? If she's innocent, no harm done. If she's guilty, you can break the news tonight."

"It sounds as though she's been a very bad girl."

"I know Schatz. She's a patriot. Maybe a bit naïve and trusting at times, but I can't see her doing something like this."

"Then what's the explanation for her copying the document?"

"Maybe we'll find that out tonight."

Rictor went silent for several seconds, then said, "Okay, we'll play it your way. But if she gives us even one reason to disbelieve her, I'll have her arrested tonight…after I call the media to let them know where and when."

Tanya said, "Unless the Attorney General objects to our plan, I'll be ready to go in an hour."

The flash drive in Ursan Awan's pants pocket felt as though it was burning his thigh. He knew about the NATO conference in Rome and that the conference delegates had been invited to participate in Carnevale in Venice this coming weekend. He had no way of knowing if the Old Man of the Mountain had anything planned in Venice. Awan felt as though centipedes were crawling around inside his stomach. *The Old Man would be crazy to miss an opportunity like this*, he thought. *Hundreds of high-level military and defense personnel from all the NATO countries in one place. And now, a shot at the Vice President of the United States.* He took a burner phone from his briefcase, put on his overcoat and his Astrakhan hat, and left his desk in Senator Schatz's senatorial offices. He walked outside, turned right at the first cross street, and placed a call to Parviz Shirazi. When Shirazi answered, Awan said, "I have a delivery. Same location in one hour," and hung up. He stomped on the phone and threw the pieces into a sewer opening in the curb.

"Were you able to clear my schedule on Friday?" Michael Danforth asked.

Major Ronald Darby said, "Yes, sir. You're booked on a flight out of Pope Field at 1800 hours on Friday. I'll have your itinerary tomorrow morning."

"Any problems with the cancellations you had to make?"

Darby chuckled. "Everyone understood except Dorothy Prescott, local chapter of the Daughters of the Confederacy president. She was quite upset about the change."

"Why? They have a monthly lunch. Couldn't we reschedule next month?"

Darby raised his eyebrows. "General, no disrespect intended, but you need to be more aware of the effect you have on the ladies of Fayetteville."

Michael shot his aide a querulous look. "What are you talking about?"

"The lovely Mrs. Prescott has a crush on you, sir. And she's not the only one."

"My God, man, she's got to be eighty years old."

Darby laughed. "I never heard there was a rule that groupies had to be a certain age."

Michael's face felt hot. He grimaced at Darby. "You seem to be enjoying yourself. I wonder when the last time was that an Army major was assigned to KP duty."

"My apologies, sir," Darby said. Then he broke down laughing.

CHAPTER 25

On a purely emotional basis, Yasmin Nizari didn't feel the slightest regret about killing her father. But on a practical level, she realized that her impulsive action in pushing the old man to his death had changed everything. With her father alive, she might have brought him around to embracing the possibility of his becoming the Supreme Leader of Iran and, maybe, the leader of the Muslim world. However, with him out of the picture, there was no one who could step into his shoes. Javad Muntaziri was a useful tool in accomplishing the Asasiyun's mission, but he couldn't replace her father. And there was no way in hell that Iran, let alone the rest of the Middle East, would accept a woman as its leader. In fact, if the mullahs learned that her father was dead and that a woman had replaced him as Asasiyun leader, they would more than likely invade the fortress and eliminate her.

She heard footsteps and turned to see Javad approaching. *He's serving a purpose for now*, she thought. *He handles the interaction with the assassins and, in bed, he takes the edge off. But soon he'll have to go.*

She realized that Ayatollah Khomeini's dream of using the Asasiyun to destabilize the West was still intact, but even if the mission succeeded beyond expectations, there was nothing in it for her. Money and power was what she wanted. But being a woman, her only hope was to acquire money. Power would never come to her.

Javad said, "What are you doing out here? The weather's miserable."

"Just thinking."

"About what?"

"About how nice it would be if we were to get out of this wind and cold and go to bed together."

Javad smiled like a child at Nowruz.

She tucked her arm inside his as they moved along the walkway from the parapet toward her quarters.

"I was thinking about the ransom money," Javad said.

She shot him a look but said nothing.

"We should use some of it to buy a place where we'll live." He showed a toothy smile. "Someplace on a beach in a country with no extradition treaty with any other."

She forced a smile and squeezed his arm. "That's an excellent idea. Let's talk more about it after the attacks on Saturday."

"I've made a list of some possible locations," he said.

I bet you have, she thought.

Seth Bridewell rubbed his temples, trying to forestall the headache he felt coming. On any given day, his department was inundated with hardware and software maintenance requests and mind-boggling esoteric projects. But since the Asasiyun had come on the scene, its workload had tripled in scope and intensity. His biggest priorities were tracking down the leak of SAP information, trying to discover who or what was behind the Asasiyun, and finding the elusive Abdel bin Hakim. They'd made progress on the leak. If that lead panned out, there would be one less problem hanging over his head.

Seth checked the clock on his computer screen and was shocked that it was already 4:00 p.m. *I've got to stop missing meals*, he thought. He yanked open a desk drawer and rummaged around until he found an energy bar. He looked at the wrapping and saw that it was two years past its prime. He stripped back the wrapper and found the bar to be as stiff as wallboard. He brought it to his nose, grunted, and tossed it in the wastebasket. He was about to go to the cafeteria when Zach Grabowsky entered his office like an errant ill wind, came around Seth's desk, and slapped a file on the blotter.

"Guess what, Seth?"

Seth rubbed his temples again. "Just spit it out, Zach."

Zach looked disappointed but quickly recovered, smiled, and tapped a finger on the file. In a slow, drawn-out fashion, he said, "We think we may have found Abdel bin Abdullah bin Mohammed bin Hakim."

Seth's burgeoning headache disappeared. He scooted his chair forward tight against his desk, flipped open the file, and stared at the photo of the man he had come to revile. "Tell me," he said.

"A huge wire order went from SBIC Bank in the Caymans to Shrikat Bank Group in Indonesia. The money went *poof*. Disappeared in the Dark Web."

"How *huge* was the wire?"

"Five billion dollars."

"Holy—"

Zach smiled.

Seth said, "What's this got to do with bin Hakim?"

"On a hunch, I hacked into the wire transfer departments of four Iranian banks, in case a five-billion-dollar wire arrived at one of them. We've known for some time that the mullahs use the four banks to handle government as well as personal transactions. Sure enough, a wire transfer from a bank in Pakistan hit Bank Pars."

"How do you know it was bin Hakim who transferred the money?"

Zach shrugged. "We don't know for sure. But we've had an eye on the account in the Caymans for a couple years. Our guy at the bank believed it was a bin Hakim account but hasn't been able to ID it as such. Besides, the account's been dormant for twenty-four months. But that all changed today with the five billion coming in from a bank in Zurich. Our contact verified that the Swiss account is in a bank that bin Hakim uses for several of his corporate entities."

"Although it's an interesting coincidence, that doesn't mean the money that went from Zurich to the Caymans was the same money that went into Bank Pars."

Grabowsky smiled as though he'd just won a Nobel Prize. "That's true, boss. But how many five-billion-dollar wire transfers happen on any day?"

Bridewell nodded. "I thought you said you'd found bin Hakim. What does any of this have to do with finding him?"

"The NSA picked up a cell phone call made in Tehran to a number in Zurich. Voice recognition software identified the caller as bin Hakim. The conversation was in some sort of code, so we can't be certain what bin Hakim was telling him. Presumably, he was directing the transfer of money. But at the call's end, the guy in Zurich asked, 'When can we expect you back home?' Bin Hakim responded that he would be home on Friday after a detour."

"So, he'll be back in Zurich on Friday. So what? There's no way the Swiss will turn him over to us. We've tried to get that done for years."

"I have a theory."

Seth felt his headache returning. He closed his eyes and waited.

"Bin Hakim owns a Swiss Premier League soccer team. I checked the team's schedule. They're playing Dynamo Kyiv, a top Ukrainian team, tomorrow in Kiev. It's a semi-final match in the UEFA Cup Tournament. Bin Hakim is a maniac about European football, but rarely goes to a game because he knows we're looking for him. I think he might make an exception and attend the game in Kiev. Being in the UEFA Cup quarter-finals is a huge deal."

"Come on, Zach. He'd be exposing himself…and just to watch a soccer match?"

Zach's eyebrows arched as his eyes widened. "I know it's a stretch, but what do we have to lose? And we have good relations with the Ukraine. They'll help us find the man and should be willing to extradite him to the U.S."

"Yeah, *if* he's in the Ukraine."

"Like I said. What do we have to lose?"

"God, I'm getting too old for this shit." After a long pause, Seth said, "Run it up the flagpole through Ray Gallegos. If he signs off on it, fine."

CHAPTER 26

"We all set?" FBI Director Stan Rictor asked after he and his driver picked up Tanya Serkovic at her Georgetown townhome at 7:30 p.m. He pressed a switch to raise the glass between the limo's front and back seats.

"You notice the way the Attorney General declined to join us tonight?" Rictor said.

Tanya chuckled. "We're on our own, Stan. If we're wrong about this, you and I should probably put in our retirement papers."

A sour expression came to Rictor's face. After a second, he said, "What did you tell Schatz?"

"That there was something we wanted to talk with her about."

"That's it?"

"Yep."

Rictor chuckled. "I'll bet me being along probably jacked up her blood pressure."

"Nah. She's a hotshot. Probably thinks we need her advice about something."

After a break in the conversation, Tanya said, "You okay with me taking the lead?"

"Probably better that way. You two have a relationship." Rictor looked out his window. When he looked back to Tanya, he asked, "Do you know if her husband's in town?"

"He's not. Skiing in Taos."

"Lucky man," Rictor said. "At least he won't have to see his wife handcuffed and carted off to jail."

"Let's not get ahead of ourselves."

"I don't want to believe that a United States Senator would commit treason."

"Like I said, let's not get ahead of ourselves."

Deborah Schatz and her husband lived in a six thousand square foot, three-story mansion near Embassy Row, a short walk from the National Cathedral. Their marriage had been a merger of trust fund babies, which had combined two inherited fortunes that amounted to a net worth in the high eight figures. When Rictor's driver pulled up to the front gate, a powerfully built man in a black suit checked their IDs, then admitted them.

Rictor said to Tanya, "Look at this place. To paraphrase Mel Brooks, it's good to be the queen."

"Stan, I keep wondering what motive Schatz would have to commit treason? She and her husband have more money than most third-world countries and she's been a hawk in the Senate. She's described organizations like Hezbollah and Al Qaeda as devil worshipers."

"You getting cold feet?"

"It's not that. This just doesn't make sense."

"Yeah, I understand," Rictor said. "I hope there's some explanation for this security breach."

Tanya shook her head. "Me, too. But if there is a mistake, we're going to come off looking like idiots and will have pissed off one of the most powerful people in the country."

Rictor tapped the side of his head. "My hair's pure white, the bags under my eyes have bags of their own, and my wrinkles resemble furrows. I was thinking about retiring anyway."

Tanya looked over at Rictor but couldn't tell if he was serious.

The tree-lined driveway meandered for about seventy-five yards, ending in a circle that bordered a fountain so elegant that it would have been at home in Rome. The residence on the fountain's far side and the coach house on the right were constructed of large stone blocks and had pitched slate roofs. Tanya and Rictor climbed a ten-step stone staircase that led up to a twelve-foot-tall double wood door. A butler opened the door before they could knock, invited them inside, and led them into a parlor that was furnished like a room from the Palace of Versailles. The senator sat in a chair that was part of a cluster of three chairs and a two-seater couch that faced a huge fireplace. The air in the room was aromatic from the wood burning in the fireplace.

Tanya looked at the senator as the woman stood and greeted them. As usual, she admired her elegance: The way she dressed, her erect posture, and the graceful way she moved. She shook the senator's hand and, as Rictor stepped beside her, said, "Of course you know Director Rictor, Senator."

Schatz smiled, shook Rictor's hand, and said, "Please sit down."

"Would you like something to drink?" Schatz asked after Rictor and Tanya had settled on a couch opposite her chair.

Tanya glanced at Rictor, turned back to Schatz, and replied, "No, thank you, Senator."

Tanya noticed Schatz's reaction to her use of her title. They'd always been on a first name basis.

"I assume you're here on official business," Schatz said. "But I have to wonder why this meeting had to be here at my home rather than at my office."

Rictor said, "We wanted to avoid any undue embarrassment for you, Senator, unless—"

Tanya placed a hand on Rictor's arm, cutting him off. She sat forward on the couch and looked directly into Schatz's eyes. "Did you see the SAP email that went out this morning about the Vice President going to Venice this weekend?"

"Of course." She bounced her gaze between Tanya and Rictor. "It surprised me, especially since POTUS is going to be in China at the same time. It's highly unusual for POTUS and the VP to be out of the country at the same time."

"With whom did you share the information about the VEEP's trip?" Tanya said.

At first, Schatz seemed momentarily confused. But her expression hardened. "That email was classified S-A-P. I know better than to share classified information." Her eyes bored into Tanya's. "What is this about?" she demanded.

"A copy was made from your account," Tanya said.

"That's impossible," Schatz said, her voice now strident.

"It's not only possible, it happened," Rictor interjected.

"I'm telling you—"

Tanya interrupted Schatz. In a softer tone, she said, "Deborah, I want you to listen carefully to what I'm about to tell you." She took a calming breath. "There is no doubt the email about the Vice President's trip to Venice was copied from your account onto a flash drive or disk. The email was sent to very few individuals. The only account that was used to make a copy was yours. Unless someone else has access to your classified email account, you are in serious trouble. I suggest you come clean now or Director Rictor will have to take you into custody."

Schatz's complexion had gone pale. Her eyes darted around, seemingly out of focus. "I'm telling you that this can't be. I would never mishandle classified information and I am the only one who has access to my...."

Rictor and Tanya looked at one another as Schatz failed to finish her sentence. They each turned their heads toward the senator, and Rictor said, "What?"

"Oh my God," Schatz said, her expression now crestfallen, her eyes suddenly moist.

"What is it, Deborah?" Tanya said.

"Ursan."

"Who?" Tanya asked.

"Ursan Awan, our IT consultant on the Intelligence Committee. He has access to my password."

Rictor's jaw dropped. "You gave someone the password to your encrypted email account?"

"Ursan does maintenance on all our accounts. My staff, committee members."

"Holy shit," Rictor blurted. "So much for password security." He took his cell phone from his jacket pocket, stood, and moved to the far side of the room. He dialed a number and, while waiting for the call to go through, barked, "Senator, I want contact information for Awan."

"I have his phone numbers, but don't have his address handy. That would be in a file in my office."

Rictor's call apparently went through. He told the person he'd called to hold, walked over to where Schatz now stood next to a window that looked out on a covered outdoor swimming pool, and said, "Here's what I want you to do, Senator."

As Rictor ordered a team of agents to meet outside the Hart Senate Office Building, Senator Schatz placed a call to Ursan Awan's cell phone. Following Rictor's script, Schatz told Awan, "Ursan, I'm calling an emergency meeting of the Intelligence Committee. I was just notified by the CIA that they've developed intelligence concerning the Asasiyun organization. I'm bringing in all my staff, too. I hate to bother you at this late hour, but I may need your assistance."

"Of course, Senator. I'll drive right in. I should be at the office by 9:15."

Schatz then called her administrative assistant and told her to broadcast-email her office staff and the Intelligence Committee's members and staff, advising them that their presence was needed at an emergency meeting at the Hart Building by no later than 9:30. "I want the email message to include the words *this is compulsory*," she told her aide.

Schatz, Rictor, and Tanya sat back down and took a minute to decompress.

"Tell me about Awan," Rictor said. "Where's he from? What sort of background investigation was done on him? What's the extent of his access to classified information?"

"He's originally from Pakistan. He came here on a student visa, went to Georgetown—where he earned a degree in Information Technology and Cyber Security—and started working at the Senate as an intern about three years ago. I was impressed with his work ethic and knowledge and moved him to the Intelligence Committee about a year ago."

Rictor looked ill. "As an employee of the committee, he would have had to go through an FBI background investigation. I wonder what we missed."

Schatz looked down at her lap. "Awan's a contractor, not an employee. I was so impressed with him that I waived the background investigation."

Rictor gaped at Schatz. Tanya felt as stunned as Rictor's expression indicated he was.

"You hired a foreign national and didn't check into his background? And he's had access to the Intelligence Committee database for over a year?"

Schatz swallowed hard and expelled a long, weighted breath.

"I need to meet my people at the Hart Building," Rictor said. He turned to Tanya. "Are you ready to leave?"

She nodded. As they stood and turned toward the door, Tanya said, "Does Awan have any family here?"

Schatz said, "He brought his mother, two sisters, and a brother over after he started working for me." A sickly expression returned to her face and her shoulders slumped.

"What is it?" Rictor demanded.

"His brother and sisters work in his consulting business."

"So, they might have had access to classified data as well."

Schatz groaned.

Tanya looked at the senator with undisguised disappointment. "Do you have contact information on Awan's family members?"

"At…at my office."

Rictor said, "Senator, get your coat. You're coming with us."

Rictor ordered his driver to ignore all traffic laws. "I want to get to the Hart Building in record time," he said.

As the driver sped away, Schatz said, "This is not going to look good, is it?"

Tanya was aghast at Schatz's question. "*Look good?*" she said. "You mean how this fiasco will make *you* look?" She shook her head and jabbed a finger at Schatz, who was seated in the back seat between her and Rictor. "How you come out looking when this becomes public information is the least of our concerns," Tanya said. "You've compromised national security, your negligence has probably contributed to the deaths of Americans and allies alike and, in the end, you will have undermined the American people's confidence in its elected leadership and in its government. No, Senator, this is not going to look *good*."

The senator covered her face with her hands. "What am I going to do?"

Tanya looked at Schatz and said, "My advice is to, at a minimum, announce that you will not run for re-election. Better yet, I recommend you resign your office…for health reasons or any other lame reason you can come up with." After a beat, she added, "I think it would be a good idea to hire the best damned lawyer you can find. I can't even begin to tell you how many laws you've broken."

Outside the Hart Building, they exited the vehicle and were met by two FBI agents.

"Go to your office with these agents, Senator," Rictor said. "I'll join you in a minute. I presume you'll have the phone numbers and addresses of all the Awan family members by then."

Schatz said, "I'll get right on it," and walked quickly toward the building's entrance.

Tanya noticed that the senator's posture was no longer erect.

Rictor turned to her. "Damn, Tanya, you were pretty rough on her."

Tanya muttered something unintelligible.

"What was that?"

"Aren't you sick of the way classified information gets shopped around D.C.?"

"Damn right I am."

"You still think I was rough?"

"Nah. I was just kidding. Wait until the Justice Department brings charges against her."

Tanya scoffed. "Nothing will happen to her. The DOJ will bury any information. She'll resign and wind up serving on multiple boards that will earn her millions of dollars. She's part of the swamp, Stan."

After a beat, Rictor said, "Just tell my driver where you want him to take you."

She had her hand on the door handle but hesitated for a few

seconds. She looked over her shoulder at Rictor. "What if every member of Schatz's staff and the Intelligence Committee shared their passwords with Awan? He'd have access to tons of personal information in addition to classified data."

"I already considered that, Tanya. But let me tell you what worries me even more. If Awan decides to lawyer-up, we might never learn what information he stole and who he passed it to."

"You want a suggestion?"

"Go ahead."

"Bring in his mother and siblings and don't charge them with anything. Segregate them, keep them in the dark about what's going on, and tell them they're in protective custody. But advise Ursan that his family members have been arrested and are being charged under the Espionage Act. Maybe he'll be willing to cooperate in exchange for his family members being treated leniently."

"I'll think about that."

"Stay in touch, Stan," Tanya said.

Zach Grabowsky and Angelina Borden were finishing up a contentious meeting with Raymond Gallegos about their presumption that bin Hakim would attend a soccer game the following evening in the Ukraine. Fortunately, the two young people had briefed Raymond on many occasions and knew that "contention" was integral to the man's management style. He asked tough questions and demanded that CIA employees do their homework and come to him fully prepared. When Zach and Angelina completed their briefing, they sat back and waited. When a minute had passed without any response from Raymond, Zach's hands began to twitch, and his knees bounced. Angelina placed a hand on his arm to try to settle him down, but without success.

Finally, Raymond looked from Zach to Angelina, his eyes like laser beams. He frowned and said, "You have some damned *fer-tile* imaginations."

Zach's heart seemed to sink into his stomach. He looked at Angelina and saw the sudden despair in her expression.

"I am confident that—" he began, but Raymond held up a hand and smiled.

Raymond said, "That was about the best damned briefing I've ever received. You two did a hell of a job. It's this kind of creative thinking we need more of around here. So, tell me, how do you propose finding bin Hakim in a soccer stadium that holds seventy thousand raving, screaming fans?"

Zach exhaled loudly. "Angelina and I talked about that. We have a Lone Wolf team out of Fort Bragg working with the Ukrainian Army's Special Operations Force. We could ask General Danforth to temporarily deploy them to work with the SBU, the Security Service of Ukraine. They could dress like Dynamo Kyiv fans and infiltrate the stadium."

"Bin Hakim will surely have armed bodyguards with him," Raymond said.

Angelina said, "We understand he travels with at least six guards. He might have even more with him in Kiev, considering he'd be more exposed there."

"So, what if shooting breaks out in the stadium? There could be many casualties among the fans."

Before Zach or Angelina could respond, Raymond said, "Let me think about it. In the meantime, I'll call General Danforth and get his support, and have him coordinate with the SBU. I'll reach out to you two later today." When Zach and Angelina stood to leave, Raymond graced them with another smile and complimented them once again.

CHAPTER 27

Ursan Awan was one of the first of Senator Deborah Schatz's people to arrive at the Hart Senate Office Building. Before he went through security inside the building's entrance, two FBI agents took him to a SCIF in the building's basement. The agents ignored his questions and demands.

When he insisted they call Senator Schatz, one agent told him, "You're the last person she wants to talk to."

As elected officials and staff members arrived at the Hart Building, they were directed by FBI agents to a hearing room. As each person arrived, his or her cell phone, iPad, and laptop computer was tagged with the owner's name, confiscated, and taken to another room.

After all staffers had arrived, a senior FBI agent addressed the group: "This is a counter-espionage operation. You will not communicate with one another while you are waiting to be interviewed, nor will you discuss with one another, or with any other person, any questions asked of you or information given to you. Anyone who violates these instructions will immediately be taken into custody and charged with obstruction and suspicion of committing treason. Do you all understand these instructions?"

The people in the room seemed stunned. They either fixed their eyes on the agent, looked around the room as though searching for an explanation from others, or mumbled. Within a few seconds, the noise in the room sounded like a crowd scene in a grade B movie.

Then one U.S. Senator on the Intelligence Committee stood, gestured at the agent, and shouted, "I object to this heavy-handed bullying. These Gestapo tactics are why I don't support funding the FBI. Explain yourselves, or I'm walking out of here." The senator twisted left, then right, and announced, "You don't need to put up with this. This is the United States of America."

Some murmuring started, but no one else stood.

The agent said, "Senator, we will explain everything to you. In the meantime, please be patient."

The senator threw up his hands, muttered something, and moved toward the aisle to the exit door. As he reached the aisle, two FBI agents bum-rushed and frog-marched him from the room.

The agent asked, "Does anyone doubt the seriousness of the situation here?"

No one said a word.

"Good. If anyone wishes to be represented by legal counsel, that is your right. But I suggest you wait until you talk with an FBI agent who will sit down with you and explain what this is about. I suspect most of you won't need counsel. This is a fact-finding exercise. I apologize for the way this has to be handled, but national security is involved and delays in this investigation could lead to serious consequences."

The agent paused for several seconds and looked around the room. "Okay," he said. "When interviewed, please don't hold anything back. We are attempting to identify…vulnerabilities that might have been created." Another pause. The agent pointed at the group of twenty-seven FBI personnel who stood along the room's back wall.

The first FBI agent on the left—a thirty-something female—called out a man's name, waited for him to raise his hand, and said, "Please come with me, sir." She walked to the door and led the man out into the hall and down to an office. This process continued until twenty-seven members or staffers had left the hearing room with agents. When an agent completed an interview, the interviewee was reminded to keep his or her mouth shut and was excused. Unless it was discovered that the interviewee had shared his or her computer access password with any other person. In those cases, the interviewees were passed along to an FBI counter-intelligence specialist who conducted a further interview.

By the time the interviews were finished, just before midnight, the senior FBI agent was armed with a list of five U.S. senators (including Deborah Schatz), two Senate Select Committee on Intelligence staffers, and two of Schatz's senatorial staffers who had, out of stupidity and naïveté, divulged their passwords to Awan.

Mark True, one of Stan Rictor's senior counter-intelligence people, entered the SCIF where Awan had been held for the past two-and-a-half hours. The two agents guarding Awan moved to opposite corners of the room behind the man. True flipped a switch that started built-in recording and video devices, recited the time and the names of everyone in the room, and read Awan his rights. When Awan opened his mouth as though to speak, True raised a finger and said, "Before you say a word, you should listen to something." He removed a miniature recorder from his suit jacket pocket, placed it on the table, and hit the PLAY button.

A stream of loud shouts punctuated by several screams filled the SCIF. Awan's face reflected surprise as he leaned back in his chair. When a high-pitched female voice unleashed a torrent of invective in Urdu, Awan's expression changed. He now looked pale; his surprise metamorphosing to fear and shock. Sweat bathed his forehead. His eyes were doe-like—wide-open and moist.

"What has happened to my mother?" he said in a dry, whispery tone.

True waited several seconds to answer, while glaring at Awan. Finally, he said, "We know you've been spying against the United States. We know you've passed classified material to a terrorist organization. Your spying has led to the murders of dozens of people. So, in addition to committing espionage, you're an accessory to murder."

For an instant, True thought Awan had suffered a stroke. He seemed to have aged decades in a matter of seconds. His complexion turned pallid and he bent over as though his spine had turned to rubber.

True said, "You live with your mother, sisters, and brother. Your siblings work with you, which, by extension, means they're parties to your crimes. We also know your mother has carried information from the United States to Pakistan on several trips. She will probably spend the remainder of her life in a federal prison, as will your brother and sisters."

True couldn't believe that Awan's appearance could get worse, but that's exactly what happened. He rapped his knuckles on the table and barked, "Look at me, Ursan."

The man didn't seem to have the strength to raise his head.

"Would you like some water?"

Awan nodded once. His gaze was still directed at his lap.

True looked at one agent. "Why don't you get Mr. Awan a bottle of water?"

After the agent left the room, True leaned toward the Pakistani and, in a calm, steady voice, said, "You have until my colleague returns to decide whether your family members will spend the rest of their lives in prison or will be allowed to return to Pakistan. Understand this, however; if you don't cooperate, none of you will ever be free again."

"We can all return home if I cooperate?" Awan said, his voice weak and plaintive.

"No, Ursan. Your mother and siblings can return. You will pay the price for your betrayal of the country that educated you and gave you the opportunity to create a successful business. The country that trusted you."

The man still hadn't met True's gaze. It wasn't until the agent reentered the room that Awan lifted his head and said, "I will tell you everything."

THURSDAY
FEBRUARY 21

CHAPTER 28

Bob and Liz took an early-morning high-speed train from Venice to Florence, where they'd arranged for a car to take them to the Florence American Cemetery seven miles south of the city. Liz's uncle, a U.S. Army Air Corps member during WWII, had died when his bomber was shot down during the liberation of Italy. She'd never known her uncle but had grown up hearing stories about him and remembered how her mother had always wanted to, but never had the chance to, visit his grave.

Although it was a crisp, cool, breezy day, the sun shone brightly, illuminating the 4,402 headstones and the monument overlooking the ground down to the pole where the American flag popped and snapped.

They walked to Liz's uncle's grave, where she placed a rose and a small American flag in front of the headstone. There was something ethereal about the cemetery. She and Bob had tears in their eyes as they looked around the hallowed ground.

"All these boys," Bob whispered. "What could they have accomplished if they'd lived? None of them got to have the lives they'd dreamed of."

"They accomplished a lot in their short lives," Liz said. "They helped save the world from the Nazis."

Bob nodded, wiped his eyes with a hand, and walked a short distance away.

Liz gave him a minute on his own. She guessed what was going through his mind. He'd reacted the same way when they'd visited the Vietnam Veterans Memorial in Washington, D.C. and Arlington Memorial Cemetery. He no longer talked to her about nightmares he might still have about Vietnam, but she knew he thought often about the men he'd served with over there.

Liz moved to where Bob stared down the hill at the American flag.

"You ready to go?" she asked.

Bob kissed the side of her head.

They took the path downhill. Halfway to the parking area, Liz said, "How about calling Michael about when he's supposed to arrive in Venice?"

"Great idea," Bob said. "He might still be at home. It's only seven in the morning in Fayetteville."

Liz placed a call to Michael's cell phone.

"Hello."

"Mike, it's Mom and Dad."

"How are things in Europe?"

"We're having a great time. How are things with you?"

"Everything's good. But what about what happened to you in Venice?"

"How'd you hear about that?"

"Are you kidding? Why didn't you tell me about it?"

"I'm getting the feeling the parent/child relationship is a little upside down. Besides, everything worked out fine."

"Oh, brother," Mike said, sounding thoroughly exasperated. He took a loud breath and said, "I need to put a bodyguard on 24/7."

Bob felt suddenly sad. He knew the experiences he'd had in the Army and working for the CIA had weighed heavily on Liz, but he hadn't really focused on the impact those experiences might have had on his son.

"We're fine, Michael," he said, then changed the subject. "When will you arrive in Venice?"

"I'm booked on a military flight out of Pope Field late Friday afternoon. After a refueling stop in England, it's supposed to land at Aviano Air Base on Saturday morning. I should be able to catch a hop from there to Caserma Ederle Army Base in Venice. Hopefully, I'll arrive there before noon."

"Sounds like a tiring trip."

"It won't be my first. I'll call you when I arrive at the BOQ at Ederle."

"No way you're staying at the Bachelor Officers' Quarters. I booked you a room at our hotel. It's our treat."

Michael started to object, but Bob cut him off. "Don't even think about arguing with me. Besides, it was your mother's idea. You don't want to go against her."

"Okay, Dad. I appreciate it. I'll take a water taxi to your hotel. I'll try to get there no later than the middle of the afternoon on Saturday."

"Safe travels, Mike. We're looking forward to seeing you." Bob blurted a laugh and added, "Your mother has arranged for a costume for you. I think you're going to look very cute in tights."

"No way."

"Hah. If I gotta wear them, so will you."

After Michael hung up, he felt guilty. He'd criticized his father for not calling him about the attack in Venice, but he'd not disclosed what had happened with Robbie at West Point. *I guess Dad's right,* he thought. *The parent/child relationship is upside down.*

At Yasmin's direction, Javad prepared an encrypted message to be sent to eleven hundred and eighty-three assassins in twenty-nine countries. The assassins were ordered to strike their targets—eight hundred and eighty-four influential men and women in NATO countries—at 9:30 p.m. Venice time, on Saturday, February 23.

Javad's hand shook as he pressed the SEND button that blasted the message into cyberspace. But it wasn't the broadcast message to the horde of agents that excited him the most. It was the messages to the hit team in Venice that made him feel euphoric. That elite crew had been constructed with eight men and two women gathered from Greece and Italy. He was confident they would succeed in their mission. He laughed as he thought about the special event's venue: Palazzo Pisani Moretta on the Grand Canal. The name given to the annual event at this palace was "The Heaven & Hell Ball."

There will be no heaven and plenty of hell for the people who attend, he thought.

CHAPTER 29

Raymond Gallegos's call to Michael Danforth at 1:00 a.m., Eastern Standard Time, had initiated a series of actions that included Michael issuing new orders to the Lone Wolf team commander in Kiev, and his coordinating with Ukraine's SBU director, the country's counterterrorism and antiterrorism force.

Raymond and Michael decided that a confrontation with bin Hakim and his people inside the stadium could lead to wholesale slaughter of innocents. They also concluded that bin Hakim would not avail himself of the privileges usually afforded the owner of a visiting soccer club. He would probably not inform the Dynamo Kyiv team owner of his presence. Which led them to conclude that he would purchase tickets in the general admission area. The man would not want to bring attention to himself.

It was Michael who suggested that bin Hakim would likely select seats as close to the ramp that ran around the middle of the stadium as possible, which would allow him to exit the facility quickly and prevent him from being trapped near the lower-level seats as the mass of fans exited after the match ended. "And I expect bin Hakim will take seats in the Swiss fan section," Michael said. "He won't want to cheer for his Swiss team surrounded by Dynamo fans."

Raymond said, "If your assumptions are wrong about where bin Hakim will sit, we could miss him entirely. But, if you're correct, we'll be able to narrow our search to a small area of the stadium."

Michael said, "I believe it's our best approach to finding the man. If we flood the stadium with police and military personnel, we'll scare off bin Hakim; or, worse, cause him to go on the offensive. I think we should post men on the ramp where it passes the visitors' seating areas. We can also station men at the twelve outside entrances and exits."

"That sounds good, Mike," Raymond said. "The one change I suggest is that we intentionally slow down traffic exiting the stadium parking lot and have police officers carefully eyeball the vehicles' occupants. That way, if we miss him inside the stadium and at the building exits, we might catch him as his vehicle leaves the lot."

"One last thing," Michael said. "Why don't we put spotters with cameras in the announcers' booths? We'll have about three hours to scan the crowd. Hopefully, anyone who notices them will assume they're simply television cameramen."

"You know this could all be a waste of time and resources," Raymond said.

Michael said, "What's your gut tell you, Ray?"

"Hah," Raymond scoffed. "Between taking Maalox and Tums, my gut instincts have been suppressed into lethargy. But to answer your question, ever since those two analysts brought the idea to Seth about bin Hakim possibly being in the Ukraine, I've had this tingling sensation running down my spine. I'd bet money they're correct."

"Good enough for me. I'll let you know when everything is set up. Keep your fingers crossed."

After getting off the phone with Michael, Raymond contacted the CIA Chief of Station in Kiev and gave him a heads-up about what was planned.

"How certain are we that bin Hakim is in the Ukraine?" the station chief asked.

"The best I can tell you is that the analysts who came up with the supposition did a thorough job. All we might lose is face, but what we might gain could be huge. I like the risk/reward ratio."

"Okay, Ray," the chief of station said. "I'll check in with the SBU and the Lone Wolf team commander and offer whatever assistance

I can."

FBI Director Stan Rictor had met with his senior people at the Hart Senate Office Building after the interviews had finished. He left a few minutes after 3:00 a.m. On the ride to his office, he called the Bureau's Joint Terrorism Task Force commander and advised him that he might need one of his SWAT teams on a moment's notice. He explained about the interrogation of Ursan Awan and what he hoped would come of it.

"I'll call you as soon as I hear from the team working on Awan," Rictor told the commander.

The commander said, "We'll be ready to go within the hour."

Rictor's driver dropped him off at the FBI building. As he entered his office, his cell phone rang.

"Rictor," he barked.

"It's Mark True, sir. This guy, Awan, is a treasure trove of information as far as it goes. He's confessed to passing classified information to a handler. He's stolen information since he went to work for Schatz. The subject matter list of the stuff he's taken is massive. He can't remember half of what he took."

"Did he keep copies of what he stole?" Rictor asked.

"We should be so lucky," True said. "Every damn thing he took was put on a flash drive and handed off to a taxi driver. All he could tell us about the cabbie was that his first name is Parviz and he speaks English with an Iranian accent. They'd meet near Stanton Park. He'd take a ride in the cab, hand over the flash drive, and have the driver drop him somewhere."

"How would the taxi driver know when Awan wanted to meet?" Rictor said.

"He'd call the driver's cell phone and tell him he needed a cab at a certain time. Then he'd dispose of the phone he used and get another one for when he'd next contact the guy. We've already traced the number. It's registered to an export-import company. The registered agent on the account is an attorney in Reston, Virginia."

"Give me the attorney's name, home address, and telephone number."

"He'll be asleep at this time of night."

"Exactly."

After he terminated the call, Rictor called the Director of National Intelligence and the U.S. Attorney General. He briefed them on what had been discovered in the interviews at the Hart Building.

Two FBI agents hammered on the front door of Eric O'Neill's home. After a minute of banging, a nervous voice from inside the home called out, "Who is it?"

One agent held up his ID card to the peephole and shouted, "FBI, Mr. O'Neill."

The man inside muttered, "What the hell?" He opened the door, leaving the security chain engaged, and said, "Hand me your ID card."

The agent passed his card to O'Neill, who took a moment to inspect it. Then the man closed the door to release the chain and reopened it.

O'Neill wore a dark gray bathrobe over pajamas. He looked as though he was having a bad hair day. "What can I do for you?" he said.

"How about inviting us in? This shouldn't take long."

O'Neill seemed to consider the request for several seconds. Finally, he stepped aside and led the agents to the kitchen, offering them seats at the counter; neither agent sat. "Would you like some coffee?" he asked. "I can brew a pot pretty quickly."

The first agent said, "No thanks, Mr. O'Neill. We don't have time for coffee or to shoot the breeze. I want you to listen very carefully. How you respond to our questions could determine how the rest of your life goes."

O'Neill's eyes bulged as he seemed to be deciding what he should do with his hands. He eventually shoved them into the robe's pockets. "What the hell are you talking about?" he demanded.

The second agent spoke for the first time. "You have a client by the name of Brothers Export-Imports. Is that correct?"

"Yes, but—"

"Are you aware your client has trafficked in stolen classified documents?"

"What? Of course not. I would never—"

"We have reason to believe your client is associated with a terrorist organization that has already been responsible for the deaths of dozens of people in more than a dozen countries."

O'Neill looked from one agent to the other.

The first agent said, "While you stand there and consider your options, I want you to reflect on something. If you tell us the names and locations of the principals of Brothers Export-Import and divulge everything you know about them, we will walk out of here and never return unless we discover that you've lied to us. If you don't cooperate, we'll arrest you on terrorism charges and haul your ass to jail."

The two agents looked at O'Neill, but when no response came from the man, the second agent removed a pair of handcuffs from his belt. As soon as the lawyer saw the cuffs, he blurted, "The company president is Yusuf Shirazi. He's in business with his three brothers: Adel, Fereydoun, and Parviz." He spread his arms. "As far as I know, they're legitimate businessmen. They hired me to incorporate their company and to register it with the Virginia Secretary of State. That's all I've ever done for them."

The first agent said, "I hope so, Mr. O'Neill. Now give us their business address and telephone number."

O'Neill went to a built-in desk in the kitchen and unplugged a cell phone from a charger cord. He punched several buttons and announced, "Here's their address and phone number. They operate the business in their home. At least, that's the only address I have for them."

The second agent wrote down the information. Then they quickly left the room for the front door. The first agent paused before exiting the house and said to O'Neill, "I presume you understand that if you call the Shirazis to warn them, we will return and arrest you."

O'Neill nodded.

As the agents rushed to their vehicle, the second agent called their supervisor and gave him the Shirazis' names and address.

CHAPTER 30

Stan Rictor called Tanya Serkovic at 4:15 a.m. "You awake?"

"Are you joking? Who could sleep with what's going on?"

Rictor said, "I sent a tactical team to the home of the people—four brothers whose last name is Shirazi—who've been working with Awan. Unlike Awan, who's spilling like a broken bucket, the Shirazis have clammed up. We can't get a thing from them. The good news, however, is that we found dozens of flash drives in a backgammon board in the back of a closet. We've just started reviewing the files on the drives, but you won't believe the stuff we've already found. Some information is so highly classified that I had to bring in a different team of investigators with 'Q' clearances to review the data."

"That doesn't sound good."

"Tanya, this is worse than I ever imagined. Although there was a great deal of sensitive information about our global relationships that would be of interest to terror groups, there was an equal amount of sensitive data that would be worth a fortune to other countries—the Russians and Chinese in particular. I have a feeling the Shirazis sold information to bad actors all over the globe."

"Thanks for the update, Stan. On our side, we're working with the Ukrainians to apprehend Abdel bin Hakim. We think he might be in the Ukraine to watch a soccer match."

"You gotta be kidding me."

"Nope. But we're not sure. One of our Lone Wolf teams was already over there. They're coordinating with the internal security service to try to find bin Hakim."

"Anything new on the cyber forensic research you and the NSA have been investigating?"

"I have a meeting with my people later today. If there's any progress, I'll let you know."

"Good luck in the Ukraine."

"Thanks." Tanya thought, *We'll need it.*

Five men and two women representing the FBI, the DEA, and the Army's Criminal Investigation Division sat around a coffee table in the living room of a suite at the FairBridge Inn in West Point, New York. The team had been assigned to the James Pointer investigation.

The team leader, FBI Agent Elyse Babaijan, had just briefed the group about what the Bureau had learned about Pointer's history. A call to the couple who had adopted Pointer had provided information about how and when they'd adopted the boy, how they'd changed his name from Mahmoud Lemontoff to James Pointer, and his passion for nursing, firearms, and hand-to-hand combat training.

"Sounds similar to stories we've heard about other assassins," DEA Agent Jim Hoffsis said. "Kid born overseas and brought here as a sleeper agent."

"That's right," Babaijan said.

"But how did Pointer get access to the Gray Death drug?" CID agent, Dolores Marquez, asked.

Hoffsis said, "Unfortunately, it can be bought on the street. I admit it's not common, mainly because it's bad for business."

"What do you mean?" Marquez asked.

"It's more likely to kill a customer than give them a high. We think we know how he got the stuff. There's a gal in this area known as Dena Death. She specializes in selling exotic drugs. The rumor is she has her own lab and manufactures what she sells. We haven't identified her but have intel that she operates as a supplier to people who want someone rubbed out. We arrested a woman in Binghamton, New York a couple years ago who poisoned her husband with what was later determined to be a Gray Death concoction. Unfortunately, the woman never personally met Dena. The wife made a phone call to a number she'd received from a street dealer. Negotiations were conducted over the phone and money and drugs changed hands through a little kid who the wife didn't know and never saw again."

"Is there any link between this Dena gal and the Asasiyun?" Babaijan asked.

Hoffsis said, "None we are aware of, but I wouldn't rule it out."

"What about a connection between the Asasiyun and the Greek church that arranged the Pointer adoption?" the second CID agent said.

"Nothing we could find," Babaijan said. "The Old Man of the Mountain apparently played the Church just like James Pointer played the military academy."

"So, we got *nada*," Marquez said.

Babaijan nodded, trying without much success to keep a sour look off her face.

Abdel bin Hakim and two security men, all dressed like laborers, left the kielbasa vendor's delivery truck as the driver backed up to the vendor's stall on the east side of the Dynamo Kyiv stadium. The vendor, an Iraqi immigrant, had settled in the Ukraine just as the first Gulf War began. Bin Hakim had used the man to smuggle contraband weapons from Russia into Iran. The man was more than willing to accommodate bin Hakim in his desire to 'slip quietly' into the stadium.

Playing his role to a "T," the vendor ordered bin Hakim and his men to unload containers of food, condiments, paper cups, napkins, and the like from the truck into his stall. When the truck had been unloaded, thirty minutes prior to the soccer match, bin Hakim and his men reentered the truck, changed into street clothes—including Swiss team colors—and left the truck. As they were already inside the facility, they were able to bypass the ticket takers at the stadium entrances and proceed to their seats in the end zone on the stadium's south side.

Four more of Bin Hakim's security men were already seated—two men behind bin Hakim's seat and two in the row directly in front of it. They were surrounded by the Swiss team's supporters.

Bin Hakim whispered in Arabic to the head of his security force, "The things I have to do to support my team."

The bodyguard chuckled and whispered back, "What's the matter, boss, you don't like sitting with the riffraff?"

"Humph," bin Hakim said.

Cameras set up in the two broadcasting booths inside the Kiev soccer stadium, on opposite sides of the field, were on live feeds to Langley and the U.S. Joint Special Operations Command at Fort Bragg, North Carolina. The cameramen had been instructed to initially film spectators as they entered the stadium. The videos were transmitted to Langley and instantaneously processed by facial recognition software.

Michael Danforth hoped the policemen stationed at the stadium entrances would recognize bin Hakim when he entered the facility, but he knew what a clever bastard the Saudi was. He was resigned to relying on the cameramen and computer software picking the man out of the crowd.

An encrypted satellite phone line was open between Langley; Fort Bragg; Captain Ronald Swayze, the Lone Wolf team leader in Kiev; and the two cameramen in the stadium. When the first fans entered the stadium, Michael said, "Here we go, gentlemen." But, almost instantly the dribble of fans turned into a torrent as thousands of people—mostly men—charged to their seats, wearing blue and white scarves, and waving pennants of the same colors. The Dynamo fans overwhelmed the small contingent of red and white-clad Swiss fans, who were relegated to the end zone section on the stadium's south side. The cameramen couldn't keep up with the flow of the crowd.

"Focus on the south end zone," Michael directed the cameramen.

As the cameras zeroed in on the Swiss fans' faces, their pictures appeared on split-screens at Langley and Fort Bragg. The cameramen slowly scanned row by row, with no hits. Then, to make their assignment even more difficult, just as the match started, rain began to fall. Spectators donned hooded slickers or draped themselves in plastic sheets. Faces in the crowd were now obscured.

"This is impossible," a cameraman complained.

"Just keep working at it," Frank Reynolds said into the sat-phone connection.

On the same line, Michael said, "The guy's right, Frank. Between the rain and the protective clothing most people are now wearing, we'll never pick out bin Hakim."

Frank groaned.

The cameramen continued to pan the crowd with no hits.

This isn't working, Michael thought. *And if this rain continues, we're unlikely to locate bin Hakim outside the stadium after the match finishes.* He watched the screen with the camera feeds. Every time the Dynamo players made a good defensive play or went on the attack, the local fans leaped to their feet, shouting, and chanting frenziedly. By the end of the first half, the rain-soaked Swiss fans had little to be happy about. They sat desultorily in their seats. The half ended with Dynamo ahead 1-0, because of a penalty kick goal.

Michael had tried to come up with a strategy for pinpointing bin Hakim in the rain-drenched, animated crowd of Ukrainian and Swiss soccer fanatics. But nothing came to mind.

With ten minutes to go in the match, the Dynamo left back spearheaded an attack against the Swiss team. He juked to his right and set up to kick the ball to a wide-open teammate marked by only one Swiss defender who had already shown he didn't have the speed to keep up with the tricky, fast Dynamo player. Just as the Dynamo left back was about to send the ball forward, his standing foot slipped on the field's slick surface. He fell on his back and lost control of the ball, which was stolen by the Swiss right mid-fielder, who then burst down the sideline. Two other Swiss forwards and the Swiss center back rushed forward in support. Dynamo had only two defenders back.

A collective gasp sounded in the stadium. The crowd seemed to have gone into shock. For a few seconds, the only noise came from the few thousand Swiss fans in the end zone behind the Dynamo goal. Then the Ukrainian fans began to shout at their team.

The Swiss right winger crossed the ball along the top of the goal box, eighteen yards from the Dynamo goal, out of reach of the two Dynamo defenders. The ball cleared the goal box and rolled to the Swiss left winger. The Dynamo defenders ran toward the ball, leaving the Swiss center back uncovered. The Swiss left winger dribbled once and rifled the ball over the pitch back into the box, toward the Swiss center back who was in perfect position. He leaped into the air, struck the ball with his head, and sent it into the left corner of the Dynamo goal, clearing the goalkeeper's outstretched hand by mere inches. A collective groan filled the stadium as the Swiss players celebrated.

The cameramen continued to film the stands. In the right half of the screen at Fort Bragg, something caught Michael's eye. It was as though an anomaly had occurred. He wasn't certain what it was but, in his gut, he felt something was wrong. He confirmed that the right quadrant showed the stadium's south end.

"Show me the south side footage from a minute ago," Michael said. "From just before the Swiss team scored, through the players' celebration on the pitch."

An A/V tech in the Fort Bragg ops center dropped the other half of the screen and showed a full screen view of the south side footage that Michael had requested. After a few seconds passed, a man dressed in a rain slicker appeared on the screen, his hands in the air, his mouth open as though he was shouting at the top of his lungs. As the footage continued, the same man became even more excited. Coincident with the goal, the man bounced up and down. But it hadn't been that man who had caught Michael's eye. It was the fact that six men surrounding him, although wearing Swiss colors, had shown no emotion at all. They stood and looked around the way bodyguards do, ever vigilant for threats to their charge.

"Freeze that frame," Michael said. When the excited man was frozen in mid-leap, Michael asked all who were linked into the feed, "Does anyone recognize the little guy in the middle of the large men?"

"Sonofabitch," Frank muttered.

"Can you enhance the image?" Michael shouted to no one in particular.

His A/V tech answered, "Give me a minute, sir."

The operations room at Fort Bragg went deathly quiet; no sound came through the open line. It felt as though there was no oxygen in the room as the technician worked to enhance the image. Less than thirty seconds went by before the tech called out, "How's this?"

Frank blurted another curse as Michael announced in a firm, calm voice, "It's him. It's bin Hakim."

"Look at the muscle around him," Frank said. "I count two, four, five—six guys in total."

Michael spoke into the open phone line to Captain Swayze, the Lone Wolf team commander: "Lone Wolf One, the target is seated on the south side, four seats in from the bottom of the tunnel that goes to the back side of the stadium. We count at least six security guards seated around him. Two in front, two behind, and one on either side of him. Do not…I repeat, do not approach targets until they exit the structure. Follow the ops order: two men will tail the targets while the rest will stage in the parking lot. Take them down hard as soon as they reach the lot."

"Yes, sir," Swayze said.

"Don't let them out of your sight," Michael added. "This guy is as slippery as they come. Expect the unexpected."

Michael had already experienced enough heart-stopping events for ten lifetimes: kidnapped as a small child in Greece, battles with terrorists trying to disrupt the Athens Olympic Games, commander of a Loan Wolf team assigned to capture terrorists who had infiltrated the United States, defusing a nuclear weapon that was seconds away from detonation, commander of the invasion force that decimated ISIS in Syria. But there was something about this operation that was causing him to feel as tense as he had ever felt before. Bin Hakim could be the key to learning who was behind the Asasiyun. If they failed to capture the man, the killings might continue in numbers far beyond what had already occurred.

Although the Lone Wolf team leader in Kiev was on a CommNet with his team members, the people at Langley and at Fort Bragg could only communicate with the commander, himself. The commo link between the CIA, JSOC, and the Lone Wolf team leader was open throughout the soccer match, but the line was quiet as the situation remained static. The participants focused with single-minded intensity on bin Hakim and his men as the soccer match continued.

With less than five minutes remaining in regulation time, the score was still tied 1-1. Each time the Ukrainian team threatened the Swiss goal, the fans became chaotic. The mass of Ukrainian supporters seemed to be a living organism that went from being subdued and exhausted to feverishly frantic.

With just two minutes left in regulation, the Dynamo team suddenly appeared to lose enthusiasm; its energy level was obviously declining by the second. Only a minute remained when a Dynamo player received the ball a good thirty yards out from the Swiss goal. As though he had lost interest in the game, he booted a low-odds, arcing shot. The ball sailed straight toward the Swiss goalkeeper who was set up to collect it with ease. But a Swiss player moved into the ball's path and blocked his goalkeeper's view. The player attempted to clear the ball, but it caromed off his foot and sliced into a corner of his own goal. The score was now 2-1, Dynamo.

The Ukrainian fans went mad. They hugged and shouted and cried and stamped their feet until the stadium swayed like a ship at sea. In the UEFA Tournament each team played an opponent twice, once at home and once at the opponent's stadium. Dynamo had tied the Swiss team in Zurich 1-1. If this game ended with the score as it was, Dynamo would win the two-game competition and advance to the semi-finals. Bin Hakim's team would be eliminated from the tournament. As regulation time ended, the officials added four minutes of stoppage time. The two teams competed as though they'd been infused with adrenaline. They'd played an intense, exhausting ninety minutes, but now appeared to be as fresh as they'd been when the game began.

As the game clock continued toward the end of stoppage time, Michael kept his gaze on the Saudi and felt a rush of pleasure as he saw the man's despair. He looked progressively sicker as the clock clicked down. It was as though his world had crumbled. Michael thought, *It's about to get a lot worse for you.*

With only one minute to go, bin Hakim abruptly stood, signaled to his men, and stormed out. He had apparently given up hope that his team would prevail, which turned out to be well-founded.

"He's on the move," Michael said into the sat phone.

"We've got him," Captain Swayze said. "Going to CommNet."

The people in the ops centers at Fort Bragg and Langley were suddenly relegated to watching the video with no access to the CommNet communications between Lone Wolf team members. And when bin Hakim and his retinue disappeared into the tunnel, the ops teams were effectively incommunicado unless Captain Swayze came on the satellite link.

"Lone Wolf Three to Lone Wolf One, I have targets moving toward Gate 5," Staff Sergeant Marco Ricci announced.

"Confirm targets moving toward Gate 5," Swayze responded.

"Roger Gate 5."

Swayze ordered the remainder of his team to set up a close perimeter outside Gate 5. The CommNet went quiet. Thirty seconds passed, then Ricci keyed his radio mic and breathlessly said, "Subjects have diverted away from Gate 5. They're moving toward the next gate down. Gate 4."

Swayze said, "Team members confirm you copied last transmission. Targets moving toward Gate 4."

Each member confirmed he'd heard the call.

Then Ricci came on the frequency again. He sounded stressed. "Lone Wolf Three to Lone Wolf team. Targets entered a vendor stall and disappeared through a rear door. I've lost visual contact."

Swayze's stomach clenched. "Where's the stall?"

"About halfway between Gates 5 and 4," Ricci said.

Swayze barked into the CommNet, "Lone Wolf Three, engage." To the rest of the team members, he ordered, "Redeploy to the rear of vendor stalls between Gates 4 and 5."

Then Ricci came back on the radio and shouted, "They boarded a white panel truck headed toward the south side of the parking lot."

Swayze switched to the open line with Fort Bragg and Langley. "Target is in a white panel truck moving toward the south side of the parking lot. Notify the Ukrainians to intercept the vehicle. We're on foot and moving to the south side lot exit."

The parking lot was filling with fans exiting the stadium. They ran in mad dashes toward vehicles as the rain now fell in sheets and cold mist descended. The Lone Wolf team members had a tough enough time with visibility, but now dodging fans and vehicles only made their job more difficult. A few people ran away when they saw the black-clad, heavily-armed men. Some seemed overcome with shock and froze in place. But because of the darkness, rain, and fog combination, most were oblivious to the team.

"Lone Wolf Three," Swayze said, "what's your position?"

Ricci, breathing heavily, said, "I think I've got the truck in sight. Twenty-five yards ahead. It's tied up in traffic exiting the lot. The exit is about seventy-five yards ahead of it. They make it to the street, we'll lose them." A second passed, then Ricci said, "Sonofa— They're bailing out of the truck and moving toward the exit on foot."

"Don't lose bin Hakim," Swayze said.

Marco Ricci increased his pace and shortened the separation from his targets to twenty-five yards. To avoid detection by bin Hakim's guards, he crouched as he ran. He guessed bin Hakim had vehicles parked near the lot's exit. He noticed flashing emergency lights a short distance ahead and guessed policemen were managing traffic on the street outside the parking area. He saw a small lot off to the right where there were dozens of parked limousines.

He diverted to the right, all the while keeping an eye on the large men who shepherded bin Hakim. Ricci knew he was taking a chance that bin Hakim and his men had arrived at the stadium by other means, but his instincts told him they'd probably come in one or more limos and transferred to the delivery truck. He was elated when his targets, still twenty or so yards from the street, turned right toward the limo lot. He was now in position to cut them off at a location that was significantly less populated than the general parking lot.

Ricci serpentined his way around the limos. The headlights of a parked car backlit the Saudi and his guards, one of whom shielded their boss from the downpour with an umbrella.

"This is Lone Wolf Three; target in limousine lot to the east of main parking area," Ricci said into his mic. "Bin Hakim and three men just entered a white stretch limo. Three other men moving to a second car: A black stretch limo next to the white one."

Ricci was now surrounded by dozens of limos. Headlights were coming on and engines roared. Bin Hakim's vehicles had an open lane leading to the street. Not waiting for orders from Captain Swayze, he ran forward, pointed his M4 CQBR weapon and shot out the rear tires of both limos. Like wraiths, shrouded by rain and fog, men leaped from the vehicles armed with pistols and automatic weapons. Ricci scurried to his right and put a parked, empty limo between him and bin Hakim's men. He unleashed a volley from his rifle over the car roof. The guards returned fire. Ricci wasn't certain if he'd hit any of them until a man screamed. He ejected the magazine from his weapon and inserted another thirty-rounder as he sought cover behind a car two rows over. He could tell from the sounds of the weapons that some bodyguards had AK-47s. The AK's 7.62 mm ammo could punch right through regular glass and vehicle bodies.

Captain Swayze's voice came over the CommNet: "Lone Wolf One: Ten seconds out."

Ten seconds, Ricci thought. *A lifetime.*

He rose and fired a short burst at a guard who ran toward him. The man's forward momentum was arrested as though he'd been hit with a two-by-four. The best that Ricci could determine was that there were still two guards engaged in the firefight. The two drivers didn't appear to have joined the battle, nor had bin Hakim. The white limo's driver tried to escape the melee, but the rear wheel rims of his vehicle dug into the muddy lot, trapping him. A few drivers in vehicles around bin Hakim's two limos reacted like stampeding cattle. They sped away from their parking spaces—some escaping, others crashing into one another in a luxury car demolition derby. Ricci found an unoccupied car and crouched behind its right front fender. He said into his mic, "I got at least two men still active. They're beside the only white limo I see. Could be a couple more. The target is inside the white limo."

"10-4," Swayze responded.

The Lone Wolf team entered the lot. As they ran forward, looking like specters from an alien world, the two remaining bodyguards dropped their weapons and raised their hands in the air. Team members forced the two to the ground, searched them, and secured their wrists and ankles with zip ties. Another team member pulled the driver from the white limo and secured him.

Captain Swayze charged the black limo and dragged its driver out onto the ground, zip-tied his wrists and ankles, and announced on the CommNet: "Driver of black limo secure."

Then Swayze and one of his men cautiously approached the white limo's right-side passenger door, threw it open, and found a man cowering on the floor. He ordered him out of the vehicle. As the man rolled onto the seat, slid across it, and dropped his feet to the ground, Swayze shined a flashlight at his face. "Well, well, Mr. bin Hakim. You've been a very naughty boy."

Bin Hakim stood, shielded his eyes against the flashlight's glare, and said, "How would you like to become a rich man?"

Swayze sniggered. He leaned over and growled, "There isn't enough money in the world, asshole." Forcing bin Hakim facedown on the ground, he turned to one of his men, and ordered, "Cuff him."

As bin Hakim was cuffed, Swayze radioed the Ukrainian SBU commander, gave him the team's location, and asked him to bring up the tactical vehicle that had transported the Americans to the stadium. When the truck arrived, the team bundled a now-blindfolded, mud-soaked bin Hakim inside, placed sound suppressor earphones over his ears, and covered his head with a black mesh bag.

While the SBU team took bin Hakim's bodyguards and drivers— four alive and two dead—to a second vehicle, the first roared off to a helicopter positioned on a vacant field a mile away. The American team with their captive boarded the chopper, which took them to an airfield where they rendezvoused with an American C47, which would transport them to a clandestine base in Lithuania where the Lone Wolf team would hand over bin Hakim to a CIA interrogation team.

CHAPTER 31

Yasmin was surprised at how shaken Javad was. His eyes bulged and his face was beet-red.

"What's happened?" she asked.

"I just got off a phone call from Tehran."

"Calm down and tell me."

Javad was overwrought to the point where he could barely put his thoughts into words.

"Take a deep breath, Javad," she told him, as she took his arm and guided him to a chair.

He sat down, bent over, and put his elbows on his thighs. After taking several breaths, he said, "It was Khavari."

"The President's executive assistant?"

Javad nodded.

"What did he want?"

"He demanded to talk with your father."

Yasmin felt intense pain in her head. It was as though electrical impulses had stabbed both her temples and traveled into the middle of her skull. "What did you tell him?" she demanded.

Javad raised up; his face was now pale, and perspiration ran off his forehead. "I told him Mr. Nizari was supervising the final directives to our agents."

"Good," Yasmin said.

"Then he wanted to know what had been done about the

Danforths."

The stabbing pain hit her again. *What is it about these Danforths that is so important?*

"Khavari was very upset about the failure in Venice. He wanted to know what we were doing about correcting that mistake. He also asked about the son and grandson. When I told him that the grandson was probably dead and the son would be killed tomorrow, he went ballistic, screaming and yelling about our incompetence. He told me, 'They must be dealt with now.' When I told him the elder Danforth and his wife would be at the site in Venice on Saturday and would be killed along with all the others, he shouted, 'I want your guarantee that they will all be dead by Saturday.'"

"How was it left?"

"I told him I would have Mr. Nizari call him back as soon as—"

"How in the name of the Prophet will that happen?" Yasmin shouted.

Javad lowered his head again. In a voice that was little more than a whisper, he said, "I couldn't think of anything else to say."

Yasmin slowly released a breath, wondering what was causing such angst in Tehran. Still confused by this American family and their importance, she paced the hallway and tried to pull a clue from the furthest recesses of her mind that would explain the Iranian President's assistant's behavior.

Javad broke into her thoughts. "Maybe the embargo the Americans imposed on Iran is unsettling the mullahs."

"What would that have to do with killing these Danforths?" Yasmin said. "Who the hell are these people?"

But something niggled at the back of her brain, and the connections between Iran and the Danforths finally sparked. She had heard for years that a Saudi diamond merchant had been a fanatic supporter of the Iranian regime and its funding of the Asasiyun. *What was the Saudi's name?* she thought. It finally came to her: "Abdel bin Hakim."

"What was that?" Javad asked.

"Nothing," she said, waving a hand at him. Her father had told her a story about bin Hakim and how his son, Musa, had been killed by a CIA operative in Brazil. *What if that CIA operative was*

Robert Danforth?

"Hah," Yasmin blurted. *Maybe bin Hakim is withholding funds from the Iranians until they kill the Danforths.* Her stomach did a little flip-flop as she considered her failure to eliminate Danforth in Venice.

She walked back to where Javad still sat and told him to find out what had happened at West Point. "If the grandson is still alive, send another agent after him."

Javad waved his arms around. His mouth opened and closed like that of a beached fish. Finally, he said, "Another agent?"

Yasmin stabbed a finger at him and shouted menacingly, "Pull yourself together."

Javad wiped his forehead with a hand. "You want to waste one of our people on a lowly cadet?"

Yasmin shot Javad a venomous look. "What did I say?" she screamed. "If the grandson is still alive, I want him eliminated. And send the best agent we have in Venice after the grandfather."

Javad stood, his eyeballs ping-ponging everywhere but on her face. He wore a confused expression. "That…that's terribly risky," he said. "If we just wait, he'll be dead along with all the others at the ball."

"I don't want to take any chances that—"

"These last-minute changes can jeopardize—"

Yasmin swung a hand at Javad's face, slapping him with incredible force. She bent over and, nose-to-nose with him, shouted, "You will do as I say. Do you understand?"

Javad looked like a little boy who had disappointed a parent. His eyes filled with tears as he touched the side of his face where she had struck him. "I'll…get…to…it," he said. "But…what about Khavari?"

Yasmin shook her head. "I'll take care of it."

Yasmin entered the operations center, which was segregated from the rest of the property so that no one could inadvertently access it. Entry required a six-digit keypad code, along with a scanned palm print.

She stood on the platform that overlooked the workstations and large screen monitors. She loved this place. It was a state-of-the-art setup that acted as the heart of the Asasiyun campaign. The location of every assassin was monitored through an encrypted satellite telephone that each agent carried, except on the day that he or she was ordered to execute a mission. On that day, the agent would destroy the phone by punching in the code 2112, which would fry the device's electronics.

Each monitor on the room's curved front wall displayed a map of a continent. Blinking blue lights on the monitors identified the agents' locations. Static white lights indicated agents whose phones had been disabled and replaced by burner phones. Static red lights symbolized agents who had died executing their missions. Yasmin knew that in some instances the agents had been unsuccessful in completing their missions. But she had no way of knowing, short of a news report, if those agents had been captured or died in failed assassinations. This was a weakness in the system her father had created, but there was nothing she could do about it now.

The operators could pull up each continent on their consoles, update the board as new attacks occurred, and reference information about each individual field agent.

Yasmin stared with satisfaction at the digital counters in the bottom left of each monitor. One counter showed the number of targets killed and a second showed the number of targets who had been assigned to assassins but had yet to be attacked. A third digital counter recorded the total number of deaths, including both targets and collateral deaths. The first two numbers totaled one thousand. She liked the symmetry of killing one thousand infidels. But she knew the number would be even higher, taking into consideration collateral damage. A warm rush ran through her as she considered the hundreds of victims in the Carnevale venue who weren't on the target list. Their deaths would enhance the shock effect.

But it was the deaths of one thousand Western leaders that would have the greatest practical impact on the Western world.

She moved down to the level where two dozen console operators sat and asked each one to pull up data on a random agent in his assigned territory. She also confirmed with each one that the encrypted messages sent to the assassins had been acknowledged.

"How is your father doing?" one operator asked. "I hope he's feeling better."

"Thank you for asking," Yasmin said, perpetuating the myth that her father was ill and quarantining himself in his quarters. "He's not quite recovered." She patted the man on his shoulder. "I'll tell him you asked about his health."

Satisfied that the staff was prepared for the events planned for the day after tomorrow, she left the ops center and went to her father's office. She went online and checked her balances in banks located in Switzerland, the Caribbean, and Panama that were originally opened by her father. *At least he had the sense to rake off some funds those fanatics in Tehran provided for the Asasiyun,* she thought. Between the $27 million her father had accumulated and the $50 million in ransom she'd extorted from the mullahs in Tehran, she was confident she would have a long, luxurious life ahead. She sent a message in her father's name to Khavari in the Iranian President's office: *I understand you called. I'm certain you understand that I am extremely busy but will call you as soon as I am able.* As a postscript, she added: *The Danforths will be eliminated.*

Now, what to do about Javad? she thought.

CHAPTER 32

Because Ursan Awan had declined the benefit of legal counsel and had advised his mother, brother, and sisters to do the same, the FBI counter-intelligence agents assigned to interrogate the five Awans were able to do so without the interference of lawyers. This allowed them to grill the Pakistanis unhampered by legal niceties. Ursan turned out to be a loyal son and brother. In return for the government not filing charges against his family members and allowing them to return to Pakistan, he shared everything he knew about his contact, Parviz, how the man had approached him, the money he'd been paid to steal classified material, and details about the information he'd stolen. Being that the FBI had the flash drives they'd found in the Shirazi house, which Ursan had passed to Parviz, they verified that Ursan was being straight with them. They were satisfied that everything they got from the other Awans was also accurate.

But the disappointment the interrogators felt was substantial when they learned that the Awans had never had direct contact with or intimate knowledge about the Old Man of the Mountain or the Asasiyun.

Stan Rictor personally followed the progress the interrogators made with the Awans and concluded that any more time spent with them was useless as far as tracking down the Asasiyun base and its assassins were concerned. And, so far, the Shirazi brothers had proved to be "true believers." Rictor was convinced that one or all the brothers had connections with the Asasiyun but, short of torturing them, he concluded they represented a dead end, too.

Rictor called Tanya Serkovic and asked for an update regarding Abdel bin Hakim.

"I was just about to check with Ray Gallegos," she said. "I'll patch him in." She connected Raymond to the call and asked, "Anything new from Lithuania? Has bin Hakim opened up?"

"The sleazy bastard…um, sorry, ma'am. The horrid excuse for a human being wants us to make a deal before he'll talk. The team leader with him believes he will spill everything he knows if we grant him immunity from prosecution. He also believes the guy will sing like a canary if we apply a little pressure. With or without an immunity deal."

Rictor knew that "applying a little pressure" was a euphemism for "enhanced interrogation methods."

"We want to avoid crossing the line here, Ray," Tanya said.

"Don't I know it."

Rictor said, "I've read everything we have about bin Hakim. My impression is that the man is sybaritic, narcissistic, and money-grubbing. I suspect he won't hold up to even the *threat* of…physical pressure. But let's hold that option in reserve. I suggest you tell him we'll waive extradition to the United States and forego prosecution against him if he cooperates. I'll message a document to you that will assure him of our agreement. Give him exactly ten seconds to agree. If he doesn't cooperate, we'll have to pursue…other options."

"I don't want any American touching the guy," Tanya said.

"Don't worry about that," Raymond said. "The Lithuanians sent over two guys who look like the offspring of a Dothraki father and a White Walker mother."

"You really want to give this guy a free pass?" Tanya said.

Rictor said, "I didn't say anything about a free pass. I just told him we would waive extradition to and prosecution in the States. I didn't say anything about not shipping him to the Saudis."

"You think the Saudis will deal with bin Hakim?" Raymond asked. "Hell, they've been protecting him for years."

"There's no way the Saudis will continue to protect him after we inform them about his support of the Asasiyun," Rictor said. "If they don't prosecute the man, we'll let the world know they're protecting a criminal who's supported a mass murder campaign. Many Western countries have already had an influential citizen murdered by the Asasiyun. If the Saudis don't cooperate, they won't sell another drop of oil to the West."

Tanya said something that Rictor apparently didn't get.

"What was that?" Rictor asked.

Tanya laughed. "You're a devious bastard, Stanley."

"Ma'am, please…your language." Raymond smiled.

CHAPTER 33

Abd al Bari Murad was born in Iraq to poor Muslim parents who taught their son the best priniciples of Shi'a Islam at a very early age. When the boy showed unusally high intelligence and an aptitude for mathematics, a local Shi'a cleric suggested to his parents that they enroll him in a *madrasa* in Iran that would help their son realize his full potential. At first, the Murads resisted sending their only child to another country. Despite the fact that Iran was a Shi'a country, the Murads considered Iran the enemy. Their oldest son had been killed by Iranian forces during the Iran/Iraq War. But, when the cleric offered the parents ten thousand American dollars, they acquiesced.

What the Murads didn't understand was that they'd just given their son to the Old Man of the Mountain and, effectively, sentenced him to the probability of an early death.

The boy's religious education continued at the Asasiyun's aerie in Iran. He also received intense training in mathematics, including algebra, geometry, trigonometry, and differential calculus, all by the time he'd turned thirteen. Initially, the boy didn't understand why he also had to spend so much time learning American English and American customs. And, being a frail child, he was extremely unhappy spending so many hours of every day on physical activities, including hand-to-hand fighting and weapons training. But he'd quickly learned to keep his mouth shut and do what he was told. Complainers and recalcitrants received severe corporal and emotional punishment. By his fifteenth birthday, he'd been indoctrinated in Asasiyun ways and had become a stone-cold accolyte of the Old Man of the Mountain.

Three days shy of his sixteenth birthday, his mathematics tutor at the Asasiyun's training center arranged to have a paper written by Murad about the Fibonacci Sequence and the Golden Ratio published in the *Academie Francaise de Mathematique*'s quarterly journal. That article established Murad as a global mathematics wunderkind, and precipitated a flood of scholarship offers from universities around the world. Although offers came from dozens of top schools in half-a-dozen countries, Murad's tutor told him he would be attending the University of North Carolina at Chapel Hill. Murad had never heard of UNC, but he knew that didn't matter. He shut up and did as he was told.

"Your name will be Barry Murad," his tutor informed him. "You'll live with a family friendly to our cause. Your new guardian will give you an encrypted satellite phone and one day you will receive instructions to perform a task that will make you famous in all of Islam."

Murad felt that being the preeminent mathematician from the Islamic world would be a wonderful way to bring honor to his country and his faith, but he'd learned to keep his opinions to himself.

For two years, Murad thought he was in paradise. He worked with the top math scholars at UNC and attended conferences all over the country. Barely eighteen years old, he had established himself as a renowned scholar. Except for rare moments when the words of his tutor back in the *Asasiyun* enclave picked at the edges of his memory, causing him to shudder and wonder what the man had meant when he'd told him he would be famous in all of Islam, he was as happy as he had ever been. But that changed one month ago when the satellite phone rang at 3:00 a.m.

"Hello," he'd answered.

"Murad, do you know who this is?"

The young man's stomach lurched, and he felt instantly nauseous. "Yes, Arbob."

"Good," the man said. "The time has come for you to bring great honor to the brotherhood, to your country, and to all those who follow the Prophet."

Murad's stomach heaved and he came close to vomiting. Bile burned his throat. He swallowed. "What is it that you require, Arbob?"

The man recited a date, a location, and a name.

For the past month, Murad had been unable to focus on his studies. His professors noticed a change in his behavior and in his ability to concentrate. But when they asked if he was ill, Murad just shrugged and told them he was fine. One of his professors came up with the theory that Murad's behavior was attributable to homesickness and hormones.

On Thursday, February 21, just before sunset, Murad boarded a bus bound for Fort Bragg. Other than a woman working on a PhD in Economics and whose thesis was titled "War & Economic Development," Murad was the only passenger on the bus who was not a UNC Army R.O.T.C. cadet. The R.O.T.C. Department had opened the trip to all students until the seats were filled. There hadn't been many takers.

The bus pulled up to the gate at Fort Bragg at 7:45 p.m. A staff sergeant boarded the bus and, clipboard in hand, read the passengers' names from a list. He checked off each name as the passenger responded.

"Welcome to Fort Bragg," the sergeant said. "We'll go to the 82nd Airborne Division's mess hall, where you'll have dinner. Afterward, you'll be taken to your rooms at the BOQ." He smiled. "The U.S. Army starts its day quite early. Someone will knock on your door at 0500 hours—that's five a.m. civilian time. Breakfast will be served in the BOQ mess hall from 0500 to 0600 hours. I'll be at the entrance to the mess hall to hand out your meal tickets. You should be in the lobby on the first floor by no later than 0615 hours to board the bus."

The sergeant handed a sheaf of papers to the R.O.T.C. unit commander who distributed them to the passengers. "These are your itineraries for your visit here. You'll have a full day tomorrow.

We'll finish the briefings and tour tomorrow at 1800 hours." He smiled again and explained that was 6:00 p.m. "You'll return to the mess hall for dinner and will be free until the following morning. After breakfast on Saturday, your bus will return to Chapel Hill. Are there any questions?"

Barry looked at the itinerary. His heart seemed to stutter when he saw his target's name. For a moment he thought he might be sick, but he swallowed hard and gulped air into his lungs.

CHAPTER 34

The recording of Abdel bin Hakim's interrogation by CIA specialists in Lithuania was sent to Frank Reynolds at Langley. Frank passed it on to Seth Bridewell, who immediately brought Zach Grabowsky and Angelina Borden into his office.

"You both did a remarkable job coming up with the theory that bin Hakim would be in the Ukraine. I just emailed a copy of the man's interrogation to you. I want you to fact check it. We need to prove bin Hakim's claim that the Iranian government is behind the Old Man of the Mountain and the Asasiyun." He looked at Grabowsky. "We have to find the money trail that goes through them." After a beat, Seth said, "And we have to identify every assassin out there. That's the only way we can prevent more murders."

"That's all?" Zach asked.

Seth gave Zach an impatient look. "Isn't that enough?"

"I was being sarcastic, boss."

"I don't process sarcasm. Now get back to work."

"We're on it," Angelina said.

Bob and Liz ate a late dinner at the Canova Room in the Baglioni Hotel Luna. It was just before 10:00 p.m. when they returned to their room. Fifteen minutes later, Bob was fast asleep. Liz wasn't as lucky. After tossing and turning for thirty minutes, she left the bedroom and moved to the small sitting room. She tried to read the book she'd brought with her but couldn't concentrate. She'd never been one to get anxiety attacks, but that's what seemed to be happening. Her mind reeled, cycling thoughts in kaleidoscopic confusion: the attack on Bob in Venice, the news about the gang of assassins who had murdered over twenty people, Miriana's comment earlier that day about the pirates who'd taken over their ship on their last family vacation, the pressure on Robbie at West Point. She tried unsuccessfully to focus on one thing at a time. She'd been in the sitting room for almost an hour when Bob joined her.

"What's the matter?" he asked.

Liz shrugged. "I can't sleep."

"What's bothering you?"

Liz's eyes teared up. She shrugged again. Finally, she said, "Something's wrong. I don't know what it is, but I've got this feeling…like something's happened. Or is about to happen."

Bob sat next to her on the couch, put an arm around her, and pulled her to him. "Something's happened to whom?" he said.

"I think we should call Robbie."

"Honey, if something had happened to Robbie, we would have heard. Besides, trying to get hold of him at the academy isn't easy. We'd probably have to leave a message."

"Then let's call Michael."

"We talked to Mike once already today."

She took a tissue from her robe pocket and dabbed her eyes. When she pulled away from Bob, she glared at him. "Since when is there a rule against talking with my son more than once a day?"

"Okay, I'll call Mike. But I warn you, he's going to think we're going senile."

Michael's cell phone went to voicemail. Bob left a message: "It's Mom and Dad. We're fine. Just wanted to check in to see how you all are doing."

"Try Robbie," Liz said. "Leave a message if you have to."

Bob blew out a frustrated breath. "He'll be at dinner. They can't take calls then. I'll try him a little later."

Liz stood. "I guess I'm just being silly. You're probably correct. If something had happened, we would have heard."

Bob hugged her again. "What do you say we try to sleep?"

Liz nodded and followed Bob into the bedroom. He diverted to the bathroom while she climbed into bed. By the time he came back into the bedroom, she was asleep.

"Wonderful," he said under his breath. "She's asleep and I'm now wide awake." He went to the sitting room and thought about calling Michael again, but decided instead to call Raymond Gallegos. He knew he shouldn't bother Raymond, and didn't want to impose on his former subordinate, but in addition to checking on Robbie, he was aching to discover if anything new had developed with the investigation into the Asasiyun.

"Hello," Raymond answered.

"Ray, it's Bob."

"Oh…hey Bob. I wasn't sure if I'd hear from you. Especially considering the time in Italy. Must be the middle of the night."

Bob was confused by Ray's comment. "What are—?"

"Everything's fine. That grandson of yours is something special."

Bob felt a chill hit the back of his neck. "What are you talking about?" His breath caught in his lungs as he waited for Ray's response.

"You don't know? I thought that's why you were calling."

"Now you've really got me worried."

"Aw shit," Raymond muttered. "There was an Asasiyun sleeper agent planted at the military academy who targeted Robbie. But your grandson took the guy down. Probably saved several lives in the process. The killer had a pad impregnated with a deadly drug concoction. Our assumption is the man was at West Point to cause some sort of serious disruption whenever his masters decided the time was right. He'd been there for a couple years."

"You're certain Robbie was the target?"

"Pretty damned sure. Remember, the initial intel we got about this Asasiyun group included Michael and Robbie's names, as well as yours."

"Have you told Michael and Miriana?" Bob asked.

"Of course."

Why the hell hasn't Michael called us? Bob thought. But he answered his own question: *He was protecting his elderly parents from further stress.*

Bob huffed a sigh. "Ever since I learned that Michael, Robbie, and I were on that hit list, I've racked my brain to figure out why the Asasiyun would care about Robbie. According to the news, every person killed so far was a senior military officer, politician, business executive, or the like. Robbie is none of those things."

"His undercover role in Syria is what we presume got his name added to the target list."

"Yeah, but how did the group know about Robbie being in Syria? He operated under an alias and his participation in the operation was supposed to be kept in a sealed, classified file."

"We think we've answered that question. The Senate Select Committee on Intelligence had an IT consultant from Pakistan working for them. The man had access to everything the committee members had."

"Oh, my Lord," Bob said. "What genius hired the guy?"

"I'd better not say. But it was the same genius who gave the consultant her passwords. The guy downloaded thousands of classified documents and passed them on to Iranians who are Asasiyun agents. We arrested the entire cell. The Pakistani is cooperating, but the Iranians are not."

Bob was tempted to ask if the person who had compromised classified information had been arrested as well but decided he would be wasting his breath. He could barely control his anger as he wondered how many individuals had been put at risk because of shoddy handling of classified material. Then another thought came to him.

"Ray, how do we know there aren't other Asasiyun agents at the academy?"

"We don't. But Army CID and FBI counter-insurgency teams are going through every employee and cadet personnel file checking for suspicious background information. They're also reviewing the files of every contractor and vendor doing business on the campus."

"Is any place safe anymore?" Bob muttered, more to himself than to Raymond.

"You know better than most that a determined enemy with massive resources, including fanatical followers who are willing to die for their cause, is damned difficult to defeat."

"To paraphrase General George Patton, let's do everything we can to *help* them die for their cause."

FRIDAY
FEBRUARY 22

CHAPTER 35

Iranian President Hassan Shabani and his executive assistant, Jalil Khavari, walked down a pea-gravel path through one of the gardens on the seven hundred forty acre Sa'dabad Palace Complex adjacent to the President's official residence in Tehran.

"What did Nizari have to say?" Shabani asked.

"His text assured me that the two Danforths would be dealt with today."

"Two?"

"Yes. I texted him back about the grandson. He believes the boy was eliminated by the agent at West Point."

"Believes? He doesn't know for certain?"

Khavari shrugged.

"You didn't talk with Nizari?"

"No. When I called yesterday, his man, Javad Muntaziri, told me he was unavailable but would get back to me. He texted me a couple hours later."

Shabani mused for a moment. After they'd walked twenty more yards, he said, "When was the last time you spoke with Nizari?"

"We have a telephone conversation scheduled on the third Monday of every month. I guess the last conversation I had with him was last month."

"Why not this month?"

"I called this past Monday and talked with Muntaziri. He told me Nizari was in a meeting and couldn't be interrupted."

Shabani stopped and turned to look at Khavari. "Has that ever happened before? That he couldn't speak with you?"

"Come to think of it, no. But I assume, what with the campaign ramp-up, Nizari must be extremely busy."

"Too busy to talk with a representative of the government that has invested over one billion dollars in the Asasiyun?"

Khavari shrugged yet again.

"I don't like it. Nizari was one of Ayatollah Khomeini's most trusted and loyal followers, and has continued to be a most important person in our revolution. I can't imagine him being *too busy* to talk with my top aide."

"What are you thinking, Mr. President?"

"I think it's time for you to visit the Old Man of the Mountain."

"That could be dangerous. We know that all the regime's top members are electronically and sometimes physically followed by the Great Satan's agents. What if someone tracks me to the Cloud Forest?"

"What if they do? Within forty-eight hours, the leaders of all our enemies will have been severely damaged. Their financial systems and markets will be in disarray. The cowards will all be begging us for peace."

CHAPTER 36

Bob had agonized over whether to tell Liz about Robbie. He knew she continually worried about her grandson, but he also knew that if she learned about it at a later date, she would be livid with him. She wouldn't see his lack of candor as him protecting her. Besides, she'd proved herself to be tough enough to handle anything over the years. In the end, he was glad he'd told her everything that Raymond Gallegos had shared with him. Her initial shock and concern turned to unmitigated anger. Their conversation had ended with, "What the hell is the damned CIA going to do about these murderers?"

It was now just after midnight in Italy when Bob again called Michael's cell number.

Michael's voice was full of worry when he answered. "What's wrong? It's the middle of the night over there."

"Everything's fine here, Mike. I just wanted to talk with you for a minute. I learned about what happened at the academy with Robbie and—"

"Listen, Dad, if you're going to hassle me about not calling, now's not the time. I've—"

"That's not why I'm calling, Mike. Just give me a minute to talk."

"Okay."

"The last I heard, the Asasiyun had murdered almost two dozen people. Their M.O. has essentially remained the same. One assassin goes after one target. The only exceptions to that have been where there were a target's family members or associates who got in the way. The targets have all been prominent men and women in leadership positions." Bob paused, took a breath, and said, "The only two targets who aren't in leadership positions are Robbie and me. Which tells me that someone affiliated with the Asasiyun has a grudge against our family."

"You were in CIA leadership not too long ago," Michael said.

"Emphasis on the word 'were.' Your position with the Army makes you a logical target. If someone is taking revenge against all of us, that makes you an even more obvious target than you are already."

"And what do you suggest I do about that?"

"First, you should bring Miriana onto Fort Bragg and put her under protection. I think this is especially appropriate if you still plan to fly to Italy this weekend. Second, I suggest you call the commanding general at the academy and have him put Robbie under protective custody. And, finally, it would be a good idea if you didn't come to Italy. You should stay with Miriana on the base until this whole business is resolved."

"Dad, you sound paranoid."

"I'm not paranoid, but that doesn't mean there aren't assassins hiding behind every bush. Son, I want you to put aside ego and machismo and take every possible precaution."

"I appreciate your concern, Dad, but this isn't about being macho. It's about doing my job. If someone in my position starts hiding, we've already lost to these homicidal maniacs."

I knew he would say something like that, Bob thought. "Just consider what I said."

"I always listen to you and appreciate your instincts. For your information, I've already talked with the commanding general at the Point. He moved Robbie and Samantha Meek to his personal quarters and assigned a security team to protect them. But I think your suggestion about temporarily moving Miriana onto the base here is a good one. I'll take care of that as soon as I get off this call. But as far as my going to Italy is concerned, I leave early this evening. I'll call you as soon as I land."

"Thanks for listening, Mike. One last thing: Don't trust anyone.

Asasiyun agents have infiltrated some of the most secure institutions in the world. Think about the number of people who enter Fort Bragg on a daily basis. One of your most trusted associates could be an *Asasiyun* agent. Maybe someone who appears innocent and nonthreatening."

"Okay, Dad. Thanks again. I'm sorry, but I have to go. We have a group of students from UNC visiting today and I've been asked to say a few words to them."

The only times Barry Murad prayed in the United States was when he was in his home, when no one but members of his host family were around. He always found solace in prayer. He wished he could pray now that he was so frightened. But he'd been taught by his tutor at the training camp that practicing dissimulation was acceptable for one's self-preservation. It would not be good if his roomate here at Fort Bragg observed him prostrate in prayer.

He'd often considered what would happen to him if he was ever called upon to execute an order from the Old Man of the Mountain. *Maybe I'll die in the process*, he'd thought many times. But, whether it was the overconfidence of youth and inexperience, he sometimes fantasized about how he would successfully accomplish his assignment, escape, and become a great Islamic hero. He'd hoped his mission would be to plant a bomb, or burn down a building, or use a sniper rifle to kill someone. However, now that he'd received his assignment and the moment of execution was fast approaching, he could no longer fool himself into believing in fairy tales.

He was unable to sleep as his mind raced through the scenarios that might occur. *Will I succeed? Whether I accomplish my mission or not, will I be killed? If I'm captured, what will happen? Execution? Life imprisonment?* He'd seen television shows about American prisons and how young men became victims of sexual deviants. His eyes now closed, he shuddered as a chill gripped him as though an icy hand had punched into the center of his chest.

"I could be one of the world's great mathematicians," he whimpered.

When someone knocked on his BOQ door at 5:00 a.m., Murad struggled out of bed. He felt as though sand had been ground into his eyes. When his roommate popped out of bed and flipped on the light switch, Murad covered his face with his hands and groaned.

"Let's go, Barry," his roommate chided him.

Barry moved to the bathroom, relieved himself, and washed his hands and face with cold water. He ran his wet hands through his short, black hair. By the time he'd returned to the bedroom, his roommate was dressed and ready to go.

"You'd better hurry, man," his roommate said, "or you'll miss breakfast."

Barry just nodded as the young man left the room. After the door closed, he locked it, went to his knees, faced east, and said an abbreviated prayer. He pulled his overnight bag from under his bed and removed a change of clothes, which he tossed onto the bed. From the bottom of the bag, he grasped the weapon his guardian in Chapel Hill had given him; removing the knife from its scabbard, he ran the four-inch blade across the back of his wrist. He was amazed at how swiftly and easily it shaved away the hair there. The two edges met in a sharp point that he'd been told would penetrate human skin, flesh, muscle, and organs.

He replaced the weapon in the scabbard and clipped the scabbard straps around his left forearm. He quickly dressed in a heavy shirt, jeans, running shoes, and a ski parka.

Downstairs, the rest of the group members were already seated at mess hall tables. Most appeared to have already eaten and were now in animated conversations. Barry wasn't hungry. *Besides,* he thought, *I'll probably puke if I eat.*

CHAPTER 37

Jalil Khavari wasn't comfortable flying to the Asasiyun enclave without a military escort. *After all*, he thought, *I'll be surrounded by some of the most vicious killers on the planet.* But the President had laughed at his suggestion that he might need protection. He looked down on the mountain fortress as the chopper cleared the tree line edge below the southern wall and landed on a helipad on the north side of a wide expanse of flat granite-rock roof. Three men and a woman stood fifty or so yards away from the helipad. Two men carried rifles. Khavari placed his hands on his knees to stop them from trembling. He sucked in a huge breath and let it out slowly. *Remember,* he told himself, *you represent the President of the Islamic Republic of Iran.*

Yasmin watched the aircraft settle onto the helipad. As her guards ran over to the chopper, she whispered to Javad, "Is everything set?"

"Of course," he answered. "As soon as we determine the frequency his satellite phone is using, the engineer will turn on a very high power jammer designed for blocking satellite communications. We'll claim that all communications are down, not just his phone."

Yasmin felt a tremor course through her. "We're so close," she told Javad under her breath. "I can't believe a bureaucrat took *this* moment to visit."

"Don't overreact," Javad said. "After all, they know that what your father and Ayatollah Khomeini planned years ago will come to fruition tomorrow."

Yasmin's stomach clenched. *Who the hell does this man think he is that he would dare tell me not to overreact?* But she stifled a sharp response and instead smiled as though she appreciated Javad's advice. She rubbed her forehead with the tips of her fingers and adjusted the black scarf that covered her hair and framed her face. She stuck her hands in the pockets of the long, gray tunic she wore over a sweater and long pants.

By the time Jalil Khavari stepped down on the helipad and followed a guard toward Yasmin and Javad, the aircraft's rotors had slowed to a laconic pace. The second armed man did as he'd been instructed and escorted the pilot to the cafeteria.

"Welcome, Arbob," Yasmin said. "We are honored to have you here."

Khavari glared down at Yasmin; his expression was imperious. "I expected to be greeted by Hassan Nizari."

"I am Yasmin, Hassan Nizari's daughter, your excellency." She expelled a shuddering breath and lowered her eyes. Her voice broke when she said, "I am distressed to tell you that my father passed away two days ago."

Khavari's jaw dropped for an instant. After he closed his mouth, the muscles in his cheeks twitched and his eyes narrowed to slits. He turned to Javad and barked, "Are you Muntaziri?"

"Yes, your excellency," Javad said.

"So, you lied to me when I called yesterday. You told me Mr. Nizari was in a meeting and couldn't come to the phone."

"Your excellency, I told Javad to tell you that," Yasmin said.

Khavari's eyes looked as though they were on fire as he turned to look directly at her. "When I want to hear from you, woman, I will tell you. Otherwise, keep your mouth shut." He looked back at Javad and demanded, "Why did you lie to me?"

Javad stammered a few words, collected himself, and said, "Everything is in order here. We are executing every iota of Hassan Nizari and Ayatollah Khomeini's plan. We didn't want you to fear the plan would go awry without Mr. Nizari. I assure you, your excellency, everything will go as expected."

Khavari pointed a finger at Javad. "Take me to a place where I can make a private call," he said. He pulled a satellite phone from his coat pocket and marched toward the roof entrance into the fortress. Once inside the facility, Khavari wheeled on Yasmin. "Get me a glass of tea. I must call President Shabani. He will be most unhappy about this development. Very unhappy, indeed."

Yasmin and Javad led Khavari through a door to the executive offices. Khavari moved to the leather chair behind the hand-carved desk that had been designed by Yasmin's father. The desk's front panel was etched with Ayatollah Ruhollah Khomeini's image. Her blood boiled as the Tehran bureaucrat sat in the desk chair, snapped his fingers, and loudly demanded, "Where's the tea I ordered?"

She moved to the desk telephone and punched in the number to the kitchen. "Bring tea and cakes to my father's office," she ordered.

Khavari whisked his fingers at Javad and Yasmin and told them to leave the room.

"What a pompous ass," Javad whispered to Yasmin after he'd closed the door behind them.

Through clenched teeth, Yasmin said, "Did we capture the phone's frequency?"

"Yes. The engineer should have already jammed the signal."

"What about our phones?"

"Everything will be jammed. He won't be able to call out."

Yasmin sighed. A noise startled her, and she turned around as a steward from the kitchen came into the corridor. He carried a brass tray holding gold filigreed tea glasses, a tea pot, a pot of hot water, a plate of tiny sesame cakes, and a small bowl of sugar cubes.

When the man stopped before them, Yasmin told him to turn the tray over to Javad and dismissed him. After the man left the corridor, she popped the hinged top of her turquoise ring, turned her hand over, and deposited powder from the recessed space under the stone into a glass. She poured brewed tea into the glass and diluted it with water from the other pot.

"Take it to Khavari," she told Javad.

When Javad opened the office door, she heard Khavari bellow, "Something's wrong with this phone. What do I need to do to get an outside line?"

"Just dial 7, your excellency, followed by the code for Tehran and your number."

"Give me my tea."

After a minute, Javad returned to the corridor.

"What did you give him?" Javad asked. "A sleeping potion?"

"Don't be ridiculous," she answered.

Then Khavari roared, "Muntaziri, get in here."

Javad reentered the office but left the door ajar. "Yes, your excellency."

"The desk telephone doesn't work. What's wrong with this place?"

She heard Javad say, "It could be the weather. I'll check on it immediately."

"You do that."

No more than a couple of seconds passed when Yasmin heard Khavari cough. The man retched, followed by a loud groan. She quickly moved inside the room and closed the door.

"Are you feeling unwell, your excellency?" she said.

Khavari's face was beet-red, and his eyes bulged. He bent over in the desk chair, clutching his stomach. Suddenly, he released an ear-splitting scream and rolled onto the floor. His body curled into a tight question mark as brown-tinged foam bubbled from his lips and his eyes rolled back in his head.

"Is there something I can do for you, your excellency?" Yasmin asked.

Khavari's only response was another long groan that began with force and dissipated to a weak exhalation that seemed to last forever.

"Would you like some more tea?" Yasmin asked.

Khavari looked up at her. "What…did…you do?" he gasped.

"I killed you. Do you have any other questions?" She laughed and spat in his face.

He moaned and curled into an even tighter ball.

Yasmin picked up the pot from the desk, pinched closed the man's nostrils, and poured scalding water into his mouth. He screamed for a few seconds, then his body convulsed as though he'd been hit with a powerful electrical charge. After a half-minute of violent spasms, he went still.

She looked at Javad and blurted a laugh when she took in his wide-eyed, shocked expression.

"In the name of Allah, what have you done?" he exclaimed. "This will be our undoing."

"Don't be stupid, Javad. Of course, the mullahs will question Khavari's death, but when we unleash the terror on the West tomorrow, it's unlikely anyone will wonder about him." She snickered. "And while those medieval bastards in the government exult about the killing campaign, you and I will be long gone."

Javad's words came across as breathless, tainted by a whine. "Where will we be able to go? Every government, including Iran's, will be after us."

Yasmin swallowed her contempt for the man and forced herself to respond unemotionally. "Leave everything to me."

"Where will we go?" he asked plaintively.

"Javad, we'll discuss all that later. Right now, we need to concentrate on executing my father's plan."

She moved around Khavari, avoiding the puddle of water and vomit near his head. She pointed down at him and told Javad, "Have his body taken to the helicopter."

"What?"

She chuckled. "Tell the pilot that Khavari became ill and died despite the efforts of our medical people. Tell him to return to Tehran."

Javad looked incredulous. "The pilot will never believe that story. The first thing he'll do is contact Shabani on his radio."

She smiled. "Do you trust me?"

Javad didn't immediately respond. For a long moment, uncertainty showed on his face. Finally, he nodded.

She patted his arm. "Good, Javad. Now, get the body out of here and send the pilot on his way."

CHAPTER 38

The intelligence the CIA team had gathered from Abdel bin Hakim had proved to be an information treasure trove. In the end, the trigger that caused the Saudi to spew information was merely the threat of turning him over to the Lithuanian interrogation team. The CIA hadn't had to negotiate a plea deal with him afterall.

Zach Grabowsky and Angelina Borden, along with a half-dozen other CIA team members, had already viewed the video recording of the bin Hakim interrogation sessions eight times. There was no disagreement about the Saudi's veracity. In addition to Iranian culpability in support of the Asasiyun, bin Hakim had disclosed a multi-billion dollar black market scheme that facilitated Iran's selling crude oil through the Russians. That scheme funneled much needed cash into the regime, which used much of those proceeds to support terrorist activities around the world.

But what sent the CIA team members' heart rates into the stratosphere were bin Hakim's comments about the Asasiyun.

"Unbelievable," Zach muttered. "They've operated since shortly after the overthrow of the Pahlavi Shah. Since Khomeini took over."

"That surprises you?" Angelina said.

"What surprises me is that we've had no inkling of the Asasiyun until just recently."

Angelina frowned. "We can't know everything that's going on."

"That's because the politicians have handcuffed us so badly

that—"

Angelina cut him off. "Let's focus on where the *Asasiyun*'s operating base is. If we can locate its headquarters, we might be able to hack its system."

"Or blow the place off the map," Zach said.

Before Angelina could respond, and just as Seth Bridewell entered the ops center, a young woman seated at a computer console shouted, "Traffic coming in from NSA."

Seth moved to the woman's station and looked over her shoulder at her computer screen. The message showed latitude and longitude coordinates, the identification code of an NRO satellite, and the time the satellite passed over the coordinates. He read the message text as the console operator placed her cursor on the coordinates, which simultaneously brought up a map on her computer and on a big-screen television mounted on the front wall. After he finished reading the text, he looked up at the screen and studied the satellite image of a mountainous, forested area. The console operator brought up detail on the big-screen, which identified the area as *Shahroud Abr* Forest. The program automatically translated the forest's name into English and showed that translation on the screen: Cloud Forest. She superimposed a topographical map on the satellite map and transformed the area on the screen to a blueprint that showed cities, province boundaries, major roads and rail lines. The map showed that the coordinates were in the north part of Iran's Semnan Province, almost on the border of Golestan Province.

"Reduce the scale," Seth ordered.

The image that the NRO satellite had captured showed the burning wreck of what appeared to be a helicopter about twenty miles outside the city of Shahrud.

"Back up the video," Seth said.

Frenetic images ran across the screen as the video reversed. When a bright light bloomed on the screen, Seth told the operator to stop. "Run it forward," he said.

Except for the *click-click-click* of the woman's fingertips on her keyboard, the ops center had gone dead silent. The satellite video scrolled forward and, after a few seconds, showed the dark image of a helicopter against the backdrop of a blackish-green forest. Then, the chopper exploded in an orange fireball and dropped from the sky, trailing black smoke.

"Holy shit," Zach exclaimed.

"Play it again," Seth said.

After the controller replayed the explosion, Seth asked the people in the room, "Anyone see a projectile hit the aircraft?"

His question was answered with shakes of heads and "No, sirs."

"Looks like the helicopter just exploded," he said.

One analyst asked, "Was the satellite slaved to those coordinates for some reason, or was it just coincidence that it captured that explosion?"

"Pull up that message from the NSA," Seth said.

When the message showed on the big-screen, the atmosphere in the room became almost funereal as the people there read it: *Our voice recognition system picked up the voices of Iran's President, Hassan Shabani, and his executive assistant, Jalil Khavari, on a telephone conversation. They discussed a trip that Khavari was taking. We later satellite-tracked Khavari to the helicopter and followed the aircraft to a location in the Cloud Forest. He was there for fifty-seven minutes before the helicopter took off again. The pilot transmitted the following message via radio: 'Jalil Khavari has died suddenly. I am returning to base with his body. Something is very curious about—' That's when the aircraft exploded and we lost the signal.*

Angelina Borden said, "What was Khavari doing at that place in the Cloud Forest?"

"The more pertinent question might be, what *is* that place in the Cloud Forest?" Zach said.

CHAPTER 39

Liz had noticed that Bob had been on edge for the last hour. At first, she thought he was thinking about the attacks against him and Robbie. But she now sensed there was something else going on.

While on the water taxi trip that morning from their hotel to the San Marco Plaza stop, she took his hand and asked, "What's going on?"

"Nothin."

She twisted slightly in her seat and glared at him. "I'm glad we're alone because I wouldn't want to embarrass you by telling you that you're full of it."

Bob met her gaze and smiled. "You read me like a book, don't you?"

"Does that surprise you?"

He leaned toward her and tried to kiss her cheek, but she pulled back, released his hand, and said, "Don't you dare ignore me or change the subject. There's something going on and I want to know what it is."

He stared down at his clenched hands as though deciding how to respond, then said, "If you were the head of a terrorist group that had targeted Western leaders and learned that hundreds of military, intelligence, diplomatic, and business leaders from NATO countries were planning to congregate in Venice, what would you do?"

"I sure as hell wouldn't ignore it," Liz said. "In fact, I would see an attack against that group as my *pièce de résistance.*"

"That's what has me worried."

Liz thought about reminding him that he was retired and that security people from all over the West would surely have considered the same thing. But she swept that aside and thought about how many times she had accused Bob of being paranoid, only to discover that it wasn't paranoia but experience and instinct that more often than not guided his thinking and actions.

"You really think those monsters would try something here in Venice?"

"Why not? From their point of view, Venice is an ideal target. Besides the gathering of Western leaders, this city is a terrorist's dream. It's surrounded by water. A solitary boat, or several boats for that matter, could deposit armed fighters at numerous locations in and around Venice. They could attack delegates to the conference in their hotels, at restaurants, or even at the Carnevale venue."

"But how would they get near any of those places?" Liz said. "Think about the security that will be in place wherever the delegates go."

"In the cases I'm aware of, the killers have been effective because, for the most part, they were sleeper agents who had been accepted as trusted friends and confidants of their targets. They could very well walk into any place where delegates gather and take out dozens or more people."

"How?" Liz asked.

Bob rubbed his chin. "I've thought about that for hours. It would be difficult to smuggle weapons into the venue because they'll surely have metal detectors installed. It will be easier at hotels and restaurants, but I don't think they'll go after people in those places. I think they'll want to go for the biggest bang possible."

"Meaning?"

"My gut tells me they'll hit the location where they can bring down the most targets at once. That would mean the carnival ball attended by the NATO delegates."

"But you said there would be metal detectors there."

"Right. But metal detectors won't pick up explosives like C-4, unless they're packed in a pipe bomb, for instance. And if an explosive isn't paired with a detonator and some sort of shrapnel, it won't do maximum damage."

"What if they smuggled in explosive devices beforehand?"

Bob gave Liz a surprised look. "You have a sinister mind, my dear."

She showed him a grim expression. "That's from being married to you for five decades. What are the likely ways that an attack would occur?"

Bob went silent for several seconds. Then he said, "First, the terrorists could be one or more armed security personnel who are beyond suspicion. They could open fire and murder dozens of people. But I don't see that happening because relatively few people would be killed before the assassin or assassins would be taken down by other security people. I mean, why infiltrate a massive venue just to murder a small number of people?"

"That's a bit cold," Liz said.

Bob held up a finger, signalling her to hold off. "Second, one of the security people with early access to the venue could plant explosives that, when detonated, would be devastating. But the building, grounds, and underwater building supports will surely be inspected by multiple security teams, including the U.S. Secret Service, and they would most likely discover planted explosives."

"What about an air assault?"

"I thought about that, as well. I called Giovanni Ventimiglia. He told me there will be a 'no fly zone' in a thirty-mile radius from the center of Venice during the ball."

The water taxi docked and Liz and Bob climbed out onto the ramp and walked to the quay. They moved toward the plaza when a thought came to Liz. She grabbed Bob's coat sleeve and said, "What if an airplane violates the 'no fly zone'?"

"Italian Air Force jets will be in the air just outside the thirty-mile limit and will have orders to take down any plane that approaches the boundary."

"What if an air force jet pilot is with the Asasiyun?"

"That's a great question. But I suspect all the pilots on duty will be native-born and will have been carefully vetted. The Asasiyun killers have mostly been naturalized citizens who migrated from

Middle Eastern countries. Sure, one pilot could be a bad guy, but it's not likely."

"How else would an attack happen?" Liz said.

"Oh God, Liz, there are so many possible ways. They could poison the food or drink, set fire to the building, machine gun the attendees as they leave—just to mention a few. But the security people will hopefully take measures that will prevent those things from happening."

"My head hurts," Liz said.

"Welcome to my world."

"So that's why you've been out of sorts?"

"Partially."

"What else?"

They were now in the center of San Marco Plaza. Bob took her arm and turned her to face him. "You know that premonition you had last night about something happening to Robbie?"

"Yes, and I was right, wasn't I?"

Bob nodded. "I think your premonition abilities are contagious. I've got a really bad feeling."

CHAPTER 40

It was a simple matter for Carlo Severino to convince his boss, Deputy Defense Minister Andreotti, that he should be an advance team member in Venice. Twenty-four hours ago, he'd taken a high-speed train to Venice and traveled by hydrofoil sixty-five miles east across the Adriatic to a cove near the south end of Piran, Slovenia, where two 500-Class patrol boats were hidden under canvas camouflage covers. Screening the two crafts was a fifty-foot fishing trawler crewed by three *Asasiyun* operatives. Also on board the trawler was an *Asasiyun* team of four men and two women. These six individuals were all naturalized Italian citizens who had each been in Italy for at least ten years. One woman was an officer with the Carabinieri, one man and the other woman were with the Guardia Costiera—the Italian Coast Guard, and the remaining men held various professional positions. All were graduates of the training camp in the Cloud Forest and experts in small unit combat tactics. The two Coast Guard officers were intimately familiar with the 500-Class patrol boats, ten of which had been donated by Italy to Libya a few years ago to enhance the North African country's ability to manage its migrant crisis. With funding and technical assistance from Iran's Revolutionary Guards Corps, two patrol boats had been retrofitted with two launch canisters for Iranian Nasr-1 cruise missiles on their sterns. The missiles had a range of twenty-two miles, and used a television guidance system. The boats had been repainted with Italian insignia and colors.

Severino went over the plan with the team and fielded their questions.

The female Coast Guard officer asked, "What should we do if we're challenged by an Italian Coast Guard boat?"

"Use the call sign I gave you."

"It's not authentic," the woman said. "They'll know we're not legitimate."

Severino scoffed. "It's the Italian Coast Guard. If you respond to a challenge with attitude, they'll never think about double-checking your credentials."

The woman scowled at Severino. "And what if they try to board us?"

"Then blow them out of the water." He jabbed a finger at the woman. "You can't allow anything or anyone to prevent the mission's success." After he made eye contact with each of them, Severino said, "Get some rest. You'll leave here at 2 a.m. on Saturday and will sail to a location twenty miles from Venice. There, you'll input the target coordinates and fire the missiles."

One man who was a winemaker in Tuscany chimed in, "You didn't mention what we should do after we fire the missiles."

"As soon as the missiles are launched, you'll sail east toward Rijeka, Croatia, in Kvarner Bay. The fishing boat we're now on will rendezvous with you. You'll board the fishing boat after you scuttle the two patrol boats. One of our agents will meet you in Rijeka and take you to an airstrip. A plane will transport you to Iran." Severino smiled at the team members and spread his arms, as though to embrace the lot of them. "You will be heroes in the mother country."

Michael had considered skipping the meeting with the people from the University of North Carolina. He'd been up since 4 a.m. and had a series of meetings before he would catch his flight to Italy. But he shook off the impulse to tell Major Darby to cover for him with the university group, and blew out an exasperated breath. *Dad always said that shirking responsibility was a trait of the weak and characterless.*

"Thanks, Dad," he muttered.

Ron Darby said, "What was that, sir?"

Michael cleared his throat and made a dismissive hand gesture. "Nothing," he said. "Let's go to the auditorium and do our dog and pony show."

"The kids will love you, General."

Michael chuckled. "Thanks, Ron. I'll keep that in mind as I rush around to make meetings."

Darby handed a file folder to Michael with prepared remarks for him to make to the audience. He said, "If you greet them and hand out the challenge coins"—he shook the box in his hand—"I'll step in after that so you can leave for your next meeting."

Michael smiled at Darby. "Thanks, Ron."

They moved to the auditorium where Michael walked behind a microphone set up between the stage and front row of seats.

"I'm General Michael Danforth, Commander of the U.S. Joint Special Operations Command. Welcome to Fort Bragg, the home of U.S. Special Forces and the 82nd and 101st Airborne Divisions. I know most of you are Army R.O.T.C. cadets at the University of North Carolina. For those of you who are already in the Advanced Corps and will be commissioned after you graduate, I want to thank you for your commitment to serve your country. Those of you who are considering continuing in the R.O.T.C. program in your junior and senior years, I encourage you to talk to your classmates who have already made that decision. I can't imagine a more rewarding career than being an Army officer.

"Before I leave you with Major Darby, who will give you a tour of our headquarters, we have a gift for each of you. Please come forward."

Michael moved to the microphone and Major Darby came over and stood to his left. As the audience members walked down the center aisle to the front, Darby handed Michael a JSOC challenge coin to give to the first student.

Barry Murad swiped his parka sleeve across his forehead. The sleeve came away soaked with perspiration. He'd gone over in his mind a dozen times what he was about to do. He hoped he'd be able to follow his orders. As the others marched down the center aisle toward the general, he forced a smile. Now the only one in the audience still seated, and about to stand, an errant thought slithered into his brain. He had a stomach-clenching, bowel-loosening sensation. The satellite telephone! He was supposed to destroy it! He'd left it in his overnight bag.

His legs wobbled as he stood. He felt light-headed. He removed his parka, placed it on the seat to his right, and trailed the group, which shuffled forward toward the general. His trembling fingers were slick with sweat and his body shook as though he'd suddenly been afflicted with palsy. He took a deep breath and let it out slowly, but the trembling continued and now his eyes had lost focus. The heads of those in front of him wavered as though they were holograms. The line stopped and Barry bumped into the boy in front of him.

"What's your problem, asshole?" the kid rasped.

"S-sorry," Barry said.

He wiped his hands on his pants and fumbled with the button on the left cuff of his shirt. As the line creeped forward, he tried again to unbutton the cuff. He looked up and saw there were only five people between him and his target. Sweat seemed to drop from every pore; his underarms were soaked. His shirt felt drenched and the sour odor of his own body assailed him. Again, he tried to open the shirt cuff, and again he failed. Desperate now, he grasped the button and ripped it off. It slipped through his fingers and shot away. The noise it made when it clattered on the floor under the seats to his left sounded to him like a chunk of hail shattering on a tin roof. He looked up and was surprised that no one seemed to have even noticed the noise.

There were now only two people between him and the general. He moved closer to the student in front of him and used him as a screen. He slipped his right hand in the left sleeve of his shirt, grasped the knife hilt, and moved it an inch from the scabbard.

There was now only one person between him and the general. He swallowed hard, prepared to shout the mantra they'd all chanted a thousand times at the training center: *Long live the* Asasiyun. But someone said something to him. At first, the voice seemed disembodied, then Barry realized it was the sergeant who had greeted them the day before. The man stood beside the last step.

"What?" Murad said, his voice high and squeaky.

"Are you all right?" the sergeant said. "You look ill."

The boy in front of Murad moved away. There was five feet of space between him and the general. The sergeant had lightly grasped Murad's right bicep and was asking him something again, but the words scattered like windblown leaves. He shook off the sergeant's hand, yanked the knife from its scabbard, and leaped forward. In the next second, he went into sensory overload: the general's squint-eyed look; the roar that came from the sergeant who was now behind him; the horrified expression on the face of the officer to the general's left; the sound that came from his own throat.

He struck at the general but wasn't certain his thrust had hit home. He pulled his arm back to strike again but was slammed to the floor with such force that he lost his hold on the knife. The air exploded from his lungs and his body felt as though his skeleton had turned to sawdust.

The activity around him seemed frenetic, in a slow-motion sort of way. A drone-like noise filled the room, but the only sounds perfectly clear to Murad were the gasps and hoarse moans emanating from his own chest and throat.

Michael felt as though he'd fallen into a freezing-cold lake. He couldn't seem to breathe, and his body had gone rigid. He'd seen the knife and had parried with his left hand and swept his right arm under the kid's raised left arm. He'd thrown his assailant to the floor and crashed on top of him. Initially, he thought the fall had caused his body to react as it had. But he felt a slick wetness on his chest. He rolled off the kid and thought, *I'll be damned*, when he looked down and saw the handle of a knife protruding from the upper left side of his chest.

He looked up and saw concern in Darby's expression. His aide knelt by him and told him not to move. He tried to tell Darby that he was fine, but his mouth wouldn't cooperate. From the corner of his eye he saw a soldier roll the kid who'd attacked him onto his stomach and pin his arms behind his back. Michael tried unsuccessfully to take in a deep breath. The effort only made the pain in his chest worse.

Darby was saying something to him, but Michael wasn't processing the words. He became only half-aware that he was being moved onto a gurney.

CHAPTER 41

Zach Grabowsky and Angelina Borden had eaten only junk food for the past thirty-six hours and hadn't slept in twenty-four. It was late, and they knew they had many more hours of work ahead. They'd initiated a "dictionary attack" against the Shirazi brothers' computers and cell phones, using "brute-force" password cracking software, which used eight million combinations of letters and words per second to crack a password.

Zach paced while he stared at his computer and listened to the hard drive hum as the cracking software seemed to agonize over its mission. After hours of processing, the software had still not discovered the password.

"Dammit!" Zach shouted.

"Will you please sit down?" Angelina said.

"Why the hell do we need the Shirazis' password? Bin Hakim already told us everything we need to know to go after the Iranians."

Angelina swiveled in her chair and looked at Zach. "You know better than that. Bin Hakim is a sleaze. If we don't have corroborating evidence, we'll be accused of going off half-cocked."

"Who cares?"

Angelina shook her head and turned back to her computer.

The six-person Asasiyun team removed the canvas covers from the two 500-Class patrol boats. After moving the covers to the fishing boat they'd been on, they lowered blue-colored panels over the boats' gunwales to hide the Italian Coast Guard insignia and placed fishing poles in brackets affixed to the sterns. They performed a quick check of the boats, turned on the engines, and sailed west from the cove. One boat followed a straight line toward Venice, while the other took a northwest heading for ten miles before turning toward the city.

The two Coast Guard officers inputted identical GPS coordinates into the missile guidance systems. They reminded the other crew members to have their AK-47 weapons ready in case a legitimate Coast Guard vessel approached them.

Once the team leaders were satisfied that their teams were prepared, they followed leisurely courses, which would eventually place them twenty miles from Venice.

Major Ronald Darby had sent a car to General Danforth's Fayetteville quarters to pick up the general's wife, Miriana. He would meet her at the Womack Army Medical Center on Fort Bragg and explain what had happened.

Darby had always been impressed with Miriana. Besides being a stunning beauty who, at fifty or so years of age, seemed at least ten years younger, she was the perfect Army wife. She was stoic and calm in any circumstance. Even when her husband was on dangerous assignments, she came across as though she were unaffected—confident and unafraid.

As he stood in the waiting room to meet Miriana, he hoped she would be just as strong as she usually was. He spotted the staff car as it pulled up outside the hospital. He fast-walked to the entrance and intercepted her as she stepped from the vehicle.

Miriana met his gaze, her eyes lasering into his, and said, "How bad is it?"

Darby spread his arms and shook his head. "We don't know yet." He turned toward the door and said, "Let's go to the surgical waiting area. They might be able to tell us something there."

Miriana followed Darby through the main waiting area, along a circuitous hallway, to the surgery section. Darby approached a counter and introduced Miriana to a female nurse seated there.

Without being prompted, the nurse stood and said, "Mrs. Danforth, the general's in surgery. All I know is that he has a punctured lung. There was some internal bleeding. The surgeon has inserted a tube into the lung to inflate it."

"You said there was internal bleeding," Miriana said. "What does that mean?"

"Of course, there would be internal bleeding with this sort of injury. But if the pericardium wasn't hit, it shouldn't be a problem."

"Um," Miriana said, followed by a long sigh.

"If you'll give me your cell phone number, ma'am, I'll call you the moment I have more information."

Miriana gave the woman her number, thanked her, and turned on Darby. "Let's go to the cafeteria," she said. "I want to know exactly what happened." Her voice broke as she added, "I have to call Robbie and Michael's parents."

As they walked down the hall toward the cafeteria, two men dressed in camouflage fatigues approached them. Each carried a holstered pistol and an automatic rifle. Darby greeted them, introduced them to Miriana, and told her, "The last thing the general told me before he was taken into surgery was to put you under guard and to move you onto the base. These men are members of a Lone Wolf team stationed here at Bragg. They'll stay with you until this thing is…resolved."

Miriana's eyes widened for a second. "I guess you'd better explain what *this thing* is."

CHAPTER 42

Most of what Miriana knew about the Asasiyun, she'd learned from watching television news and reading Internet postings. Michael had filled in some blanks over the past week. But the fact that her father-in-law, her son, and now her husband had been targeted by the group completely bewildered her. Her throat felt tight and the anger building inside her made her chest feel as though it was encased in a metal band. She cleared her throat and took a drink of water while she waited for her son to return her call. Twenty minutes had passed before his call came in.

"Hey, Mom, you just caught me on my way out the door. What's—"

"It's your father, Robbie. He was stabbed and is in the base hospital." Her voice broke momentarily as she tried to continue. She coughed. "He's in surgery. Hopefully, I'll know more soon."

Robbie didn't immediately respond. Finally, he said, "I'll get there as soon as possible, Mom. I'll have to—"

"No, I don't want you to leave there. It's obvious that you, your father, and grandfather are all targets of this *Asasiyun* group. I don't want you traveling."

After another pause, Robbie said, "You can't be alone right now." Before she could object, he added, "I'll ask the commandant if he can arrange transportation."

Miriana thought, *I'll call the commandant and insist he doesn't allow Robbie to leave the West Point campus.* "Okay, Robbie. I'll call you as soon as I know more about your father."

Robbie took calming breaths as he tried to deal with the mix of emotions that boiled inside him. His worry about his father and being so many miles away made him want to scream. He was concerned for his mother, too. He knew how strong his parent's relationship was and how much they depended on one another. The thought that his father's injuries might be fatal brought tears to his eyes. Layered on top of these emotions was a bone-chilling anger. What made his anger so torturous was the fact that there was no available physical target to release it on.

After her phone call to Robbie, Miriana called Bob and Liz. Bob picked up on the first ring. "Hello, Miriana."

Miriana muttered something that sounded unintelligible to her. She tried to clear her throat, with limited success. Her voice rasped, "There's been an attack. It's Michael."

"What happened?" Bob asked.

Miriana didn't want to break down and did her best to control her voice, but her words came out harsh and dry. She cleared her throat as she heard her mother-in-law in the background ask, "What's wrong?"

Finally, in stuttering speech, Miriana related what had happened to Michael.

Bob had put his cell on speaker, so Miriana heard Liz clearly say, "We'll catch the first flight we can to North Carolina."

Miriana cleared her throat again and, in a strained voice, said, "Call me when you know your arrival time."

"Of course, honey," Liz said. "Does Robbie know?"

"I already called him. But I don't want him to leave West Point right now. He's safer there than here."

Robbie opened the front door of the commandant's residence and crossed the porch to the sidewalk where two armed soldiers waited. He had just reached the cement when Samantha Meek burst from the residence and called, "Weren't you going to wait for me?"

Robbie stopped and turned, gave Samantha a wan smile, and mumbled, "I need to go to the commandant's office."

Samantha hurried to Robbie's side and kept pace with him as he strode toward Washington Hall on Thayer Road. "What's going on?" she asked.

Robbie stopped again and turned to face her. "My father is in the hospital. He was stabbed by someone who was probably a member of the Asasiyun."

"Oh my God, Robbie," she said. "I'm so sorry."

"Thanks, Sam." As he began walking again, he said, "I don't get it. First my grandfather, then me, and now my father. If these people can get to my father and me on military bases, we must be dealing with something completely different than we've seen before. You need to keep alert. There could be another assassin here at the Point."

She tipped her head at the armed soldiers trailing them. "That's why we have our own bodyguards."

"They might not be enough against a determined enemy."

She nodded, tapped his arm, and stepped to the curb to cross the street. "Let me know about your father."

"I will."

One soldier branched off with Samantha, waiting beside her as a Jeep approached. Robbie and the second soldier continued toward Thayer Road. They were ten yards away from Samantha and her guard when the Jeep suddenly veered, jumped the curb, and sped toward them. Robbie's guard pushed him away, sending him sprawling onto the grass beside the sidewalk. The guard reached for the .45 caliber pistol on his hip. He had barely cleared the weapon from its holster when the Jeep thudded into him, spiraling the man into the air and out onto the middle of the street.

As Robbie scrambled to his feet, he saw the vehicle race toward Samantha and the other soldier, who grabbed Samantha and rolled with her out of the vehicle's path. The Jeep blew past them, dropped back onto the road, skidded to a stop, and began to turn around.

Robbie glanced at the injured soldier. The man lay in the street and wasn't moving. He spotted the man's pistol lying beside him. As the Jeep had almost completed its U-turn, Robbie rushed to the road, snatched up the weapon, disengaged the safety, and faced the charging vehicle. He dropped into a half-crouch and aimed the .45 at the Jeep's driver. He fired until the slide on the .45 locked backward. Just before ramming him, the Jeep diverted to Robbie's right, leaped the far curb, and crashed into an oak tree.

The soldier with Samantha ran over to Robbie, took the pistol from his hand, and shouted at Samantha to call the MPs and have them send an ambulance. Then he ran to the wrecked Jeep and carefully approached the driver's side. Robbie followed him and saw the driver hanging face-up halfway outside the open vehicle door. Despite the man's gaping mouth, open-eyed blank stare, and the hole in his forehead, Robbie recognized him. *What the hell?* He thought. *It's Jim Ross.*

"You know this guy?" the soldier asked.

"Yeah. He's a third-year cadet."

"Sonofabitch," the soldier exclaimed.

CHAPTER 43

Brigadier General Stevens arrived at the incident site just as the ambulance drove away with the injured soldier. A half-dozen MP vehicles blocked both ends of the street and a Criminal Investigation Division team was inspecting the ruined Jeep and the dead driver.

Stevens spotted Danforth and Meek, along with one of the soldiers he'd assigned to protect them. He approached a Chief Warrant Officer who headed up the CID team and asked, "What's the injured man's condition?"

"The paramedics told me he has two broken legs, sir. They think his pelvis is fractured, as well. He was conscious when they transported him, but in severe pain. They administered morphine."

"Chief, when you finish up here, come to my office. I want a briefing as soon as you can. This thing has international implications, and I'm sure the FBI, CIA, and the White House will want to be brought up-to-date."

"Yes, sir."

"Who was driving the Jeep?"

"The man had no ID on him, sir. But Cadet Danforth told me he's a third-year cadet named James Ross."

Stevens was momentarily stunned. He knew Ross. The young man was a standout on the academy soccer team, and in the top five percent of his class academically.

"How did this go down?"

The CID captain said, "All we know now is what the soldier and the two cadets told us. They were walking up the sidewalk over there when the Jeep jumped the curb and charged them. The two soldiers, Matson and Foles, pushed the cadets out of the way. The injured soldier, Foles, unholstered his pistol, but was struck by the Jeep before he could fire it. The Jeep went past them, stopped, and did a U-turn. As Ross drove back at them, Danforth ran over to Foles, picked up his pistol, and fired at Ross."

Stevens looked over at Danforth and slowly shook his head. *Amazing.*

The captain grimaced. "Danforth emptied the full clip. He hit Ross four times. Two others went through the windshield and exited the rear Jeep canopy. Wherever the other two rounds went, I just thank God there was no one on the street behind the vehicle." Then the warrant officer added, "The two soldiers are real heroes. They prevented both Danforth and Meek from being struck by the Jeep. And if Danforth hadn't had the presence of mind to grab Foles' pistol, who knows what the outcome would have been?"

"Okay, Chief. I'll leave you to your duties."

Stevens walked over to Danforth, Meek, and the soldier named Matson. The three saluted Stevens, who returned their salute and told them to stand at ease.

"You okay?" Stevens said.

The three replied in unison: "Yes, sir."

The general nodded. He noticed that the three young people all had wide-eyed stares and were having difficulty standing still. *Adrenaline overload*, Stevens thought. He looked back toward his residence. "How about we all go to my place?"

Danforth and Meek were temporarily living in the general's residence, but Matson had never gotten closer to the general's quarters than the front sidewalk. His already wide eyes seemed to bulge.

Stevens noticed the young man's discomfort. "I would be honored to have you in my home, Sergeant. It's not often I have the pleasure of welcoming real heroes there."

Matson's mocha-colored complexion darkened. He seemed nonplussed, but finally said, "Yes, sir, but I'd really like to go to the hospital and check on Foles." Tears came to Matson's eyes. He wiped them away with his fatigue shirtsleeve and said, "We're good buddies, General."

Stevens placed a hand on Matson's arm, and met his gaze. "Let's go to my place, sit down for a little while, and then you and I will go together to see how Sergeant Foles is doing."

Matson gave Stevens a glowing smile. "I'd like that, sir."

As soon as Raymond Gallegos learned about the attack on Michael Danforth, he called the Fort Bragg Base Commander and told him he wanted General Danforth's attacker sequestered in a cell where he could communicate with no one. He reminded the man to check for a poison pill implant in the attacker's mouth, and told him, "I don't want him questioned by anyone. I'm sending an interrogation team to your location."

Raymond dispatched a CIA interrogation team—Patrick Kinsella and Linda Swatek—to Fort Bragg on a Gulfstream Executive Jet. While on the flight to Fort Bragg, the two agents studied a profile the CIA had prepared on Barry Murad. Although the file didn't contain much information, they did learn he was only eighteen years old, was a world-class mathematician, and had been sponsored by a couple in North Carolina when he'd immigrated to the United States two years earlier. The report noted that another interrogation team had been sent to interview that couple.

They were met by the base commander's aide and driven to the Fort Bragg Prison. At the prison, the two CIA agents exited the vehicle and were met by an MP who escorted them to a block of six cells. A second MP sat on a chair facing the only occupied cell. He stood as the CIA team approached him. The agents stopped and stared at the prisoner, whose hands were cuffed behind his back; a black hood covered his head and shoulders. Leg shackles bound his ankles.

Kinsella said to the first MP, "You have the key?"

"Yes, sir." The MP handed it over.

Swatek told the MPs to take the prisoner to an interrogation room. They watched the two men take Murad from the cell and frog-march him down the corridor, through a security door, to a room with a one-way window; a small metal table and four metal chairs were bolted to the floor. A ceiling fixture shone blindingly bright light on one of the chairs. The room was equipped with an audio/visual recorder that could broadcast an interrogation to anywhere in the world.

The MPs placed Murad on the chair under the flood light and secured the leg shackles to a metal ring embedded in the concrete floor.

"Take off the hood," Swatek ordered, "then leave us."

One MP removed the hood before the two of them left.

The prisoner bent his head and closed his eyes against the glare. He groaned and tried to shift his body to the side, but the manacles allowed him only limited movement.

Kinsella studied Barry Murad's face. His eyes were red and puffy, and there were dark circles under them. He had expected him to have the look of a stone-cold killer but was surprised that he looked so young and innocent—so distraught and afraid. He reminded himself to not be influenced by the kid's appearance. Afterall, he'd tried to murder a senior Army officer. Kinsella knew that he and Swatek were now an integral part of a huge investigation with massive implications. Assassins had already murdered twenty-two people. They'd been briefed about the Asasiyun and the belief that hundreds more might be targeted by the group. Barry Murad might be the key to identifying the terrorist group's master plan.

He drummed his fingers on the table, which caused Murad to squint at him.

"You failed, Barry," he told him. "General Danforth is alive." He let that sink in for a moment. "He'll soon be released from the hospital." Another pause. "I guess, in a sense, you lucked out. Instead of the death penalty, you'll only spend twenty-five years in a federal penitentiary." Kinsella chuckled. "You'll be very popular among the men at that prison."

The boy's eyes widened for an instant but blinked shut against the light.

"You have a chance to reduce your sentence if you talk to us."

Murad's eyes opened again. They were doe-like. Tears leaked onto his cheeks. He opened his mouth as though to speak, but all that came out was a rasp. He tried to clear his throat, but still could not form intelligible words.

Swatek stood and opened the room's door. She told the MP outside to bring water for the prisoner. She waited until he returned, thanked him, and shut the door. She uncapped the plastic bottle and placed the opening against the boy's mouth. He drank greedily, ignoring the water that dribbled over his chin and onto his shirt. He pulled his head back after he'd consumed a third of the bottle and coughed.

Swatek sat. She and Kinsella stared at Murad and watched his Adam's apple bob and his eyes blink several times. After a few seconds, he dissolved into soul-wrenching sobs.

Kinsella said, "Why'd you do it, Barry?"

The boy cleared his throat again. He looked down at his hands. "I didn't want to do it. I just wanted to study mathematics." He swallowed hard. "I didn't have a choice. They told me they would kill my parents if I failed."

He broke down again, tears flowing as though a dam had broken. In a squeaky voice, he said, "My poor *baba* and *mader*. They will die because of me."

Kinsella saw an opening and went through it. "Where are your parents?"

"In Dhi Qar, in southern Iraq."

"Here's what we're going to do for you, Barry. You tell us everything you know about the Asasiyun and we'll try to protect your parents."

A hopeful strain now in his voice, Murad said, "How can you possibly protect them?"

"We have military units in Iraq that we can send to bring them out of the country."

"You'll bring them here to the United States?"

Kinsella shrugged. "Depends on what you tell us, Barry."

"Can you turn off the light?"

CHAPTER 44

The recording of Barry Murad's interrogation was transmitted to CIA Headquarters, where a standing-room-only crowd observed the one-hour session. Attendees included Frank Reynolds, Raymond Gallegos, Seth Bridewell, and a twenty-person team from Bridewell's Directorate of Digital Innovation. One of Seth's team members stood at a whiteboard while the interrogation was conducted and wrote down key "finds."

At the end of the interrogation, Seth mounted the dais, pointed at the whiteboard, and said, "What should be added to the list there?"

Zach Grabowsky announced in his foghorn voice, "We now have confirmation that this is an Iran-funded operation. Murad validated what we heard earlier from bin Hakim. Although the training center site was kept secret, even from the students there, Murad's information indicates it may be in Semnan or Golestan Province. He told us that some day-workers spoke with an accent from that region."

"Good observations, Zach," Seth said.

Raymond said, "Remember that midair explosion the NRO satellite recorded? That occurred in Semnan Province? We've had suspicions about the fortress sitting in the Cloud Forest in that particular province."

Frank said, "To lend credibility to that location, the last NRO satellite pass, just an hour ago, showed an enormous cluster of heat signatures emanating from that fortress. The place is an underground hive of activity. Also, the satellite detected a large volume of electronic communications activity."

"Was any of it recorded?" Tanya asked.

"Unfortunately, no. It was all encrypted."

"Okay," Tanya said, "is there any reason to reject the fortress as the Asasiyun training site? Any other sites we should be looking at?"

"Just to play devil's advocate," Raymond said, "the terrain that Murad described could be any number of locales in the Caucasus. But we might as well see what we can find out about that fortress."

"What about Murad's comment about the number of Asasiyun agents?" Frank asked.

Seth said, "From our analyses based on the intel we gathered earlier, we'd extrapolated the number of possible assassination targets to be in the thousands. But Murad told us that rumors abounded at the training site about one thousand people being targeted by an equal number of assassins. He heard the phrase 'The Glorious One Thousand' spoken on several occasions. He assumed that meant there were one thousand assassins." He paused a second. "Which means there are an equal number of people targeted for assassination."

"Assuming Murad told the truth and that the rumors he heard were even close to being correct," Frank said.

"Anyone doubt that Murad told the truth?" Seth asked.

Frank said, "Both interrogators, Swatek and Kinsella, believe he was one hundred percent candid. I'm inclined to agree with them."

"We've got more than we've ever had before regarding this investigation," Seth told the audience. "I suggest all department heads get with their people and summarize our conclusions and recommendations. If you'll send them to Gary"—he pointed at his employee at the whiteboard—"by no later than 1700 hours today, we'll collate all your reports into a final draft that will be sent to the DCI." He waited a few seconds and asked, "Anything else?" When no one responded, he announced, "Good work, folks. Let's get on this. You all know what's at stake."

After the others, except for Frank and Raymond, left the room, Seth stepped down from the dais to the first row of theater seats and collapsed into one.

"You okay?" Raymond said.

Seth waved a hand in response, as though to say, "I'm fine." He tried to put on a confident expression but, between worry and fatigue, he suspected he'd failed in the effort. He stood with obvious effort and looked at the two men. He knew the continuation of all their careers at the Company could be in jeopardy if they didn't pull a rabbit out of a hat…and damn quickly. It was bad enough the CIA hadn't come up with any meaningful intel about the Asasiyun before the killings began, but they also had no viable plan to put a stop to the murders. He thought, *Going to POTUS and recommending a military strike against Iran would probably not go over well and might do nothing to stop the assassinations.*

"Any other thoughts?" Seth asked.

"To state the obvious," Frank said, "these assassinations have already had a debilitating effect on Western countries, including our own. The stock and bond markets are in the tank and consumer spending is on a downward spiral. Confidence in our political leadership is at an all-time low. The only bright spots are the personal protection and arms industries." He laughed but there was no humor behind it. "Every politician is trying to blame the people on the other side of the aisle. They're all running scared about the next election."

Seth blurted a laugh. "Cleaning house in the U.S. Congress might be a good thing."

Raymond ignored Seth's comment. "Let's concentrate on tactical and intel matters. The Joint Chiefs are already pushing for a massive military operation against Iran. Whether you agree or not, that's not our business. Neither are the political implications. We need to figure out how to stop the assassinations."

"Our people are busting their asses on just that," Frank said. "I won't promise you they'll figure it out, but I will tell you we have the best and brightest working on it."

Raymond sighed. "I know, Frank," he said. After a couple of seconds, he added, "Just before coming in here, I was advised there was another attempt on Robbie Danforth's life. At first, it made no sense to me. I mean, why would the Asasiyun send two killers after a kid? His grandfather and father being targeted, I get. Even with Robbie's role in Syria last year, his being attacked once, let alone twice, just doesn't compute. Targeting him seems personal."

There was silence in the room for a good thirty seconds before Frank exclaimed, "Sonofa...."

"What?" Seth said.

"We screwed up," Frank said. "When we interrogated Abdel bin Hakim, we assumed his support of the Iranians and the Asasiyun was based on his anti-Western and pro-Islamic biases. But I'll bet they weren't his only motivations. What if the Saudi made taking out the Danforths a requirement of his support for Iran and the Asasiyun?"

"Which tells me that Bob, Michael, and Robbie will never be safe as long as the Asasiyun are active," Raymond said.

Seth Bridewell, Angelina Borden, and Zach Grabowsky gathered in Seth's office. Seth looked at Angelina and Zach. "You two look like three-day-old pizza."

Zach grimaced. "That comes from working for a heartless boss and worrying about trying to identify a horde of mass murderers who might alter Western civilization as we know it."

Angelina said, "I find your description of Zach creative and accurate, but I resent you likening *me* to left-over fast food."

Seth chuckled. "I want you both to go home, shower, and get a few hours' sleep." When Angelina appeared about to object, Seth raised a hand. "That's an order. You'll be a hell of a lot more productive after some rest."

Zach groaned as he struggled to his feet and looked down at Angelina. "Come on. I'll drop you off at your place. If you want, I'll pick you up later."

Angelina stood and took a step toward the door. But then she turned back to Seth and said, "How the hell are we going to stop this?"

Zach said, "We could obliterate Iran, but that probably won't stop the assassins if they've already received their marching orders."

Seth groaned. "We have to figure out how to cut communications between the Asasiyun leadership and the assassins."

"Not good enough," Angelina said. "As Zach just said, if the assassins already have their orders, cutting communications between the killers and their bosses won't do a thing to stop them. We must discover if the assassins have been given their orders and, if so, find a way to either communicate with them and revise those orders, or learn where they're located and eliminate them."

"Aw, jeez," Seth said. "You two get out of here. I'll see you at ten o'clock. Try to get some sleep."

"Oh, sure," Zach said.

CHAPTER 45

It took Bob over an hour to make reservations on an American Airlines flight from Venice to Raleigh-Durham International Airport, with a connection to Fayetteville Regional Airport. Consumed with worry about Michael and exhausted from anger at the Asasiyun, he walked to the elevator to go through the checkout process in the lobby. Just as the elevator car door opened, his cell phone rang. He backed away from the elevator and looked at the phone screen: Raymond Gallegos.

"Yeah, Ray," Bob answered.

"Bob, I just got off a call with one of our people in the Ukraine. At my request, he pressured Abdel bin Hakim who we have in custody over there."

"Who the hell is Abdel bin Hakim?"

After a beat, Raymond said, "You remember Musa Sulaiman?"

The Sulaiman name conjured up images Bob had stored away in the deepest recesses of his brain. Musa Sulaiman was the last "wet job" he'd done. He'd tracked the guy down in Brazil, followed him into a *favela* that made the worst ghetto in the United States look like a five-star resort, and shot him. Though Sulaiman had been a mass murderer, Bob got no pleasure from "wet work." But he'd been able to rationalize killing Sulaiman because, if the man had lived, he would likely have been responsible for countless more acts of murder and mayhem.

"I'm listening," Bob responded.

"Sulaiman's birth surname was bin Hakim. He was Abdel bin Hakim's son."

Bob didn't acknowledge that he had learned about the father/son relationship from Eitan Horowitz. "Okay," he said.

"The son was an early Asasiyun acolyte. The father has been a major Asasiyun financial supporter, as well as a donor to other extremist organizations."

Bob's stomach seemed to flip as he anticipated what Raymond was about to say next.

"Bin Hakim just admitted that a quid pro quo of his continued support of Iran and the Asasiyun was the murder of your family."

Bob dropped onto a banco in the elevator lobby as nausea hit him. He sat dumbfounded.

Raymond said, "I talked to Miriana a few minutes ago. Mike is in recovery. Surgery went well and, subject to no infection, he should be released on Monday or Tuesday."

Bob coughed and massaged his throat to prevent his emotions from hijacking his voice. Finally, he said, "Liz and I have reservations on a flight out of here at 5:00 a.m. We should be—"

"There won't be any flights in or out of Venice for at least the next twenty-four hours. The Italian government is about to declare a no-fly zone within twenty-five miles of Venice until further notice. They're scared witless about what could happen with all the NATO reps there."

"Dammit," Bob muttered. "I presume Michael and Miriana are under protection."

"Oh, yeah. Miriana was moved to quarters on Bragg. Men from a Lone Wolf team are escorting her everywhere. A full team has been stationed at the hospital."

"What about Robbie?"

"Same thing at West Point. They've tripled his protection detail after what happened there this morning."

At first, Bob thought Raymond was referring to the attack in Robbie's dormitory. But then his stomach did the flip-flop thing again when the words "this morning" hit home.

"This morning?"

"Oh."

"Dammit, Ray. What happened?"

"A cadet at the academy tried to run over Robbie and Samantha Meek with a Jeep. They're both fine."

"You're telling me the Asasiyun tried twice to murder my grandson?"

"Yes. But it was Abdel bin Hakim who was pulling the strings. He's obsessed about getting revenge for his son's death. That's mainly why I called you. Bin Hakim's not ever going to issue orders again. He'll spend the rest of his life in prison. But the mandate to take out you and your family has already been issued, and we have no idea how to put a hold on that mandate. We don't know if the Asasiyun will send other killers after any of you. I want to move you and Liz out of your hotel to a safe house."

When Bob didn't object, Raymond said, "There will be an armed team at your hotel within the hour. They'll escort you to your new quarters."

Zach Grabowsky had thought about getting in bed but by the time he'd showered and shaved, it was already a few minutes after 7:30 p.m. He would have to leave his apartment at 9 to pick up Angelina and make it to Langley by 10.

What's the point? he thought.

He booted up his laptop and, using a secure line, accessed the files the CIA had built on the Asasiyun and on the assassinations that had already taken place. He looked for commonalties among them. After an hour, he'd concluded that there were no similarities among the killings. The assassins had eliminated their victims using just about every method of murder possible: explosions, shootings, knifings, poisonings, traffic accidents, etc. One victim was even taken out with a bow and arrow.

"The link is not the way the murders happened," he muttered. "It's something else."

Zach continued perusing the files. When 9 p.m. arrived, he closed his computer and screamed a string of expletives that would probably generate a complaint to the building manager from the neighbor next door. "Screw her and the horse she rode in on," he whispered.

As Angelina got into the passenger seat, Zach asked, "Get any sleep?"

She scoffed. "Not a minute. But at least I was able to shower. I was getting a bit gamey there."

"Tell me about it."

Angelina punched his arm and laughed.

"What did *you* do while you should have been sleeping?" he said.

"Went over some files."

"You, too?"

"Come up with anything?" Zach said.

"Not a thing. You?"

"Yeah. A bigger headache than I already had. I tried to find something common to all the hits. But I got zilch."

"I got worse than zilch," Angelina said. She fluttered her lips. "The only common thing I came up with about some of the killers was that investigators found satellite phones in their residences. The internal workings had been fried. Apparently, the phones were booby-trapped. I guess the assassins were ordered to destroy them before they went off on their missions."

"Huh," Zach grunted. "I didn't think anything about that. What about the SIM cards?"

"Destroyed or missing."

"Were the phones all the same? I wonder if they were manufactured by the same company. If so, were they the same model? Did any of the serial numbers survive?"

"I don't know. The reports didn't specify. But what does it matter?"

Zach shrugged. "Hell, I don't know. Maybe we can contact the manufacturer, who could give us the buyer's name."

Friday evening traffic was a mess. Zach didn't pull his car into the CIA lot until 10:10. By the time they reached the ops center, it was almost 10:30. He expected Seth to chew him out for being late, but their boss just nodded at them and went back to whatever he was doing.

Zach whispered to Angelina, "This place is like a morgue. It's depressing."

Angelina frowned and whispered back, "That's because no one has a clue about what to do to stop the destruction of the Western world."

SATURDAY
FEBRUARY 23

CHAPTER 46

As the speedboat carrying Bob and Liz approached the intersection of two canals, Lorenzo De Luca, the head of the security team accompanying them, pointed at a high stone wall on their right. There was a large, rusty gate behind a decrepit-looking boat dock set into the middle of the wall.

"Is the back of the property of your new home," De Luca said in his heavily accented English.

Bob just nodded in response.

The speedboat turned right at the canal, which defined one side of the property, and then turned right again at the next corner of the property. The walls on each side blocked any view of the grounds behind them. But, from the front, a three-story building was clearly visible. The windows on that side were set back inside arches that gave the building a distinctly Moorish appearance.

Bob followed two armed men off the boat and onto a fifteen-foot-deep cobblestone walkway; he turned to take Liz's hand to help her out of the bobbing craft. Sandwiched between two pairs of armed men, they moved toward a solid iron gate set into the eight-foot wall on the front. Bob noticed a boarded-up building under rehabilitation that was cheek-to-jowl with their building's left side. An armed guard slid open the iron gate a few feet so that they could all enter the grounds. Lawns and gardens encompassed at least two acres inside the walls. The early morning sun highlighted multiple statues of the Virgin Mary and other Catholic saints planted on the lawn and along dirt pathways that ran around the lawn's outer edges, several yards back from the perimeter walls.

"What is this place?" Liz asked.

De Luca said, "Is a convent. There are only eight sisters in this Order. They live in a wing secluded from rest of building. We use as"—he paused as though he was trying to come up with the correct words— "how you say…safe place?"

Bob said, "Safe house."

"*Si*, safe house," De Luca said. "We use as safehouse and pay money to nuns." Then he said, "This is very nice place but, *per favore*, you no go outside." He gave them an apologetic look.

Bob nodded and followed Liz and two guards to a second-floor suite that was richly furnished and equipped with modern electronics, including a computer, a printer, a big-screen television, and a stereo system. When the guards placed their luggage on the floor inside the door and departed, Liz told Bob she was going to take a shower.

What a mess, Bob thought. Then he walked downstairs and suggested to De Luca that they walk the property.

"You no need to worry about nothing, Mr. Danforth. We have things under control."

"Humor me," Bob said.

Thirty minutes later, Bob returned to their suite. He found Liz standing before a shallow balcony framed by double doors. Dressed in a robe with her hair wrapped in a towel, she had her arms folded across her chest, her back to Bob, her posture rigid.

"I'm sorry, honey," he said. "I know how much you wanted to attend the ball."

She turned and held out a hand, with the index finger and thumb spread barely a half-inch. "We came this close to attending Carnevale," she said. She smiled. "But I don't want you apologizing. This isn't your fault." She squinted at him. "It's those bastards, those psycho maniacs who think nothing of murdering innocent people." After a beat, she said, "Did you call the Ventimiglias about our change of plans?"

"I did. They were disappointed but completely understood. I asked Giovanni if there had been any thought about canceling the events for the NATO delegates. He told me he'd recommended that, but the Prime Minister overruled him."

"You still think the terrorists will target the Carnevale ball?"

"Hell, I don't know, Liz. But if I were the Asasiyun leader...."

For a reason he couldn't fathom, Zach Grabowsky repeatedly turned his attention to his cell phone. It was as though his subconscious was trying to tell him something, but he couldn't make whatever it was rise to the surface. He glanced over at Angelina and recycled through his memory what she'd said during their car ride back to Langley.

At one point, his stares got on her nerves. "What are you doing?" she barked.

He threw his arms up. "Tell me again what you said about the assassins' telephones."

"Jeez, Zach."

"Come on, Ange. Tell me again."

Angelina said, "Wherever a phone was found, it was a satellite device. Its electronic components had been fried and, sometimes, the phone had been smashed to bits. The SIM card was either missing or destroyed."

He raised a finger, telling her to hold on for a second. He moved the headphones draped around his neck over his ears, stood, and walked around the area. He snapped his fingers to the music that only he could hear, ignoring the stares of other employees.

Seth Bridewell exited his office at that moment and stopped next to Angelina's desk. "What's with *the Grabowsky*?" he asked.

Angelina pointed at a sign on Zach's desk that read: Genius at Work.

Seth joined the others as they watched Zach move in a circuitous route around the ops center. After a couple minutes had passed, the others went back to their computer terminals and Seth turned to go back to his office; suddenly a shout shattered the room's relative quiet, and Zach ripped off his headphones and threw them into the air. He didn't bother to catch them. Instead, he sprinted to his desk and tapped maniacally on his computer keyboard.

Angelina scooted her chair over to Zach's desk, while Seth stood over them and looked at Zach's computer screen.

Zach pulled up the file about the attack on General Danforth. He skimmed through it until he came to the section of the CID report on Barry Murad's belongings. When he came to the entry for the satellite telephone, he stabbed the screen with a finger, wheeled around in his chair, and shouted at Seth, "I need that phone."

"Calm down, Zach, and tell me what's going on."

"The Murad kid who tried to kill General Danforth screwed up. As far as I know, he's the only assassin who didn't destroy his phone. If I can get that phone, I can snatch the *key* from it. With the *key*, I can break through the encryption protection on the source of communications that went out to the assassins in the field."

"What the heck are you talking about?" Seth said.

Zach shot his boss a condescending look, paused a beat, then said, "In cryptography, a key is a parameter that determines the functional output of a cryptographic algorithm or cipher. The algorithm would be useless without a key. In encryption, the key is the process of changing plaintext into ciphertext, or vice versa during decryption. These technologies combine to protect information…and the parties to communications. If I can grab the key, I might be able to decrypt the Asasiyun communications system."

Seth was smart enough to not take umbrage with the sarcastic way Zach pronounced the word *key*. Working with creative geniuses took a massive amount of patience.

"And what happens if you can decrypt their system?" Seth asked.

Zach rubbed his hands together. "Then we'll hack it and suck out every byte of data."

"You're sure about this?" Seth asked.

"Kinda," Zach said.

"God save me," Seth muttered.

CHAPTER 47

After hearing from Seth Bridewell regarding the satellite telephone found in Murad's overnight bag, Raymond Gallegos called the base commander, Lt. General Paul Cameron, at his residence on Fort Bragg at 5:30 a.m.

"I need you to get the satellite phone you found in Murad's bag here to Langley as quickly as possible. And, for God's sake, don't let anyone play with it."

"I'll get right on it," Cameron said. "Anything else?"

"Yes. What's Murad's emotional state?"

"He's done nothing but cry since he was interrogated. I think the kid is sorry for what he did."

Raymond scoffed. "Or he's sorry he got caught."

"I can't reconcile the kid's personality and academic background with his being an Asasiyun killer."

"General, I need you to put your top CID interrogator and Murad, along with the telephone, on the same plane. Have your CID guy ask the kid about the telephone, about how communications worked, etcetera. Tell your guy to call me from the plane if he gets anything more from Murad."

After a hesitation, Cameron said, "What about the FBI? They have an office in Fayetteville."

"We don't have time to play games here. And the last thing I want is for the FBI to read that punk, Murad, his rights, and wind up having him get legal counsel. He'll clam up and we'll get nothing out of him."

Raymond knew he had crossed the line in his conversation with General Cameron. The CIA had no law enforcement function and was mainly focused on overseas intelligence gathering, with only limited sight set on domestic intelligence collection. But he had a gut feeling that he didn't have time to waste. He decided to risk violating Murad's rights versus risking losing the assassin in the legal morass that normal law enforcement channels would create. He thought about advising Tanya Serkovic about the conversation he'd just had but decided that would only put her at risk of political reprisal. He'd leave her with "plausible deniability."

He went to his office and tried to concentrate on other duties but, after an hour, donned his overcoat, gloves, and a scarf, and left the CIA building. He walked around the grounds and wondered what he would do if he was fired by the Company. He had some money in the stock market, but not enough to retire on. The thought of working in academia as a geography professor made him momentarily depressed. He had been out in the cold and dark for over thirty minutes when his cell phone chimed. He looked at the screen but didn't recognize the number. He thought about ignoring the call but figured so few people had the number that it had to be someone he knew.

"Hello."

"Mr. Gallegos, I have the information you requested."

Raymond didn't recognize the woman's voice. And it sounded distorted.

"Are you there?" the caller said.

"Yes. What information are you referring to?"

The woman ignored Raymond's question. "Are you ready to copy?"

"Go ahead."

She recited a number, then said, "That's the only number the kid knew that connected him to the organization. We are due to land at Dulles in fifteen minutes. I'll hand over the kid and the satellite phone to your representatives."

Raymond had written the number the woman gave him on the back of one of his business cards and told her the names of the employees he'd dispatched to Dulles to meet the plane from Fort Bragg. "You will give the phone to Ms. Toney. Agents DiMonaco and Middleton will transport your passenger. Did you get anything else from him?"

"He told me he had been given the name of his target a month ago. That gave him time to research the general and to plan a trip to Fort Bragg." After a second's pause, she said, "By the way, he asked how the general was doing. He seems remorseful about what he did."

"You believe him?"

After several seconds, she replied, "Yeah, I do. He claims he was told that his parents—"

"I know. His parents would be killed if he didn't perform. Tell him his parents are being transported to a Saudi air base. They're safe."

As Raymond returned to the building, he thought, *I guess that woman is as concerned as I am about the line we just crossed.*

He rushed to Seth Bridewell's office, caught the man napping at his desk, and shook him awake. He read off the numbers from the back of his business card to Seth, who wrote them on a legal pad.

Seth looked up at Raymond with a questioning expression.

"That's the number for Murad's handler."

"Hot damn!" Seth exclaimed. Then he shouted, "Zach!"

Yasmin felt as though every nerve in her body was electrified. Time seemed to have slowed to an unreal pace. She looked at the wall clock in the Asasiyun operations center and huffed a mighty sigh as the second hand crept around its face.

"You should get some rest, Yasmin," Javad said. "It's still hours before we have to make the call."

Yasmin looked around, concerned that one of the dozen workers in the ops center had heard Javad treat her like an impatient child. Apparently, they hadn't. She turned on Javad, skewered him with an ice-cold stare, and somehow restrained herself from screaming at him. She took a breath, released it slowly, leaned toward him, and whispered, "I know exactly what time it is and when we will call the agents. What concerns me is that we've heard nothing about the Danforths." She made a noise that sounded like half-growl, half-moan.

Javad shrugged. "Perhaps the Americans are suppressing news of those assassinations. Think of the impact news like that would have on the American people. If assassins can hit targets on secure military bases, no one is safe." He chuckled. "I'll bet you our people performed their assignments."

"And Tehran hasn't contacted us about the helicopter crash. What do you think about that?"

Javad shrugged. "Accidents happen."

"Or the mullahs suspect us, but they don't want to risk upsetting our plans so close to the execution date. But they'll come after us once tomorrow comes to a close."

Javad showed Yasmin a condescending smile. "We'll be heroes tomorrow. They'll have no reason to punish us, regardless of what they know or suspect."

"What about the Danforth grandfather in Italy?" Yasmin asked shrilly.

Javad merely shrugged.

"Get the backup cell phone numbers of the agents we sent after the Danforths. Call them."

Javad's eyes widened and his mouth gaped. "Please, Yasmin, we're just hours away from realizing the dream. We shouldn't make any calls until 9:30 Venice time."

Yasmin was aggravated that Javad was correct. She stormed from the ops center.

Luigi Donatello, an AISE senior director, could barely breathe. He'd received instructions to eliminate a man named Robert Danforth. The man's wife, too.

Donatello had been an Asasiyun sleeper agent in Rome for twenty-six years, since he'd come to Italy as an exchange student, assumed the identity of a deceased infant, and adopted the boy's name. He served in the Italian Army and later worked at the intelligence agency when it was still named Servizio per le

Informazioni e la Sicurezza Militare (Military Intelligence and Security Service). He'd risen through the ranks and had never been called on by the Old Man of the Mountain to do anything other than provide classified information.

But that all changed twenty-four hours ago when he received a text instructing him to eliminate the Danforths in Venice. The Danforth name rang a bell, and he'd remembered why after only a couple of minutes. He'd seen the name on the official invitation list for one of the Carnevale events that had been vetted by AISE. The Danforths were to be guests of Giovanni Ventimiglia, a former AISE hotshot. Donatello hadn't had much interaction with Ventimiglia before the man retired, but he'd always hated him for his aristocratic bloodline and his world class wealth. He thought about targeting the Danforths at the ball but decided it would be nearly impossible to eliminate the man and his wife and then escape. Besides, his instructions were emphatic: *Take out the Danforths NOW!*

He'd been given the couple's hotel name. But after he arrived in Venice, called the hotel, and asked to be connected to their room to determine if they were in, he'd learned they'd checked out.

"Did they leave a number where they can be contacted?" Donatello had asked the hotel operator.

"I can't give out that information," the operator told him. "Would you like to leave your name and number in case they call for any messages?"

Donatello hung up and fumed. *What are those idiots thinking?* he thought. *They risk losing a highly placed agent in the Intelligence Service by turning me into a common killer. Now, they want me to kill a man and his wife on a moment's notice.* He huffed and dropped into the chair behind the desk in his Venice hotel room. His stomach rumbled and he felt as though he might need to run to the bathroom. *What will the Old Man of the Mountain do to my family in Shiraz and to me if I don't complete this mission?*

Then an idea came to him. He noted the time on his cell phone: 10:15 a.m., and rushed from his room. It took fifteen minutes to walk to Piazza San Marco. He entered a costume shop and told a clerk he wanted to buy a mask for a man.

"The Medico della Peste (the Plague Doctor) mask should be

perfect," the clerk said. He pointed at a mask with a huge golden bird-like beak, crowned with black feathers. "It will be an ornament that can be displayed on a credenza or a wall."

"Perfect."

Donatello waited for the next water taxi to arrive and boarded it. The ride from the dock to the Danforths' hotel was supposed to take twenty minutes. But the trip took half-an-hour because the weather had worsened and wind gusts buffeted the boat, causing it to pitch and yaw. Stinging rain pelted the craft, drumming loudly on the windows. By the time the craft arrived, Donatello felt queasy. He climbed onto the hotel's covered dock, burped a bubble of bile, and unsteadily made his way up a flight of steps to the lobby.

He moved to a young woman seated at a desk, raised the bagged mask to show her, and said, "Mr. Robert Danforth ordered this mask from Bonato's Maschere Autentiche e Costumi. I believe he wanted it for the ball tonight. Can you see that he receives it immediately?"

The woman tapped her computer keyboard. After a minute, she looked up at Donatello, and said, "I'm sorry, but Mr. and Mrs. Danforth checked out earlier."

Donatello feigned distress. "Oh dear," he exclaimed. "My boss will kill me. I was supposed to deliver this to the Danforths yesterday, but I didn't have time. What am I going to do?"

As he'd hoped, the young woman shot him a sympathetic smile. "Perhaps they left a forwarding address. Our records show they weren't supposed to check out for another four days. They might still be in Venice and just moved to a hotel closer to the ball venue." She went back to her computer, tapped at the keyboard for a few seconds, and looked back up at him. "They did not leave a forwarding address." She looked around as though to be certain that none of her co-workers were in earshot, then leaned forward. "I do have Mr. Danforth's cell phone number. Perhaps you could call him and deliver your package to wherever they are staying now."

Donatello smiled at her. "You're a lifesaver. Thank you so much."

As he departed the hotel, he called the signals intelligence section at AISE, gave an employee there the personal identification code number of a mid-level AISE employee named Claudio Monteleone, recited Danforth's cell number, and said, "This is pertinent to the Asasiyun investigation. The number I gave you is for a cell phone I believe is in Venice. I want to locate that phone. As soon as you can track it, call me." He gave the woman the number of his burner phone...and waited.

CHAPTER 48

It was dark out when CIA Agents Mike DiMonaco and Huson Middleton escorted Barry Murad to a Company safe house in Reston, Virginia. They removed the black hood from his head and uncuffed his hands.

DiMonaco's cell phone rang as Middleton directed the boy to a straight-backed chair at a four-top kitchen table. DiMonaco answered the call, listened for a few seconds, then handed the phone to Murad. "It's for you," the agent said.

Murad's eyes widened in surprise. He accepted the phone, said, "Hello," and listened for a few seconds before wailing something in Arabic and breaking down in tears.

DiMonaco heard shrieking on the other end of the call. After he allowed Murad to talk for a couple minutes, he grabbed the phone, terminated the call, and said, "Your parents are fine. They're safe in the hands of a U.S. Army unit in Saudi Arabia. They'll be transported to Landstuhl Army Hospital in Germany. Assuming you cooperate fully with us, you might be able to see them after they're transported to the United States."

Murad stared at the agent, who glared back.

"I already told you everything I know."

Middleton sat down across from the boy. "You know that's not true, Barry."

Murad dropped his gaze to his lap.

271

"You have thirty seconds to decide how you and your parents will spend the rest of your lives. If you don't work with us, we'll send your family back to Iraq and you'll be an old man before you even have a hope of being released from a federal prison."

DiMonaco, standing next to Murad, leaned in, and said, "It's time to let it all out, Barry."

Murad said, "I don't know much more than I already told you."

Middleton said, "Much more? In other words, you have been holding back."

Murad blinked, then looked up at DiMonaco who continued to hover over him.

"Okay, okay," he said. "I understood that I would be part of a massive, coordinated attack. When the assassinations began a couple weeks ago, I was surprised. I anticipated everything happening at once." He shrugged. "I'm kinda surprised that hasn't already happened."

"How did you know who you were supposed to target?" Middleton said.

"I received a call. I was given the name of my…assignment. I was given several weeks to learn about him and plan my attack."

"Is it your impression that this would be the way all assassins and targets were matched?" DiMonaco said.

Murad shrugged. "Yes…I guess."

"What? Why the hesitation?" DiMonaco said.

"Well, as I just said, the single attacks that happened over several days really surprised me. They used to talk about 'massive strikes' and 'maximum psychological impact.'"

Middleton asked, "So, why do you think the attacks so far have been one-off versus coordinated?"

Murad shrugged again. "I've thought about it more than once. At first, I thought there had been a change in strategy. But that didn't make sense. I mean, the Old Man of the Mountain has worked on the plan for decades. It was originally conceived of by Ayatollah Khomeini. Anything the Great Ayatollah put in place is akin to law set down by Allah. No one would countermand what Khomeini wanted, even after his death."

"You think a massive attack is still in the works?" DiMonaco said.

Murad nodded.

"Do you think the date for that attack has been set?"

Murad seemed to consider the question for a few seconds. He looked from DiMonaco to Middleton. "I think the Old Man of the Mountain has a date in mind, but if the assassins knew that date, I can't believe there wouldn't have been a leak by now. After all, the odds against one thousand people keeping the same secret are enormous. I built a formula for a similar situation last year. The odds that a secret will be disclosed go up exponentially with each twenty-four-hour period that passes after the secret is initially shared."

Middleton and DiMonaco stared at one another. Middleton said, "You believe the Asasiyun leader has a date in mind, but hasn't disclosed that date to his agents?"

Murad nodded again. "Yes. I suspect the assassins might know who their targets are. They would be given time to research them and plan their methods of attack. But they wouldn't execute the attacks until ordered to do so by the Old Man of the Mountain."

"So, this massive attack could happen today or months from now?" DiMonaco said.

"Today or tomorrow would be a better guess than months from now."

"Why?" Middleton said.

Murad hesitated for a long beat. He looked at the agents again, his eyes narrowed, his lips tightly compressed. Finally, he said, "Our instructors told us we have spies embedded in many governments. They know everything you know. Which means they know or will soon know that you have me in custody. They'll also know if you plan to retaliate against them. They won't take the chance that you'll undermine their plans. They'll act before that can happen."

"How will the Asasiyun leadership turn the assassins loose?" Middleton asked.

"All the Old Man of the Mountain has to do now is give the attack order. Probably by text." A sickly smile momentarily crossed the boy's face. "If the others are informed of their targets' names like I was, then they have researched their locations, habits, family members, acquaintances; and probably know where they will be at any given time on any given day." The sickly expression again—now more grimace than smile. "People are creatures of habit."

Middleton nodded. "But you told us you received a phone call, not a text."

Murad frowned. "I wondered about that." He shrugged. "It was like…I don't know. There was something different about my assignment. Like General Danforth was a…special target."

"Special? How?" DiMonaco asked.

"I don't know."

"So, the Old Man of the Mountain will text his agents about the date and time to strike?" DiMonaco said.

"Probably. I think the text will include a date and time and words in Arabic that mean *you will strike a blow for our people.*"

"Will the message to all the assassins be transmitted from the same number you gave us earlier, the one for your handler?" Middleton asked.

Murad tilted his head to one side as though to indicate he wasn't certain. Then he raised a finger and said, "But, if I have to guess, I think the order from the Old Man of the Mountain will go out via a broadcast text message to all the field agents simultaneously if the attacks are to be coordinated to occur at the same time. For instance, I assume the message will tell the agents they should execute the attacks on their targets at a certain time in a specific time zone."

CHAPTER 49

Zach Grabowsky and Angelina Borden, working with a team of CIA and NSA communications experts, with assistance from the National Reconnaissance Office, were able to track the telephone number of Barry Murad's handler to a satellite telephone located in the Cloud Forest in Northern Iran's Semnan Province.

"Sonofa—" Zach exclaimed, but Angelina stopped him with a cautionary look. "I was going to say sonofagun," Zach said, with a sheepish expression. He turned toward Seth Bridewell. "As if we needed further confirmation. There's no doubt the Iranians are behind the Asasiyun and that they're based at that fortress our satellites filmed."

Seth said, "I'll notify Ray Gallegos. In the meantime, we need to hack that phone." He turned to one of the NSA contingent and asked, "How long will it take to pull the memory and especially the contacts file from that phone?"

"Assuming we can catch someone on the phone when it's in use, and assuming the NRO can position a satellite on top of the Cloud Forest, and assuming we can identify the encryption key, we can suck all the information out of that phone in a second. We can upload the data to the satellite, which will transfer it here. But what do you expect to capture from that phone? There might be nothing but calls between the phone's owner and his mother. And how will you get him to use the phone?"

Seth called Ray Gallegos, updated him, and said, "I need Murad brought here as quickly as possible."

Luigi Donatello held his breath as he punched in the Danforth cell number on his burner phone. He let out the breath when a man answered, "Hello?"

"Mr. Danforth?" Donatello said.

"Yes. Who's calling?"

Donatello gave Danforth the same name he'd previously used of the mid-level functionary in AISE's Rome headquarters and said, "We're calling all the people on the Grand Ball invitation list to confirm their attendance and to determine the approximate time of their arrival at the venue. As you can imagine, with all the NATO personnel attending the event, security will be quite tight. We don't want all the guests to arrive at the same time." He coughed an abrupt laugh. "We don't want them standing outside in a long line in this nasty weather we are having."

"I see," Bob said. "What did you say your name was again?"

"Claudio Monteleone, signore."

"Apparently, Mr. Monteleone, you weren't informed that my wife and I will not be able to attend the ball this evening."

"I'm sorry to hear that, Mr. Danforth. I hope you and Mrs. Danforth are not ill."

"No, we're fine. But thank you for your call."

"Not at all," Donatello said. "I hope there wasn't anything wrong with your previous hotel that required you to leave before your planned checkout date."

"No, everything was fine. Thank you," Danforth said.

Donatello said, "Arrivederci," and terminated the call.

A call came in from the woman in AISE's Signal Intelligence Department five minutes after Donatello hung up with Danforth. He answered by again giving the woman the hacked personal code number of Claudio Monteleone, and abruptly said, "What did you get?"

She provided him with the phone's location, including the canals that bordered that location. He was about to hang up when she said, "That location is a convent, signore. Strange place for the Asasiyun."

Donatello ended the call, pulled up a map app on his phone, and inputted the convent's address.

After his conversation with the man named Claudio Monteleone, Bob reclined on the couch in their suite. He hadn't slept more than a couple hours after they'd been escorted to the convent and thought he'd try to grab a couple hours sleep on the couch, rather than disturb Liz with his tossing and turning that had characterized his sleep since he'd been targeted for assassination earlier that week.

But his mind seemed to be on an out-of-control merry-go-round. His nerves were on edge as he rehashed the phone call from Monteleone. Something just didn't ring true about that call. He closed his eyes and tried to focus, fighting through fatigue. The first thing about the call that seemed off was Monteleone's reference to their checking out of their hotel before their planned departure date. *No one is supposed to know that we checked out of the hotel*, he thought. The second thought he had was that he had already called Giovanni Ventimiglia and explained why they wouldn't be able to attend the ball. One thing he had learned about Giovanni was that he was a stickler for detail. The Italian had told him he would call the ball office and pass on his regrets. He suspected that Giovanni would have also called whichever government department oversaw security at the ball and inform them to delete the Danforths' names. The third question that came to Bob's mind was about how Monteleone had gotten his cell number. All his concerns could be explained away. Perhaps Monteleone was an overzealous employee who had called the hotel and finagled information. Perhaps Giovanni had included his cell phone on the original invitation list. And maybe Giovanni hadn't yet called the ball committee and security. He could be waiting for a decent hour to do so.

However, the more he focused, the more suspicious he became. For a long moment, Bob second-guessed himself. How many times had Liz accused him of being paranoid? But the familiar twinge of suspicion had now grown to something bigger. Something was wrong.

Bob left the room and sought out the head of the security detail. He informed him of the call and of his suspicions. The chief security guy told him that he would alert his men.

Bob called Giovanni's cell number. When Giovanni answered, he apologized for calling so early.

"I've been up for hours, my friend. What can I do for you?"

Bob asked, "Did you notify the ball organizers and AISE about Liz and me not attending the ball this evening?"

"Of course," Giovanni said. "Why do you ask?"

Bob's stomach did a small flip-flop. He explained his reasoning and suggested Giovanni check up on an AISE employee named Claudio Monteleone.

"I'll do it immediately and will call you back as soon as I know something." Before he signed off, Giovanni added, "You know this could all be nothing more than bureaucratic bumbling."

After a pause, Bob said, "I understand. But something seems off."

CIA agents Mike DiMonaco and Huson Middleton, with Barry Murad in tow, drove at breakneck speed from the Company safe house in Reston to CIA Headquarters. They were met by a four-man security team in the underground entrance and ushered at quick time to the operations center.

Raymond Gallegos stepped from a small conference room when they arrived. "Come with me," he told Murad, then led the way back into the conference room where Seth Bridewell, Zach Grabowsky, and Angelina Borden waited. On the center of a table was the satellite telephone found in Murad's belongings back at Fort Bragg. Murad stared at the phone as though he recognized it, but didn't speak.

Raymond pointed at a chair and barked, "Sit!" He took a chair next to Murad, shifted it so he faced the young man, and began. "How do you feel about trying to murder General Danforth?"

Murad closed his eyes and muttered, "I didn't have a choice."

"Look at me," Raymond blurted in a threatening voice. When Murad opened his eyes, Raymond growled, "I didn't ask you why you did it; I asked you how you feel about what you did."

In a weak voice, Murad said, "Not good. I hope the general will recover."

"You're damned lucky that he's doing fine. Now you're going to do something to show us whether you're sincere about what you just said." He pointed at the phone. "You're going to call the number you gave us and tell whoever answers that you killed General Danforth, that you escaped, and that you are waiting for further orders."

Murad slowly shook his head. "I don't think they'll believe me. As I told the agents earlier, the Old Man of the Mountain has spies inside your government. They've probably already informed him that the attack on the general failed and that I am in custody."

Raymond didn't want to disclose to Murad that Ursan Awan and his family members, along with the Shirazi brothers, were all locked up. Of course, the Asasiyun might have other operatives buried deep inside the U.S. government, but there had been no announcement or report filed about the attack on Michael Danforth or the apprehension of Murad. Putting all of that aside, he just wanted Murad to make the call. The assumption was that his telephone number would be recognized, which would, hopefully, cause the call to be answered. That might not be correct if someone had informed the Asasiyun of Murad's failed attempt to kill Michael Danforth, but he was playing the odds that had not happened. And he had nothing to lose.

"You let me worry about that," Raymond said. "All you need to do is what I told you to do."

Murad's eyes widened and seemed to sparkle. Raymond looked at the young man's expression and sensed he was happy to cooperate.

"What language are you supposed to use?"

"Farsi or Arabic."

"Okay, let's do this," Raymond said. He turned to Zach and said, "Dial the number." He looked back at Murad. "I speak both languages."

"I understand," Murad said.

Zach dialed Murad's handler's number, pressed the speaker button, placed the phone on the desk, and stepped back.

Murad cleared his throat and looked around at the others as he waited for the call to be answered. His expression changed after the fifth ring—his face turned red and the muscles in his jaws twitched.

Raymond had hoped the plan would work, but as the phone continued to ring, his hopefulness waned. By the ninth ring, he was about to call it off. But, as the next ring began, a male voice barked in Farsi, "What is your message?"

Murad answered, "This is 9-8-1. My mission is accomplished. What are my orders?"

After a pause, the man said, "Wonderful. We wondered what had happened. There has been no news."

"The Americans apparently don't want it publicly disclosed. Bad for morale."

"You are safe?" the man asked.

"Yes."

"Where are you now?"

Murad seemed momentarily flustered, but, after a couple seconds, said, "In a car outside Fayetteville."

Then the man's tone changed. "Why are you using this phone? You were supposed to destroy—"

"It was a mistake. I will do so immediately."

"No, don't do that. We will be in touch." The call was terminated.

As Zach and Angelina ran from the office into the heart of the ops center, Murad expelled a nervous laugh, and looked at Raymond. "Was that okay?" he said.

Raymond stood. "Yeah."

Seth asked Raymond, "Do you want him taken back to the safe house?"

Raymond considered the question. "No, let's keep him here for a while." He glared at the young man. "He might be of further assistance."

Murad was led out to where DiMonaco and Middleton waited. "Keep him handy," Raymond told the two men. "Maybe you could all get something to eat."

After the two agents and Murad exited the ops center, Raymond surveyed the activity at and around several computer stations, then addressed Seth, "You think it worked?"

"You want my best guess or a guarantee?"

"What's a *guarantee*?" Raymond said. "I've been here for years and I've never experienced anything close to a guarantee. I hope my conclusion that the Asasiyun doesn't have anyone else buried inside our intelligence community is correct."

Javad rushed to Yasmin's office as soon as he ended the call from Abd al Bari Murad. He burst into the office and shouted, "We got the general."

She shot him a questioning look.

"General Danforth in North Carolina."

"That's the best news I've heard today. Anything from Tehran?"

He shook his head. "No."

"Does that surprise you?"

Javad had wondered about the lack of communication from the mullahs. Not one had called to pressure them about taking out the Danforths or about the helicopter explosion. "A little, I guess. But it's probably because they know we are about to release the assassins."

"Perhaps," Yasmin said.

Javad had already had this conversation with her several times. He didn't want to revisit the topic. "I'd better check on things in the operations center," he said. "The messages will need to go out soon."

CHAPTER 50

It was after 11:00 a.m. and Bob hadn't heard back from Giovanni. He'd been unable to sleep since he'd called him. Liz had found his pacing aggravating, but rather than complain about it, she'd decided to go outside to the gardens. Despite the cold, she found the quiet a nice reprieve from the tension in their room. She tried to identify the bushes in the garden, but stripped of their flowers and leaves, that was almost impossible. On top of that, worry about Michael and Robbie intruded. She'd tried to reach Miriana on her cell, but her call went directly to voicemail. The same thing happened when she tried to reach Robbie.

What a bust this vacation is, she thought.

About to call Giovanni again, Bob's phone rang. He recognized his old friend's number.

"You learn anything?" Bob asked.

Giovanni didn't immediately respond. For a moment, Bob thought he'd put him off, and apologized for being so abrupt.

"No, no, it's okay," Giovanni said. "I was reading an email that just came in. I tracked down the man who you said called you: Claudio Monteleone. He's a mid-level manager at AISE. Only been there a couple years."

Bob exhaled sharply. "So, it makes sense that he might be assigned to call people attending the ball."

"That was my initial reaction," Giovanni said. "But I called a friend at AISE and asked her to find out for sure. It turns out that no one had been assigned to call ball attendees. On top of that, Claudio Monteleone is out on leave. His wife gave birth two weeks ago. A call to the young man by an AISE investigator probably boosted his blood pressure. Bob, your instincts were correct. The call you received wasn't legitimate."

"But for what purpose?"

"I thought about that. The only thing I can come up with is that someone wanted to locate you through your cell phone. I think I should request that another special ops team be dispatched to your location."

"I don't think that's necessary, Giovanni. I already have more than enough protection."

"Okay. But please tell your security people about what I learned. They need to be on high alert."

"I will," Bob said. "But let me ask you something. If someone wanted to track me through my cell phone, they would need the technological capability to do so. Besides AISE, what other agencies here in Italy would have that capability?"

Giovanni muttered, "Santa madre di Dio. Who doesn't have that capability! It could have been someone in the Carabinieri, the Polizia di Stato, the Guardia di Finanza, the army, the navy. It goes on and on."

Luigi Donatello paid one hundred Euros to a gondolier to take him on a thirty-minute tour of the Ghetto Cannaregio area. As the gondola turned onto *Rio Madonna Dell' Orto*, Donatello spotted two men off to his left on a walkway between the canal and a high stone wall that fronted a three-story building. They were doing nothing to disguise their purpose. They were obviously guards. From the bulges under their coats, he had no doubt they were armed. As the gondola drifted past, Donatello glanced in their direction and confirmed the address he'd received from the woman in AISE's signals intelligence section. A metal gate was inset in the stone wall to the right side of the building. There was no visible entrance on the structure's front side, so Donatello assumed there was a building entrance behind the gate. After they'd passed the building, he asked the gondolier if a canal bordered the back side of the property.

"*Si*, signore. Would you like to go there?"

"Yes."

They went under a footbridge, turned left into another canal, and then left again to the back side of the property. There was a walkway on this side, too, and a loading dock with a padlocked metal door in the stone wall there. A four-story building that appeared to be under renovation bordered the fourth side.

Donatello found that his inspection confirmed what he'd seen when he'd viewed the property on Google Earth. He would have to approach from the rear. But the building was set back from the property's rear by an eighty-yard-long expanse of lawn and gardens. There was no way he would be able to cross that area in broad daylight without the guards spotting him. Unless they were preoccupied at the building's front side. He would have preferred to operate after dark, but his orders hadn't given him that option. He was to kill the Danforth couple as soon as possible.

In his hotel room, he retrieved the bag with the mask he'd bought and a small suitcase. He took them outside, hired another gondolier to deliver them to the address where Danforth was located, and told him the delivery had to be made at exactly 11:15 that morning. He walked away from the gondolier and approached a man seated in a speedboat.

"I'll pay you two hundred Euros for one hour of your time," he said.

The man laughed. "Are you planning to rob a bank?"

Donatello smiled back at the man. "If I was, do you think I would tell you?"

The man laughed again. "When would you like to leave?"

"In ten minutes. I have to get something from my room."

Donatello went back inside his hotel, took the elevator to his room, and changed his clothes. He put on a loose pair of black pants and crepe-soled shoes, picked up a soft-sided athletic bag, and went back outside. He handed the bag to the boatman, stepped down into the speedboat, and told the man where he wanted to go.

Settled in a seat behind the driver, he averted his gaze when they approached the gondola that he had hired earlier. He again looked away when they went by the convent building.

"Go under that bridge and turn left," he instructed the boatman.

Once behind the convent property, Donatello pointed at the dock. "Pull in there," he ordered.

When the boatman had nosed the bow toward the metal door in the back wall—placing the speedboat's left side flush against the small dock—he cut the engine to idle. Donatello tossed the athletic bag onto the dock, hopped from the boat, and secured the bow and stern lines to cleat hitches.

"What now?" the boatman asked.

Donatello removed a silenced pistol from the bag. He saw the surprise on the man's face just as he fired. But that was the man's only reaction as a bullet punched a hole in his forehead, dropping him like an empty sack onto the deck. Donatello reached over, cut the engine, and made certain the man's body wasn't visible above the boat's gunwales. Satisfied, he slipped a bolt cutter from the bag and removed the lock from the metal door on the back of the convent property. He looked at his watch: 11:10.

One security guard at the convent's front gate put a hand on his holstered pistol in a shoulder rig beneath his coat when he spied a gondola turn into the canal and then approach the convent. Gondolas were a common sight here, and the guard wasn't particularly concerned, but he knew what his responsibilities were and reacted as though the boat presented a threat. He alerted the second guard who turned to stare at the gondola.

"Not another damned gondola," the second guard muttered as he, too, reached for his pistol.

But unlike the other crafts that had cruised down the canal, this one slowed as it came closer.

"Ciao, signori," the gondolier called out. "I have a delivery for Signore Dan-forth."

The guards immediately went on hyper-alert. They had been told that no one knew the Danforths were here. Each man released the grip on his holstered pistol, pushed back one side of his leather coat, and swung free an Uzi machine pistol cradled in a sling under his right arm.

"*Fermarsi*," the first guard shouted, ordering the gondolier to stop. "Raise your hands."

The gondolier shot his hands in the air, all the while yelling, "*Cosa c'è che non va?*" (What's wrong?)

The boat continued to drift, crunching against the cement canal wall, throwing the gondolier off-balance. He fell backward into the boat, his eyes wide as the two men aimed their weapons at him.

The first guard told his partner to search the gondola as he continued to train his weapon on the frightened gondolier.

As the second guard jumped into the gondola, a massive explosion erupted. His and the gondolier's bodies were blown apart. Pieces of wood from the gondola, along with chunks of concrete from the canal wall, became supersonic shrapnel that lacerated the first guard. His body was shredded; his blood painted the convent's front wall.

Luigi Donatello felt the blast's pressure, despite the distance from his location to the far side of the property. The ground shook and the little dock creaked and swayed. He quickly put his shoulder against the metal door and shoved. It budged a couple inches, but not enough for him to slip through. He heard shouts from the front of the property and assumed the security people on site were going there. He slammed into the door, driving it open another twenty or so inches. The godawful screech of its hinges seemed to careen across the yard and gardens, but no one had apparently heard the sound. He raced toward the convent, using trees for cover. On the left, just inside the front gate, was a building entrance. He noticed that the front gate hung slightly askew.

Three men, each carrying an automatic weapon, burst from the building entrance. They ran to the gate in single file. The first man stopped at the gate, peeked through an opening, and sped around it. The other men followed.

Donatello saw a door on the building's right rear and sprinted to it. It was locked. After peering through a glass panel in the door and seeing no one in the apparent kitchen, he kicked the door handle, broke the lock, and threw the door open. He slipped inside and padded through the kitchen to a marble-floored hallway that led past a dozen or so closed doors. Shards of glass and small chunks of stone and plaster littered the floor. A heavy haze of smoke and dust lazily floated in the air. As he went down the hall, he heard voices, which became louder the further he went. A door was open at the far-left side of the corridor. He made his way there and peeked inside a room. A cluster of frightened elderly women huddled together, apparently praying. Donatello quickly skirted the opening and stopped at a door at the end of the hallway. He kicked this door open too, and entered a foyer-like space. He found two more doors, each with shattered glass sidelights. The one on the right accessed a foyer that appeared to lead to the door from where he'd earlier seen the security guards exit. The other door accessed a staircase. He carefully opened that door and climbed the stairs.

Bob had left the sitting room to place a call to Raymond Gallegos, leaving Liz reading a book on her e-reader when a blast occurred. The explosion blew out the glass in the doors that opened onto the balcony and caused plaster to fall from the ceiling in great chunks. Framed paintings crashed to the floor. He heard Liz scream and was about to run toward the sitting room when she burst into the bedroom.

"Are you okay?" he said.

In a trembling voice, she answered, "Yes, I'm fine."

He took her hand and pulled her toward the balcony. Now holding both her arms, he shouted, "We've got to get out of here."

"Where are the guards?" she asked.

"I imagine they've responded to the explosion and are out front." *Or they could all be dead*, he thought.

Wind blowing through the broken balcony doors fluttered the curtains. The temperature in the room had probably dropped twenty degrees.

"I'll check the hallway and the stairs to the first floor," Bob said. "I'll be right back."

Bob cracked the door open and looked up and down the hall. No one. He crept into the hallway and fast-walked to the door leading to the staircase down to the nuns' quarters. The sidelight next to the door had been shattered. He peered through the space and saw a man armed with a pistol hovering near the bottom of the stairs. The man abruptly stopped when he saw Bob looking at him, but quickly recovered, pointed his weapon, and fired. A bullet thudded into the stair riser just below Bob's feet. He raced back to his room, slammed the door shut, locked it, and dragged over a heavy desk chair. He propped the chair under the doorknob and moved into the bedroom. After snatching the sheets from the unmade bed and tying them together, he secured one end of the sheets to a bed footpost and tossed the other end over the balcony railing. When he looked at Liz, he was surprised at how calm she seemed.

"We're going to climb down the sheets?" she asked, sounding a bit incredulous.

Before he could answer, someone slammed into the room door. The door held, but Bob knew it wouldn't for long.

"Go," he rasped at Liz. "I'll follow you down. Don't wait for me. Get to the back of the property as fast as you can. There's a gardener's shed back there. Hide inside. I'll join you."

Another crash against the door.

Bob watched Liz swing a leg over the railing as he ran to the suite door. He threw his back against it just as someone hit it again. The door popped open an inch, but the chair held. The attacker slammed into the door again, this time moving the chair a few inches. Bob heard the man curse in Italian as he hit the door again. Bob momentarily lost his balance but gathered his legs under him and rolled the chair aside. He heard heavy breathing through the small gap between the door and the jamb, then the sound of footsteps. He guessed the intruder was about to charge the door again. Bob anticipated his charge and leaped backward as the man crashed into the door again, throwing it open. The man staggered into the room, his momentum carrying him halfway to the balcony. But he quickly regained his balance and twisted around just as Bob swung a fist at him. The man blocked the blow with his left arm, shouted angrily in Italian, and backed away.

Bob stepped forward, about to swing again, but stopped when

the man pointed the pistol at his chest.

The man smiled and seemed ready to say something, when a frenzied scream came from behind him. He whipped around and brought his pistol to bear on Liz whose head poked above the bottom of the balcony floor. She ducked down as the man fired. In that instant, Bob ran forward, dropped his shoulder, and rammed into the man's back, knocking him off his feet, and sending him through the door space and head-first over the balcony railing.

Bob rushed to the railing and saw the gunman's body draped over a marble fountain. He was shocked to see Liz perched on a six-inch-wide ledge, five feet below the balcony floor. Her fingers, bright with blood, gripped the edge of the balcony.

"Pull me in," she cried.

"There could be others with that guy down there. Climb down."

She grabbed the sheet, wrapped her legs around it, and slid down to the patio. Bob followed her, despite pain in his right shoulder, and held Liz's arm as they ran toward the gardener's shed. But as they went past the iron gate in the back wall, he noticed it was no longer locked.

"This way," he said.

They exited through the back gate and found a small dock with a boat tied to it. Liz approached the boat, but suddenly stopped and pointed at the body inside.

Then sirens sounded in the distance. By the time a security man found them, dozens of motorboats had come up the canals that bordered the convent. Bob's adrenaline high had long since dissipated and his nervous system seemed to be short-circuiting. His hands shook as he removed glass shards from Liz's hands and then ripped strips from his shirt to use as bandages.

The police helped them into one of their boats. An officer told them they would be taken to Signore Ventimiglia's casa.

How that was so quickly arranged confused Bob, but he was too exhausted to ask. Seated in the back of a Polizia di Stato boat, wrapped in blankets, accompanied by three members of their private security detail, Bob put an arm around Liz and kissed her cheek. "That was quite a shriek," he said.

She burrowed into him. "I scared myself."

The security detachment chief requested that they turn over their cell phones to him. When they did so, he removed the SIM cards, smashed the phones under his boots, and tossed the debris into the canal. Bob didn't object. He had a sinking feeling that it could have been his phone that had led the assassin to the convent. He felt sick about possibly being culpable in the deaths of two of the guards.

After they sped through the network of canals for several minutes, Bob asked the security chief, "Why are we going to the Ventimiglia home?"

The man shrugged in that distinctly Italian manner and replied, "Those are my orders."

Bob leaned into Liz. "I hate to tell you this. Our things are back at the convent, including our ball costumes. Even if we were able to go to the ball, we couldn't go now."

Liz scoffed. "You're probably thrilled." She smiled and said, "Wouldn't matter, though. I've had enough excitement."

One guard leaned in and said, "Excuse me, but I couldn't help overhearing. Don't worry about your things. Everything will be delivered to the Ventimiglia's."

"Thanks for nothing," Bob said under his breath.

CHAPTER 51

Raymond Gallegos joined Seth Bridewell who paced around the CIA Operations Center, which was eerily quiet, except for tapping on keyboards and an occasional expletive.

"Any progress?" Raymond asked.

Seth frowned. "You'll be one of the first people I call."

Raymond patted him on the arm. "I know that, Seth. It's just that I can't focus on anything else."

"I know. I have the same problem."

Raymond looked around at the men and women in the large room. "My God, you ever notice we're surrounded by kids?"

Seth chuckled. "You just noticed? Grabowsky and Borden are only in their late twenties. The others here call them Dad and Mom."

"I guess that makes us their grandparents."

"You got that right."

"Okay, Seth. I'll get out of your hair."

As Raymond turned to leave, someone shouted, "Hot damn!"

Raymond whipped around and gave Seth a hopeful look. But Seth had already rushed over to where half-a-dozen employees now stood around a young woman seated at a terminal.

Zach Grabowsky separated from the group, looked at Seth, and pointed a thumb back over his shoulder. "Sasha broke in." He turned back to the terminal and told the others there to make room. When the people spread out, Seth saw a stream of letters and numbers cascade down the terminal screen.

"What do you have, Sasha?" Zach said.

Without turning, the young woman said, "It's the names and telephone numbers from that satellite phone we got from Murad."

"How about locations?"

"No, Zach," Sasha said. "The only data on the phone are telephone numbers and names. No addresses. Not even cities."

"What about area codes?"

Sasha slowed the scrolling of the data lines and touched her screen. "Notice that all the numbers include the digits 8-8-2-2-6. The first three indicate the international network. The last two identify the telecommunications service provider, also called the network operator. I don't recognize the network operator ID."

Zach said, "See the two numbers in front of the 8-8-2-2-6? Those are the country codes. The problem with them is that, for instance, the country code for the US and Canada are the same, with no differentiation by city. Unless a sat phone user has saved a caller's number in their contact list, there's no way to know who's calling."

"So, we know a name on your list might be in North America, but we can't narrow down the location?" Seth said.

"We could make calls to each number and ask them where they're located," Zach suggested.

Everyone around the terminal stared at Zach as though he were crazy.

He raised his hands in surrender. "I was just kidding."

"How do we get the addresses?" Raymond asked.

"We have to hack the network operator database," Angelina said.

"Can we do that without being detected?" Raymond said.

Angelina said, "Based on our observations to date, these people have a highly sophisticated system. They'd probably be able to detect an intrusion. If they did, they'd shut us out. And they probably have a backup system they can go to."

Zach said, "If they discover they're being hacked, they'll probably immediately release the killers. Hell, they may have already done that anyway."

No one had a response. Zach's comment seemed to cast a chill over the room.

Finally, Raymond said, "How much time would you need to access and copy their database?"

Zach spread his arms. "Once inside the database?"

"Yeah," Raymond answered.

"With our systems here, we could theoretically copy a lot of data in a few minutes. Maybe longer if their database is huge."

Raymond pulled Seth Bridewell aside, out of earshot of the others. "If I get you a few minutes, you need to extract every byte of data out of the Asasiyun's system."

"Whoa, wait a minute. I can't be sure we'll be able to do that."

Raymond narrowed his eyes and poked a finger at Seth. "If you can't get it done, I can guarantee you that a lot of people will die."

Seth groaned. "What are you going to do?"

"Better you don't know. Just get your people ready."

Raymond called Frank Reynolds from his cell as he rushed toward Tanya Serkovic's office. "I need you to meet me and the DCI," he said.

"What's the subject of the meeting?"

"Trust me. I don't have time to explain."

"What did you tell the boss about why you want to meet?" Frank said.

"I haven't talked with her yet."

"You know she doesn't like surprises."

"Yeah, I know. And she's going to hate this one."

When Frank and Raymond barged into Tanya's office, she said, "This can't be good. What's up?"

Frank looked at Raymond. "It's Boy Wonder's show. I'm here for moral support."

"Sit down," Tanya said. As an afterthought, she added, "Maybe I should get Cliff Hansen in here, too."

"Probably a good idea," Raymond said.

Tanya called Hansen, asked him to come to her office, and settled into her desk chair. "Have you thought out whatever it is you're about to ask?"

Raymond looked at his watch. "Yes, Boss. For the last four

minutes, anyway."

Frank exclaimed, "Holy Mother of God," as Tanya sank a bit lower in her chair.

It took Raymond ten minutes to provide background about the hack of Murad's satellite telephone, what he wanted to do to hack the Asasiyun's computer system, and how he wanted to accomplish it.

Predictably, Cliff Hansen thought Raymond's request was half-baked and replete with risk, including the possibility of starting a war with Iran.

"I thought about that," Raymond said. "I just can't come up with any other way to prevent the murders of maybe a thousand people."

To assist Raymond, Frank said, "And we can't bomb the crap out of that fortress in the Cloud Forest. We destroy the place and we'll never identify the assassins or where they're located."

Tanya now sat erect in her chair. "Are you certain Seth's people can hack the Asasiyun's system?"

"No, ma'am. But I'm certain that if we don't try, we'll have no chance of preventing whatever it is they have planned."

"Well, if you're going to risk starting World War III, why not just drop an invasion force into the area?" Cliff said.

"You're right, that would definitely start a war. But, more importantly, the Pentagon would want weeks, if not months to prepare. We don't have that kind of time."

"How much time do you think we have?" Tanya asked.

Raymond shrugged. "Hell, I don't know. But I doubt if it's weeks or months. The kid who attacked Mike Danforth thinks something is imminent."

Frank said, "We could be talking about hours. Don't forget all those NATO people in Venice today."

"When do you want to do it?" Tanya asked.

"Now," Raymond said. "We have long-range cruise missile prototypes that can be launched from F-18s. All we need to do is slave them to the target and give the order to fire."

"Prototypes?" Tanya said. "Are you referring to the LRASM integrated on an F/A-18E Super Hornet?"

"Yes, ma'am," Raymond said. "The Long-Range Anti-Ship

Missile."

"They're not in production and they're designed as anti-ship weapons," Cliff Hansen said.

"DARPA's been adapting them for air-to-surface use and there's an aircraft equipped with an LRASM on a carrier in the Mediterranean."

"Have they tested them in that configuration?"

"A few times."

"God save me," Tanya said. "By the way, you haven't mentioned two little hiccups in this plan of yours. If I remember the statistics correctly, the combined range of the plane and the missile would possibly necessitate flying and refueling over unfriendly territory. That's bad enough, but we'll need to get POTUS to approve the order."

"The plane will have to fly and refuel over Turkey," Raymond said.

Tanya turned pale. "Like I said, unfriendly territory."

Raymond spread his arms. "What choice do we have?"

After she told Raymond that he had thirty minutes to prepare a briefing document, Tanya called the White House and asked for a video conference with President Stanley Webb at 12:30 p.m. When POTUS's Chief of Staff began to tell her the President wouldn't be available until Monday, Tanya invoked the emergency code that indicated a crisis was impending and which, she knew, would grant her access to the President regardless of where he was or what he was doing. She hated using the code, but she had complete faith and trust in Raymond Gallegos. She had been momentarily reticent about risking so much of her own reputation on Raymond's scheme, but she'd quickly scrubbed any hesitation. Now, as she waited for her conference with President Webb, a slim worm of doubt entered her mind. Before the worm could turn her thinking around, a message flashed across her computer screen: *Iran's Leadership Claims They Know Nothing About Asasiyun Group.*

"Lying bastards," Tanya muttered.

When Raymond rejoined Tanya and Cliff, he told them, "I emailed you both the briefing document."

Tanya pulled up Raymond's email, read it aloud, and looked at Cliff.

"Sounds okay," he said, but he looked skeptical.

She checked the time—12:30. Turning on the big-screen monitor on her office wall, she sighed and said, "Here goes."

Right on time, President Webb walked into the Oval Office and sat behind his desk. The Secretary of Defense, the Director of National Intelligence, the Vice President, and Webb's Chief of Staff followed him into the office and took seats opposite him. Tanya was amazed once again at how much POTUS had aged since he'd taken office. His hair was now completely white, and his wrinkles looked more like crevices.

"Good afternoon, Madam Director," Webb said.

"Good afternoon, Mr. President. Thank you for making time for me on such short notice."

Webb made a dismissive hand gesture. "I understand we have something serious to discuss."

Tanya advised that Cliff Hansen, Frank Reynolds, and Raymond Gallegos were in her office. "I'm going to turn this over to Mr. Gallegos."

Raymond briefed Webb on what he wanted to do.

POTUS listened without interruption. When Raymond finished, he said, "Let me summarize. You want to drop ordnance close enough to a remote facility in northern Iran to get the attention of its occupants. You don't want to hurt or kill anyone; you just want the people there to hunker down while you hack their system and copy their files."

"That's correct, Mr. President."

"And you believe you can get the information you're after in two minutes."

"Yes, sir."

"And what if the technical people there don't seek shelter? And what if they destroy their files as soon as our bombs hit?"

"Then we would have accomplished nothing," Raymond said.

"That's not quite true, Mr. Gallegos. We will have initiated a daisy chain of events that could precipitate an international conflict." After a beat, Webb added, "Actually, that will probably happen anyway, whether or not we get the information we're after."

Tanya felt momentary sympathy for Webb. His expression and posture were perfect representations of someone bearing the weight of the world. She raised a hand to stop Raymond from responding and said, "Mr. President, we have no doubt the Iranians are behind the Asasiyun group. Regardless of their reaction to our attack, we will be able to show the world Iran's culpability in this murderous campaign. Compared to a relatively benign bombing attack that doesn't target people, the Iranians have orchestrated a vicious, psychopathic assassination operation. We'll save hundreds, if not thousands of lives, and we could mine a vast trove of documents from the Asasiyun system hack."

"Assuming the hack is successful," Webb said.

"Yes, sir."

"That's a big assumption."

Tanya thought, *That's the understatement of the century.*

"And you'd like an answer by when?"

"Yesterday," Tanya said. She coughed a humorless laugh. "We don't believe we can afford to put this off. We are very...concerned about Venice being a target while the NATO representatives are there."

Webb said, "I haven't heard anything from you that backs up that belief. It sounds as though you all are operating on instinct rather than facts."

Tanya nodded several times. She said, "That's about right, Mr. President. But we do know that almost two dozen VIPs and family members in Western countries have now been assassinated. Our analysts estimate that there could be at least one thousand sleeper agents about to be turned loose. We learned from a captured Asasiyun operative that a very large number of people were trained by the group and are probably sleeper agents in dozens of Western countries. He told us that he heard the phrase, 'The Glorious One Thousand,' on many occasions. This might confirm our analysts' estimates. The phone we hacked had well over one thousand different numbers in its memory. Every one of those numbers could represent an assassin. What we're trying to do is identify the locations of those people."

Webb appeared to try to smile, but his expression was more of a grimace. "This still comes down to you wanting me to make a decision to drop bombs on a sovereign nation that would see our actions as justifiable provocation to retaliate against us. And you want me to make that decision based on beliefs, instincts, and assumptions, and very few facts."

Tanya thought, *That's about right.* She wondered if she was about to lose the argument. More on impulse than on clear-headedness, she blurted, "If we fail in this mission, Mr. President, I will resign my position and announce that I took action unilaterally."

Webb's eyes seemed to become lasers. The muscles in his jaws twitched. "I'll get back to you as soon as possible," he said, pointed a remote at the monitor in the Oval Office, and clicked off the screen.

The others in her office looked stunned. Before any of them could say something, she spoke: "I'll get back to you all as soon as I hear from POTUS."

CHAPTER 52

Yasmin's knees jackhammered; her feet bounced on the office floor. She stood, hoping she could walk off her nervousness. Her emotions ran from exhilaration to abject terror; from raging anger to total serenity. But it was anger that predominated. What she was about to accomplish would be the greatest triumph that Iran and the Muslim world had ever had. Nothing that Cyrus, or Ashurbanipal, or Nebuchadnezzar, or Darius, or any of the region's great kings had accomplished could compare to what she was about to do. If she were a man, she could realistically aspire to become the new emperor of a modern Persian Empire. But her own people would never accept a woman as their leader. All she would come away with after the successful completion of the Great Ayatollah's vision would be world class wealth. Her anger grew as she thought about how that wealth had been accumulated. Her father had stolen monies intended to fund the Asasiyun mission, and she'd kidnapped rich men's children. But that wealth wasn't enough compensation for the accomplishment of a heroic task.

She walked off her nerves and sat at her father's desk as Javad entered the office. She suppressed her contempt for the man. The more familiar their relationship had become, the more Javad had presumed importance and authority. The more he presumed, the more her contempt grew.

She told herself, *Soon, I'll be rid of you.*

"Four hours to go," he said.

Yasmin felt a manic flutter in her stomach. "Yes," she said.

"I suggest we give our people a break to eat something and maybe relax a little. They have a long, tense evening ahead."

She nodded. "Good."

Giovanni and Anna Ventimiglia came out onto the concrete path between their home and the canal when Bob and Liz arrived. As soon as Liz stepped from the boat, Anna put an arm around her and quickly escorted her inside. Giovanni introduced Bob to five AISE agents detailed to provide protection. The five men went off to reconnoiter the property while Giovanni and Bob went inside to join Anna and Liz.

"Are you okay?" Giovanni asked once they were inside the foyer.

"We're fine," Bob said. He smiled at Liz. "If it weren't for her, I might not be here."

"Nonsense," Liz said. She turned to Anna. "Thank you for having us."

"It's our pleasure," Anna said. "I am so sorry about what has happened to you both. This is not the welcome visitors to Venice usually experience."

Liz hugged Anna and whispered, "That's because the usual visitor to Venice is not named Robert Danforth."

Anna giggled, as Liz released her and stepped back. "Your things will be brought here." She looked momentarily embarrassed, then asked, "I assume you haven't changed your mind about attending the ball?"

"I think I've had enough excitement. But you and Giovanni must go. I don't want our being here to keep you away from the ball."

"We'll see," Anna said. "Come, I'll show you to your room."

After the ladies left, Giovanni took Bob into a salon, poured him a whiskey, and said, "Let's sit. I have information for you."

Bob sat on a couch, took the drink, and downed a fourth of it. He set the glass on a table and half-turned to his right to look at Giovanni who sat on the other end of the couch.

"We identified the man who tried to kill you. His name was

Luigi Donatello." Giovanni's face had turned red. "He was a senior director at AISE."

Bob's breath caught in his chest. He hadn't expected to hear that.

"The man was a long-time agency employee," Giovanni continued. "Almost nineteen years. Before that, he served in the Army. His background investigation was pristine. But we've now discovered that we really have no idea where he came from. It appears he took over the identity of a boy who died as an infant. His past, before his military service, is apparently fiction." Giovanni shook his head; he wore a dismayed expression. "He must have been an Asasiyun sleeper agent for over twenty years."

"You know what surprises me?" Bob said. "The Asasiyun sending a man like Donatello to kill me. I mean, the guy must have been an important asset for them. Probably provided them with a lot of sensitive information over the years and could have continued to do so for many more. Why waste an asset like that on a retired CIA employee?"

"I can come up with two answers," Giovanni said. "One, someone very powerful badly wants you dead. In fact, from what I've learned, someone wants your entire family dead. You must have done something in your past that precipitated this sort of reaction."

"I know the answer to that one. The personal vendetta is all about the death of Musa bin Hakim, the son of the wealthy Saudi, Abdel bin Hakim."

Giovanni nodded. "My second theory is that the Asasiyun was willing to risk losing Donatello because the organization itself is expendable."

"What do you mean?"

"I've thought a lot about this," Giovanni said. "I suspect the Asasiyun has an end game. When it accomplishes that end game, it'll go away."

Bob said, "We could be talking about surviving assassins, hundreds of instructors, language teachers, support staff, and the like. How do they just *go away*?"

"The majority of the assassins are on suicide missions. The instructors and non-critical support staff have probably already been disposed of. They couldn't leave those people alive. If they had, it would have taken only one of them to talk and we would have heard about the group a long time ago. I suspect they eliminated an employee as soon as he or she was no longer needed."

"That would serve the Iranian regime's best interests," Bob said. "Eliminate every person that could tie the mullahs to the Asasiyun."

"That's right. Even if no one will believe the mullahs if they claim they had nothing to do with the Asasiyun, there would be no one alive to contradict them. At least, that's how I believe the mullahs would think."

That's probably correct, Bob thought. *The Iranians don't know the CIA has interrogated people who placed the Asasiyun headquarters in Iran.*

"And the mullahs will take maximum advantage of the disruption in the West caused by the Asasiyun," Giovanni said.

"The Iranians know how to play a long game," Bob said.

"Yeah, they do. But what we should focus on is what the hundreds and hundreds of killers are going to do to commit suicide. They'll take out a huge number of Western leaders."

Bob felt intense frustration. He didn't like being on the outside. *I wonder what they're doing back at Langley about all this*, he thought.

CHAPTER 53

What else should I be doing? Tanya thought as she paced her office. But she couldn't make her mind focus on anything other than the impending call from POTUS. The minute hand on the clock on her desk seemed to move in slow motion. Twenty minutes had passed since the video call. She visualized the Oval Office, the President's advisors throwing objections at him. The more she imagined the scene, the more pessimistic she became.

Another ten minutes passed. Her legs had become so shaky that she went to her chair and plopped down onto it. She closed her eyes, propped an elbow on a chair arm, and rested her head in her hand. Taking long, deep breaths to calm herself, she had just about concluded she'd lost the argument, when her phone rang. Her assistant told her that the President was holding.

"Yes, Mr. President."

"It's a go, Madam Director. Turkey will allow our pilot to overfly their airspace, but they'll file a complaint with the UN Security Council after the fact, pretending we violated their airspace without their permission. They don't want to appear as though they supported an attack on a fellow Muslim country. One other thing. They will fire on the plane if it spends more than two hours over Turkey."

Tanya wanted to shout for joy. This was as good as she could have expected. Instead, she said, "Thank you, Mr. President. I will—"

Webb interrupted. "If the mission succeeds, what do you suggest we do with the fortress in Iran?"

"Once we have the information we need, I recommend we destroy the facility's electronics, including all their communications equipment."

"Won't that require a bombing run? That's not acceptable at this—"

"No, sir. We can get it done with an electromagnetic pulse burst from an NRO satellite."

Webb didn't immediately respond. Finally, he said in a gruff, even voice, "I don't appreciate stunts."

"Mr. President?"

"I don't want my key people threatening to resign over failed missions, and I sure as hell don't need them to take the fall for my decisions. As old Harry Truman said, 'The buck stops here.' Don't ever do that again."

"Yes, Mr. President."

"Now get that information we need. I'd hate to learn I overruled my entire national security team's advice on a losing cause."

"Yes, sir."

Tanya ordered her assistant to call in Cliff Hansen, Frank Reynolds, and Raymond Gallegos. The three men arrived within a few seconds of one another and gathered in front of her desk, looking like children waiting to be told that Santa Claus was on his way.

"We have a green light from POTUS," she said. She stared hard at Raymond. "I emphasized that time was of the essence. The President responded accordingly. He's already informed the Joint Chiefs and the Secretary of the Navy. The aircraft should be ready to take off within the hour." She leaned back in her chair and rubbed her hands over her face. When she looked back at Raymond, she said, "I expect you to make this happen."

"Yes, ma'am," Raymond said.

She made a slight tip of her head. "You should know that President Webb made this decision against the advice of all his advisors, including the SECDEF. I suspect every one of those bureaucrats would love to tell POTUS 'I told you so.' We don't want that to happen for multiple reasons which I assume you can figure out for yourself." She stood and handed Raymond a copy of a directive wired from the White House. "That includes the contact information for the aircraft carrier's captain."

"I'll get right on it."

"Keep me informed every step of the way."

Raymond rushed down to one of the SCIFs at Langley and used encrypted communications equipment to contact the captain of an aircraft carrier with the 6th Fleet in the Mediterranean. He neither used the man's name nor gave his own. He recited the code name for the mission—Silver Flash—the authorization code provided by the White House, and the target's coordinates.

"Expected time of engagement?" the captain asked.

"ASAP," Raymond answered.

An F/A-18E Super Hornet armed with a Long-Range Anti-Ship Missile had been covered with a tarpaulin since the missile had been mated to the aircraft weeks before. The Navy and the Defense Advanced Research Projects Agency wanted no unauthorized photographs taken of the aircraft/ordnance configuration; nor did they want sailors aboard the carrier gossiping about it. As the plane was moved to the carrier elevator, the captain ordered all non-essential personnel to quarters. Only a skeleton launch crew remained on the carrier deck. In addition to the LRASM, the plane had been modified with conformal fuel tanks, which replaced the drop tanks usually on the aircraft. This added three hundred miles to the jet's range and reduced its radar footprint.

The missile's guidance system had been programmed to strike coordinates that were two hundred yards from the western wall of the compound in the Cloud Forest. The weapon would have to fly to the outer limits of its modified three hundred and fifty mile range, which meant the aircraft pilot would need to fly to a spot north of Erzurum, Turkey, release the weapon, and immediately head north toward the Black Sea; there, a KC-135 aircraft near the coast would refuel his plane.

The one thing about his mission that truly worried the F/A-18E's pilot was the two hour time limit that he'd been given over Turkey. He knew that would be cutting it close. *I guess that's why the squadron commander talked to me extensively about electronic countermeasures and evasive maneuvers,* he thought as he taxied to his launch position on the carrier deck. He swallowed hard as he remembered that his commander had also asked him if his will was up to date.

At the end of the runway, the pilot clicked on the satellite camera inside the cockpit and performed a radio check with the carrier tower. He knew that every word he spoke from that moment to the end of his mission would be heard by his squadron commander on the carrier, CIA executives in a SCIF at Langley, and members of the Joint Chiefs at the Pentagon.

"We have an ETA for the aircraft to arrive at launch location of 1527 hours EST," a voice announced over the SCIF overhead speakers. "Impact on target should be at 1559 hours."

Tanya "rogered" the transmission from the carrier's tower. She checked the digital wall clock: 1316 hours, Eastern Standard Time, and told Seth, "You need to make sure your boys and girls are alert and ready to initiate the hack immediately after the missile hits."

Seth shot her a "thumbs-up" and exited the SCIF.

She turned toward Raymond and saw the tension that seemed to have turned his body rigid. His lips moved as though in prayer as he stared at the screen that showed the pilot inside the jet. Tanya walked over to Raymond and touched his shoulder, which caused him to jerk.

He turned and said, "Yes, ma'am?"

Tanya smiled at him. "Don't worry, Ray. Everything's going to work out fine."

"As far as this op is concerned, I think you're correct. What worries me is how the Iranians will respond. Israel is within range of their nuclear missiles. So are a number of our military facilities and ships in the Middle East."

"You hack the Asasiyun computers and get the information we think is there, the Iranians would be crazy to respond to a missile blast that doesn't create a single casualty. Once we let the world know those bastards are already responsible for the Asasiyun murders and were planning to assassinate as many as one thousand or more people, they'll have no place to hide. Retaliating against our missile strike would only make their position worse. They may be crazy, but they sure as hell ain't stupid."

CHAPTER 54

"You're certain?" Iranian President Hassan Shabani said.

General Ardashir Tahami, head of Iran's Ministry of Intelligence, maintained his usual stoic expression. Other than a slight shifting of his feet, he could have been a statue. "Mr. President, I wish I could give you guarantees. I can't. But I can tell you that something is wrong. In fact, I have several concerns. There is no evidence that Mr. Khavari's helicopter was attacked externally. It appears to have just exploded in mid-air."

Shabani stood and moved to the window. His back to Tahami, he said, "So, an explosive device may have been planted aboard the aircraft."

"That's our best guess. We will be able to determine the cause as soon as our team reaches the site. But, as you know, it's secluded and mountainous. And the weather has worked against us. It began snowing last night. We will have to helicopter our investigative team in once the weather clears and, perhaps, lower them in if we can't find a landing site nearby."

Shabani turned. "You said there were other concerns."

"Yes, Mr. President. We have been unable to contact the Saudi, Abdel bin Hakim. The crude oil we planned to transfer to his ships for transport to Russia is still in storage tanks. His ships haven't arrived."

"What about the money he promised?"

"It didn't arrive either."

"The transfer was contingent upon the deaths of some people named Danforth. Maybe he's holding up funds until—"

Tahami blurted, "I personally looked into that. There has been no news about the deaths of anyone named Danforth. When I called the Asasiyun headquarters, to see if they had heard anything, I was told no one was available to speak with me."

"That's impossible."

"I agree, Mr. President. My instincts tell me something is wrong there. I think that, if there were explosives placed on Mr. Khavari's helicopter, it could have been done by someone at the Asasiyun fortress."

Shabani felt his face go hot. "Anything else?"

"Yes, sir. Our cell in Reston, Virginia has gone silent. We can't contact any of the Shirazi brothers and haven't received intelligence from them in days. They also missed a hand-off yesterday to our diplomat there."

Shabani's bowels churned as he considered the meaning of all this bad news. "Do you think the Americans discovered the cell?"

Tahami blinked and his lips compressed. Shabani knew that this was about as expressive as the general ever got. *He's worried,* the President thought. *Which means that I need to really be worried.*

"We're looking into it," Tahami said.

Shabani tried to slow his breathing. He turned back to the window. "Are the attacks still on?"

"As far as we know," Tahami said.

The jet pilot checked his instrument panel. He saw he was three minutes from launch point. He continued to maintain radio silence. His electronics kept the tower on the carrier informed of his location, and much more. His stomach felt queasy as he remained hyper-alert. He was fast approaching the two hour time limit, and he still had to fly north to the Black Sea after releasing the missile.

When he reached the launch location coordinates, he fired the LRASM and banked to the north as he dropped altitude. He pushed the plane's collective to maximum speed, less concerned about fuel consumption than about getting into a dog fight with one or more Turkish F-16C Fighting Hornets while he was low on fuel. He knew he had a superior plane, but he was almost as concerned about shooting down a NATO ally's jet as he was about being shot down himself. *It's a crazy world*, he thought. *Gotta get permission to overfly an ally's territory and then get threatened with obliteration for exceeding a time limit over that country.*

He tapped a finger against his fuel gauge and saw he had less than thirty minutes of fuel remaining. *I'm barely going to make it*, he thought.

After the LRASM dropped from the F/A-18E's underbelly, its rocket motor ignited. The twenty-five-hundred-pound weapon mated to a Tactical Tomahawk Weapon Control System for guidance and, boosted by an Mk-114 motor, flew a planned, low-altitude profile to its pre-determined endpoint three hundred and seventeen miles to the east. It slaved to the coordinates programmed into its guidance system and sped eastward.

At first, Yasmin Nizari thought an earthquake tremor had occurred. Earthquakes were not uncommon in Iran. Then she heard screams and the pounding of feet in the hall outside her office. She leaped from her desk chair and opened the door to the hallway. She was almost knocked down as workers maniacally jostled with one another while they ran down the hall, toward the underground shelter. She grabbed a woman by the arm and pulled her into the office.

"What's happened?"

The woman couldn't seem to form words. Yasmin slapped the woman's face and shouted, "Calm down. Tell me what's happened."

"A bo…bomb. We are being attacked."

She shoved the woman back out into the hall, where she was immediately knocked down and trampled. She spotted Javad to her right, coming down the hall toward her. He pushed his way through the crowd, which had suddenly stopped moving as people stacked up at the underground shelter door at the corridor's far left end.

"We need to take shelter," Javad shouted as he entered her office. He grasped her arm and tried to pull her outside.

She shook her arm loose and yelled, "Tell me what's happened."

"A rocket or missile landed near the west wall. The next one could hit the fortress. We have—"

"It landed outside the wall?"

"That's right. Come on. We—"

"Was anyone hurt?"

Javad tried to grab her arm again, but Yasmin stepped back.

"Do you wonder why, considering modern guidance systems, a missile would land outside the wall?"

"That's ridiculous. No weapon is foolproof. There's always human error. Come on, we have to go down into—"

"Shut up!" Yasmin shouted. She turned away as she processed what she'd been told. Something didn't seem right. She turned back to him and rasped, "They want our data!"

"What are you talking about? Who wants our data?"

"How the hell do I know? The Americans, the Israelis, the English. It could be any of our enemies."

"There's no way anyone can hack us. The ops center people will shut down the system the second they detect an intrusion."

"*If* they're still in the ops center and haven't fled for their lives, just like all those idiots out there in the hall."

Javad seemed momentarily confused. But a light appeared to go on behind his eyes. He cursed and stormed from the office, barging into the men and women choking the hallway. "Out of my way," he screamed.

Yasmin trailed Javad as he parted the crowd. It took them over a minute to break through to the ops center. They found the door there unlocked and the center vacant.

"In the name of Allah and all that's holy," she muttered. She raced to the nearest console.

Zach Grabowsky personally piloted the Asasiyun database hack. He triggered the hacking software fifteen seconds after the missile impacted near the fortress. As Angelina had told him earlier, there was no point in waiting to initiate the hack any longer than that. If the people manning the computers didn't flee within the first fifteen seconds, they probably were there to stay.

He held his breath as the hacking software kicked in, and prayed that nothing would obstruct it. He breathed out when a FILES UPLOADING message came on his computer screen. He took another deep breath and held it, anticipating at any moment that one of the Asasiyun computer experts would realize what was happening and shut down their system. He had become lightheaded by the time he realized the hack was proceeding as planned. He raised his arms above his head in triumph as others in the CIA Operations Center seemed to have collectively stopped breathing.

FILE UPLOAD COMPLETE popped up on Zach's screen. He placed his cursor over a button in the hacking system that read: SANITIZE INTRUSION. He clicked his mouse and watched the button blink for ten seconds before it was replaced by a message that told him he had erased any evidence of his having been in the Asasiyun database.

Angelina, seated next to a Farsi-speaking female IT employee named Nasrin, immediately accessed the data Zach had extracted from the Asasiyun system. They searched the file names, looking for something that might include information about the group's assassins. Nasrin read aloud from the file menu, translating as fast as she could. They were five minutes into scanning the files when Angelina yelled, "Stop. What was that last one?"

"*Our Glorious One Thousand*," Nasrin said. She placed a finger on the screen. "It's that one."

Angelina opened the file and waited for Nasrin to read the contents.

"I think this is it," she said. "It has names, with addresses and telephone numbers from dozens of countries."

"Are the countries all in the West?" Angelina asked.

Nasrin scanned the list again. "Yes."

"One other thing," Angelina said. "See if the name Barry Murad is on the list."

After fifteen seconds, Nasrin said, "There's an Abd al Bari Murad."

Angelina shouted, "Zach, we have it."

Zach turned until he spotted a relieved-looking Seth Bridewell. "Seth," he shouted, "we need those Farsi speakers in here now."

Then Zach called out, "Listen up," so that all the employees in the room could hear him. "Angelina is going to email each of you a list. The Farsi translators will pair up with you as we discussed earlier. When your translator gives you information from your list, you will immediately email that information to the contact you were given in your assigned country. They are waiting to hear from us. You will share with that person the names, addresses, and phone numbers of all the Asasiyun operatives located in that country. Questions?"

When no one responded, Zach moved to Seth and, in a soft voice said, "You might want to let Mr. Gallegos know."

Seth smiled and pointed over his shoulder. Zach saw Raymond Gallegos standing in a back corner speaking into a cell phone. Seth said, "Probably letting the DCI know."

CHAPTER 55

Yasmin's heartbeat slowed when she discovered no evidence that the database had been breached. She told herself they'd been damned lucky and thought about how much pleasure she would get from seeing every man and woman in the building executed as soon as the mission was complete.

"Is everything okay?" Javad said.

"No thanks to the idiots who were supposed to protect the system at all costs. Go find those morons and bring them back here." She stormed out of the center as a couple of employees returned. She shouldered one of them aside and cursed at him. A second man jumped out of her way and scurried to his console.

Javad followed her out. "That missile attack has me worried. Why only one missile? If someone wanted to do real damage, they would have launched multiple weapons at the fortress, not one into the trees. I think you were correct. Someone wanted to frighten us. If that was their intent, they succeeded."

"Yes, but I checked the database. It's secure."

"Yasmin, I'm not a computer expert, but what if a hack did occur and the hacker was able to conceal the intrusion? Maybe we should push up the time for starting the attacks?"

She thought about that for a moment. "That could ruin our plans in Venice. The people there probably won't be at the ball yet. Those targets are too valuable to miss."

"We planned the attacks for 9:30 p.m., Venice-time, because the crowd at the ball should be at its largest then. Why don't we move up the time a couple of hours? Sure, we'll miss some NATO people, but we'll get enough of them to have a major impact."

Yasmin nodded as she considered Javad's suggestion. Finally, she said, "I agree. Now get the rest of those cowards and put them back to work."

Tanya and Raymond found the CIA Operations Center a circus of sound and movement. Telephone conversations, dialogue between translators and computer operators, people shouting at one another, and rapid typing on keyboards made the place resemble a trading room at a Wall Street brokerage firm during a market collapse.

"How can they hear one another?" Tanya asked.

Raymond chuckled. "They're kids. They're used to noise."

"Show me where we're collecting feedback from the foreign intelligence agencies."

"Over this way," Raymond said. He led Tanya down four steps to a twenty by twenty-yard space equipped with twenty-nine manned workstations, each of which included a desk, a chair, a computer terminal, and a multi-line telephone console. At each station, a staff member wearing a headset was engaged in an animated conversation. The wall in front of the area was, in effect, a huge electronic screen that showed columns with the names of all twenty-nine NATO countries in alphabetical order, a government employee contact name in each country, and the contact's phone number and email address. On the screen's right side was information that the hack of the Asasiyun database had yielded: the names of assassination targets and names of Asasiyun agents in each country. The last column showed sequences of numbers separated by commas.

Raymond pointed at the wall. "The first five columns are self-explanatory. The numbers in the last column indicate the status of the assassin shown in the next-to-last column. Go to the first line: Albania. The number one indicates an assassin has been captured or killed. The number two signifies the assassin has not been located, three means the target is under protection, four is for targets who have not been secured, and five is for targets who have been killed or wounded. You will note that there are no fives on the screen, which tells me the Asasiyun leadership has not yet turned their killers loose."

"Which also probably means the group is not aware of what we've accomplished to date," Tanya said. "Sooner or later that could change."

"That's right. That's why we need to fry the electronics at that place in the Cloud Forest."

"I'll give the order when the time is right," she said. "But if we do that prematurely, it will be like telling them that we know what they're up to. They could switch to another system and turn their killers loose before we can locate them."

Raymond nodded. "By the way, did you hear there was another attempt on Bob Danforth's life?"

Tanya blew out a loud breath. "Oh, yeah. I arranged to have Bob and Liz moved to the home of an old AISE ally. Hopefully, what you're doing down here will put an end to all of this."

As Tanya moved to an office where she could escape the bullpen's noise, she noticed the time on a digital wall clock: 1400 hours. She thought, *It's already 7:00 p.m. in Italy. I wonder what Bob and Liz are doing now? Some vacation they're having.*

A doctor had just left the Ventimiglia residence, having cleaned and bandaged the glass cuts on Liz's hands and examined Bob's shoulder, which turned out to be bruised but not broken. The painkillers the doctor gave Liz had made her drowsy, so she had excused herself and gone up to their room. Anna, Giovanni, and Bob moved to the solarium where the last of the evening sun cast an eerie glow through massive bay windows that almost touched the fourteen-foot-tall ceiling. Dust motes danced lazily in broken rays of sunlight that made the wicker furniture and the marble floor gleam.

"Would you like something to drink?" Anna asked. "Perhaps a glass of prosecco."

Before Bob could answer, Giovanni said, "My dear, I suspect Roberto would prefer something stronger."

Bob smiled and shot Giovanni a grateful look.

Giovanni stood and moved to a bar built into one corner, opened a bottle of prosecco, and filled a flute for Anna. He poured two fingers of scotch into two glasses. After he served the drinks, he returned to his chair, raised his glass toward Bob, and toasted, "*Per la tua salute.*"

Bob coughed. "Toasting to my health is probably not a good bet." He breathed in the scotch's smoky aroma, swallowed a healthy portion, set the glass on the lamp table on his right, and said, "Don't you have to get ready for the ball?"

"Giovanni and I decided to pass on the ball this year," Anna said. "We'll stay in and have dinner with you."

Bob looked from Anna to Giovanni. "Please, don't do that," he said. "Liz and I won't be the best of guests. We're both exhausted. We'll feel awful if you skip the ball because of us."

Giovanni made a dramatic Italian hand gesture and scoffed, "We've attended dozens of balls. There will be another one next year." He laughed, then shot Bob a toothy smile. "Besides, there's always more excitement being around you."

"I feel terrible about this," Bob said.

The hand gesture appeared again. "Before you become overwhelmed with guilt, perhaps I should explain the conditions of the dinner tonight."

Bob saw mischief in Giovanni's expression. He looked over at Anna, but her expression was inscrutable. "You now have me worried," Bob said.

"Oh, there's nothing to be worried about, my friend," Giovanni said. "In fact, I believe you will be thrilled about our surprise. Anna, why don't you explain."

Competing emotions battled inside Bob's head. He appreciated what Giovanni and Anna were doing. He knew Carnevale was the grandest annual event in Venice, and Anna and Giovanni's families had been active and important participants and sponsors of the ball for many decades. Despite what they'd told him, he knew missing the event was a sacrifice. But Giovanni's *surprise* hadn't left him with a warm, fuzzy feeling. And, at this point, he wasn't sure how Liz would react. They were both spent. Between lack of sleep, emotional and adrenaline overload, and injured bodies, all he wanted to do was rest. *I imagine Liz will feel the same as I do*, he thought.

He found her curled up on their bed, her iPad next to her, her breathing slow and deep. He padded across the carpet as softly as he could, but she stirred, opened her eyes, and showed him the smile that won his heart over fifty years earlier.

"Sorry, I tried not to wake you."

"That's all right. I should get up. I'm not being a very good guest."

"Giovanni and Anna have decided to pass on the ball and host a dinner here. And they want us to dress in our ball costumes."

Liz scooted backward, sat up, and leaned against the headboard. She clapped her hands like an excited child. "That's wonderful." She smiled again. "Is that okay with you?"

He suppressed a groan, put on as big a smile as he could muster, and said, "Tights and all." Then he chuckled and said, "I hope you can control yourself."

"Oh, I'll be fine. It's Anna I'm worried about. She might swoon over your legs."

"You are so bad," he said.

CHAPTER 56

With the personnel back at their workstations, Javad announced, "Our great Order has planned for this moment for over forty years. Thousands of loyal supporters have worked to bring us to this moment. But you are the tip of the spear that will pierce the heart of our enemy. You each know your assignment." He looked at the wall clock and saw it was now 6:00 p.m. in Venice. He thought, *Our Glorious One Thousand are about to be released, but Venice will be the blow that will have the greatest impact.* He felt as though the temperature of his blood had risen; heat surged through him. He'd never been more excited in his life. "It's time to unleash our people on the corrupt West." He raised a fist and shouted, "The Asasiyun will be victorious."

The men and women in the room leaped to their feet and repeated the mantra, chanting it until Javad pumped his hands, cajoling them to settle down. He again looked at the clock. *Only ninety minutes until zero hour.*

Javad continued: "When the Venice clock reads 7:30, you will each transmit our founder's message to our agents' satellite phones."

Javad knew that nine hundred and seventy-eight satellite telephones would receive the message. An equal number of men and women—and perhaps many more innocent friends, family members, and/or associates of those targets—in twenty-nine Western countries would be targeted shortly after the message's transmission. To account for those targets who were in Venice and not in their home countries where Asasiyun agents were located, Yasmin had amended her father's message to his agents. Nizari's words were: *The Old Man of the Mountain Sends His Love to His Children!* To this, Yasmin had added: *If your target is not available, find a suitable alternate.*

Carlo Severino was one of the few Asasiyun agents who had known in advance that the mass attacks would occur today, February 23, at 9:30 p.m. His part of the mission—the annihilation of hundreds of NATO representatives—was perhaps the most important of all. He'd estimated that the two 500-Class patrol boats' captains would have plenty of time to make the trip from Piran, Slovenia to their assigned positions, arm and launch their weapons at 9:30, and then escape to Kvarner Bay, Croatia, where they thought they would be met by compatriots who would spirit them to Iran. Severino had already sent agents to Croatia to eliminate the boat crews upon their arrival. Severino was too valuable an asset to be compromised if a crew member was apprehended and decided to talk.

But Severino had been surprised when he'd received a text message earlier that day ordering him to initiate the attack on the carnival ball venue at 7:30 that evening, two hours earlier than originally planned. He hated last-minute changes. And he knew meeting the new timeline would be difficult. *But not impossible,* he thought.

He smiled at the image that came to mind: the missiles impacting the Palazzo Pisani Moretta, obliterating a significant portion of the NATO cadre.

He inspected his costume in the full-length mirror in his hotel room and buttoned the ornate vest. A bubble of disgust rose from his stomach. The decadence of the entire Carnevale was abhorrent to him. *What would the Old Man of the Mountain think if he saw me dressed like this?* he wondered. But he knew his job was to do whatever it took to accomplish his mission.

He glanced at the bedside clock: 6:15 p.m. Forty-five minutes to get to the Palazzo Pisani Moretta, make an appearance, conduct a brief conversation with his boss, Paolo Andreotti, and then quickly vacate the building. He would shelter in a nearby building and, after the attack, stagger into the debris and carnage, pretending to be stunned. With the loss of most of the Italian Defense Ministry's hierarchy, he would be assured of a promotion to a position in which he could dramatically influence Italian and NATO intelligence and military policy.

Severino patted the scabbard on his left hip. The dagger there was supposed to be part of his costume, but he'd honed the blade to a razor's edge. *You never know*, he thought.

About to leave his room, his cell phone rang.

"*Pronto*," he answered.

"Carlo, it's me."

"Secretary Andreotti, I am on my way to the palezzetto. I—"

"I'm glad I caught you. I've been invited to a private dinner this evening. My wife isn't feeling well, so I'd like you to join me. I think you'll enjoy this."

"But—You're not going to the Grand Ball?"

Andreotti blurted a laugh. "I've been to a dozen of those extravaganzas. I find having dinner with former AISE Director Giovanni Ventimiglia a much nicer way to spend my evening than being jostled by hundreds of crazed revelers."

Severino thought for a beat. *This sounds like a much better alternative than going to the ball. I can't ask for a better alibi than Andreotti. The only negative is my boss won't be killed in the missile attack. But I can make that happen at another time.*

"Will there be others at the dinner?"

"Yes. Many people you will know and others you should get to know. A retired American intelligence officer and his wife, Robert and Elizabeth Danforth, will also be there. I think you will enjoy meeting them. Mr. Danforth had an illustrious career. The dinner is essentially in their honor."

Severino's heart skipped a beat. He thought Danforth had already been killed. Luigi Donatello was supposed to manage that. "What's the address, Minister Andreotti?" he asked.

Bob forced himself to smile, but he knew he wasn't fooling Liz. As they took the curved staircase from their floor down to the first level, Liz took his arm and said, "I appreciate you being such a good sport." She glanced down at his legs and chuckled. "You know, you really do have great legs. You should wear tights more often."

Bob let his smile slip away and scowled. "If I didn't love you so much," he said.

She pressed his arm against her side and whispered, "I suppose posting photos on Facebook of you in this costume is out of the question."

Bob glared at her, feigning anger. "You have a sick sense of humor."

"Just promise me you won't say anything to me in Italian. I might not be able to control myself."

"Ha, ha, ha."

When they reached the bottom of the stairs, Bob looked down at the brocade curled-toed slippers, the sequined coat that hung to his mid-thigh, and the purple tights. He adjusted the multi-colored vest that was a size too small and put a finger under the silk shirt collar, pulling it away from his neck. He had a sudden fear that he'd been set up. *What if Giovanni and Anna aren't in costume?* he thought.

Just then, the Ventimiglias came into the foyer. They were decked out in what Bob thought were outlandish outfits. But it was the way that Giovanni's face was made up that surprised Bob. Giovanni doffed his feathered hat, bowed to them, and said, "*Buonasera, amici miei.*"

Anna's gown was bright pink and had a football-sized cameo embedded in its front skirt. Her pink-tinted wig towered two feet high, with ringlets that framed her face. She held a fan in one hand and a scepter in the other.

Bob was about to laugh, but Liz short-circuited his reaction as she stepped toward their hosts, effusively complimenting them.

"You look quite debonair," Giovanni told Bob.

"And very handsome," Anna said.

"How do you like the tights?" Liz asked as she pointed at Bob's legs.

Anna giggled. "It would be inappropriate for a married woman to comment on a man's quite shapely legs."

"Aw, jeez," Bob said.

Giovanni came to Bob's rescue, took his arm, and said, "Let's go into the salon."

Bob said to Giovanni, "Do you do this every year?"

"Absolutely. It's the highlight of my year."

Bob shot his friend a suspicious look. "Really?"

Giovanni whispered, "Of course not. This is one of many things I do to keep Anna happy. I assume you can relate to that concept."

Bob again felt guilty about contributing to his friends missing the ball. "Anna must be crushed about missing the ball. I'm so sorry that things turned out the way they did."

Giovanni said, "When you can't attend one ball, you go to another."

"Meaning?" Bob asked.

Giovanni threw open the doors to a small ballroom. Liveried waiters stood at attention holding silver trays of wine glasses. There were about twenty costumed people in the room; a string quartet in one corner played baroque music.

"Oh my God," Bob blurted.

"Calm down, my friend. You know most of the men in here. Half of them are retired NATO intelligence types and the other half are senior defense officials—some retired, some still active."

"I thought this was a private dinner."

Giovanni laughed. "It is. When everyone arrives, we'll only be forty people. That's Anna's idea of a small, private dinner."

"Aw, jeez," Bob said as he once more adjusted his vest.

CHAPTER 57

Carlo Severino agonized over what his boss had told him. As he departed his hotel room and took the elevator down to the canal beside the building, he remembered the emphasis that Hassan Nizari had placed on eliminating the Danforths. *What the hell do I do?* he thought. About to signal a boatman, he reversed direction and used his sat phone to call the number for the fortress in Iran.

A man answered. "What do you need?"

"I need to talk with our leader."

"That's impossible. As you can imagine, he is quite busy. Perhaps I can assist you."

"Who is this?" Severino demanded.

"That's unimportant."

Severino hesitated for a moment, then said, "I just learned that Robert Danforth is still alive. I am on my way to an event that he will also attend."

There was silence on the line for five seconds, then the man said, "You must end this Danforth business. He must be killed."

"Are you telling me you want me to kill Danforth?"

"No. I'm telling you to have someone do it."

"There's no way I can assign someone at this late hour."

"Then you must take on the task."

"That's insane," Severino shouted. When he noticed people looking at him, he lowered his voice. "That would jeopardize my position here. Everything I've spent years working on. There is no way—"

The call was disconnected.

Eitan Horowitz had never cared for boats. Having become violently ill on a sailboat when he was eight years old, he'd avoided anything that traveled on water. So, he wasn't happy about being ordered to board a fishing trawler that not only rocked in the turbulent Adriatic Sea but stank of fish. The weather had deteriorated in the past two hours; rain pelted him as he walked the deck to breath fresh air and cleanse his sinuses of fish stench. Each time he passed a place on the ship's stern, he looked up at the flashing, pole-mounted red light that indicated the Iron Dome Anti-Missile Defense System was armed and ready.

Horowitz had heard rumors that Mossad, in collaboration with the Israeli military, had placed Iron Dome systems aboard fishing trawlers, cargo crafts, and other non-military ships. This was a Top Secret program that provided an extra measure of protection against enemy missile attacks aimed at Israel. He wasn't aware of any of the ship-based systems ever actually being used.

God forbid, he thought, *that the first time the system is used it happens in the territorial waters of another country. It will create an international incident of dramatic proportion.* He exhaled loudly and growled, "Why the hell do they need me here? I don't know *bubkes* about missiles."

But he knew the answer to his question. It was intelligence that he'd acquired that informed Mossad about the conversion of the 500-Class patrol boats from rescue craft to armed, tactical boats. A man in Libya who he'd recruited as an informant had passed that information to him. When the boats left Tripoli and sailed north, his agent had warned him. The confluence of events— armed patrol boats moving toward Venice where hundreds of NATO representatives were attending Carnevale—seemed like too much of a coincidence to be overlooked. Horowitz had recommended to his supervisor that he warn the Italians, but the man wasn't confident in the intel that Horowitz had provided and didn't want the Italians to wonder how Mossad had learned of the conversion of

JOSEPH BADAL

the boats. Horowitz guessed that his supervisor, who he thought was a pompous ass, had ordered him aboard the trawler as punishment. His antipathy for boats was well-known within Mossad.

Despite being drenched and chilled, he committed to making another circuit of the deck. As he finished and moved toward the ladder that led below decks, he decided to stop at the little camouflaged cube that housed the air defense command center, its commanding officer, Moise Dohan, and an array of electronic equipment that baffled Horowitz.

"Moise," Horowitz said, "how are you doing?"

Dohan shrugged. "It's like watching paint dry."

The two 500-Class patrol boats dropped anchor five hundred yards from one another. The two captains readied their weapons—inputting target coordinates and arming the high-explosive warheads. They had already received messages directing them to launch their missiles at a new time: 7:30 p.m.

The first boat's captain radioed his counterpart on the second boat: "We're ready to launch."

The second captain advised that his crew was ready, as well.

"On my countdown," the first captain said. The man counted down from five to one. The two boats fired their weapons simultaneously, momentarily lighting up the night sea as the missiles roared skyward, reached the apogee of their trajectories, then turned down on a path to the Piazza Pisani Moretta.

Horowitz once more looked around the air defense command center, said a silent prayer of thanks that he didn't have to spend his time cooped up in a box, and told Dohan, "I'll leave you to it. I have to get out of these wet clothes before I catch pneumonia."

As Horowitz turned to leave, a siren blared and Dohan said, "I'll be damned."

"What is it?" Horowitz asked.

"Sit down and shut up," Dohan said.

Horowitz sat and watched Dohan lean forward and stare at a green screen.

After a solid ten seconds, Dohan slowly shook his head. "You

326

spooks may have finally gotten something right."

"What is it?"

"Those boats your people warned us about just launched four missiles. Looks like they're headed for Venice."

"My God. What the hell are you going to do about it?"

Dohan rasped. "Watch, my friend." He tapped the screen in front of him. "My tracking radar has locked on all four missiles. As soon as the computer confirms the missiles are heading for Venice, an electronic message will go to the weapon management and control unit, which will predict the missile impact points and, based on that information, decide whether to engage. If it engages, it informs the missile firing unit, which launches our missiles to intercept the incoming ones."

"My God, Moise, shouldn't you be doing something besides lecturing me about your system?"

The officer snapped his fingers. "I'm just a spectator. The electronics have it under control."

"Are you kidding?" Horowitz said.

His back still to Horowitz, Dohan said, "I thought you Mossad cowboys were fearless; supposed to be cool under fire."

Horowitz groaned and muttered, "Asshole."

The officer laughed. "Let's step outside and watch the show."

Outside the cube, the rain had intensified, now falling in sheets. The officer pointed toward four barely visible launch pods at the ship's stern. Horowitz had just turned to look in that direction when flashes of bright light illuminated the ship's stern and then shot skyward. When the missiles disappeared in the night sky, Horowitz asked, "What now?"

"They engage the incoming missiles."

"You say that as though you're absolutely certain."

The officer turned and opened the door to the cube. "Ninety percent certain," he said as he went inside.

Horowitz had a sudden sinking feeling. "If one missile hits Venice, it will be a disaster."

The officer took his seat at the console. "Let's watch and see what happens." He pointed with his left hand at an area on his screen. "Those are the incoming missiles." He touched the screen with his other hand. "Those are my babies."

Horowitz leaned over the officer's shoulder and watched the two sets of four missiles converge on one another. In a matter of a few seconds, four light bursts showed on the screen. The officer turned, brushed his hands together, and said, "All done." He smiled at Horowitz. "Now what should we do about those patrol boats?"

"Why don't we let the Italian Navy deal with them?"

CHAPTER 58

Carlo Severino had been shocked to learn that Robert Danforth was alive. There had been news coverage about an explosion at a convent in Venice. He wondered for a moment if that had something to do with an attempt to kill Danforth, but a follow-up news story posited that the explosion had been caused by a gas leak.

He felt befuddled as he boarded a gondola to take him to the Ventimiglia residence. He had tried to find a speedboat, but only gondolas were available. The ride in the little boat was a miserable experience as the waters in the canal rocked the craft. Then it began to rain again, and the temperature dropped. The gondolier passed him an umbrella and a blanket. But he still felt chilled by the time he arrived at the Ventimiglia's at 7:30. As the gondola docked, he looked up at the sky in the direction of the Carnevale venue, expecting to hear explosions and to see the night sky illuminate. Yet, there was nothing but gray sky and falling rain.

He ran to the residence and was immediately granted access by two burly, black-suited men guarding the entrance. Inside, another man asked him for his name, checked it against a list, then welcomed him.

"Please come this way," the man said.

Severino took several calming breaths, swiped a handkerchief over his forehead, and thought, *What the hell do I do now?*

As a Ministry of Defense senior official, Severino had been

in many elegant homes but, from what he saw as he was led from the entry to the grand salon, none of those homes could compare to the Ventimiglia residence's grandeur and elegance. He stood in the salon doorway and slowly moved his gaze from left to right, astonished by the room's glittering brilliance. For a moment he thought he had gone back in time, to a seventeenth century gala attended by the glitterati of that time. The classical music being played by a string quartet only enhanced the moment. He spotted his boss, Paolo Andreotti, in the middle of the room, deep in conversation with two men. Andreotti met his gaze, smiled, and waved him over.

"Carlo," Andreotti said. "Let me introduce you to our esteemed host, Mr. Ventimiglia, and his guest, Mr. Danforth." He leaned conspiratorially toward Severino. "Mr. Danforth is a great friend of Italy and worked for many years with Mr. Ventimiglia on very... sensitive matters."

Severino half-bowed and thanked Ventimiglia for welcoming him to his home.

"It's our pleasure, Mr. Severino," Ventimiglia said. "Your service to our country is much appreciated."

Severino bowed again. He moved his gaze to Danforth who stared back at him as though analyzing him. He felt naked under the man's scrutiny. He swallowed hard, coughed once, and said, "Are you enjoying your vacation here in Venice, Mr. Danforth?"

"Very much, Mr. Severino. It's been an...exciting experience."

"I'm pleased to hear that. Venice is a jewel of a city."

"Yes, it is."

Andreotti tapped Severino on the arm. "Come with me, Carlo. We've taken enough of our host's time."

As the two men walked away, Bob watched them until they disappeared in the crowd. "Mr. Severino seems nervous," he told Giovanni.

Giovanni chuckled. "I get that a lot. People always assume we intelligence types either know more than we do or that we're analyzing every word and expression."

Bob nodded. "Perhaps I should find Liz before she thinks I

abandoned her."

"Good idea," Giovanni said.

CHAPTER 59

As of 8:30 p.m., Venice-time, because of the intelligence provided by the CIA to NATO country authorities, nine hundred and forty-five Asasiyun agents had either been taken into custody or killed in the process of trying to execute their missions.

By 9:00 p.m., assassins assigned to the remaining thirty-three targets had fulfilled their missions. They were successful because of failures by local authorities, or the targets were unable to be warned because they'd turned off their cell phones and had traveled away from their homes.

Reports about the plot flooded the airways and became international news. The Islamic Republic of Iran's senior leadership were past the point of being apoplectic. Ayatollah Sayyid Noori Hamadani, the country's Supreme Leader, was the only man in the Supreme National Security Council conference room who didn't speak while the others around him tried to place blame on one another.

After twenty minutes of manic squabbling, the Iranian President, Hassan Shabani, who was also the Security Council's chairman, ordered the people in the room to cease their bickering.

It was almost midnight in Tehran when Hamadani stood at his place at the head of the table, bent over and whispered something to Shabani; then, without another word, he walked out. On the way to his car, he called the Iranian Revolutionary Guards Corps commander and ordered him to arrest several Council members. *Better they take the blame*, he thought.

In his vehicle, Hamadani used his cell phone to search for information about Venice, but there was still no mention of an attack on the carnival ball venue. Although there were thousands of postings about captured Asasiyun killers and the assassinations that had occurred, nothing came up about an attack in Venice. He threw the phone across the back seat and thought about the debacle that the Asasiyun program had created. He was certain his country was about to suffer as it hadn't suffered since Genghis Khan had invaded ancient Persia. *If only a few agents are captured and cooperate with the West, our role will become common knowledge*, he thought. He came close to cursing the Grand Ayatollah Khomeini but stopped short of that blasphemy. He shouted at his driver, "Take me home."

After the Supreme National Security Council adjourned, Iranian President Shabani retired to his office and wondered how long it would take the Supreme Leader to target him for failing to do his job. He was shaken to the point of despair. His position as the elected head of the Iranian government was dependent upon his success in demeaning the West and avoiding embarrassment for Iran. Both of those foundations of his position had been weakened, if not destroyed. His first instinct was survival. He knew the only hope he had was to shift blame for the colossal failure that was now globally common knowledge. His voice broke as he shouted for his assistant.

"Yes, Mr. President," the man said as he scurried into Shabani's office.

"Call the fortress in the Cloud Forest."

"Yes, sir." The man rushed from the office. Minutes later, his assistant returned. "No one answered my call."

"What do you mean?" Shabani roared.

In a tremulous voice, the assistant said, "I tried the radio as well as the phone, sir. There doesn't appear to be anyone there."

Shabani took a moment to consider what this meant. Then he said, "I want General Jafari here immediately."

Yasmin Nizari stormed along the Asasiyun fortress' parapets. Her shouts and screams echoed off the surrounding hills, bouncing back as though ridiculing her. *This is not good*, she thought. *It's all undone.* She moved along the parapet edge and looked down at the spot where her father's body was buried. "It's all your fault," she screamed. "You abandoned me when I needed you most. You should have listened to me."

Javad Muntaziri stood near the roof entrance into the fortress and peeked out from behind a half-wall. His heart sank and his fear rose as he listened to Yasmin's irrational rantings. He turned and entered the building, made his way down to the cells, and ordered the guard to release the children held there.

The guard hesitated a moment and looked as though he might object.

Javad grabbed him by the front of his shirt and shouted, "I want those children released and I suggest you get as far away from here as possible." He paused a second and added, "Unless you want to explain our failures to the Supreme Leader."

The guard snatched a ring of keys from a hook, unlocked the cells, and shepherded the children to where Javad waited. Then the guard rushed off and disappeared around a corner.

The children were wide-eyed. Some cried. Others shook with fear. They hung back as though Javad meant to do them harm.

"Listen closely," Javad said. "You will find your coats in a locker down that corridor. Get them, then go to the door at the end." He stopped and looked at the tallest boy. "Can you drive?"

The boy nodded.

"There's a van there. The keys are in it. Follow the trail through the forest to a village. It's a long drive, but you'll be safe once you reach the village."

The children moved away like zombies. They were deathly quiet.

Javad climbed the stairs, past the now-abandoned operations center, past the vacant office level, past empty rooms where recruits had attended classes, back to the roof of the complex. He shouted for Yasmin, but the wind blew in gusts that threw his words back at him. He stepped out from behind the half-wall and looked toward the parapet where Yasmin usually walked. She was still railing against those she believed had failed her: her father, Ayatollah Khomeini, the current Supreme Leader, and on and on. She cursed the Americans and the West, in general. He advanced toward her and, in an even tone, said, "Yasmin, we should leave. Our failure will bring the Ayatollah's wrath down on us."

"You," she shouted. "It's all your fault. If I'd had someone with me who—"

Javad moved to within inches of her. Her eyes seemed to gleam as though a light glowed behind them. It struck him that she had gone mad. *How did I ignore all the signals?* he thought. As he turned around, he heard the *whup-whup-whup* sounds of multiple helicopters and knew his instincts had been correct. They needed to flee this place while they had the chance.

He ran toward the roof entrance but stopped after twenty yards and turned back to Yasmin, wanting to give her one more chance to escape before the helicopters arrived. But before he could say a word, she removed a pistol from under her jacket, aimed it, and fired at him. He felt a massive shock wave in his chest and staggered backward until he fell. The last thing he saw was Yasmin's psychotic, gleaming eyes.

CHAPTER 60

At first, Bob thought Carlo Severino might be shy. Every time he looked at the man, Severino's face flushed and he dropped his gaze. Then Bob thought the man might resent the presence of an American in the company of some of Italy's top leaders. But, on second thought, neither explanation seemed to make sense. Arrogance, rather than shyness, and the ability to hide their feelings were watch words of senior defense types. *There's something else going on with Severino*, Bob thought. He'd also noticed that Severino was drinking heavily. *Not smart to get drunk in the company of your boss.*

The seating arrangement at dinner placed Severino on Liz's right. An Italian Navy admiral sat on her left. Bob was on the other side of the huge table, down eight chairs from Liz. His view of Severino was minimal, at best. But when he glanced again at the man, Severino seemed to shrink inside his costume. Despite the distance between them, Severino's voice carried to Bob. The more he drank, the louder he became. And Bob noticed something in the man's voice. *Maybe an accent*, he thought. *Not Italian. Something else. The way he pronounces "Salute!" every time someone makes a toast, or when he says words like signore and signora. There's a slight sibilance in the man's "S's."*

Giovanni Ventimiglia sat at the head of the table to Bob's right, six seats away. Anna Ventimiglia was at the other end of the table, thirteen seats to Bob's left. The bowls from the *primo* course—buridda, a seafood soup—had just been cleared and waiters were now pouring white wine in one of seven wine glasses at each setting. Giovanni happened to meet Bob's gaze. He must have seen something in his expression because he tilted his head to one side and slightly spread his hands apart. Bob tipped his head toward the dining room entrance, said *"Per favore scusami,"* to the guests on either side of him, and pushed back his chair. He left the room and made his way down a hall. Giovanni joined him a moment later.

"Is something wrong?" Giovanni said. "Are you okay?"

"You'll think I'm crazy, but what do you know about Severino?"

Giovanni squinted at Bob for a good five seconds. "Why?" he finally asked.

"I've got a feeling about—"

"You've got a feeling?"

Bob felt his temperature rise, but he forced calm into his tone. "I may be retired, but I'm not dead. Don't tell me your instincts died on the day you retired."

Giovanni pumped his hands at Bob. "My apologies," he said. "I don't know much about the man other than Andreotti thinks the world of him. Apparently, the man's a genius."

"I apologize for taking you away from your guests, but I need you to do something. Would you talk with Andreotti about Severino's background?"

Giovanni gave Bob the long, silent stare again. "You're sure about this?"

"I'm not sure about anything. All I can tell you is there's something off about the guy."

"Name one thing that's off."

"He's nervous; won't look me in the eye." After a slight hesitation, Bob added, "Remember when we were introduced, and he asked me how I was enjoying my vacation? How did he know I was here on vacation?"

Giovanni scoffed. "He's nervous because he's surrounded by some of the most powerful people in Italy. Hell, I'm nervous. And, as far as his question about you being on vacation, why else would you be here accompanied by your wife?"

"Okay, I'll give you that. But there's something else. The more he drinks, the more his pronunciation of the letter 's' is wrong. I don't think he's a native Italian."

"So, he has a lisp."

"He didn't have it before he started drinking. He makes his 's' sound the way…Iranians do."

Giovanni blurted a laugh. "You think Carlo Severino, a senior man in our Ministry of Defense, is a spy?"

"My God, Giovanni, have you been paying attention to what's been going on? Highly placed, trusted people have turned out to be Asasiyun agents."

Giovanni's eyes narrowed and his lips compressed into a tight line. Before he could respond, Bob apologized and said, "Please, Giovanni, talk with Andreotti."

"You're asking me to ask Severino's boss if his right-hand man is a spy for a vicious terrorist group. What do you think he's going to say?"

"Better he finds out now than later after more people are murdered."

Giovanni muttered something in Italian, told Bob to return to the gathering, and walked back into the dining hall to Andreotti's place at the table. Bob heard him tell Andreotti that he had a phone call and then watched him lead the minister out of the ballroom.

Bob forced himself to sit calmly, despite his electrified nerves. Every minute that passed only ratcheted up his angst. He tried to avoid staring at Severino. When he did glance in the man's direction, he saw that he was becoming more animated and voluble.

Giovanni and Andreotti had been absent for nearly fifteen minutes when they returned. Giovanni moved up to Bob's side of the table, chatting up the guests, while Andreotti went to his own chair. When Giovanni stopped at Bob's place, he dropped a folded piece of paper in Bob's lap and continued along the table.

Bob unfolded the paper and looked down at it: *According to the ministry's records, CS was born in Siena, attended secondary school there, and attended university in Rome. He joined the Ministry of Defense after a three-year tour in the Italian military. Andreotti asked a woman at the Ministry to verify each of these activities. I expect her to call back soon.*

Bob had lost his appetite and couldn't do justice to the *secondo*—veal, and the *contorno*—mixed vegetables. The *dolce* course was about to be served when a security man came over to Giovanni, whispered in his ear, and then followed him out of the room.

Giovanni picked up the telephone receiver, "*Pronto.*"

"*Signor Ventimiglia, e Sara Cortone che chiama.*"

"Yes, Miss Cortone."

"I checked on Mister Severino's background. Everything looked fine—"

"That's good news, Miss Cortone. Thank you for your help."

"Excuse me, sir. I wasn't quite finished."

Giovanni felt his stomach clench. He said, "I apologize. Please continue."

"I researched his history in reverse order. Everything was fine until I checked his secondary school records. The school digitized all their classes ten years ago. When I pulled up the class that Mr. Severino was supposedly in, there was no student by that name. Then I called all the Severinos in the Siena area, where Mr. Severino is from. One woman told me she had a son named Carlo who died before his first birthday. When I asked her for the baby's birth date, she gave me the same date as Mr. Severino's."

Giovanni's stomach discomfort now escalated to pain. He thanked Sara Cortone, hung up, and moved to the security man. He explained what he'd just learned and told him, "We need to escort Severino from the room with as little commotion as possible." He had a sinking feeling when he pictured the knives at each place setting.

The security man used his wrist mic to call a member of his team and ordered the man to join him. Then he asked Giovanni to go to the dinner table and to not do or say anything that might alarm the guests. After Giovanni returned to his seat, the guards moved into the dining room and almost casually advanced toward Severino.

Bob saw the men move along the opposite side of the table and tried to catch Liz's eye, but she was absorbed in a conversation with the admiral on her left. Then Bob's heart seemed to leap into his throat when Severino turned and looked toward the two security men. He wobbled a bit as he stood, then reached down to his left side and pulled out a bejeweled dagger with a blade that was at least eight inches long. He seemed to steady himself, wrapped his left arm around Liz's neck, and placed the dagger blade under her chin. He yelled at the security men to stop where they were as he dragged Liz from her chair.

Liz's height and her costume screened most of Severino from Bob's view. Severino backed up from the table and moved toward Anna Ventimiglia's end of the room, where a door led out onto a balcony overlooking a canal. A few guests screamed, but, for the most part, they sat stunned and silent. When he reached the room's far end, Severino shouted, "You, Danforth, come here."

Bob, who was already on his feet, walked quickly toward Severino. "Let her go," he said. "Take me instead."

"How noble," Severino said. He laughed. "I don't know how or why you're still alive, but that ends tonight."

Bob was now six feet from Severino. The security men had drawn pistols and pointed them in the man's direction. But they had no shot without endangering Liz.

"Get on your knees," Severino shouted at Bob.

"Let her go," Bob said again.

Severino took the knife from Liz's neck and pointed it at Bob. "Shut up," he yelled. "Get on your knees."

The look in the man's eyes frightened Bob. He looked desperate, fatalistic, as though he had nothing to lose. Bob moved to his knees and raised his hands.

Severino released his arm from around Liz's neck and pushed her forward, sending her into the back of Anna's chair. Liz cried out as she hit the chair and fell to the floor. Bob saw her roll over and try to get to her feet, but her dress was cumbersome and hindered her effort to stand. He dropped his hands and reached toward her, but Severino had rushed behind him and now had the dagger against his throat. He used his other arm to lift Bob to his feet. Although Bob couldn't see the security men, they'd apparently moved toward Severino because the man screamed, banshee-like, and ordered them to stay where they were.

Bob saw the desperate expression on Liz's face as Severino moved in her direction, dragging him toward the balcony door.

"I may not get out of this," the man said into Bob's right ear, "but I'll join Allah in paradise. Your death will ensure that."

The dagger slipped and Bob felt it slice his skin. Blood dripped down his neck and under his collar. An irrational thought came to him: *I'm going to die in this stupid outfit.*

He decided that he wasn't going to allow Severino to take him out easily. About to reach up to grab the man's arm, Severino screamed as though he'd been poleaxed. The man's killing hand dropped away allowing Bob to strike backward with an elbow and then spin away from his grip. As he turned to face Severino, he looked down and saw Liz's bandaged hand wrapped around one of the six-inch-long pins that held her plumed hat in place. She was pressing the pin into Severino's thigh and rocking it back and forth. Severino's knife hand was now raised above his head, about to drive the weapon into Liz's back. Bob leaped at the man and stretched to snare his hand, but before he could do so, gunshots exploded, sending careening waves of sound through the room. Severino took a step back, then dropped as though his bones had turned to sawdust; his face was now a red mask.

CHAPTER 61

Eight helicopters landed in sequence on the soccer field within the fortress walls. As one chopper offloaded a Revolutionary Guards Corps squad and then took off again, the next aircraft landed and offloaded its squad. Each assigned to a specific part of the property, the squads spread out and aggressively infiltrated the facility. They shouted as they kicked in doors and invaded rooms. But their efforts to intimidate the occupants were for naught. There were no occupants. Within twenty minutes, they'd swept the entire fortress and, other than a dead man and a raving woman, the place had been abandoned.

The senior Iranian officer on the ground radioed General Homayoun Jafari, the IRGC commander, who was in a helicopter hovering over the fortress. "There's no one here, General, other than some half-crazed woman who's babbling about how people betrayed her."

"Who is she?" Jafari said.

The officer on the ground chuckled. "She claims to be the leader of the Asasiyun. Sir, she's out of her mind."

Jafari said something the officer didn't understand. Then he told the officer, "Throw her out of there. The last thing we need is a delusional woman on our hands. Then place the explosives. You have thirty minutes before the helicopters return to pick up your teams."

President Stanley Webb had listened to his cabinet members for forty-five minutes. Intellectually, he agreed with the suggestions they'd made about actions the United States should take against Iran for its support of the Asasiyun. Emotionally, he wanted to retaliate against Iran in a manner that would send a message the mullahs would not soon forget. What he hated the most about his job was that every decision he made minimized emotion and maximized rational thought. A quote from George Bernard Shaw came to mind: "The reasonable man adapts himself to the world: the unreasonable one persists in trying to adapt the world to himself. Therefore, all progress depends on the unreasonable man." *This job won't let me be unreasonable*, he thought.

"So, we're agreed," Webb said. "We'll increase the sanctions regimen already in place, with an emphasis on embargoing their oil and gas exports." He looked at Christine Luongo, his Vice President, and told her, "I want you and the Secretaries of State, Commerce, and Energy to explain to the European Union how we'll replace the oil and gas they've been buying from Iran. Then I'll call the key heads of state and explain how we expect them to support these sanctions."

Before Webb returned to the Oval Office, he pulled the Chairman of the Joint Chiefs of Staff aside and asked, "General, what would it take to destroy the enemy fortress?"

"I love your question, Mr. President, but that's a moot issue."

"Why's that?"

"I just received a text message. The place just imploded."

"How?" POTUS asked.

"If I had to guess, the Iranians sabotaged it."

"Clever bastards," Webb said. "Destroy the evidence. I suspect the next thing they'll do is claim they knew nothing about the Asasiyun or its training facility. That the entire thing was a rogue operation."

"Already done, Mr. President. Iranian President Shabani just did an interview on MSNBC. It was a masterpiece of deflection and professed innocence."

"I don't suppose he had anything to say about the hundreds of captured Asasiyun agents who are spilling their guts about Iran's role in all of this."

The general laughed. "No, Mr. President. Not yet, anyway."

Despite the success of taking out the missiles fired by the patrol boats in the Adriatic Sea, Eitan Horowitz was miserable. The weather had gotten even worse. High winds and torrential rain battered the trawler as it sped south, pitching and yawing in high seas. Before the Italian authorities captured the patrol boat crews and discovered they were Asasiyun agents, the trawler captain wanted to be as far away as possible.

Horowitz had already thrown up everything in his stomach. Now dry heaves racked his body. He was supine on his bunk when his satellite phone rang. He groaned, pressed the CALL button, and said, "What?"

"Is this Eitan Horowitz?"

"Yes, who's this?"

"Eitan, it's Prime Minister Sabin."

"Oh, my God," Horowitz said.

The Prime Minister laughed. "Eitan, I want to congratulate you on the success of your mission. You have made our NATO friends very happy."

"Thank you, Mr. Prime Minister."

"Are you okay? You sound...ill."

"No, no, I'm fine."

"That's good. As soon as you return home, I want you to pay me a visit. We will have a conversation over lunch. I'm sure you've missed our fine Israeli food."

Horowitz felt bile hit his throat. He leaped from the bunk and ran to the toilet.

CHAPTER 62

It had been two hours now since the security men had shot and killed Carlo Severino and Italian Carabinieri had transported Severino's body and questioned guests at the dinner, that Bob noticed Liz's bandaged hands still shook. Seated beside her, he lightly touched her right arm to comfort her. She showed him a wan smile but couldn't hold it for more than a few seconds.

Their hats, masks, wigs, vests, cloaks, and other paraphernalia discarded on a chair at one end of the Ventimiglia sitting room, Bob, Liz, Giovanni, and Anna lounged on facing sofas. Liz was the only one drinking water; the others held glasses of scotch.

Bob downed his drink, looked at Giovanni, then Anna, and said, "I think it's time for us old folks to hit the sack."

Anna smiled. "Excuse me?"

Bob laughed. "I guess that's not translatable to Italian. I think we need to go to bed."

Giovanni stood, took Anna's hand, and helped her to her feet. "That sounds like a very good idea." He looked at Liz whose gaze was fixed on her glass. "I can't apologize enough for what happened tonight."

Liz looked up; her expression momentarily confused. Then she said, "From what I've heard, the Asasiyun were masters of deception and intelligence. I can't imagine what you could have done to prevent any of this. My God, that man had worked for the

Defense Ministry for years."

Giovanni tipped his head as though to show appreciation for Liz's statement. "Anna and I are distressed about...." He spread his hands in a way that told Bob and Liz he couldn't come up with words that appropriately expressed his regret.

Liz leaned forward and placed her glass on the coffee table. She stood and moved to Giovanni and Anna. Hugging them in turn, she stepped back next to Bob; her eyes brimmed with tears. He wrapped an arm around her as she put her head against the side of his shoulder.

After the Ventimiglias went to their bedroom, Liz hugged Bob, burrowing her face into his chest. Her body shuddered with sobs.

"What's wrong, honey?" Bob said.

She made a dismissive hand gesture. But finally she said, "I almost lost you...again."

"Not even close," he said.

She pushed off him and took a step backward. "What are you talking about?"

"I was never even worried. After all, I had you to protect me." He held up two fingers. "You saved me twice on this trip."

Liz coughed a laugh and moved back into Bob's arms. "You're an idiot." Then Liz leaned into him and said, "Maybe we've had enough of Venice for a while."

"Probably a good idea to return home. See how Michael and Robbie are doing."

Liz kissed Bob's cheek. "The thought never crossed my mind," she whispered.

Yasmin Nizari had been astonished by the noise and force of the blast that destroyed the fortress. *Good riddance*, she thought.

Besides the cold, it now snowed as though the sky had opened and decided to blanket the earth. She wasn't dressed appropriately for the weather: sweater, silk slacks, and flats. She shook as the cold penetrated her bones. Her feet no longer pained her; they were numb. She knew the storage building near the training field where war games had been conducted was just ahead. There would be winter clothing there; perhaps cases of bottled water, too. The thought of the money she'd transferred to an account in the Caribbean gave her the persistence to carry on. *Just another half-mile or so,* she thought.

Her arms crossed over her chest, she stumbled into a clearing, talking to herself, imagining the life she would lead with the money she had. She thought she saw the shape of the storage building in the distance, but she couldn't be certain. "Perhaps…it's more…than a…half-mile," she mumbled, her teeth chattering, her body shaking.

Then a movement to her right startled her, making her heart leap. She felt a rush of heat that was quickly displaced with bone-chilling cold. *What was it?* she wondered as she scanned the barely discernible tree line in the distance. She took a tentative step forward toward the storage building when movement on her right startled her again. A massive form moved from the trees into the clearing. It was shrouded in a haze of falling snow. At first, Yasmin thought it was an apparition, then maybe a *jinn.* But as the figure came closer, she realized with relief it was a stag with a monstrous rack.

Suddenly feeling warm, she grimaced and said, "Are you…the one my…father…watched from the…parapets?"

The stag continued to look at her as it moved closer. Through the snow screen, she noticed its breath coming in great clouds of steam.

As she waved half-heartily at the animal, she thought, *Take care of yourself. I must go now.* She tried to move forward, but her body seemed immobilized. *Maybe I should rest for a few minutes,* she thought. *No, that's not a good idea. I must move on.*

But a voice stopped her. She looked back at the stag. "Did you say something?"

"It's me, Yasmin."

"Fa…ther?" she said. "Is…it…you?"

"You're stuttering, daughter. You must be very cold."

"Yes, Fa…ther. But I'll…be…fine." She tried to raise a hand to point at the storage building, but her arm seemed too heavy to lift.

"Come over here, child. I'll warm you."

Yasmin thought, *I must get to the building.* But the offer of warmth was too seductive. For an instant, in a moment of clarity, she wondered: *How can I be having a conversation with my father?*

Isn't he dead? But her blood-starved brain couldn't seem to process the thought to its conclusion.

The stag huffed a huge breath, expelled a great cloud of steam, then turned and moved, as though in slow motion, back toward the tree line.

Wait, Father, I'm coming, Yasmin thought. She felt as though she was moving on stumps as she stumbled toward the forest.

The voice came again: "Are you coming, child?"

Yes, Father. But I need to stop for a minute. She thought she might have spoken the words, but she wasn't certain. She dropped to her knees and rolled onto one side.

I'll just rest for a minute or two. Wait for me, Father. I'll be right there.

*

A PERSONAL MESSAGE TO THE READER

Dear Reader:

Thank you very much for reading "The Carnevale Conspiracy," the 7th book in the *Danforth Saga*. I have wanted to write a story based on Hassan-i Sabbah, known in the West as The Old Man of the Mountain, for years. He was the founder of the Nizari Isma'ili state and its *fidā'i* military group, known as the Order of Assassins. What if a new order of assassins was created to target Western political, military, and business leaders? And what if many of those leaders from over two dozen Western countries were gathered for a NATO conference in one location?

Obviously, because this is fiction, I could have located the NATO conference anywhere in the world, but I fell in love with Venice when I visited the city in 2018, and decided to place the Western leaders there during *carnevale*. My protagonists, Bob and Liz Danforth, on the vacation of a lifetime in Venice during *carnevale*, find themselves enmeshed in The Old Man of the Mountain's diabolical plan. As with other books in the *Danforth Saga*, "The Carnevale Conspiracy" is inspired by historical events that, I hope, added to the richness of the plot and to your reading enjoyment.

I cannot overstate my appreciation for your support of my work. If you enjoyed "The Carnevale Conspiracy," I hope you will read my other books. Also, I would very much appreciate you spreading the word via word of mouth, email, and social media to your friends about my novels. I would be especially grateful if you would consider posting a review of "The Carnevale Conspiracy" on Amazon.

If you would like to have a conversation, please feel free to email me at josephbadalbooks@outlook.com. I read my email every day and respond personally. I look forward to hearing from you.

Thank you again,

Joe

ABOUT THE AUTHOR

Joseph Badal grew up in a family where storytelling had been passed down from generation to generation.

Prior to his literary career, he served six years in the U.S. Army, including tours of duty in Vietnam and Greece, from which he received numerous decorations.

After his military service, he worked for thirty-six years in the banking & finance industries and was a founding director and senior executive of a New York Stock Exchange-listed company for sixteen years.

Joe is an Amazon #1 bestselling author, with 17 published, award-winning suspense novels. He has been recognized as "One of The 50 Best Writers You Should Be Reading." He was named 2020 Writer of the Year by the Military Writers Society of America, is a two-time winner of the Tony Hillerman Prize for Best Fiction Book of the Year, a three-time Military Writers Society of America Gold Medal Winner, an Eric Hoffer Prize Winner, a four-time "Finalist" in the International Book Awards competition, and a top prize winner on multiple occasions in the New Mexico/Arizona Book Awards competition.

He writes a regular column titled "Inspired by Actual Events" in *Suspense Magazine*.

Joe is a member of Croak & Dagger, Sisters in Crime, Military Writers Society of America, International Thriller Writers, Public Safety Writers Association, International Crime Writers Association, and Southwest Writers Workshop.

To learn more, visit Joe's website at www.JosephBadalBooks.com.

CPSIA information can be obtained
at www.ICGtesting.com
Printed in the USA
LVHW011358230721
693510LV00015B/1026

9 780578 8814